"Lou Kilzer is simply the best detective I have ever worked with, ever met or, I believe, ever to ply the trade of journalism." – *John Ullmann, former Executive Director, Investigative Reporters and Editors, USA.*

This book is dedicated to Alex and Xanthe, and to all the fabulous souls of the Denver Press Club.

FATAL
REDEMPTION

A mystery thriller

LOU KILZER & MARK BOYDEN

ENIGMAS
PUBLISHING
North America & Europe

An Enigmas Publishing book

Enigmas Publishing
244 Fifth Avenue, Suite E-265
New York, NY 10001-7604, USA
Tel (+1)(0)212 726 2402
and
27 Old Gloucester Street,
London WC1N 3AX, UK
Tel: (+44)(0)203 143 3184

enquiries@enigmaspublishing.com

www.enigmaspublishing.com

The edition published in the USA by Enigmas Publishing 2014

A catalogue record for this book is available from the United States Library of Congress

ISBN 978-0-9928068-0-4

eBook ISBN 978-0-9928068-1-1

Set in 11pt Big Caslon

Printed in the United States of America by Edwards Brothers Malloy, Inc.

Contents

"When you have eliminated the impossible, whatever remains, however improbable, must be the truth."
– Sherlock Holmes, *The Sign of the Four*

ACKNOWLEDGEMENTS

I would like to give thanks to my relentless copy editor, demanding critic and lifetime love and partner, Liz Kovacs. Liz pulled some all-nighters getting this into shape. Where she gets the energy is anyone's guess. My oldest friend Mark Smith of Montrose, Colorado, gave sage advice as did my friend from Moscow (now living in Denver) Vitali Konjoukov.

- Lou Kilzer, USA

With deep gratitude I wish to acknowledge the contributions to this book by Richard Thomas, Sophie Bolesworth and Zoe Boyden: Richard for total support and sustained energy in bringing this manuscript to publication, Sophie for the splendid cover, and Zoe for encouragement and a keen eye for perspective.

- Mark Boyden, UK

Prologue

MR. Wood cut his lights and aimed the SUV down the last one hundred yards of rutted blacktop. He stopped near a junkyard fence, got out, stretched, lit a cigarette. Considered.

It was 3 a.m. in Commerce City, a north Denver suburb unknown to any tourist map. A nearby rendering plant that baked cattle blood down to fertilizer was belching vapor. The air was thick. Every time he came here Mr. Wood thought he was going to puke.

Seventy-five yards away was a two-story house. What little paint remained was bubbling and chipping off. Lights burned in an upstairs window. Other windows were boarded up. There were five Harleys parked outside, four more than Mr. Wood would have liked. But the key one was sitting, as usual, under a forty-watt yellow bulb. The custom cruiser painted with skulls and flaming red arrows belonged to Bow Hendricks. Big Bow. Bow was the national enforcer of the Sons of Khan motorcycle gang, a designated and ruthless killer. Nobody fucked with Big Bow Hendricks if they valued living.

Mr. Wood intended to change that. He had been here in the shadows near the bikers' clubhouse every night for ten days, sequestered by the fence, watching, timing, making mental notes. By now, it should have been routine. But going from watching to doing was not routine, Mr. Wood knew. He could not pretend he was not scared. More than the day Sister Rachel told him as a boy about the fires of Hell. More than when he learned his father was going to die. More than ever before he was entering a space he had only ever dreamed about. This was real. His stomach churned.

I must be crazy, Mr. Wood thought. Insane. Who but a madman would risk a successful career to pursue an unnatural obsession? It's what Mr. Wood had asked himself the day before as

1

he walked around his middle-class neighborhood, twenty miles away, checking with himself again why he was going to rip apart what little remained of his Catholic conscience. And he had kept coming back to this: Why not?

The question was part of a deeply personal agony that had started ten years earlier, when Mr. Wood had been shocked by actions he felt could not have been committed by anyone born in the image of the Christian God.

Sure, Mr. Wood knew all about Pascal's wager: believe, just in case there is a God. What was there to lose? Fuck that, he thought. Pascal was just another sophist. To Mr. Wood, even if there was a God, there was no evidence that he gave a damn what a human being did or believed. So he kept coming back to this: Why not?

When Mr. Wood first started planning to cap Big Bow, he told himself he had justice on his side. Bow was a badass. He had chosen Bow primarily because there wasn't a chance in hell the cops would put an ounce of effort into finding Bow's killer. If they did, it would only be to give the killer a medal. No, Mr. Wood's priorities were basic: to get in his first kill and escape, and then see how it felt. After that, Mr. Wood didn't know what could be in store, hadn't given it a lot of thought. Surely he would want to do it again. And surely he would not want to get caught.

He had a vague notion that he might be able to turn a dime now and then if he became any good at it. Or maybe it was nothing to do with money at all. Maybe he just wanted to become the perfect killer. He didn't know for sure and at the moment he didn't care. Right now he was content to feel what he would feel.

A sudden movement below shook him out of his meditation. Two bikers came noisily out of the clubhouse, stumbling drunk. They passed a bottle between them, snorted some speed, got on their Hogs and wobbled down the road. Good, Mr. Wood thought. There were now three bikes left. Three Sons. Two men usually stayed at the club overnight, he knew. Big Bow was never one of them. Bow would be out next.

Mr. Wood leaned on his SUV and threw down his cigarette.

This was it. It was time. Could he do it? He reached inside and grabbed his 30.06. Could he cross the line? Or was he just another pussy? He leveled the rifle at the target.

Minutes later, Big Bow walked out. He sent a stream of shit-brown chewing tobacco towards a gutter and slid onto his Hog. He wore full outlaw-biker regalia, including his treasured purple wings – a badge that said Big Bow was a member of an elite group, one of those who had had oral sex with a dead woman.

God, how I hate these filth, Mr. Wood thought. Ridding the world of a man like this will be a pleasure.

Bow inserted his key into the ignition – but just like on the other nights he didn't fire up right away. Instead he reached into his jacket for a cigar. Twice he tried and failed to light it. On the third try he got it going. He leaned back.

As Bow sat there breathing in the scent of blood, Mr. Wood's finger touched the trigger. Suddenly his heart calmed. The ringing left his ears. He had his answer.

Bow finally reached again for the ignition. It reflected a glint of silver moonlight. The shot echoed around Commerce City, sharp and definitive, and Big Bow Hendricks fell like a stone, a bullet clean through his head. He would never have known a thing.

Mr. Wood did not hurry away. He knew the two bikers still in the club were just like other bikers, tough as a group but can-dyasses in small numbers. They would not rush out to take on a high-powered rifle. No, the bikers would wimp out. Probably call the cops.

Mr. Wood stood looking at the dead biker a moment, sprawled over his collapsed blood-spattered machine. Then he turned to the SUV, tossed his rifle inside and got in. He waited again, savoring the moment, feeling a peace like he had never known before.

He turned on his lights and put the truck in drive. As he drove slowly away he felt the remnants of his Catholic guilt seep away. He felt free, he realized, and happy, and strong. And right.

I can do this, Mr. Wood thought. He would sleep soundly tonight.

1. Red Alert

REUTERS+Late News+Washington sources reported
yesterday that President Lawrence Naslund's re-
election prospects have suffered a further serious
setback following more revelations on Capitol Hill...

PRESIDENT Lawrence Naslund sat alone in the front passenger cabin of the helicopter. He balled fists and wondered how he
had ever gotten into this mess. Then he remembered: Texas.

It had been easier back in Chicago where Naslund had been
something of a prodigy. No one had expected much from the skinny, mixed-race kid. But he had been edgy from the start, picking
a fight with a fourth grader when he was a year younger. It was a
time of life where a year was forever. Somehow Buddy Naslund
had won. And that, more than anything else, had stamped
Naslund's future.

He became popular, and then clever, qualifying as a lawyer and
making his name fighting unpopular causes. His rise from mayor
to state governor to Democratic presidential candidate had had
an air of inevitability about it. At 45 he had become the youngest
president since Kennedy, sweeping all before him. And like Kennedy he was held in some awe. Voters expected a lot from him. He
expected a lot from himself.

Naslund's helicopter appeared over the White House, hovered,
set down on the South Lawn. It was 8 a.m. Saturday. Naslund
saluted the Marines as he walked off. Reporters, rumpled and un-
happy, shouted questions.

"Will you dump the vice president?"

"Impeachment, sir. Have you heard the talk?"

"Where is the First Lady?"

Naslund smiled and waved. Like Reagan, he pretended not to hear. He cupped his hand to his ear, shook his head, and strolled toward the West Wing. Pissed off. Inside the portal a woman in a liquefying gray suit and raven black hair took his hands. Linda Orvez had been the country's youngest federal judge when Naslund tapped her to head the CIA. Ever since, anytime charity work took Mrs. Naslund out of town, Linda Orvez seemed to be needed for a briefing at Camp David. There were already rumors.

"Larry," Orvez said as she leaned into the President. "We will get through this." Her tone was a mix of devotion and manipulation.

The politics were clear: Larry Naslund's administration of high expectation was reeling from disclosures that the vice president's brother was in a joint venture with Russian mobster Dimitri Ivanov. The brother's take: a reputed $1.6 million. Worse, a secretary had told it all to the Washington Post.

Worse still, she said the vice president had known about it all along.

To Naslund, Vice President Rutherford "Jesse" James was just like LBJ – immoral, ruthless and one bribe away from being destitute. And, like Kennedy, Naslund had picked the older man because he needed Texas, Rutherford's home state. Naslund hoped only that he wouldn't pay the same price as Kennedy. He needed to act fast. And smart.

When the president and Orvez got to the Oval Office, FBI Director Roger Hamilton and Secret Service boss Michael Strange shot to their feet. Naslund nodded recognition, examined papers on his desk, mumbled. He went to a window, hands clasped behind his back.

"OK," he said, "I called you here to discuss the obvious. My vice president has his head up his ass and it threatens everything we're working for. How do we get it out?"

No one answered.

"Roger," asked Naslund, "who the hell is this Dimitri Ivanov?" Jaw clenched, eyes unsmiling.

"A billionaire. Maybe the top mafia figure in Russia."

Naslund grunted, pensive. The Russian mafia was no laughing matter. "But what did he think he was buying?"

"Sir, he has his own box at the Bolshoi, acquires every van Gogh he can find, and moves everywhere with impunity. He has illusions he can buy politicians."

"Illusions, my ass," said Naslund. "My vice president comes cheap."

Hamilton turned crimson.

"OK," the president said. "So how do we contain this mess?"

"Sir, you can point out that your administration has fought Ivanov all along," Hamilton said. "We set up the Russian Organized Crime Task Force just last year."

"Yes, we set up a task force," Naslund said, unimpressed.

"Sir," said Orvez, "We could become proactive."

Naslund stopped pacing. Hamilton and Strange exchanged a glance. This part seemed rehearsed.

"Mr. President, if you go after Ivanov no one will be able to say you went limp because of the vice president."

"I'm listening," said Naslund. "We hit him here?"

"Sure. But that might not be enough of a message. He thinks he's safe. We need to show him we can hit him on home turf."

"In Russia?"

"Yes," Orvez said. "But carefully. He's Putin's pal. But we can attack his men. It will be dangerous, of course. We will need deniability if anything goes wrong."

"You can do this?"

"Sure," said Orvez.

The president looked at Hamilton and Strange. If either man objected, they weren't showing it. Mostly they looked relieved that someone had a plan.

"Well, Linda, this is interesting," said Naslund. "How do we start?"

Linda Orvez laid out her plan. Then the President gave it a name: "Project Shutdown."

2. Denver Don

DANNY Dicerno – sixtyish, pudgy with salt and pepper hair and a couple of relevant scars on his face – bounced twenty-something Stacy on his lap while trying to stab a morsel of Italian sausage. Stacy giggled and cooed and let her too-short red skirt ride a little higher. For a north Denver stripper in one of Danny's clubs, Stacy was just fine, all the boys said. Not used up.

Dicerno was in the corner booth at Capricio's, a bar and restaurant along 38th Avenue that was in his wife's name, though she had never set foot in the place. It was Friday evening – girlfriend night for the capos and soldiers that made up Dicerno's ever-shrinking La Cosa Nostra family.

It was a sad testament to the health of Denver's mob that made guys would now and then arrive girl-less. Dicerno had sunk to having a stripper or two drop by to service his luckless crew. In the old days women were falling all over each other to make contact with the guys. Quality women, too, not just trailer trash and junkies like now.

The thought depressed Danny. Time was marching on and it didn't care who it screwed over. A shame how things were turning out. Back in the 60s the mob meant something. "Our Thing" had been special, alive. You went to St. Mary's on Sunday, listened to the priest in a language you didn't understand, and then had lunch with the boys and their wives, kids everywhere running wild. No one cared much about a hustle or a bad-guy hit as long as it all stayed in the family. Then Rudy Giuliani and the other fed do–gooder assholes decided to crack the whip. And what did they get? Chaos, Dicerno thought – Colombian and Mexican and biker gangs that had not an ounce of honor and would kill if you farted too loud. And then came the real jerks, the friggin' Russians who knew even less honor and would kill you even if you didn't

7

fart. They would kill you for the fun of it alone, the brutal, moth-erfuckin' cunts.

Still, Danny never lost hope that Our Thing would someday make a comeback – as soon as someone in the White House woke up. And there was hope. The current occupant – some dipshit idealist from Illinois named Naslund – was at least sounding OK. He had announced a crackdown on motherless Russians. But that was just for show, they said on CNN. His vice president was hooked up in some scandal involving Russians and now every-one in Washington was running around playing innocent. Who the fuck did they think they were kidding? Those were balls the Russians had, got to give them that, Dicerno thought. Who today but the Russians would even dream of doing a number on the vice president? Danny shook his head at the thought. Back in the good days the Italians used to have balls too – back when Sam Gianca-na, the best of all the Outfit's bosses, sent his main squeeze to fuck Kennedy right under Jackie's nose. Back then, the mob knew how to get things done.

Danny put his hand on Stacy's pink thigh and moved it upwards towards treasure. Stacy stopped cooing and started taking deeper breaths.

Danny had heard that some of the boys were complaining that he lived in the past. Well, yes, he did – and so fuckin' what? There was a time when Danny would whack anyone who raised a doubt. Now you couldn't go around whacking just anybody, because who was there to fill in? Everyone today was a goddamned freelancer, anyway, doing his own thing. It started years ago when the dude on HBO crafted Tony Soprano, Dicerno felt. Tony went to see a shrink with good legs because Carmella had him by the short hairs. Fuckin' right, Danny thought. That says it all.

Danny had thought of seeing a shrink, himself. He had read a chapter about abnormal psychology, and had decided he had an affliction called passive-aggressive disorder, except he was a little too much on the aggressive side of the equation.

Danny reached Stacy's crotch. Shaved and no underwear, just

as he liked. And she was already wet. Oh man.

The least he could do was teach the boys a thing or two about the past. Maybe it might rub off. So Danny kept Capricio's just like it had been since Danny was a tadpole rounder and Capricio's was Nick the Greek's joint. The Greek had fallen behind on some gambling debts and had to be taken care of. So Danny took it over, but made sure to keep it like old Nick had done, a fuck-the-feds kind of place. The waitresses tended towards the fat and jolly side while the bartenders looked a little dangerous. And it smelled of cigars and cigarettes – to hell with Denver's anti–smoking Gestapo. At least the DPD didn't enforce that law at Capricio's. Cops had some nostalgia, too. Best of all, on the jukebox, you could still select "Mack the Knife." And somebody had.

That never failed to bring back memories, the best Danny Dicerno ever had. The very best had happened back in '83 – and every year that passed, it just got more dreamlike. Even today the young squirts talked about it in whispers. Danny was then all of 32, intent on getting loaded on the day he made capo and got his own crew. Felipe Spilotro had lured him to Capricio's with the promise that he had scored some high-priced goods – watches or some shit like that. The goods weren't the point. Danny knew it was bull but played along. After all, it was Felipe. If Danny had had a brother he couldn't have bested Felipe. No way. As kids they had swiped cars together and bonked the cheerleaders side-by-side. They had been together when Danny made his bones by killing some jerk named Alfonso. Felipe helped bury the bastard.

So Danny had expected a surprise party, with some hungry broad jumping from a cake or something, but he got more. In spades. When he entered there was a not-so-bad band and babes and plenty of scotch boosted from God knows where. After his eyes adjusted, Danny could hardly believe what he saw. The Chicago Outfit had sent its underboss to celebrate with Danny, and the Outfit was like God. Danny was big time. Had to be. What more proof was there than The Outfit?

But that was not all. As soon as everyone was good and liquored up, the underboss had tapped a crystal carafe until all had quieted. He was like some fuckin' conductor.

"We have a friend of ours passing through," the underboss said. "So I invited him over."

You should have heard the gasps as the man emerged from the back, took over the mike and belted out the sweetest "Mack the Knife" that had ever been sung. Then he grabbed Danny and Felipe, hoisted a good stiff drink, and asked the Good Lord to watch over "Our man, Daniel." One of the wise guys had snuck in a camera – usually as welcome around Capricio's as the clap – and shot the picture of a lifetime. The moment Danny took over from Nick the Greek he had the picture framed and hung behind the bar. It showed Sinatra himself, drink spilling a bit, with one arm around Danny and the other around Felipe, all three with blurry, wasted, happy eyes. Sinatra! Yeah, so he was, in fact, just passing through. And so he did owe Chicago an arm and a leg. So fuckin' what? Who could top Sinatra?

Stacy was going bonkers right there in the back booth as Danny's face broke into a wide involuntary grin at the memory, her yelps seeming to keep rhythm with an Old Blue Eyes CD as she worked her crotch against Danny's probing fingers. By the time it got to "I Did It My Way," Stacy was pulling on Danny's zipper and he was seriously thinking of taking a blow job right there at the table, fuck your mother. But then Jimmy Fresno entered, and Danny's hard-on went south in an instant.

Danny had sent Jimmy to check up on some rumors about Felipe, none of which had a chance in hell of being true. Still, Felipe was acting strange and the boss had to check – if nothing more than to show he was still on the game, treating everyone equal and crap like that.

It had been a month since the feds had busted Felipe on some bullshit charge, and the jabber mouths were jabbering.

Felipe had gone down a couple times before, spent a year or two in the joint, and always emerged unscathed with his wicked grin and that devil gleam in his eyes. That's exactly what would go down here, no sweat, Danny was sure. But the boys, most of whom didn't even know what honor meant in Our Thing, kept talking. One rumor said the DEA had found Felipe with five keys of coke, but Danny didn't believe it. Coke was off limits, always had been. No way Felipe Spilotro was dealing that shit. Anyway, who was going to throw the first stone? Even if Felipe had fucked up, he would get lawyered up and laugh it off. Danny would settle things down with a good talk.

Still, the rumors had a life of their own. Danny had seen it before. The boys were like a bunch of girl scouts on a camping trip, scaring themselves with ghost stories. One scary tale had the feds pushing for the Big Bitch – life without parole. Nonsense.

Danny thought it was going just as planned when Felipe got bonded out two weeks earlier. And all the talk would have ended right there if Felipe had used Mr. Goldfarb as his attorney, like every other one of Danny's friends. You couldn't beat the Jew in court, Danny said. Everybody knew that. But Felipe had always been an independent SOB and had hired his own shyster, one that no one knew. Danny had shrugged it off. Felipe was Felipe, after all. The boys would soon learn a lesson.

Then the call came.

Felipe left a message that he had decided to celebrate his release by taking a vacation. He was going to Hawaii with the wife. The boys hadn't liked that, and, to be truthful, neither had Danny. It was one thing to get nabbed by the feds, but another just to take off. Felipe must have a screw loose, Danny thought. Some of his men were even saying that Felipe had flipped. No way, thought Danny. Still, Danny had to check. Right?

Jimmy slipped into the booth opposite Dicerno and Stacy. Danny's hand had stopped exploring.

"Danny, bad news," Jimmy said.

Dicerno's veins froze. Shit.

"You, go," he told Stacy.

"Aw, Danny, we was just gettin' started."

"Now!" Dicerno shouted. Others in the restaurant turned to

look, and, seeing that Dicerno was agitated, turned quickly away. Stacy scurried off, almost crying. What had caused this?

"Bad news?"

Jimmy couldn't look Danny in the eyes. He shredded a napkin. He seemed miserable.

"Talk," said Dicerno.

"It's Felipe," said Jimmy. "He's taken a deal."

"Ah, Jesus," Dicerno lowered his head and shook it side to side. "This certain?"

Jimmy nodded. "I had Red sniffing, and a dumb shit in the U.S. Attorney's office braced him. Threatened him with witness tampering."

Red was Danny's enforcer, mean, dedicated to Danny, stupid.

Danny put down his cigar.

"Follow me," he ordered Jimmy, and headed for the back exit.

No one would ever confuse Jimmy Fresno with Albert Einstein. Or Tom Cruise. With skin the color and composition of bread-mold, black trenches hanging under his eyes and retreating black hair, lacquered back, Jimmy looked just a millimeter removed from one of the panhandlers on Speer Boulevard holding out signs and asking marks for money. But Jimmy Fresno's greatest goal in life was to help Danny Dicerno, and there were very few like that anymore. Danny would have preferred a *consigliere* like Don Corleone had in the Godfather movie, someone smooth as a 17th Street lawyer. But this was Denver in a new millennium. You took what you could get.

Outside, Dicerno walked without saying a word, staring at the cracks in the sidewalk. At Pecos he headed south.

"He's turned state's evidence? That's what you're saying?" Dicerno said.

"That's it, Danny."

"Gonna take me down?"

"You're the only reason the feds are bargaining."

Danny observed another set of cracks. Then he paused and lit a new cigar.

"You know what they say about shooting the messenger, Jimmy?"

"No Danny. Who's the messenger?"

"You."

Jimmy looked puzzled. Danny could be real weird at times. Shooting the messenger – where'd that come from? Didn't make Jimmy feel real good, either.

"Ah, shit, Jimmy. Fuck us all."

Danny turned away and Jimmy didn't know what to do. He was hoping Danny didn't have a gun.

Dicerno stood for a minute, not saying a word. Then his right hand went to his eye, like he had gotten a piece of dust in his contact, except Danny didn't wear contacts. Jimmy wasn't sure what was happening. Danny walked a couple of steps with his back still turned, digging at some more dust that must have gotten into both eyes. He let the cigar drop.

"He was like a brother."

"I know," said Jimmy.

After another minute, Danny took a deep breath and turned.

"OK, Jimmy," he said. "Who do we have that can smoke the motherfucker?"

"That's a problem, Danny. He's in the Witness Protection Program. No one can get to him."

"Gotta be someone," said Danny Dicerno.

3. Stop Press

SALLY Will soaked in a lion-pawed Victorian tub, bubbles up to her chin, nipples protruding proudly, smoking a thin black cigar. Two glasses of white Bordeaux were stacked precariously on a ledge, one nearly empty, the other cold and dripping. Sally let the ends of her short blond hair touch the water. Osmosis did the rest. Her hair was soaked. Sally liked the smell and feel of smoke and sweat and suds. Her iPad played some sweet Enya on Pandora.

Also soaking up water was the bottom of the Denver Post, the Denver daily that had survived the great shakeout and the one Sally hated most. Sally drew the paper close and blew a near perfect smoke ring at an article about the murder of some loser named Big Bow Hendricks and the biker dustup it had caused. The ring hit and scattered against the black letters like they had been mowed down by a tiny atom bomb.

Sally drained the rest of wine glass one, and reached for number two. She flipped pages, getting the paper soggier. She flicked more ash onto the tile floor.

At 27, Sally was the youngest national correspondent for the Chicago Tribune. She had a plum beat – Denver and the Rocky Mountains.

She worried now that she had been scooped.

Lou Elliott knocked on the door.

"You still alive?" he asked.

"Not sure," said Sally.

Lou walked in, waving a hand in front of his face.

"Jesus Christ, Sally. It smells like a Turkish brothel in here. I thought you gave those up on New Year's."

"I did," Sally said, looking up only momentarily from the paper. "But that asshole friend of yours is driving me to distraction." She sent more ash crashing to the tiles.

"Brad Johnson?"

Sally gave him a "who else?" look.

Lou sat his six-foot-three frame down on the side of the tub, his black polo shirt wilting. He began to gently massage Sally's shoulders.

Sally was drop-dead beautiful, everybody agreed. Most who saw her for the first time, took her as a model, or a TV talking head. Never a print journalist. She was five feet ten with deep blue eyes, full lips and a strong jaw. Even without makeup, which she rarely wore, she could hush a crowd just by walking through the door. But she hated that. She wasn't an object.

"And what is Brad writing?" Lou asked.

"Some bull about a biker war."

After a minute, Sally began to relax, the fight slowly leaving her. Her hand drooped over the tub and the cigar plopped into a small puddle and fizzled out. Then the paper crashed down. Sally lowered her head.

"Ah, Lou. That feels good."

"The cigars, Sally..."

"You're right. They're history. A little more pressure, honey. Right there. Left a bit. There. Yes."

Lou's massage eventually included her biceps and then, slowly, her breasts. Sally caressed Lou's left hand just after it had touched a very hard nipple.

"Do you have time for this?" she asked.

"Sally, you ask the strangest questions."

An hour later, Sally walked out onto the balcony of Lou's 20th story Denver condo. She had on one of his teal dress shirts. A double espresso had replaced her white wine. Lou had beaten her there only moments before, wearing swim trunks and a bathrobe. It was chilly. Neither seemed to notice.

"Well, that was certainly nice," said Sally.

Lou looked amused. "Nice? It was fantastic, you ungrateful lady. What do you suppose the neighbors think?"

Sally smiled. "That you have a large, unwieldy cat with issues?"

"I'm afraid their imaginations might run deeper."

"Voyeurs," Sally said, reaching for a cigar but then pulling back as Lou shook his head.

Lou's dog, Tika, sleeping nearby, seemed to stir.

For Lou, this was month two of the affair, and he had no hint about how long it would last, or even if it should. He had sworn off love after his first, Becky Sue. And that resolution had made life simple. His women friends were of the same mind: no tie-downs, no relatives, and no kids. Then Sally appeared.

His biggest fear, one that came to him at night when he thought he had tucked everything away, was that he would fail Sally. Like he had failed Becky. That was a problem.

Sally went back inside and returned with the soggy Denver Post.

"Sherlock," Sally said as she sank into the sofa beside Lou and handed him the paper, "What do you make of this?"

Lou was a former FBI supervisory agent who now ran his own investigations agency. He had short, wavy dark hair, a George Clooney jaw, and a nose that suggested it had seen the business end of a fist. Sally liked to call him Sherlock.

Lou studied the paper. Brad Johnson was reporting that there was a full-fledged biker war going on. He recounted that someone – probably a Hells Angel hitman – had killed Big Bow Hendricks, and five minutes later two scared-shitless Sons had dialed 911.

"We're under attack!" one had shouted. "The Hells Angels have us pinned down!"

According to Johnson, the Commerce City cops found no Hells Angels when they got to the clubhouse. Instead, there was a dead 300-pound biker, a shell casing, and a filterless cigarette butt. A typical biker dusting.

Afterwards, wrote Johnson, the Sons regrouped. They reasoned that only the Angels had the balls to kill their national enforcer. Soon, a north Denver Angel named Barracuda Mike was eating Tombstone Pizza with two of his meth pushers when a

100-pound black powder bomb blew up under his trailer, sending Barracuda and his friends to an ugly end. Now five other bikers had been killed and police said they were worried.

"Bow Hendricks?" Lou said as he read the name.

"That's right," said Sally. "You know him?"

"Knew of him. He was a monster."

"Hard to hit?" asked Sally.

"Hard to, no. Crazy to, yes. Brad's right. There could be a big war. Bow was the national enforcer."

"Damn," Sally said, knowing she'd lost out on a good story. She lit a cigar.

Lou shook his head.

"Suggestion?" Sally said.

"You could go knock on their door."

"Whose door?"

"The Sons."

"Jesus, Lou. I thought you sorta liked me."

"I sorta do."

"Just knock on their door?"

"No, you'll need an invite. There are bikers dumber than snail piss that would kill you for a pack of gum."

"An invite?"

"Sure. I'll set it up with the president of the Sons."

"Now I believe that you have lost your mind."

"Sally, I bet if you called the Son's president, he would be flattered. His name is Sonny Sumpter. A greaseball, sure. But one with a rare half-brain. I once had an encounter with him. Look, if Sonny invited you out to the club, no one would lay a finger on you. No telling what you might find out."

For a moment Sally looked at Lou as she would a stubborn mule. Then a light went on. Maybe it could work. And Lou wouldn't have suggested it if there was any real danger, she reasoned.

"Do you have a number?" Sally asked.

"Christ, must I do everything?"

Lou grinned and got up to fetch it, but Sally blocked him with her index finger.

"OK," said Sally. "Time to fess up. Take me inside and tell me about that Turkish whorehouse first."

Later, doubly satisfied, Sally shoehorned herself into a pair of faded Levis and a cashmere turtleneck. When she returned, Tika's ears stood up. Sally reached down and gave her a scratch and Tika's tongue dropped out.

"Damn dog is lazy and worthless," said Lou. "They raise Akita's in Japan to hunt and kill bear. But something got mixed up in the genetics, I guess, because this one couldn't take down a mouse."

"Come on, Lou," said Sally. "Tika actually growled at the Chihuahua in Washington Park last week."

"Yeah, and when the Chihuahua growled back, Tika took off like the Republican Guard."

Sally lit a new cigar.

"Sally!" remonstrated Lou.

But Sally simply put on Tika's chain and went out, smiling defiance.

4. Moscow Night

JASON Mede, one of Linda Orvez's agents, was told that Boris Slavnik, a Russian copper tycoon and arms dealer, would contact him near one of those special places that give Moscow its spooky charm. Jason was to go to a gray hotel off the Prospect Kachikov in the Gerovski section of south Moscow near the Olympic Stadium. It had no name, no street address. Two decades after the Evil Empire ended, Russia was still Russia.

As he entered the 13-room hotel, a large-boned Russian woman with a soft patch of chin whiskers greeted Jason. She was sitting behind a tiny metal desk she dwarfed. He spoke to her in Russian.

"Anyone else here?" he asked.

"An Italian businessman on the second floor. You are on the first floor, 1A. Please turn off all lights when you leave."

"Fine," said Jason.

"And hot water is between five and seven in the morning and nine and ten at night."

She crossed her heavyweight-champion arms and studied how the Westerner would take this abomination. She seemed surprised by Jason's indifference.

Regular VIPs would have stayed at the Marriott or another five-star, but Jason was no regular VIP. His cover said he was a gangster, just like the Italian businessman must have been. Except for the first rank of gangsters, men like Jason roamed in the shadows, stayed at no-name hotels.

This hotel was long associated with a scientific institute, which was itself long associated with a Bohemian nightclub. If he got the signal, Jason would soon be visiting the nightclub.

Jason's instructions were clear. He was to sit and wait. If a red poster were put up on the building across the street, he would proceed.

Every half an hour he looked through a small slit in his curtains. No red poster. With wolf-gray eyes and a sinewy body, Jason paced and chain smoked Marlboros and wanted desperately to crack open a bottle of Black Jack he had managed to get through customs for a mere $5 bribe. An American faith healer was on the black and white TV promising everlasting riches. All you had to do was touch the screen.

Jason hummed "Happy Days are Here Again."

He took another look through the curtains. Still no poster. What he wanted to do was get drunk and forget this stunt. It was a fool's errand for idiots.

Two more hours passed. He glanced at his watch: Nine o'clock. It was getting dark. Maybe the mad hatters in D.C. had regained their senses, Jason thought. He took a long drag on his cigarette, and then had one final look outside. And there it was. A red poster. The President's Operation Shutdown had begun. Well, fuck me, Jason thought.

Jason had been deep cover for the CIA for years. He had traded Russian commodities ranging from wood, copper, AK-47s and SAM missiles for pennies on the dollar in the great burglary that happened to Russia after the Soviet Union went bankrupt. Now his masters in Langley had told him that he would lose all that carefully scripted legend to perform one last great operation. He was to kill Slavnik and a visiting Sicilian associate – no doubt the Italian businessman upstairs. And then he was to get out of the country, fast. The CIA had his documents and tickets and cash.

What the hell, Jason thought. Time to start the carnival.

At 9:30, as dark came and a chill filled the air, Jason met Slavnik and the Sicilian outside the nightclub, only fifty yards from the no-name hotel. Jason and Slavnik hugged like long-lost brothers.

"Jason, you little rogue," Slavnik said as he planted a wet one on Jason's cheek. He patted the rest of Jason, always careful about bugs.

"When are you going to get fat like us? Do all those American girls burn up that many calories?"

"You should come to America and see," Jason said. "They'd even get a fat old slug like yourself in shape."

"Hear that, Frankie?" Slavnik said to his Sicilian friend. "There's still some hope for fat Russians."

They chuckled and Slavnik introduced Frankie to Jason.

The nightclub was a typically Russian-only affair. It was dark, loud, and expensive. But the most surprising thing about it was the service. It was tolerable.

Jason's story was that he had come to buy a new shipment of three thousand AK47s and a like number of rocket-propelled grenades from Slavnik. A month ago that was exactly what he would have done. But with Project Shutdown, things had changed.

Jason, Slavnik and the Sicilian drained bottle after bottle of Georgian brandy. By the fourth bottle Frankie the Sicilian began to ogle the blonde Russian beauty on stage belting out unique renditions of "Hello Dolly," getting half of the lines right.

"Well, hello, Dolly. Well, hello, Dolly, It's so nice to have you backwards where you belong," she sang, licking lips.

It turned into a great night. Backs were slapped. Seven courses of food were served. Then scotch and oysters appeared.

The whole operation almost came to naught when Frankie decided he just had to have the Russian beauty and charged backstage during a break, only to be manhandled by a couple of bouncers.

"Let me go, you cocksuckers," Frankie shouted in Italian. "Don't touch me!"

Slavnik jumped up and strode like a general to the bouncers. He told them his name. The bouncers let Frankie loose. Slavnik was an important man. If Frankie wanted to screw the Russian beauty, the damn lady had better be ready to get screwed, Slavnik explained. The bouncers saw the logic and turned away.

Slavnik and the unsteady Frankie returned to the table and all seemed like it had been before. Slavnik hoisted his glass of scotch.

"May we be friends till the end of time!" he said.

They clinked glasses. Frankie quickly spilled half of his scotch down his chin and onto his shirt.

"And may we stay drunk forever," he said, as he gobbled his first oyster, and then quickly sucked down another.

Then things got sideways. Frankie's face turned sunset red. Too much brandy, Slavnik thought.

"He's not going to be sleeping with any Russian beauty tonight," roared Slavnik. "These wops, they're like little girls, they can't hold their liquor."

Slavnik scarfed down two more oysters. He roared again when Frankie fell over backwards, just like in the song. Crazy wops. This was one of the funniest nights of his life.

Then the fun stopped. Slavnik put his hands to his throat, suddenly not feeling so great himself. He gave Jason an accusing glance, and then he started to gag. He, too, tumbled over.

"Call an ambulance!" Jason screamed, leaping to his feet and knocking over the table. "These men have food poisoning!"

When the nightclub staff looked on wide-eyed, too scared to move, Jason stormed off as if to call the ambulance himself, yelling: "You are going to pay for this!"

Jason headed down the back stairs, but did not stop to call any ambulance. A black car was waiting. Jason got in. And disappeared.

Project Shutdown had won round one.

5. Bikers' Truce

SALLY Will, dressed in a black pinstriped dress suit, parked her red convertible Miata outside the Cajun Tavern in Commerce City, just a half mile from the Son's clubhouse. Some two dozen Harleys and another dozen pickups adorned the dirt lot. It was night. Two 300-pounders picked their rotting teeth and silently watched her from the shadows.

Lou said this would work, but Lou was nowhere in sight. She wondered if this was such a good idea after all.

What the hell, she told herself as she slipped out of the car. You can die any time.

Then she thought, damn you Lou.

An Old-West style swinging door led to the dark interior of the Cajun. As Sally approached, the two big teeth pickers folded in behind her. No escaping now, girl, Sally told herself.

Inside, she found the gang already gassed. But the drunks gave her wide berth, like she had an invisible shield, just as Lou had said. But the invisible shield only blocked out physical contact. Visual and olfactory assaults carried on unabated. The boys leered. Several licked their lips. One managed to get his tongue up over his nose. The underside had coarse purple vessels. Several bearded bikers rubbed their crotches and arched their hips towards Sally. One started to hump a barstool. Another dangled his dick. The smell of beer piss, chewed tobacco and vomit was everywhere. Sally managed not to gag. On the juke-box someone played a Garth Brooks song about having friends in low places.

The invisible shield seemed to protect a booth where two men with well-trimmed beards sat with another man sporting a blond ponytail and wearing a suit. Sonny Sumpter, president of the Sons, sat on the other side. Sonny's head lolled back and his eyes were glazed. His hair could have been brown or black or blond-it was too greasy to tell. It spiked out randomly. Some sticky brown liquid oozed from his mouth and onto his jacket. He was clearly coming down from too much speed.

Swell, Sally thought. He's my protection. Lou, she thought, we need to have a talk.

The man with the suit and pony tail rose as Sally approached.

"Miss Will," he said, extending a hand. "Stan Markson."

Sally noticed a wedding ring.

"I represent the Hells Angels Motorcycle Club." Markson handed her a business card.

Sally was confused. Why was an attorney for the Angels at a Sons biker bar? The two neatly attired bikers added to the confusion by introducing themselves as vice presidents of the Angels.

"Sally," Markson said, "there have been some misunderstandings. We're going to try to get those resolved. After Lou Elliott called Sonny, who I believe is a bit wasted..."

"I'm not wasted, you fuck," Sonny said with surprisingly good diction as he raised his head from the table. "Hey, Magpie," he shouted to one of the leerers. "Get the lady some wine."

"Sonny, we ain't got no wine," protested Magpie.

"A Budweiser would do," said Sally. Soon a King of Beers materialized.

Sonny wiped some of the sludge off his face and threw the napkin down. "Fuckin' speed," he said. "Upsets the stomach."

"Sally," Markson said, "after Sonny called to say that a Chicago Tribune reporter was coming to interview Sonny about the big 'biker war'" – Markson made quotation marks with two fingers on each hand – "I saw a chance to take advantage of it. You provide neutrality, you see. Nobody will get killed with a reporter around. We can have a peace conference."

Sonny appeared to follow this with interest, but decided to change the subject.

"How the hell does a nice lady like you know a mean sonofabitch like Lou Elliott? You know, he busted me a couple times. He even busted my nose." He laughed at his own joke.

Sure enough, the nose was bent. But Sonny seemed to wear it as a badge of honor.

"And it wasn't a sucker punch, either," he added. "The man's an animal."

Then Sonny leaned over. In a conspiratorial whisper he said, "Those creeps over there have mud for brains and would kill you for a dime. I'm surprised that you had the *huevos* to come in this hell hole."

He let out a long, acrid burp.

"Fuckin' speed," he said.

Sally reached into her jacket and pulled out a cigar. Markson lit it.

"I eat *huevos* for breakfast. I'd even eat yours," she said to Sonny, blowing out one of her expert rings.

Sonny stopped dead, as did everyone. All looked at Sally. Who was this lady to come in here and talk trash to the president of the Sons of Khan? And Sally was thinking the same thing. Jeez, Sally, where did that come from? But she tried to appear calm despite her pounding heart. She blew another perfect smoke ring.

Then Sonny started to laugh, and everybody joined in. The verdict seemed to be that to come in here and talk like that to Sonny meant you were one hell of a lady.

"Lou Elliott knows how to pick 'em," Sonny opined, hefting a toast to Sally.

"OK, Sally," said Markson, clearing his throat. "These are the rules. This is a peace conference. You are here to record it. Make it real."

"So is the war off?" asked Sally.

"Yes," said an Angel. "You guys," he nodded towards Sonny, "read in the paper that there was going to be a war and you believed it. We were never going to fight you. We never wanted your turf. Bow Hendricks must have been hit because he was getting into someone's poontang."

"Poontang, my ass!" Sonny said as he rose threateningly. One of the Angels slipped a hand inside his jacket.

25

"Boys," Sally said. "Calm down. Sonny, why would the Angels even be here if they didn't want peace?"

Sonny stared directly into the eyes of the Angel in front of him. Then his brow furrowed.

"Fuckin' speed," he said, dabbing at his shirt.

"So," Markson said. "Do we have a truce?"

"What choice do I have?" Sonny asked. "I could kill these two assholes," he said, looking at the Angels. "But they could bring in a thousand more to toast my walnuts. You guys say you don't want Colorado?"

"Sonny," an Angel said, "we never wanted Colorado. Just a place to park. The war was a newspaper story, that's all. We didn't touch Hendricks."

"Bet the fuck you did," said Sonny.

"Think what you want."

"I will," said Sonny, but there was no steel in the voice.

"So we're agreed?" asked Markson. "Have we kissed and made up?"

"Yeah," said Sonny. He paused, shaking his head. Then he reached out his hand to the Angels. "The war's over."

"Hold it, guys," Sally said as she dug in her purse. She got out a digital Kodak.

"I need to shoot this."

The shot wasn't greatly framed, and it was a little fuzzy. But it told a story. Sonny and an Angel were shaking hands. They had big smiles.

The Denver biker war was over.

6. Another Hit

MR. Wood sipped a latte at a downtown Starbucks, reading the Chicago Tribune and Sally Will's remarkable story. When the biker war first started he had hoped that they would continue killing themselves forever. But there they were, on the front page, Sonny Sumpter looking totally zonked, shaking hands with a Hells Angel. The Angel was grinning like he had just won the lottery.

Mr. Wood put down Sally's story and pulled out a clipping of a story in the Denver Post by Brad Johnson. It concerned an event that had happened six weeks before.

The headline: "Coke Ring Busted, Linked to Mob."

The story read:

> Denver police and federal agents Thursday said they had arrested five men with 25 kilos of cocaine, the largest Colorado coke bust in seven years.
>
> Two of the men, Giorgio Ferrara, 38, and Dominic Mora, 41, were employees of The Velvet Touch, a downtown tavern owned by Felipe Spilotro, reputed underboss of the Dicerno crime family.
>
> Contacted at the Velvet Touch, Spilotro said he had "fired the two bums" a month ago. Danny Dicerno, reached by telephone at his North Denver restaurant, said he didn't know of the men arrested, and only had a "social-like knowledge" of Spilotro.
>
> "I don't know where you guys come up with this mob crap. I own a small restaurant and sell cheese on the side. Go f... yourselves."
>
> Official sources, however, say Dicerno and Spilotro had been associated for at least twenty years. Spilotro's attorney disagreed.

"Maybe they meet at church," he said. "Big deal."

Police sources scoffed at the comments.

"What puzzles us," said one commander "is why a Dicerno man may have been involved with drugs. That had always been off limits."

Mr. Wood knew this was true. The Denver mob had always allowed rounders to traffic narcotics, as long as they paid a cash tribute. But made guys were not supposed to get their hands dirty. Judges hated narcotics more than murder, racketeering and prostitution.

Mr. Wood also knew this: When the police and feds busted Ferrara and Mora it wasn't because they cared a hoot about Ferrara and Mora. They just wanted to flip those two to get Spilotro.

Ferrara and Mora both flipped within 24 hours.

But the game wasn't over when Spilotro was charged. The man the cops really wanted was Danny Dicerno. To get Dicerno, they needed help from Spilotro. It was a wonder how fast a man facing life without parole suddenly could forget the mob's honor code. And Spilotro had.

Danny Dicerno was in trouble.

Mr. Wood figured he could help Danny out. Karma, he thought. Just when he was wondering who his next target would be, fate up and placed it right in front of him.

Mr. Wood finished his latte and left. He thought of Sally Will and her fine scoop. She was a talent, he thought. Would go far. He had marveled that she actually had the guts to go into the biker bar. Impressive.

He ambled down 17th Street, blending in with the bankers, lawyers and accountants, and considered his problem: He had a service he wanted to sell and he knew a buyer who would want to buy. The problem was that Danny Dicerno didn't know him. That's the way Mr. Wood wanted it to stay.

It was a puzzle.

Mr. Wood was considering the predicament as he walked into

a Barnes and Noble. Just inside the door there was a collection of discounted books and some free community papers. He paused to look at the discounts and then caught a glimpse of the North Denver Weekly. The front-page headline read: "Italian Businessmen to Hold Ball." Interesting. He picked up one of the papers and read on.

The businessmen were holding a masquerade ball to inaugurate an Italian June Festival. Everyone was invited. Even the police chief would be there. It was going to be a grand event.

On the jump page Mr. Wood found a list of other notables who would attend, and their spouses. One of those expected was "Restaurateur Daniel Dicerno."

Bingo.

7. Long Shot

AFTER her scoop, Sally did what she always did when she was beating the odds. She gambled more.

"Ah, Miss Will," said Andy, an old black tout-sheet hawker, as Sally rounded a corner at the Paradise Park Dog Track in Commerce City. "Ain't seen you in 'bout a month. You quinellin', girl?"

Sally smiled.

"Yeah, you be quinellin'. Damn, you be winnin' all da money."

And quinella-ing Sally was. It is a seductive bet. You pick dogs to place first and second as a team, the order doesn't matter. Most bettors pick three dogs and "box" them. Betting all three possible combinations. Three tickets. Three dogs. Three ways to win. The payout was usually good.

Sally didn't bet on whims, or because a dog looked good or had a great name. That was for losers. She had a system based on wins, weight and wagers. Old Andy was always trying to get Sally to tell him the system because he knew she routinely beat the track. But Sally wouldn't tip her hand.

When the horn sounded for bettors to place wagers on race four, Sally had just put down her calculator. She was going to box Mi-Ai, Oshkosh Dan, and Proud Father. It was a triple A race – the best dogs – and Oshkosh Dan and Proud Father were considered long shots.

Tonight, Sally Will felt particularly lucky. She placed a $120 bet.

Sally groaned when Mi-Ai stumbled out of the gate. He was her only short-odds dog. No way the other two could place first and second. Sally had almost dropped her tickets when the crowd began an unexpected cheer. She turned around, but didn't catch the dogs crossing the finish line. It was then that Andy raced to her.

"Miss Will. Bet you had 'em, right? Long shots. Oshkosh Dan and Proud Father?"

"What do you mean?"

"The 3-7. Bet you had the 3-7 combo."

And that's exactly what she had.

Sally was suddenly four thousand dollars richer. One bet. One Costa Rican vacation.

Sally drove home full of adrenalin.

Thinking of Lou. Meeting Lou was as unusual as the love affair it turned into.

They had met on his deathbed. By then, Lou was already famous.

He had quit the FBI while he was flying high. One day he was offered the job of assistant agent in charge of the New York office. It was a ticket to the top. But the next day, Lou not only turned it down but also quit the Bureau entirely. He hung out his shingle, "Elliott Investigations" and didn't look back.

No one understood why.

Lou had soon been hired by a Denver tycoon to find his kidnapped daughter. Lou and the kidnapper had agreed to meet up Turkey Creek Canyon, but somehow things had gone wrong. Both men had guns. Both men used them. Neither should have lived.

Lou had somehow crawled over to the kidnapper and persuaded him – again, no one knew how – to give up the girl's location. Before slipping into unconsciousness, Lou had told a deputy about the girl. She was buried in a box equipped with a garden hose for breathing next to an abandoned cabin in the White National Forest.

If not for Lou, the girl would have died.

The kidnapper did die minutes later. An ambulance managed to get Lou to a hospital, but he had lost too much blood. Doctors believed he was brain dead and put the dreadful letters DNR on his chart.

The case became an overnight nationwide sensation.

"Former FBI Official Near Death," said the New York Times. "Docs: Pull Hero's Plug!" screamed the New York Post.

The story got better. One afternoon, an unsuspecting nurse entered Lou's room and nearly fainted when Lou roared: "I want you to get this goddamn thing out of my you-know-what."

It was said that the nurse had recovered in time to help some other nurses extract the catheter.

Sally was one of the first reporters to interview Lou while he was still at Denver General. Their eyes had met, and that was pretty much that. Lou, just back from the dead, asked Sally out on the spot, even with IVs still plugged into both arms.

"You've got to be kidding," Sally had said.

"Well, I didn't mean today."

"That's good."

"Maybe tomorrow?"

"Mr. Elliott, you are recovering from a gunshot that nicked your aorta and collapsed a lung."

"They didn't tell me about the aorta."

"Christ," Sally said.

The date didn't take place the next day, but it did take place.

And from then on, it had been wildfire.

8. Red Mist

RUSSIAN detectives determined that Boris Slavnik and Frankie the Sicilian, the two men Jason killed at the Russian nightclub, had perished from the consumption of shellfish that unfortunately, but naturally, carried paralytic toxins. It was probably from the oysters. An accident. Case closed.

Their police bosses, who knew better, were not displeased with the verdict. To them, it was just another mob hit that they didn't have to waste their time investigating. They wished all the *vor v zakone* – the Russian mob bosses – were as creative as the American killer named "Jason." Life would be easier.

But the Russian mobsters weren't fooled by the official version, nor had the police bosses expected them to be. The mobsters didn't know exactly what was happening, but they knew accidents like this didn't just form out of dust.

Something was changing.

Three of the top bosses met at Lubyanka Square in the center of Moscow. It was dank, overcast. The men wore dark trench coats and carried umbrellas. The black concrete stand that once supported a statue of Iron Felix Dzerzhinsky – the first head of the Soviet secret police – stood ominously close. The statue had been torn down shortly after the revolution in 1991, but its spirit still hung over the square like a cloud of poison gas. Even decades after the Soviet Union collapsed, this was still a place Russians avoided with resolve. Nothing good happened at Lubyanka Square, and certainly nothing good happened inside the building that it fronted – the Lubyanka, former headquarters of the KGB and now home to the new Russian intelligence service, the FSB.

In the courtyard of the Lubyanka was a prison. For most of the twentieth century, it was mankind's heart of darkness. No one knew for sure just how many men and women Stalin put to death inside the Lubyanka, but certainly it ranged into the tens of thousands. Millions more had been condemned by decrees drafted behind the Lubyanka's yellow stone walls by monsters known as Yogoda, Yezhov and Beria.

Now, Russian mobsters were trying to replace the secret state organs as the font of terror in Russia. It was still unclear which side would win out, or if the two would one day merge. The three Russians meeting in the square were apparently unmoved by the Lubyanka and its demons. Maybe they felt more at home here, among the ghosts.

These were hard, unsmiling men.

Dimitri Ivanov was in charge, head of the most feared organized crime operation in the world. To an outsider, he could have been any Western businessman – dressed in a sharply tailored overcoat above an Armani suit. His black hair was combed back, and he had a small birthmark pigmentation on his right cheek. Not a big man physically – he was five feet nine and weighed one hundred sixty five pounds – Ivanov was nevertheless imposing. His sharp, blue eyes missed nothing.

Three bodyguards in thick coats with bulges under their arms stood fifteen yards away, glancing at any movement in the square, however slight or seemingly innocent. If they were afraid of the Lubyanka, they didn't show it either.

"He was meeting with an American when this happened," Ivanov said of Slavnik. He pulled up his coat collar. "What do we know of him?"

A man named Gregory, sporting a walrus mustache and a sable hat, said, "He was a trader. Slavnik had done business with him for years. He was a crook, just like Slavnik. This makes no sense. Why would he kill his major Russian partner? He's certainly not going to get any of the goods."

"Something is wrong," Ivanov said. "Why don't you check with your friends over there?" Ivanov nodded toward the Lubyanka. "They might know."

"But what if they are the ones behind it?" asked Gregory.

"I thought of that of course," Ivanov said. "Those people don't kill in public. Far easier to do it in the basement. No, I think it's another group that's out to hurt us. Maybe a new Russian gang. Or..." He paused.

"Or what, Dimitri?" Gregory asked.

"No," Ivanov said, shaking his head as if ridding it of a particularly unpleasant thought. "Just check."

Ivanov's eyes narrowed as he looked across at the Lubyanka. A part of him wished the threat was coming from there, but his instinct told him otherwise. He would investigate and he would be ruthless in protecting his substantial vital interests.

9. Hidden Depths

BACK from the track with the loot stashed, Sally slid into bed beside a slightly snoring Lou. No need to wake him, she thought. He will be happily surprised in the morning.

Sally fell to sleep dreaming of Oshkosh Dan being knighted by the Queen of England. Old Andy the tout man stood at her side wearing a jeweled crown.

An hour later, Sally began to stir. She turned over and instinctively brought her arm around Lou. Except Lou wasn't there. The void was enough to wake Sally. She lay with her head flat to the pillow and peered into the darkness to find the time. A digital alarm stared back with angry red glowing sticks, reading: 2:00 a.m.

I'm hungry, was the first thought that registered. Sally stumbled out of bed and headed towards the kitchen. It was then that she realized that the light to Lou's study was on. And Lou wasn't in bed. Ergo...

But hunger was the major motivator and Sally continued to the fridge and poured herself a giant glass of milk. More cobwebs cleared. What was Lou doing? She had a guess.

Sally quietly opened the study's door. There sat Lou, chin on his fists, peering over a chessboard with some of the pieces already toppled to the side. His concentration seemed absolute. He hadn't noticed her.

This is the strange man that I have fallen for, Sally thought. Big, tough, Lou Elliott. Playing chess at 2 a.m.

She approached Lou from behind and gently began massaging his shoulders. He only slowly came out of his trance.

"Ah, it's you Sally," he said, as if to imply there could have been someone else.

"I'm it," said Sally.

Lou patted her hand and then glanced at the board again.

"Who is it this time?" Sally asked.

"Third game," said Lou, "Fischer-Spassky, Reykjavik, July, 1972."

"And which one of the chess giants are you?"

"Right now, I'm looking at Bobby's eleventh move. Look at what he does," as if Sally played chess. Lou picked up Bobby Fischer's black knight and moved it to the side of the board, a lonely space known as h5, seemingly away from any meaningful action.

Lou shook his head, bewildered. "I sit in Fischer's place and I ask, 'How did he ever see that?' Bobby has just moved an important piece away from the center of action. It looks like a dumb move, and goes against theory. But then I go and sit in Boris's spot, and I can't find a way to refute it."

"You big lug," Sally said, hugging Lou from behind. "Why do you do this?"

"Misplaced hope."

"Come on," Sally said. "Let's get some air."

On the balcony, Sally decided to find out a little more about this strange man. She was direct.

"You had just been appointed the assistant big wig in the New York office – and you just blew it off. No one does that."

"I had my reasons."

"So did John Hinckley."

"I got tired of political bullshit?" It was a suggestion and Sally wasn't having it.

"Quit the FBI to be a private investigator for no reason? I would rather believe in O.J."

Lou said nothing.

"I'm waiting," Sally said, crossing her arms.

"Oh, Sally, why don't we go inside and annoy the neighbors instead."

But Sally didn't move. "Come on."

Lou drew in a breath. He knew that Sally couldn't be denied. At least, not totally.

"Sally, there's not much to tell. Grew up in Connecticut. Came west. Decided to stay. That pretty much covers it."

"Lou, I wasn't born yesterday."

Lou did his head-scratching thing.

"Bare bones?" he asked.

"Better than nothing." Lou cleared his throat.

"Well, my father was a successful Wall Street banker who had bad habits, you could say. I never liked him."

"That's hard."

"Not if you knew him. Particularly after the way he treated mom."

"Meaning?"

"He was a jerk. Every time mom went to the city, my father brought one of his bimbos home. Didn't much give a shit what we boys thought. Or mom. She knew. Pretended not to of course."

"And?"

"My two older brothers thought nothing of it. Guess they were like him. Besides, he had the money."

"But you were different?"

"No, just money stupid. I wasn't onboard," Lou said. "And that somehow just impressed him. He took to calling me 'my little rebel'."

Sally studied the lines on Lou's troubled face as he talked. "By my senior year at private school, when I actually towered over him, I went to calling my father 'my little Nazi.' Once I even said it to his face, earning me a bloody lip."

"So what happened?"

Lou was talked out. "Another time Sally."

"No. Now."

"No, Sally. Not now."

He said it with sudden unbending resolve and she knew she would get no further then. He knew more about her than she knew about him. Though Sally wanted to know all about Lou, she held her own cards just as close to the vest. Lou, however, had managed a peek inside.

The facts he had were hometown: Greybull, Wyoming. Early

occupation: tomboy. Education: full scholarship to Brown. Degree: cum laude, comparative literature. Ambition: make it big.

On the way back to Wyoming, she had stopped over in Chicago and got hooked up with a weekly newspaper and fell in love with ink. Eventually she applied to the Chicago Tribune and was laughed out of the newsroom. But she didn't give up. One night she went trolling for a job and had an inspiration. She would go after a person, not just a job. And there was one person who had fascinated her. Mel Campbell was the Tribune's national editor. A black and careless Vice Lord member as a teen, somehow acquitted of manslaughter at 21. And then the missing years, until he graduated from Northwestern University in the 70s with an honors degree in journalism.

"What I did back then is private," Mel had simply told a reporter for an alternative weekly.

"Isn't that a double standard as a journalist?" the reporter had asked.

"Sure as shit, lady," Mel had replied.

Sally loved it. Mel knew what it was like to start with disadvantages, Sally figured. He wouldn't care about her lack of experience as long as she was good.

So Sally decided to avoid the rules of applying to the Tribune and instead tracked Mel down at Mike's Pub, a watering hole for the editor and his cronies. In one detail that Lou savored Sally said she marched up to Mel, handed him her clips and said, "Mr. Campbell, my name is Sally Will, and I'm going places." She was 22.

Mel Campbell could see the pit bull in Sally, because that's what he had been, exactly. He had taken a thin black cigar out of his mouth and hired Sally on the spot – as a night police reporter, bottom of the barrel.

Three years later, Mel gave her a job on the national desk. Soon she was in Denver.

Lou knew that Mel had become something of a father figure to Sally. She worshipped him.

But of her own father, Sally was as closed as was Lou about his secret, Becky Sue. Sally wouldn't go there. Lou knew that whatever it was, it was deep. He didn't know if he wanted to go there either.

10. Fall Guy

JASON, the man who had poisoned Slavnik and the Sicilian in Moscow, arrived in Billings, Montana, a changed man. His hair had gone from brown to red, and his eyes from gray to brown. He had sprouted a beard. He had a limp. He wore cowboy boots. About the only thing that hadn't changed was his first name. But his last name was now Ison. Moscow nights were now far in the past.

A big lumberjack of a man named George Phillips met him at the Frontier Airlines gate.

"Jason!" exclaimed George, wearing cowboy boots and a flannel shirt. "My God, you look good."

The newly minted Jason Ison hugged this man whom he had never seen before. "And you, too, George. How are the kids?"

"Fine, fine."

They headed down the concourse, laughing, backslapping. Jason's new friend must have weighed 250 pounds, and it wasn't baby fat. The back slaps stung. Maybe the Company did know something about protecting agents who had crossed the line, Jason thought.

They kept up the old-friends act as they retrieved Jason's baggage. People noticed the happy duo, but their glances didn't linger. Long-lost friends. Nothing more.

George and Jason hauled the luggage to a Ford Expedition, and then took off for Thompson Falls. The town was just a dot on the map in far-west Montana, the spot where the climate of the Pacific Northwest meets the climate of the Rockies. It can be warm in January and cold in July. Schizophrenic country.

"You're going to love it in Thompson Falls," said George as they left Billings. Jason thought he caught some irony in the tone.

"You a hunter?"

"No," said Jason.

"You'll become one. You'll find deer, elk, moose. Anything you like."

"That's great."

"Unfortunately, beaver is in short supply." George roared.

Jason shook his head. He wondered if this meant he would be reduced to watching reruns of "The Simpsons" on Saturday nights.

"You? How do you entertain yourself?"

"Me?"

"No. Your invisible rabbit," Jason said. He had become grouchy.

"I just come up here when I have to," George said. "I live in Denver. Fly up in the Company's Piper. You, though, you get to stay. Lucky devil." He roared again.

Fuck me, Jason thought. Five minutes passed. "George, what's my cover?"

"The dimwits haven't told you?"

"That's why they're dimwits."

George blasted his horn at the clueless cow that had wandered onto the blacktop. It didn't even look up.

"We've got a front here called New Company Logging," George said. "God's truth. New Company. I'm sales VP. Anyway, and this will also surprise you, it actually turns a profit."

"No shit?"

"No shit."

"So I'll be chopping down trees?"

"Only in your dreams," George said. "You're my new assistant. My on-location man. And I'm a hard taskmaster. A real jerk."

"I bet."

George looked at Jason, grinning.

"Actually, you'll never see me. Here's the score: You will pretend to be busy. And that's the toughest part, because you have nothing to do. If there's a Book-of-the-Week Club, you should join."

"Christ," Jason said, pushing his seat back a notch. "I used to be an international smuggler of dope and bullets."

George laughed, his big frame heaving.

"From drug smuggler to dweeb. What a racket we're in."

"I find it less than funny," Jason said.

"I find it more than funny."

The cow finally ambled off the road. George hurtled down the highway going eighty five, oblivious to nonexistent Montana lawmen.

Jason considered his predicament. He was here because he had followed orders. Twelve years in the Agency, and he had done his first "wet" job. Slavnik and the Sicilian. At the director's personal orders.

George could see consternation on Jason's face. He tried to help.

"Cheer up, friend. The culture shock only lasts a year or two."

The jest didn't help. Jason sat silent for the rest of the journey, wondering if he would ever get back into the game.

In the end, he would. But not in a way he ever imagined.

11. Face Mask

MR. Wood had a masquerade ball to attend – the Italian June Festival – and he needed a disguise.

The Denver Yellow Pages listed twenty eight costume shops, from the high-end in Cherry Creek to low-rent on south Sheridan. Mr. Wood didn't think twice. In Cherry Creek there would be video surveillance. But on south Sheridan, no way. He headed for Sheridan.

Stella's Magic and Mask Shop was crunched between a tattoo parlor and a Chinese take-out joint. Pasted on the window of the entry door was a huge picture of Bela Lugosi, fangs dripping with blood.

Mr. Wood walked in, jingling an invisible bell. A rotund woman in a 1950s pink dress and black horn-rimmed glasses sat smoking a cigarette, ignoring him as she flipped through *People* magazine. He figured she was Stella.

He wasn't looking for any mask in particular. Just something serviceable for a masquerade ball. On display were masks of world leaders of old: Churchill, Stalin and Hitler. And there were masks of Madonna, Bin Laden and Elvis. Many of Elvis. He almost took one of those, but then noticed one under the shadows of some of the costumes. He thought he recognized the face. He picked it up. Ted Bundy, one of America's most notorious serial sex killers.

Why not?

He brought it up to Stella, who sucked in the cigarette. She grimaced, almost snarled. Maybe, Mr. Wood thought, Stella did not depend on return business.

"You want to buy Bundy?" Stella asked.

"If it's for sale."

"It's been for sale for ten months. No one ever bought it."

"I guess today that ends."

"Are you some sicko?"

"Stella, honey, I'm not a sicko. I'm just like Ted."

Mr. Wood wasn't smiling. He looked straight at her.

Stella's eyes got circular. Her mouth opened.

"How much?" Mr. Wood asked.

Blood rushed to Stella's ears, face. She dropped her cigarette. Her hand shook.

"It's free, man, just get out of here," she said.

For a moment, it looked like she was going to make a run for it.

"No," Mr. Wood said. "How much?"

"Five dollars."

Mr. Wood took out one of Stella's cigarettes from a pack she had left on the counter, lit it, and put it back in Stella's mouth.

Stella remained motionless, but for a tremor in her right cheek. The unsucked cigarette bobbed. This man was dark.

Mr. Wood was quiet for a moment. Then he said: "Stella, you are one beautiful lady," and winked. On his way out, he left a ten dollar tip.

Stella liked the tip.

Maybe I misjudged him, she thought. But her hand trembled holding the bill.

12. Stepping Out

MR. Wood arrived at the festival in blue jeans and a black t-shirt, wearing the Bundy mask. The restaurant, Belagio's, had a band playing rock outside on the patio and another playing mostly country inside. At least half the crowd had taken the masquerade theme seriously: Warlocks, witches and Vegas dancers joined Donald Trump, Batman and Miley Cyrus. People were drunk, loud, happy. But for the body heat it would have been a cool night.

Attending were politicians, consultants, businessmen, several locals and plenty of barely legals. It was a cash bar, and cash was flowing. Mr. Wood wanted a drink. Needed one. Decided against. To drink he would have to remove his mask. That would not do. He decided to stay on the periphery, looking for Danny Dicerno.

A young lady in a short black skirt came by carrying a tray of hors d'oeuvres. She stopped to let him take one, but he declined.

"Sorry, no" he said.

She winked at him and sashayed on. Ted Bundy had his way with women.

The band played a Pam Tillis tune about a young woman in Memphis falling in love with a boy from a Faulkner novel. Then came YMCA. That sent the crowd roiling. Mr. Wood spotted the chief of police joining a conga line, three sheets to the wind. Someone handed the chief a mask. It was one of the three little piggies. The chief roared and put it on.

There would be few DUI traps tonight, Mr. Wood thought.

Finally, Mr. Wood spotted Danny Dicerno. He was near a side entrance, a drink in one hand and a cigar in the other, chatting with two big bruisers. He seemed sedate, his foot keeping time with the tune.

Mr. Wood noticed Dicerno had a defining scar that went from

his right ear to his chin. He wore an open collar pink silk shirt. It showed off his gold chains and rings.

Suddenly, Mr. Wood had second thoughts. Killing Big Bow Hendrickson was one thing. Approaching a Mafioso, with an offer, was quite another. Maybe I should wait, he thought. What's the rush? A drop of sweat snaked down his back.

Then a sense of recklessness returned. This is what I wanted, Mr. Wood told himself. What the hell.

He walked, too slowly he sensed, towards Danny Dicerno.

Dicerno took note. Crooked his neck. Thought: who is this guy wearing a mask of a lawyer, or something. Why is he going to invade my space?

Mr. Wood hesitated, and then took a final forward step.

One of Dicerno's men was immediately at his back, patting him down. Another goon's eyes were glued to Mr. Wood's hands.

"Mr. Dicerno," Mr. Wood said, "I wonder if I could have a moment of your time? I have a proposition I think will interest you."

"Who da fuck are you?" Dicerno asked, lowering his cigar and looking at the silly mask as though he could see through it with X-ray vision. The bruiser behind Mr. Wood looked up. If Dicerno gave the word, Mr. Wood would be out of Belagio's with a foot in his back. A few in the crowd stopped to watch. Most didn't.

"Clean," said the thug.

"I said, who da fuck are you?" Dicerno's smile had left him. He didn't like interruptions.

"Mr. Dicerno, my name is Mr. Wood. I'm serious," he said. "Give me five minutes. What do you have to lose?"

"Five minutes of my goddamn time. Now get da fuck out."

Mr. Wood had to pounce. Now or never.

"Mr. Dicerno, you've got a big problem. Someone is on your case."

"Yeah. You."

"No, someone else," said Mr. Wood. "Felipe Spilotro. I know where he is."

"I know where he is, too," said Dicerno. "Vacation. Hawaii."

47

"Is that where they keep protected witnesses?"

Dicerno almost dropped his drink. He quickly looked around. Who may have overheard this madman?

His men waited for the word. Dicerno didn't give it.

"Not here," Dicerno said finally, nodding towards the door.

They headed out to an alley.

A dumpster was piled high, and smelled it. There were glints of broken bottles. The music seemed muffled, distant. It was dark, suddenly cold. Mr. Wood didn't know if he would make it to see another day.

Dicerno leaned against a brick wall, lit another cigar.

"You know you are one crazy bastard," he said. "You could be dead."

"Mr. Dicerno, please. Spilotro."

"What about him? Hardly know the motherfucker."

"Funny, he says he knows you very well."

"Let me see your face. I wanna see your face," Dicerno said as he grasped at the Bundy mask. Mr. Wood grabbed Dicerno's arm. The thugs looked at each other. One took out a blade. One word, and this prick was history.

"If you see my face, I walk," said Mr. Wood. "Spilotro will testify against you and you will face the needle."

Dicerno hesitated, and then looked again at his guards.

"Why don't you boys go get some drinks?" he said. They exchanged dumb looks and lumbered off.

"Walk with me," Dicerno said.

Mr. Wood was hoping that they would go out to the street where there were lights. But Dicerno had something else in mind. He walked to the dark dead-end of the alley. Mr. Wood's heart was beating almost as loudly as the bass drums.

"Now, Mr. Wood, talk to me," Dicerno said.

"You naturally think that I'm a cop and this is a setup," Mr. Wood said.

"Got that right."

"I'm not."

"Sure," said Dicerno. "You're my fairy fuckin' godmother."

"Mr. Dicerno, listen. You know that cops can do a lot when they go undercover, but commit a felony they cannot."

"Bullshit," said Dicerno. "I know a dozen who have."

"OK," Mr. Wood conceded, "but not murder."

Dicerno lowered his cigar. The man had a point.

"What I'll do," Mr. Wood continued, "to prove I'm real, I will kill someone of your pleasing. Not Spilotro. That'll cost you. But someone else, someone easy. To prove a point. Then you'll know."

Dicerno: "This is insane."

"No. This is business. I want $100,000 for Spilotro."

Dicerno paused, sucked on the cigar, and then looked back at the man in the funny mask.

"You got some balls, I'll give you that," he said. "But I ain't sure you got brains. How da fuck do you know where he is?"

"You will learn that I do," said Mr. Wood, "but never how."

Dicerno put the cigar back in his mouth. It was no longer lit.

"In this dream of yours, how does it come down?"

Yes, Mr. Wood thought, I'm about to close the deal.

"Have some gofer leave a note at the bottom of the Westword news rack outside the Sawadee restaurant on Boulder's Pearl Street Mall. The Westword rack is filled every Thursday. I'll get it, read it, and burn it. Then you will see results."

"After that?"

"After that, you will pay me for Spilotro."

A jet headed for Denver International Airport flying low overhead shook the ground and seemed close enough to crash.

Dicerno looked up. The plane roared away.

"And how do I contact you?" Dicerno asked.

Mr. Wood had thought this one through.

"Put a yellow rose in a vase. Place it in the southern window of Capricio's. When I see it, I'll go to the Westword box. Leave your message there."

"This is crazy."

"Very."

13. Paper Drop

AT Capricio's Danny Dicerno, in a white suit, blue shirt and a Jerry Garcia tie, was picking a nugget of pasta out of a rear molar. He bounced another 22-year-old North Federal stripper on his lap. Jimmy Fresno was at his side.

"This guy, last night, he was a riot," Dicerno said. "I mean, must have balls as big as Texas. Wanted to be a hitman."

Jimmy said: "No shit?"

"Yes, shit. Wearing a goofy mask of some lawyer or something. I thought you were supposed to wear somethin' scary at a masquerade-fuckin' ball. But no. Some lawyer. Strangest thing I ever seen."

"You know who he was?"

"Not a clue," said Dicerno. "Hitman. For the love of Christ."

"Yeah. Strange."

"Jimmy," said Dicerno, "who in our outfit is particularly worthless? I mean, a fuckup. Someone no one would miss? No family. Nothin'."

Jimmy Fresno squinted, trying to think.

"There's Bruno at the Lay Lady Lay on Pecos," he said. "He's run the place into the ground. Wrecked the club's limo. Twice."

"You're right. He's what they call a liability."

"You want to fire Bruno?" Jimmy asked.

"No, Jimmy. Bruno's OK. But I want you to do somethin'." Dicerno sprinkled more Tabasco into his Bloody Mary and took a gulp. Then he told Jimmy about the Westword box.

"Just put it at the bottom of the rack, Jimmy. Someone will pick it up."

"Who?"

Dicerno pulled the toothpick from his mouth and slammed it down on Jimmy's hand. Jimmy yelled.

"You askin' questions now?" Dicerno said. "Never mind who

the fuck who!" The pick had hit an artery and blood was spurting. Jimmy wrapped his hand in a napkin.

"The Westword box," he said. "I'll be there."

"That's good, Jimmy."

Jimmy carried the envelope to the Pearl Street Mall. He was wearing a corduroy suit, a too-short purple tie and zip-up black boots. He didn't like the mall. It was filled with street actors, and hippies, and upper-class folks. Mixing. It wasn't natural.

Jimmy passed one man on stilts entertaining a crowd. Jimmy almost knocked him over.

"Don't worry," the man told the audience. "Every village has one."

The crowd exploded.

Jimmy thought the asshole was making fun of him, but didn't understand exactly how. It was nuts. The world was going fast down the shitter, Jimmy thought.

Finally, Jimmy tracked down the Sawadee, saw that the Westword paper box was right where Dicerno said it would be. Taking a long breath, he carefully placed the envelope at the bottom of the stack.

Then he left. Fast.

14. Blow Job

BRUNO Palermo had tattoos from his size-19 neck down to his toes. He had a trailer in Brighton, north of Denver. His girlfriend was a pimply young Mexican who spoke almost no English. On weekends, Bruno amused himself by beating her, and her four-year-old son. He thought that taking a cigarette to the kid's feet was a blast.

No one liked Bruno. No one would miss him.

It was 10 p.m. Thursday when Bruno left the Lay Lady Lay, drunk. It was four hours before closing time, but he didn't care. Let the girls rip off the joint. Who gave a shit? Most of the loot was going to Danny Dicerno, anyway. Fuck him.

There was a slight breeze, a clear sky, little smog. Perfect.

Bruno had saved Ben Franklins all week and he now could afford a fuckin' serious North Federal Boulevard blow job at Maggie's Best, right around the corner.

Mr. Wood knew this. He had done his homework.

Still, he was not happy. Killing Bruno was not challenging. Big Bow at least had taken nerve. Yet, there was this: Bruno was a made guy, and rules said made guys were off limits. Mr. Wood was about to kill a member of the Mafia. That counted. Didn't it?

At 11:30 Bruno emerged from Maggie's, a grin on his face. One of his shirttails was out. He stumbled toward his Ford Bronco.

Mr. Wood wondered how a person in Bruno's condition could even get it up. But Bruno's demeanor suggested that he had made a real go of it. Viagra, Mr. Wood figured.

Bruno stopped by the Bronco's left front tire and let his pants fall down to his ankles. He had to take a pee.

Mr. Wood stomped out a Dunhill and walked up to Palermo. "Hi," he said.

Bruno smiled. He thought Mr. Wood was just another john.

"Yeah, dude," Bruno said, "A man's gotta do what a man's gotta do, right?"

"Got that right," said Mr. Wood, as he raised a silenced .22 to Palermo's head and pulled the trigger five times.

By the time police arrived, the lights at Maggie's Best were out, the street deserted.

No witnesses.

Lt. Steve Brandon sat at the Mile High Grille with a steaming cappuccino. It was 1:30 a.m., two hours after Mr. Wood had killed Bruno Palermo.

Brandon looked over the late night revelers parading on 32nd Avenue. A waitress, in her mid-20s, cleaned off the next table. Her toned body rode well in tight clothes. Her hair was black and her complexion baby pink.

She glanced at Brandon. Smiled.

Brandon's radio crackled.

"Yeah, D-80 here," he said.

"D-80, we have a 10-2, North Pecos, in the alley off 52nd. Uniforms are there. Can you respond?"

"Sure."

The waitress looked at Brandon. Her eyes lingered. She wrote out the check.

"Something bad happened?" she asked.

"Nothing for you to worry about. Maybe I'll catch you later."

"We close at two," she said.

Brandon winked. She smiled.

Brandon swung his SUV into an alley, pulling up behind flashing blues and reds. He ducked under yellow tape and walked up to Bruno Palermo.

Bruno was face up, arms splayed outwards. His brown eyes were wide open and had an expression of puzzlement, like he was saying: "So this is it?"

"This is surely it," Brandon said under his breath.

The crime scene tech told Brandon: "Looks like small caliber hits in the front and side of his head. Professional."

Brandon took one step back. Appraising.

"Fuck you mean?" he said. "This is a greaseball-loser-killing."

"Five shots?"

"Have you any idea who this prick is?" Brandon said.

The tech started to get nervous. Brandon was a legendary detective. Took no prisoners.

"I just mean, it looks professional," said the tech.

"Listen, dick brain," Brandon said, "The mob doesn't pay hitmen to take out losers. That's Bruno Palermo. He's so big at being a loser his dog left him. He simply ain't worth the lead that took him out."

Brandon kicked some dirt.

"Mob hit, my ass," he said.

Brandon lingered for only 30 minutes, giving instructions. Then begged off.

Detective Scott Kirkpatrick, a new homicide dick, came up to the tech.

"What's up his ass?" he asked.

"Don't know."

Brandon parked outside the Mile High Grille and watched the waitress put up the "Closed" sign. It was 2 a.m.

Fifteen minutes later, she shut the door and walked towards her car. Brandon pulled up, rolled down his window.

"You have time for a drink?" he asked.

The young woman jumped.

"You startled me," she said.

"Sorry." Brandon shrugged. He looked almost sheepish. Unthreatening.

"Come on," he said, "You can listen to my official police radio."

He winked again. He seemed so nice. And he was a cop. She thought: "Why not? Go for it."

15. Shell Shocked

JASON Ison, the CIA man stuck in Montana, sat at the bar at the Nobody Saloon in Thompson Falls, a Black Jack Daniel's in hand. It was nearly midnight. Two guys were playing eight ball, three others plopped quarters into an illegal video poker machine swiped from the reservation, and more men were scattered about. The Juke Box played John Denver's "Leaving on a Jet Plane." There was not a woman in sight.

"You're new around here?" the bartender said to Jason.

Jason looked up.

"How'd you guess?"

"You have that lost, shell-shocked look."

Jason swiggled his drink.

"Shell-shocked huh? What's the cure?" he asked.

"Sorry, mister," the bartender said. "There's no cure. But to treat the symptoms we like to get plenty drunk."

He poured a little free Black Jack into Jason's glass.

Dicerno was back at Capricio's the evening after Bruno Palermo was killed. He was polishing off a plate of tortellini and sea bass. Jimmy slipped into the booth, excited.

"Boss, I just heard that Bruno got wasted last night."

"He's drunk all the time, Jimmy."

"No, Danny. I mean wacked. He's dead."

Dicerno put down his fork slowly.

"Mother of Christ," Dicerno said, crossing himself. "Where'd this happen?"

"Outside Maggie's Best. The papers say the cops don't have a clue."

"Fuck, Jimmy. What's this world coming to?"

"I know, boss."

Dicerno ate a bit more fish. Was Jimmy really that stupid? Dicerno thought.

Guess so.

16. Italian Roast

SATURDAY morning. Sally was trying to get back to sleep while Lou sat up on the bed, reading the Denver Post. He seemed puzzled.

"Why Bruno Palermo?" he asked.

"What?" Sally said, perturbed.

Lou said: "There is a metro brief that this mob loser, his name's Bruno Palermo, was gunned down execution-style last night. I've known him for years. Have friends that went to school with him. He was a total flake."

Sally buried her head in a pillow, saying, "Sure hon. Now buzz off."

Lou gave Sally's fanny a little tap and got out of bed to make some coffee. Minutes later, Sally began to smell Italian Roast. That was too much.

Sally got up, headed to the john and emerged five minutes later. Like magic, she was a new woman, wearing one of Lou's shirts. She shagged a coffee cup of her own.

"You are a piece, Lou. Got me up early Saturday because of a grade-B homicide."

"Sorry," Lou winked.

Tika came rushing into the room, wagging her tail and fawning over Sally.

"I guess after I get over my sleep deprivation, I'll take you out for a walk," Sally said to Tika.

"Make sure she's not attacked by the Chihuahua again," Lou said. Sally scratched Tika's ears.

"Don't listen to him. I know that when you ran from that beast you were just doing it a favor."

Lou sighed and went back to reading.

"Tika, get your leash," Sally commanded. With this, Tika dashed towards the basket where the leash was kept, losing control and skidding four feet past.

"If we ever get married will you let me sell Tika to the Koreans? They know how to treat worthless canines," Lou suggested.

"Tika, you should eat Lou."

Tika seemed happy at what Sally had said.

Sally ducked inside to dress. Soon she emerged in tight blue jeans and flannel shirt, both of which looked very sexily nice, in a country casual kind of way, Lou thought.

"Is that killing of Bruno what's-his-name anything important?" she asked.

"Probably not. But it makes you wonder about human intelligence. Who would risk prison for taking out Bruno Palermo?"

"What was his angle?"

"He was a club manager for the Danny Dicerno gang."

"Was he a made guy?" Sally asked.

"Yeah, but just. Maybe Dicerno got mad 'cause he wrecked the club's limo."

"They kill people for bad driving?"

"Possible."

Sally gave Lou a peck on the cheek: "We'll be back by one. You still want to go fishing tomorrow?"

Sally had been hoping that she and Lou could get away for some serious trout fishing. She had a secret spot near the headwaters of the Colorado River.

Sally gave Lou an "A" for effort. Otherwise, she had to admit, he was an abject failure. Lost all her flies, caught nothing. Didn't have it in him.

"What I would really like to do is catch a fish."

"I'm sure you have it in you."

"If Galileo can figure out gravity, I can catch a fish."

"That's the right attitude, honey," Sally said. "Mindless optimism."

17. Dead Letter

IT was noon and Danny Dicerno was dead asleep. A girl was crumpled fetal-like beside him, faintly snoring. They were in Dicerno's north Denver bungalow, the one he kept for his mistresses and crooked poker games. His legal family lived in a posh Adams County subdivision called The Farm. If one mapped Colorado's population of successful cons, swindlers, and sideways politicians, the Farm would be shown in red – like the angry thunderstorm on a weatherman's screen.

There was a noise. Something.

Dicerno wasn't fully out of a perplexing dream when his left eye opened. Some part of Danny's mind that was street smart had heard something even though the rest of his brain remained oblivious. As Danny's left eye slowly started to close, suddenly both eyes opened wide. There was a noise at the door. Someone was fucking around.

Dicerno leapt out of bed, grabbed a .45 from the nightstand, threw open the door. He found himself leveling the big piece of metal at the forehead of ten-year-old neighbor boy, Stevie.

"What the..." Danny said as he lowered the gun. Stevie's eyes were the size of pizza pans. A little yellow puddle was forming at his feet.

"I just, ah. I just, ah, ah," the kid said, and Dicerno caught a whiff. The kid had done more than pee his pants.

"Listen, Stevie, I'm sorry," Dicerno said. "Your mom is going to kill me, she finds out. But you shouldn't be messing with my door like that."

"Well, ah, this man see, he gave me twenty dollars to put this letter, you know, in your mail slot. 'Cept I couldn't find a mail slot."

Dicerno took the envelope and started to read. When he realized what it was he stopped, telling the boy to stay right there.

Though Stevie had the urge to run, he also had the urge not to make this man angry ever, ever again. He stayed.

Dicerno quickly returned with a twenty dollar bill. He gave it to the kid, saying, "Don't tell your mom. Got it?" He patted Steve's head. "OK?"

Stevie ogled the bill.

"Sure, Mr. Dicerno."

"What did this man look like, Stevie?"

"Man?"

"The guy with the letter."

"Oh, that guy. Yeah well, he had on one of those brown delivery man uniforms. He said he wanted me to make this delivery. I thought it was funny, but gosh..."

"OK, Stevie. Now what did he look like, I mean the face, you know?"

"He was a white dude," Stevie said. "He wasn't ancient or anything."

To Stevie, ancient could be anyone as old as his thirty-year-old dad.

"Hair color?" asked Dicerno.

"I just saw a brown hat. You know, delivery man."

"Eyes?"

"He had two," Stevie shrugged.

Hopeless, thought Dicerno. About the only thing the kid saw was the twenty dollar bill.

"Can I go now, Mr. Dicerno?"

"Sure. But remember. This is our secret."

"Yes sir," and Stevie took off at a gallop. Mom would never know about Mr. Dicerno's machine gun or bazooka or whatever it was. But the neighbor kids sure would.

There had been rumors about Mr. Dicerno. Now Stevie knew that every one of them had been true. He felt in his pocket for the bill, and then for the other twenty dollar bill the man had given him to make the delivery. And he smiled. Wait until he told the other kids!

Inside the bungalow Dicerno unfolded the note. It read:

"Mr. Dicerno:

"I did what I said I would do. And I'll do that other job. One hundred large, fifty large up front. Put it in the box next Thursday afternoon. Denominations: $100.

"If anyone is watching I'll see them and the deal is off. That would be bad, Mr. Dicerno. For both of us."

It was signed, "Mr. Wood."

Danny Dicerno, still in his underwear, went to a pantry and got some matches. He took the note over to the kitchen sink and created an ash. By then, the lady in bed stirred.

"Honey," she said. "What was all that racket? It's not even one o'clock."

Danny didn't respond. He went to the fridge, popped open a Coors and picked up the phone.

Jimmy had not been told what was in the package the boss gave him, but he had a pretty good idea. And he didn't like it. Money gave him the willies, especially when it was the boss's money and he was responsible for it.

The Pearl Street Mall was just as crazy as before. There were artists and actors and some kids smoking pot and cops that didn't care. Jimmy got the chills. As inconspicuously as he could, he took the package from a brief case, looked up and down the street, then put the package at the bottom of the newspaper stack. He headed out. That was the boss's order: Don't hang around. Don't try to see who picks it up.

"If you screw this up, you know that rendering plant up on 58th? You'll be dog food," Dicerno had warned. Jimmy knew he was right. Dicerno had turned someone into dog food only last year.

Mr. Wood, disguised as a latter-day hippie, observed all this. He had been there for hours and was certain he would have picked up on any spotters. He followed Jimmy a ways until he was certain Jimmy wasn't doubling back, then went to the Westword rack and collected the package. It felt nice. Five hundred one hundred dollar bills had a happy heft.

President Lawrence Naslund had his team assembled: Orvez, Michael Strange from the Secret Service and Roger Hamilton from the FBI. Their project to crush Ivanov's Russian mob was off to a good start. Jason's killing of Boris Slavnik had cut heroin traffic to New York by 25 percent and that, in turn, had fathered headlines about government success in fighting Red Mafiya. The head of the DEA took credit for the slowdown, saying Naslund's asset forfeiture program was largely responsible. Everyone seemed satisfied.

But the president had just a sliver of a doubt. He had received reports that Ivanov's men were asking the Russian FSB a lot of questions about Jason. Did they know he was CIA? If so how?

"We've got Jason out, right?" the president asked.

"He's out," Orvez assured him. "He's at one of our front companies in northwest Montana, a logging concern."

"So he's safe?"

"From the FSB, yes."

The president paused. "But not safe from others?"

"Maybe not."

"You mean Ivanov."

"Yes, sir."

"Come on, Linda. Do you think Ivanov would have the nerve to come into this country and hit an American agent?"

"Not if he's sane, sir."

"So?"

"Maybe he's not sane."

18. Home Free

FELIPE Spilotro had been in the Witness Protection Program for only two months. A thin man with brown, piercing eyes, dark hair combed straight back, and a body-builder's physique, Spilotro had risen to number two in Denver in part because he was Danny's boyhood friend, but even more because he could do one thing better than anyone else in Dicerno's organization. He was a stone-cold killer. He took care of problems.

But now he was a problem.

He knew Dicerno would go batshit when he learned of his defection; would hire someone to try to kill him. But that would not work. Spilotro was in the Witness Protection Program. Home free.

He liked the spot the U.S. Marshals' office had found for him and his wife: Savannah, Georgia. He appreciated the city's rhythms and decadence, and he was adjusting to the humidity. He had read "Midnight in the Garden of Good and Evil," and thought the garden might have been the park in front of his apartment. It had a green-bronze statue of some Southern Civil War hero in the middle and enough flowers to deck a Rose Bowl float. He liked the sensation of living near the garden of good and evil.

Spilotro knew he could score in Savannah under his new name – Donald Russell. It was great cover. If any of the locals looked into his past, they would find the spotless record of a man with a solid Social Security number and top credit rating. He was clean. Spilotro already had some scams lined up.

The only thing he had to do to achieve all this was to bring down Dicerno. Piece of cake.

But until then, Spilotro knew he had to live by new, distasteful rules. He had to stay clean, something he hadn't experienced since he was ten years old.

The feds had rented him a decent apartment in a stately three-story converted mansion in the historic district, right next to the little park. And the marshals had found Spilotro a job as an assistant manager of a riverfront barbeque dive named Natasha's Pit.

Spilotro didn't understand how straights lived like this. But, hell, he could take it for a year or so. Besides, there were all sorts of women in this wealthy, sweaty town ready to fuck you to death. No strings attached. Not bad at all.

Mr. Wood sat down on a bench in the park outside of Spilotro's apartment. There were a few children making a racket and pigeons expecting a handout. An old, long-bearded drunk in camo and sandals lay snoring on a nearby bench.

Mr. Wood was troubled. Where could he kill Felipe Spilotro?

He had first thought he would kill him where he worked. Bad idea. Savannah has a long stretch of bars, restaurants and clubs that snake along the riverfront, 30 feet below a bluff where the rest of the city sits. Natasha's Pit was at the bottom of the bluff. The riverfront's lone cobblestone road allowed only one car at a time to pass, and then in only one direction, and very slowly. Even people on foot had trouble finding a way down to the teaming front. To get a gun in there Mr. Wood would have to park blocks away and walk. Not an easy task when the city's standard attire consisted of shorts and T-shirts.

Natasha's Pit was out.

Killing Spilotro where he lived was the only real choice but that, too, wouldn't be easy. Traffic in the historic district also moved at a crawl. And there were plenty of people and cars and occasional cops around. Mr. Wood took a drag on a two-espresso hit of Americano and contemplated his predicament. No lights went on. Fifteen minutes later the drunk shifted sides, disgruntled pigeons sought another sucker, and Felipe exited the apartment, in jogging clothes.

That's just great, Mr. Wood thought. Yesterday Spilotro didn't jog at all. The day before it had been at 11 a.m., and before that it had been at noon. Made guys are unpredictable, Mr. Wood thought.

Maybe he could kill Spilotro at night. Maybe.

Mr. Wood walked to his pickup, headed for his motel. On the way, he spotted at least three drivers pulled over by the cops. Not good.

Inside his room, Mr. Wood reclined on his bed, hands behind his head, staring at a bug on the ceiling. CNN played on TV in the background. World Sport was showing soccer from England. A fresh-face young man called Alex was reporting.

The bug began to crawl. Without looking away, Mr. Wood hit the previous channel button on the remote. It was Fox News. Geraldo was on, talking about discovering a meteor from Mars that contained life, probably advanced life – maybe even human-like life. Out of this world. The bug stopped, as if to listen.

Then it dawned on Mr. Wood. He was being far too conventional. By the time Geraldo signed off, he had his solution. A bomb.

It had some downside, no doubt about that. Bombs drew vast amounts of attention, and Dicerno wouldn't want that. Everyone would suspect Dicerno was behind the hit. But then, Mr. Wood reasoned, everyone would suspect it anyway, however Spilotro was killed. Besides, the contract didn't dictate the means of Spilotro's demise, only its certainty.

Best, a bomb wouldn't be deterred by Spilotro's unpredictability. Once attached to his car, the bomb could wait him out while Mr. Wood was miles away. Home free.

19. Southern Belle

THE next morning, Mr. Wood drove to a Jacksonville gun show and purchased fast-burning black powder, an electric detonator and a pipe with screw-on caps.

"Fixin' on doin' a tree stump, are we?" said a prune-faced man with an ancient pipe from behind the counter.

Mr. Wood knew the man was not as dumb as he tried to appear. After all, he was selling five dollars of pipe and caps for one hundred and twenty dollars, a markup that would embarrass even Bill Gates.

"I jus' gonna test my bubba-in-law's sense a humor," said Mr. Wood in a serviceable Southern accent. The old man nodded.

"Bet it'll be a real surprise," he said.

After the gun show, Mr. Wood stopped by a hardware store for wires, a nine-volt battery and a clothespin.

He had designed the device in his mind while Geraldo was on. It was simple: He would wrap a wire around one of the ends of the clothespin. That wire would lead to the negative end of the battery, and another went from the positive end to the detonator inside the pipe bomb. A final wire led from the detonator to the other finger of the clothespin. If the two ends of the clothespin touched, the connection would close, the detonator would ignite and the bomb would explode.

Although he had never made a bomb before, this one would be far more sophisticated than the one that took out Barracuda Mike.

The day before he planned to strike, Mr. Wood went to a branch of the Savannah library – one that didn't have cameras – and used a PC to write out a letter for Mrs. Spilotro. It was a gamble. It read:

"Dear Mrs. Russell,

"I'm sorry for what happened, but if it makes you feel any better your jerk husband had been poking my wife. He got what he deserved."

If nothing else, this little note would give the feds something to think about. Maybe Dicerno might even appreciate the effort. Mr. Wood made sure he mailed it so the postmark would be dated before Spilotro was blown to bits.

Savannah bars don't close until 3 a.m. so Mr. Wood first thought of planting the bomb sometime after that, when no one was left on the street. But then he thought – no one but me. And the cops. He would stand out. Better, he reasoned, to hide in plain sight.

He decided to go to Spilotro's car, wherever and whenever it might be parked, disguised as an auto mechanic called on to solve a problem. He wanted to be obvious, attracting more attention but less suspicion.

It worked.

Spilotro arrived home at 1 a.m. Friday morning, parked a block away from his apartment, just in front of a Jeep Wrangler and behind a Dodge Intrepid. He stretched and ambled towards the apartment. He had an almost weightless gait.

Mr. Wood pulled his pickup beside Spilotro's car at 1:40, making no attempt to hide. Instead, he double-parked, causing a few motorists to honk and one drunk young woman to shout: "Stupid fuck."

He got out, wearing a hat and uniform, moved to the back of the truck, reached in the bed and got out a red toolbox. Anyone observing would assume the toolbox contained tools. This one contained a bomb.

Using magnets, he attached the bomb to Spilotro's car, right under the driver's seat.

Some late night stragglers, drunk and indifferent, wandered by. Didn't think a thing. And wouldn't remember much, either. A patrol car passed by. Didn't stop.

Mr. Wood put the clothespin trigger under the front passenger-side wheel.

As he wiggled his way from under the car a young man and his drunken girlfriend were watching. Mr. Wood looked up the legs and into the glazed eyes of a good-looking blonde in a very short skirt.

"Man," she said, "you got a boner on. Like a fuckin' rattlesnake."

Mr. Wood had not been aware of this, having been concentrating on lead wires and detonators. But it was true. He was pumped.

"Excuse me Miss, my job excites me," said Mr. Wood, and winked.

"Perhaps you could teach Billy Jack here how to use tools."

Gratefully, Billy Jack was too drunk to follow the conversation. Mr. Wood winked again, and got into the truck.

He rolled down his window. The pretty lady was still watching. Mr. Wood momentarily wished he had not just planted a bomb under the car of a protected witness. He was sure he could shed Billy Jack. And then it would be all imagination. But it was now too late for that.

"Honey, I'm sure Billy Jack tries hard," Mr. Wood said.

"Unfortunately, not hard enough."

It was her time to wink, and walk on, arm-in-arm with Billy Jack.

Mr. Wood sped away, knowing he had left behind a witness. Bad form. But he was somehow certain that she would not testify against him. He would be right.

Mr. Wood boarded a Jacksonville plane to Baltimore, and then purchased another ticket to Denver. The whole operation had cost Mr. Wood about three thousand dollars – a chunk out of the fifty grand he had been paid so far. In the future, he resolved to demand expense money.

He also thought of the blonde lady in Savannah with the short skirt and the open invitation. If I ever get back there, he told himself, I'm going to do something besides murder. Savannah seemed to be one hell of a town.

It was just before 1 p.m. Friday. Felipe Spilotro had breakfasted late at Le Peep and then had a Fat Tire beer at Bad Bob's. Now, it was time to head to the riverfront.

The city wasn't half bad, he thought, his wife was still with him, and he really loved the shiny new red Buick he slipped into. The feds were chumps, suckers, easy marks. Soon he would lead a crew. And what could they do about it? Life was good.

He put the key into the ignition and put the car into reverse. The explosion woke up that part of Savannah that was still asleep. Windows shattered half a mile away and from every direction came a chorus of car alarms. Some of Spilotro's blood splattered on the statue of the Southern war hero. The coroner was able to collect most of the rest of the protected witness's body. But part of his face was never found.

Spilotro's autopsy was perfunctory. No one thought he had died of cancer.

20. Imperfect Day

THE president was alone is his office at 7:30 a.m. The curtains were open. It was a beautiful day, cool and dry. Sometimes the job was worthwhile, he thought. A robin landed on a windowsill and blinked at the President of the United States.

Then Charlie, the president's secretary whom he had brought with him from Chicago and who always wore a necklace with a cross, poked her head in.

"Ah, Charlie, what is it?"

"This was sent over from the U.S. Marshal. The messenger said it was VTS." It was the president's shorthand for "very top secret". He liked his shorthand initials.

Damn, the president thought. There goes the perfect day. He read the message and hit the intercom.

"Charlie, get hold of Linda, Roger and Michael. Tell them to get here PDQ."

"What is it, Larry?" asked Orvez, who arrived first some thirty minutes later. She touched the president's hand with hers, letting it linger.

"Well, it's not World War Three," he said, returning her touch. "But it's not good."

Hamilton and Strange hurried into the Oval Office an instant later. The president and Orvez disengaged. Naslund motioned them all to sit.

"We have a problem," said Naslund, still standing. "A major witness against some western state's mob boss got himself blown up down in Savannah."

Orvez was the first to talk: "It happens, sir."

"No," the president said, "this has never happened before. This man Spilotro was in the Witness Protection Program."

Orvez moved her hand to her mouth.

Hamilton said, "Jesus."

Strange seemed the most upset.

"The program is our jewel," he said, standing. "If it goes we could lose our best prosecutions. Even those against these fucking Russians."

That was exactly what the president was thinking.

He went over to the window where the robin had been and looked out on the White House lawn. No one said a word.

A minute passed, and then the president turned around.

"Maybe we are jumping to a conclusion," he said.

Still, no one spoke.

"Is it possible that the bombing was unrelated to the mob case?" the president asked.

It was Hamilton's turn to respond.

"Possible, sir, but..."

"Yes," the president said, "It is possible. I agree. Maybe this Spilotro guy pissed someone off down in Savannah."

"That's right, Mr. President," Orvez said. "Best not overreact."

The president held the eyes of Linda Orvez long enough to have the other two men exchanging glances.

"Get on this, Roger," Naslund finally said. "Top priority. If there is a leak in the program, plug it immediately. Do whatever it takes. But if there is a simpler explanation, find that out, too. And fast. Understood?"

Hamilton nodded.

"Report back soon, Roger."

Everybody stood to leave.

"Oh, Linda," the president said as they reached the door. "Could I have one more word with you?"

21. Tearful Arrest

SALLY could list her favorite places. After a newsroom, there were four contenders: Wyoming's Wind River Range, her secret fishing hole at the birthplace of the Colorado, the dog track, and the Denver Botanical Gardens. She didn't know why she was partial to the gardens. Maybe it was the tropical conservatory where the air was heavy and moist and came with an almost sweet scent of tropical rot. It was like traveling five thousand miles away from the Rockies in a couple of minutes.

The conservatory seemingly had almost every rainforest tree and plant, all housed under a misty canopy. Even in January, visitors got drenched in sweat in less than five minutes. As a kid, Sally had read a National Geographic story about Costa Rica and its virgin beaches. Until she could fly to San Jose, the conservatory would have to do.

She parked the Miata down the block and headed in. She had some thinking to do. Lou was bugging her. Sally had had flings in the past but nothing serious. Now she feared she was growing emotionally dependent on one guy. That couldn't do, could it?

She had never given her heart to any man, save her father. And that love ended up shipwrecked, broken. Since then, love was to Sally something silly poets made up. Wasn't serious. Wasn't real. Teenagers love, adults persevere. And she always thought she would end up persevering with someone as insanely ambitious as she. That wasn't Lou.

Sally walked and pondered and walked some more, but even the tropics couldn't inspire Sally with an answer to Lou. Damn it all, she thought. It was so much easier before. Sally finally emerged, patting her forehead with a handkerchief. Her blouse glued wet to her body.

She headed down a dirt path between rival flowers beds, letting

Colorado's dry air cool her skin. Finally, next to an array of Indian Paint Brush, she turned on her iPhone, expecting nothing.

Ten missed calls, all in a row. Trouble.

They were all from Mel Campbell, her mentor, the national editor of the Tribune. Oh, boy.

Sally didn't bother with the messages. She called Mel.

"Campbell."

"Mel, it's Sally. What's up?"

"Where have you been? People have been trying to get you like crazy." Mel sounded harried.

"I took a walk. Did I miss the sky is falling or something?"

"Remember Daniel Dicerno?"

"Sure. We talked about this, Mel. I'm going to cover his trial if he gets indicted."

"Not anymore."

"OK. I give up. What's the punch line?"

"Someone blew up the chief witness against him."

"So? Dicerno is a gangster. Big deal."

"The witness was in the federal Witness Protection Program.

"Christ!"

Sally shot from the gardens and raced to her Miata. A thunderstorm was approaching, threatening hail. But Sally didn't even raise the top as she peeled out and headed to North Denver. She needed to get to Capricio's before any other reporter. A killing of a protected witness was hot, top of the A wire. And there was only one man who had the motive and possibly the means to do it.

Sally didn't know if Danny Dicerno would be at Capricio's, but it was her best bet.

A dozen ignored red lights later Sally screeched to a stop in front of Capricio's and jumped out. As she raced to the door, she was appalled to see Brad Johnson of the Post rushing in from the south. They met at the door.

"Shouldn't you still be under your rock?" Sally asked.

"And to think, I used to respect Lou Elliott."

"OK, listen," Sally said. "We're here because the TV guys can't find dung in a feedlot. Let's make the most of it."

"You first," said Brad. He held open the door. Brad followed Sally in.

Dicerno was at his spot with two young women, one at each side. A couple of serious men sat across the table. He looked up, caught sight of Sally, lifted an eyelid. Kept smiling.

Brad spoke first.

"Mr. Dicerno, I'm Brad Johnson from the Denver Post." Brad thrust his hand at the mob boss. Dicerno looked at Brad's hand as if it were covered with leper sores.

"So?" Dicerno said.

Then Sally extended her hand, saying "And I'm Sally Will from the Chicago Tribune."

Dicerno took a sip of wine, still appraising Sally. Setting down his glass, he took her hand.

"And what attracted the attention of a lovely Chicago journalist to a humble North Denver cheese wholesaler?"

Brad cut in, "Well, sir, you..."

"Let the lady fuckin' talk," Dicerno said with enough authority to make Brad take a step back.

"Excuse my language, ma'am," said Dicerno turning to Sally with mock courtesy. "Now, what is your question?"

Sally took a cigar from her purse. Dicerno studied Sally. What an interesting female, he thought. And what a body. He took out a lighter and lit her cigar.

"Well, it seems there has been an unfortunate...," Sally paused, "...accident involving Felipe Spilotro. And it occurred to one of my crazy editors that this might not have come to you as the worst news of the day. And my editors, with their tiny little minds, don't believe in coincidences. I mean, Spilotro was the key witness against you. But now you may be off the hook."

Sally launched a world-class smoke ring.

Dicerno watched it in total admiration. Then cleared his throat.

"You want someone take care of these editors?" Dicerno said, acting deadly serious. For a moment everyone was silent, then some rounders at a nearby table broke into laughter. Everybody else joined in.

If Dicerno was behind the Spilotro hit, and Sally didn't doubt it for a moment, he certainly wasn't sweating it. The two strippers continued to drape themselves over the boss, but their eyes followed Sally like magnets. Competition.

"Did you do it?" Johnson asked.

"Do I look like I'm in fuckin' Georgia?"

"You know what I mean."

"So I'm supposed to say 'Damn, you are some great investigative reporter. Did ya bring the cuffs?'" All the guys roared at that.

The strippers continued focusing on Sally.

"Still, sir, there are these editors," Sally broke in. "I gotta feed them some red meat."

Dicerno appraised Sally a little more. And Sally returned the effort. She knew his reputation, but he didn't appear a threat here, even in his own lair. The word "avuncular" came to her mind.

"OK, Miss Sally Will of the Chicago Tribune," said Dicerno, "You want a quote, I'll give you a quote. Take this down: I'm glad that lying son-of-a-bitch is dead. And no, I had notin' to do with it. That's it."

Sally was not quite done. She took out a business card and extended it towards Dicerno.

"Editors also say I should leave this with everyone I interview, just in case they want to confess, or something."

Dicerno looked at Sally again, a long, piercing probe of her eyes. Then he slowly took the card, and smiled.

"If I goin' to confess, pretty lady, you will be the first one to know." He winked. Again, there was laughter. "Now, go tell your editors that Danny Dicerno says 'fuck off.'"

Sally and Brad at least had a quote, which was more than anyone else had. The problem, as Sally saw it, was that Brad had the quote, too. But there was one good thing, she thought. It hadn't hailed.

Susan Spilotro, a 31-year-old brunette mother who had had the misfortune of marrying Felipe Spilotro, returned from the funeral home to her and Felipe's Savannah apartment after making final arrangements. There really weren't too many outstanding issues. If any of Felipe's friends showed up for the funeral, and she doubted any would, they wouldn't get to see him. There wasn't enough left of Felipe to show.

Sue walked around, wondering what that was at the pit of her heart that seemed so empty. The quiet gave Sue the chills.

In the kitchen, she spotted some of Felipe's notes still on the refrigerator. "Get Jr. to dentist." "Don't forget tooth fairy." And: "The IRS bastards want our returns again. Don't they realize that something's 'changed'?" She laughed at that.

In the living room she sat down in Felipe's old too-plump recliner and picked up a framed 8x10 photo of Sue, Felipe and Felipe Jr. on the beach at St. Augustine, Florida, taken only weeks before. It was right when Felipe had entered the witness program and before anyone suspected he had done so – a time when he had told Dicerno that he was taking his family to Hawaii on a sudden vacation. There was Felipe putting two bunny ear fingers behind Junior's head, and Sue, in her black bikini, smiling happily. It hadn't been easy, transforming her family into the "Russells," but Sue hadn't cared. Finally, Felipe was out of what he had always referred to as "the life," and into something with a future. And, for all his faults, dammit, Felipe had turned over a new leaf. He was going to be there for Sue and Felipe Jr.

But then "the life" had reached out one last irrefutable time and taken Felipe away. Nothing's right, Sue thought. A tear drifted down her left cheek.

Sue put the photo down and considered some of the mail piled on the stand. Had she picked it up? She couldn't remember. What did it matter? It was mostly junk – coupons, contests, bullshit. One from the IRS she put aside. But there was a strange one, with weird block writing. Interesting. She opened it. It read:

"Dear Mrs. Russell,

"I'm sorry for what happened, but if it makes you feel any better your jerk husband had been poking my wife."

Sue checked the postmark. And went crazy.

"Felipe, you goddamned sonofabitch! You goddamned sonofabitch! You goddamned sonofabitch!"

Pictures and windows were broken. Police were called. A tearful arrest was made.

22. News Break

FBI Director Roger Hamilton and Russ Covington, head of the U.S. Marshal's office, met in a private suite in Denver's Brown Palace. It was 20 minutes before a press conference downstairs was scheduled to discuss the Spilotro bombing. Both men knew media sharks were circling.

"What do we say, again?" Hamilton asked.

"Say we don't know if there's a leak. We're working on it," Covington said.

"Sure. You saw how well dumb looks worked after Hurricane Katrina. They're going to want a head on a pike, Russ."

Covington looked sour. The phone rang. Covington picked up. He started nodding his head. Then a smile consumed his face.

"Thank God," Covington said, putting down the phone.

"What?" Hamilton asked.

"The president is like a psychic," said Covington. "He got his wish. That was Savannah. They have one Susan Spilotro in custody. Seems she went totally nuts when she got a letter."

He filled Hamilton in.

"You sure the postmark was before the bombing?" asked a cautious Hamilton.

"It's confirmed," Covington said.

The smile bug bit Hamilton. "Well, well," he said.

"How do we play it?" Covington asked.

"We play hard to get, of course," the FBI director winked.

Blinding lights, shouts and the sound of a water pitcher shattering greeted Hamilton and Covington as they entered the conference room and walked to the front.

Covington winced when he saw an FBI man placing the Bureau's seal on the podium. Hamilton, somehow, had gotten him the good word.

The media roar leveled off to that of a 747 jet engine by the time the two men stepped up on stage and walked over to the mike. There was a scrum for position by the reporters, photographers and beefy TV cameramen. Elbows were thrown. The words "fuck you" emerged as a bruiser with a shoulder cam squeezed out a pencil-thin reporter holding a tiny notebook. All the networks were carrying it live.

Sally was not to be denied. She pushed herself toward the front and even the meanest looking network man let her slide by.

"Ladies and gentlemen, please," said Hamilton, stepping onto a small stool so he could look over the podium. He held out his hands and patted them in front of him, like he was telling a recalcitrant dog to sit. It didn't help. The roar continued.

Sally got off the first question.

"Mr. Hamilton. The United States used to say the Witness Protection Program had never lost a man. Now it has. How did it happen?"

Hamilton smiled and shook his head. "There are many reasons for murder. Let's not jump to conclusions," he said.

"Or maybe there's a leak," hammered Brad Johnson. "Have you subpoenaed Daniel Dicerno's phone records?"

"Well," Hamilton said, still serene. "We don't know if there's a leak. Besides, you know there're rules about not ever contacting certain people. Maybe he broke them. I don't know."

That stoked the fire. Hamilton could see it shooting from the journalists' eyes. They could see a cover-up in the making. Yet Hamilton still smiled. Reporters wondered why. Everyone shouted out questions at once.

Somehow, Hamilton heard Sally's: "My sources say Spilotro never would have talked about his location. They say it had to be a leak in the U.S. Marshals' office. Where will your investigation start?"

"Well, that question shows that it is dangerous to rely on sources that know nothing about the case, young lady," Hamilton said.

"I'll give you an example," said Covington, stepping up to the mike and trying to drive Hamilton from his stool. Hamilton held his ground.

"The day before the bombing," Covington said, "the bomber sent a letter to Mrs. Spilotro."

The room quieted. Reporters sensed news.

"She didn't get it until afterwards," Covington said. Hamilton looked a little irritated to be sharing the podium.

"I'm not going to discuss its contents," Covington said, leaning toward the mike. "But it suggests the motive might have had nothing to do with the Danny Dicerno case."

After a moment to let this settle in, a man from ABC asked: "What sort of motive?"

"It could have been jealousy over something that happened there, in Savannah," Hamilton blurted, adding disingenuously. "Now I'm not going to say anything more about it."

"Jealousy over what?" asked Paula Jennings from the local Channel 9.

"I'm sorry, Miss," Hamilton said. "We have an ongoing investigation."

"Over SEX?" shouted someone from the back.

Hamilton grabbed the sides of the podium and slowly waved his head back and forth, like he was thinking. It was a convincing act. Then, after the cameras had plenty of time to showcase his deep reflection, Hamilton intoned one word:

"Yes."

It was like pouring gasoline on an open flame. Questions piled one upon the other. A few were answered. But the big news was out: Authorities were looking at a local angle for the killing. Sex was involved. There was no evidence yet of a leak in the Witness Protection Program.

Eventually, Hamilton and Covington made it offstage, still smiling.

As he watched on TV, so was the President of the United States.

Lt. Steve Brandon watched the press conference from the homicide room at police headquarters. He had his feet up on a desk and was drinking a Coke. He also had a cigarette going, which wasn't allowed. A couple of homicide dicks watched, too.

Detective Scott Kirkpatrick, considered one of the department's Young Turks, appeared disgusted.

"Yeah, right," he said. "Sex. Are they nuts? It was a bomb. And it blew our Dicerno case to smithereens."

"Maybe," Brandon said.

"What maybe?" Kirkpatrick said. "I say we go over to that restaurant he owns and roust his greaser ass. Show him how irritated we are."

Brandon pushed away from the desk with his feet and stood. "Good idea, dickhead," said Brandon. "His lawyer has a court order, remember? We can't question him about Spilotro."

"How about Bruno Palermo?" Kirkpatrick said. Another detective's body language was telling Kirkpatrick not to push it.

"Who?" asked Brandon.

"You covered it. The guy gunned down at Maggie's Best."

"Kirkpatrick, you should have your tiny brain given over to research. Bruno was so low on the food chain he could only look up."

"He was a made guy."

"So?"

"Only a boss can order the whacking of a made guy."

"You're a romantic, Kirkpatrick. Those rules went out in the 1960s. By the way, we have anything on Bruno?"

"Five hollow-point .22s to the skull," needled Kirkpatrick. "From a distance closer than a gang bang. In my book, professional."

"You guys slay me," Brandon said. "Ten-year-old kids in that part of town carry .22s. Again, leads. We got any?"

"No. And this Spilotro shit isn't helping," said Scott Kirkpatrick. "Witnesses are starting to call the Witness Protection Program, the witness prevention program."

Lt. Brandon smiled. That's a good one, he seemed to be thinking.

"Still, I want to know everything," he said. "Anything at all that has to do with either Palermo or Spilotro."

Kirkpatrick and the other detective exchanged glances. Why would the lieutenant care about Palermo after what he had just said?

Didn't compute.

23. Pay Off

MR. Wood still was worried. Danny Dicerno had become the talk of the nation. Mr. Wood swore to himself that the next one he did, if there was a next one, must be very subtle. Something few would notice. Poison, he thought. He had read somewhere that a Russian mobster had been killed with shellfish toxin and that the authorities still couldn't figure it out. Whoever did that was good, thought Mr. Wood.

Then he thought of immediate issues. Should he approach Dicerno right now with a message in the news box? Or should he just leave him alone? Fuck that, he said. I want my money.

"I expect the rest," Mr. Wood wrote in the note he left at the bottom of the Westword box. "Next Thursday. You know where."

That was it.

Hell, he was audacious, writing such a note to Danny Dicerno. Mr. Wood considered going back and snatching it away. But then he thought, no, I should tough it out. He really wanted the money. And he could feel the adrenalin running through his veins. But it was time now to be extra careful. Mr. Wood was sure the feds had Danny Dicerno thoroughly bugged, tapped, followed. All the fed agencies seemed to be involved. Maybe they would have one of their military drones overhead, circling.

He arrived at the Pearl Street Mall early, looking like Willie Nelson when Willie Nelson was young. He had on a beard, long greasy brown hair, tattered clothes, and a torn guitar case. The guitar was a leftover from college, where Mr. Wood had played a little folk music. He could still strum a tune, but his voice wasn't what it had been. But so what? No one on the Mall had paid for a concert.

He set up some thirty yards from the Westword box and watched what was happening in all directions. No one would wonder why a performer would turn from side to side. He was being respectful to the public.

Mr. Wood played some of Willie's favorites: "Georgia," "On the Road Again," "Whisky River." A crowd gathered. God, Mr. Wood thought, these folks must have tin ears. But then he recalled that Willie didn't exactly have such a good voice himself. Maybe bad pitch was part of his art.

That's when he spotted Jimmy walking down the Mall, another package in his hand. No one was following.

Jimmy's head seemed to have shrunk, like he had no neck. He looked glum, worried. He went directly to the box, slipped in a package, then left. Didn't look around.

Mr. Wood played on for another twenty minutes, watching if anything seemed out of place. Nothing did. He stopped and the crowd dispersed. Some people gave him a thumbs-up, and a few dropped bills into his guitar case. He sat alone for a while and looked at the news box. Should I go for it? He asked himself. What were the chances that the message system had been compromised? He waited and saw nothing suspicious. No tells. His heart raced. Anxiety washed ashore. It was either do it now, or let some lucky Boulderite find a fat bag of cash. That would not do.

Mr. Wood walked casually up to the box and pulled out the package. There was no reason to be secretive. If the feds were there he was history. If not, what did he care if someone saw him making a pickup at a news box? He put the package under his arm, picked up the guitar case and walked down the mall.

There were no sirens, no shouts, and no Hellfire missiles. He had done it.

When he got in his car, he counted out another five hundred one hundred dollar bills. There was also a typed note: "Mr. Wood, nice touch with the letter. If I need your services again, I will use the yellow rose."

Let's hope, Mr. Wood thought.

Lou got a call from the Post's Brad Johnson. He wanted to meet at the Denver Athletic Club on Friday. He had something to run by the former FBI man.

"Besides," Brad said, "I want a grudge match."

Brad was talking about their frequent racquetball games, ones that Lou won almost every time with a deadly trick shot.

"Sure," Lou told Johnson. "I love to see you miserable."

Lou's membership at the DAC was an extravagance, he realized. But it was his best defense against love handles.

24. Dog Rescue

TO Sally, her stories on Dicerno, Spilotro and the mystery letter from Atlanta were second rate. Everyone knew about the car bombing, the feds' inference that it wasn't related to their Witness Protection Program, and Danny Dicerno's colorful comments. Granted, Dicerno's quotes had only been reported by the Chicago Tribune and the Denver Post, but that was one outlet too many. Sally had no use for the Post. She was frustrated – in both senses.

Compounding a bad day, Lou had left a message on her cell that he would be working late on a case. Dinner canceled.

Sally walked out on Lou's balcony. The sun was settling against the great slab of the Front Range. There was a small cooling breeze, cloudless skies. But there was a cloud over Sally.

It had started, as it had so often long before, with an imperceptible tightening in her gut. A bit of tension. When her heart rate picked up, Sally began to notice. No, she told herself, that's behind me. She had beaten it. Then her world dimmed, the city sounds below became hollow, her heart more uncompromising. Goddammit girl.

Sally headed back in and threw open the fridge door. There was a half empty bottle of Chardonnay. She poured herself a glass, then turned away. No more booze. Not now.

What I need is a distraction, Sally told herself. She went to the bedroom and thought briefly about masturbating. But then fetched her hidden bundle from behind the mirror, slipping five hundred dollars into her purse. The doggies could rescue her better than her pussy, she decided.

On the way to Paradise Park, Sally tried not to feel her pounding pulse or sense the perspiration building on her face, hands, back. Four years ago she had taken a yoga class to try to get on top of these panic attacks. Steady breathing and guided imagery were the tricks, she had learned. So Sally breathed slowly and tried to think of an event in her past where she was truly at peace. She always came back to the same one.

It was her first dog, Frank, a black cocker spaniel. She loved that dog so much, and Frank tried to love her back. He learned to fetch, roll over and even walk on his hind legs. But that had been pretty much his full repertoire. She recalled how Frank had looked so proud of himself when he successfully finished any trick.

Sally thought that the guided imagery might be working, because her heart seemed to slow a fraction. She put in a CD, Serkin playing "Moonlight Sonata." It almost worked.

Then Sally's memory moved on, no longer pleasant. She recalled how her dad, Mr. Lester Will, had brought Frank home as a puppy, maybe nine-weeks old, and how Frank had howled so much in protest in the evening that Sally had begged her dad to take him back. It was obvious the dog's heart was broken. But her father said that the puppy would get over it. Then Lester Will, a Wyoming small-time banker, went in his study. Even at 11 years old, Sally knew that dad had a bottle in his desk.

The dog yelped all night, keeping Sally worried and awake. But dad slept right through it. He never left his study that night. He often never did any night.

Suddenly Sally's heart was at full gallop. She felt cold, almost lost.

Andy, the tout-sheet hawker, spotted her as she came through the door. He was excited.

"Miss Sally, you be goin' long shot again? Tell me what you got, Miss Sally. I be needin' a break somethin' fierce."

The knot in Sally's stomach had become a steel claw. Her breathing was shallow. She couldn't stop and talk, not even to harmless Andy.

"Andy, I haven't even studied the program," is all she could say as she brushed by.

"This ain't like you, Miss Sally. Somethin' wrong?"

"No, Andy, I'm fine."

Except maybe the panic, Sally thought. It had been more than two years since the last attack, and Sally had thought they were gone for good. Now, out of nowhere...

Sally knew it had to do with her father, her Hercules and Apollo, the man she had wanted to please. Then, while Frank was still a puppy, Sally's father had gone away and dad's tomboy was alone. And afraid.

Sally wondered if Franklin Roosevelt realized how close to the truth he was when he said that the only thing one had to fear was fear itself.

Sally went into a restroom and bathed her face. She looked into her cool blue eyes. What is wrong with me? She asked. I'm with a man I think I love, someone strong and interesting. I've got a great job. I have a future. But there, in the pit of my stomach, unforgiving, unrelenting, undeniable tension.

Sally thought of the five hundred dollars she had brought along, fully intending to blow it all on one race. Right, that will help. Maybe she should just go to the bar and get a double gin. That would send the tension scampering, she knew.

But it would come back, eventually, and harder than ever. Sally had wondered if this tension is actually what drove people to alcoholism. It certainly had been in the case of her father. He explained his drinking as a kind of sleeping aid: "Self-medication, honey."

Sally had a theory. You can drink all you want when you're happy. No sweat. But drink to get rid of that tension, that steel claw, and you're on the slippery slope.

What Sally wondered most – feared most – was what she would do if this tension struck her when she really had something to be frightened about? Would she freeze up when she needed to stay calm? She hoped she would never have to find out.

She splashed her face again. An older woman came in, looked at Sally, and quickly left. Sally splashed one last time, briefly studied her face in the mirror and dried off. I'll wait this one out, she told herself.

When Sally emerged from the restroom, she still had the knot in her belly. A little water and reflection wasn't going to change that. But she had regained her resolve. The five hundred dollars she had brought would not be leaving her purse. The cruel master would not win the day.

Andy spotted her as she headed for the exit. "Miss Sally, you ain't goin' to bet?"

"Right now, I'd rather eat scorpions," she said.

"So, ah, maybe you can help me?"

Andy's big brown eyes were beseeching.

"You want me to call a race, Andy?"

"You done read my mind, Miss Sally."

"OK, Andy. Just once."

"It's the seventh, just after the one right now startin'. 'A' dogs. I'm picking two, seven, eight. Here, Miss Sally, what you think?"

Sally took the proffered program with all the statistics, examined it carefully, got out her calculator and began to peck. Two minutes later, Sally handed the program back to Andy.

"I think you're right about the two and eight. But seven looks wrong. Go with the five."

"You sure?"

"Andy, nothing's sure. You asked me for my best bet."

Andy nodded, and then bowed slightly.

"Thank you, Miss Sally," he said, and headed for a betting cage.

When Sally turned to go out the exit, she saw a man she thought she recognized but couldn't place. Sally sensed it had been recent but he must have changed his appearance, somehow. She filed it away.

Out in the parking lot, Sally heard noise from the crowd slowly increase. The seventh race was underway. She started for her Miata, parked in a lonely spot two hundred yards away. Suddenly, the crowd erupted. It was the type of sound that came after a long shot finished in the money.

It was cool. A thin mist was in the air but Sally could clearly see the tote board. A minute passed while officials examined the photo finish. Then it came on: Two and Five had won, a thirty-to-one chance. Andy would be happy tonight.

For some reason – and Sally wished she knew why – the tension eased as she headed back to Denver. Maybe just driving had done it? Maybe helping Andy? Maybe it was nothing?

Who knew?

25. Panic Attack

LOU was alarmed when Sally entered the condo, her hair a wreck, her clothes rumpled.

"Jesus, Sally, what happened? You look..." his voice tailed off.

"...like shit," Sally finished as she plopped down on the couch. "I know. I look like the Union Army at Fredericksburg."

"Sick?"

"Yeah, Lou, sick. Sick in here," Sally said, pointing to her head.

Lou took off his reading glasses and moved from his recliner to Sally's side, taking her hands.

"Sally, what is this about? What can I do?"

"Ah, Lou. You can't do anything. This is a father-daughter thing. Roots."

Sally's father was a subject off limits, Lou knew. That she had even brought it up was exceptional.

"Tell me what you want, Sally."

"Some things happen and after those things happen everything is lost and can never be changed."

"Sally?"

"A panic attack, Lou. I thought I was over them. It has to do with my father."

Lou softly pressed her hands into his.

"It hit like lightning," Sally continued. "First in two years. It's still here, somewhat." Sally patted her belly.

"My guts are still in a knot."

Lou reached over and took Sally in his arms.

"Have you sought help?" he asked.

"Yeah, I've gone there. There's nothing to be done."

"There are drugs," Lou said.

"All they do is make you numb," Sally said, pulling away and looking Lou in the eye.

"I went to the race track to try to get it under control. That maybe helped."

Lou wished he didn't know what Sally was talking about, but he did.

"Sally, honey, I know about fear. Comes out of depression. I've been there myself."

Sally shook her head, clearing her senses.

"Come on," she challenged, "Big stud Lou Elliott knowing fear? You're the guy that went up Turkey Creek Canyon to get that kidnapper. Not an ounce of panic in your soul."

"That was more stupid than brave, Sally."

Lou put his arm around Sally and could feel a deep shudder. She was recovering, but she wasn't home yet.

"Sally," Lou said, "I know this. You cannot just will yourself out of a panic attack. But talk helps."

Sally said nothing.

"So talk," Lou urged as gently as he could.

Sally wasn't about to talk. The knot was still too tight. But she was curious.

"Who was she, Lou?" Sally asked.

"She?"

"The woman who caused the depression."

"Sally, we're talking about you."

"We were. Now we're talking about you."

"Not ready for this," Lou said.

"Just a name, Lou."

"Drop it, Sally."

Suddenly, Sally's racing heart slowed.

"No," she said. She hugged Lou.

Lou looked down.

"Name," said Sally.

"Becky Sue," he said. "And I got her killed."

26. Drop Shot

A MAN and a woman in yellow Gortex jackets, hiking boots and backpacks walked through a mountain pasture near Thompson Falls, Montana. They appeared to be in their late twenties and in good shape, laughing, walking hand-in-hand — as ordinary a sight as there can be in Western Montana. It was a lazy summer afternoon, meadowlarks sang and a doe with her fawn grazed a hundred yards away. The effect was pure Norman Rockwell.

The couple moved into the heavy woods, and immediately a transformation took place. They dropped their packs, and turned their jackets inside out, revealing camouflage. All business now, the man opened his backpack and took out a radio transmitter. He fiddled with the dial and then tapped on a keyboard. Moments later, he barked out some numbers which the woman wrote down. Then she ripped out a page from another book, and decoded the message. Satisfied, she took out a lighter and destroyed both sheets.

The two buried their packs under some downed tree limbs and brush, but kept their rifles, side arms, binoculars, and an iPhone with Google Earth and slowly made their way through the rugged woods, checking the coordinates every two minutes. The light under the canopy was poor and, despite their training, it proved impossible to avoid stepping on things that made noise. Every twig that broke sounded to them like a gunshot.

After twenty minutes they neared a clearing. Crawling on their stomachs, they got to the edge of the woods. The woman examined a distant sign through the binoculars. It read: "New Company Logging."

They had found what they were looking for. Now it was time to watch and wait.

They wanted to make sure Jason Ison was alone.

The day after her panic attack, Sally awoke completely relaxed, as if nothing had happened. There was no knot in the belly, no dimmed vision, no inexplicable worry. She was just the Sally that everybody knew. A rock.

Lou had left early for an appointment with a client. She thought of Lou's story. "And I got her killed," he had said of Becky Sue. What did that mean? He had said no more and refused to despite her blandishments.

Sally ground up some Kenyan beans, put a French press to work, then headed for the balcony, still in a bathrobe. This was the scene of the crime, where the attack had begun. Sally felt nothing but the breeze and the sun's reflection from the mountains. She sipped coffee, refocused. She would figure out Becky Sue later. It was time for work.

Spilotro and Dicerno. How had that come down? Who had blown Spilotro to tiny bits?

Although some of her gullible colleagues believed in the jealous husband bit, Sally didn't. Jealous husbands use guns in the heat of passion. A bomb, and a good one? No chance.

Dicerno was behind it. There was not a doubt in Sally's mind. That friendly mobster with his bimbos and heavies had managed to break into the Witness Protection Program. How had the old man done it?

Sally ran through what she knew of Danny Dicerno: Head of a dying La Cosa Nostra family - runs prostitution, loan sharking and gambling rackets - has wife in Adams County, girlfriends elsewhere - faces capital murder indictment - takes care of that by killing key witness against him. Well, she thought, there must be something else she knew.

Then she sensed something vague. There had been a Dicerno employee, Bruno something. He recently had been killed, execution style. The guy Lou was muttering about one morning when she was still hanging onto sleep. Bruno something had been hit outside of a place called Maggie's Best, a massage parlor.

Palermo, Bruno Palermo. That was it, she recalled. She wondered if Palermo was to be another witness against Dicerno. She put that question at the top of her list.

Lou met Brad Johnson at the entrance of the Denver Athletic Club, a place that resembled some cubist nightmare. The original architecture was constructed in the late 1800s. Subsequent architects built additions, with scant attention to the original. They were parts thrust together, as if Dr. Frankenstein had designed it.

"Ready to lose?" Johnson asked Lou as they shook hands. His hazel eyes seem to be saying he had something up his sleeve.

"What? Is Kane Waselenchuk here?"

"I got a surprise for you, big guy," said Brad.

"Let me guess. You wrote a story not requiring a correction?"

"You'll see."

"The suspense is killing me."

Brad flipped Lou the bird.

They headed for the locker room, changed and prepared to go to the courts. Brad, at five-eleven and 170 was maybe in the best shape of his life. He smiled as he bent down to take a racquet out of his gym bag. It was a new black-metal job. Looked expensive.

"A new canon?" Lou asked.

"No. It's harmless," Brad replied. Actually, Brad had paid nearly two hundred dollars for the little racquet that a sports magazine had claimed would "kill" any ball in its way.

"It doesn't look harmless to me," said Lou.

"This is going to lighten my heart." Brad smiled.

Lou looked just a little worried at his adversary's new weapon. But only a little. Johnson had lost nine straight matches. Would that suddenly change?

Lou's worry didn't last past the first volley. As usual, Lou mostly stayed in the center of the court while Brad scampered around like a water bug on a creek's surface, chasing Lou's famed drop-dead shot. He tried so hard, ran so fast, dove so much, that Lou had little doubt how he stayed in shape. The younger man was raining sweat before Lou even began to glisten. It was a best-of-five match.

Lou had taken the first two. Brad stood at mid court, hands on his knees, wheezing. A terrible ache in his side.

"You ready?" Lou asked.

Brad just shook his head yes, already defeated. And ten minutes later that's exactly what the score showed. Game over. Threat ended. Technology routed.

Johnson held his side as they walked to the locker room. When Brad sat down, he looked at the racquet like he would an Anthrax letter.

"You win these games on the cheap," Brad moaned as he stripped down. "You only have that one stupid shot."

"No matter what they say, Brad, I think you could become competitive," poked Lou.

"Goddammit," Brad shouted, as he slammed the nice new racquet down so hard on the bench that it was no longer worth anything like $185. Then Brad slumped to the bench, reddening–embarrassed that he had let Lou under his skin. Lou was also taken aback. He knew firsthand that Brad was competitive. But why ruin a perfectly good racquet just because you never learned to play the game? Chill, Brad, he thought. And Brad did.

"Sorry, pal," Brad said, looking at the warped racquet. "It was fine while it lasted."

Then he started laughing. And so did Lou. And pretty soon they were both laughing like idiots. And when Brad tossed the racquet into the trash, they erupted again.

On the way out of the club, Brad turned to Lou.

"Actually, there was one thing I wanted to do with you tonight besides boosting your immeasurable ego," he said.

"Ask," said Lou.

"The Spilotro thing. I'm sure it was Dicerno."

'Naturally."

"Naturally?"

"Sure. But now prove it. You will get no help from me, even if I had some to give. Which I don't."

"Sally?"

"Sally."

"So the rumors are true," Brad said. He appeared to pout, defeated from all directions.

Jason Ison sat back in an oak rocking chair in the main office of New Company Logging, thumbing through a *Playboy* magazine. There was nothing else to do.

It was just after dusk. A few moths raced around his reading lamp. A few more landed in his kerosene trap, and squirmed around. If he had been attentive, Jason might have noticed that the crickets outside had stopped chirping. But the CIA man was not attentive. This was Montana, after all. Nothing happened here.

He flipped a page. Then he heard a knock at the door. And then another. Soft. Nothing unusual, he thought. One of the loggers was wondering about his paycheck, probably. He put down his magazine and ambled to the door. What time was it, ten? A little late, but what the hell. He didn't bother to look through the peephole because there was no peephole. This was Montana.

When he opened the door his eyes moved from a young woman to a young man. And then back to the woman. Her green eyes, even in low light, were like whirlpools. He had never seen such emerald, mesmerizing eyes. He began to smile a welcome. Then he noticed her gun.

The president was sitting at his desk reading what he considered to be an infantile talk he was scheduled to give to a group of boy scouts. It was a part of the job he detested. The photo ops. The sound bites. The endless stupid meetings.

But not everything was bleak. There had been only a few editorials and limp excuses for scoops about the Witness Protection Program possibly being compromised. Most focused on Felipe Spilotro's car bombing alone and his insatiable appetite for sex.

Federal agents had done their jobs, finding that Spilotro had continued his philandering ways even after entering the program. At least a dozen hookers and very drunk coeds had confessed to bedding with Spilotro. Who was to say how many married women had done the same? Maybe a jealous husband had done him in, the president considered. But then he thought: jealous husbands don't use car bombs.

He hoped someone in his administration would be smart enough to find the leak in the Witness Protection Program before someone else got killed. The president also was buoyed by the war on Ivanov. All sorts of crime statistics had kept pouring in showing all was going well. The FBI had rolled up a dozen key players in Brighton Beach and Miami. Two others in Denver had been arrested. The vice president's problems were off the front page and the Russian mob was in retreat. Bullet dodged.

The president took a pack of forbidden Marlboros from a side drawer, tapped one out and lit it. Just as the first wave of nicotine relaxed his lungs, Charlie buzzed.

What now?

"Charlie, I'm trying to work on an important speech. What?"

Linda Orvez phoned and said she was headed over. Something important. She has Hamilton and Covington with her."

Jesus, not again. This could not be good. The president stubbed out the Marlboro.

"What do you mean he's missing?" the president thundered. "You said there could be no problem!"

The agency heads looked at each other. The president seemed to be forgetting their last conversation.

"Maybe," the president said, "he just scampered off."

"Sir, he didn't like Thompson Falls, but we don't think he took off," said Covington. "He wasn't the kind."

"So?" asked Naslund.

"It must be the Russians."

"What Russians?" the president demanded.

"Not the FSB," said Covington.

"Then who?" the president asked.

Orvez cleared her throat.

"Ivanov," she said.

"Impossible," said the president.

Orvez moved forward. She put her hand on the president's and softly squeezed it. Hamilton and Covington looked on, wide-eyed.

"Mr. President," Orvez said, "I'm sorry. Mr. Ivanov may be even stronger than we expected."

"OK," Naslund said, slowly pulling away. He brushed back his hair. "This Jason guy, what's his new name?"

"Ison, Jason Ison," said Orvez. "What does he know?"

"He was the man that carried out our operation against Slavnik," said Hamilton.

"That I understand." The president looked at Hamilton like he had just flunked a first-grade spelling test.

"If Jason tells them a wet operation was authorized at the highest level," Orvez said, "they could come after me."

She paused, then said: "Or they could come after you."

That gave President Lawrence Naslund pause.

"Me?"

"They don't think straight, sir. They're crazy."

"Then," he said, "we will take the fight back to them. We will stop these bastards in their tracks."

27. Rat's Eyes

THE kidnapping team's black Econo-Line van rumbled down a dirt road outside of Ten Sleep, a Wyoming hamlet with two churches, three bars and an Ace Hardware. The sun was setting, lighting up the snow pack on Cloud's Peak. Tensleep's 305 citizens were heading for bed.

Katya, the crew boss with the emerald eyes, soaked it all in, thinking she must buy a postcard of this place and send it to her mother stuck in Murmansk, where everything was gray and life frozen. The radio was playing something Katya had learned to call Country and Western, which seemed to deal in pickup trucks and drinking and something that Americans called cheatin'. Katya was surprised that so many American women sang openly about these things, but then she realized she had a lot to learn about this crazy country. She tried to relax, because in minutes she knew the real work would begin.

Waiting in a house atop a red butte was a very special person, someone Ivanov ranked at the top. It would be awful, Katya knew, but then again the American was a criminal who had sinned against the greatest man Katya knew. Dimitri Ivanov was depending on her and Katya would not let him down.

The van pulled onto the gravel driveway a mile from town, and stopped by a lonely ranch house. Here, Katya knew, there would be no neighbors to hear the screams, no chance of escape, no hope at all.

Katya's four male comrades hauled Jason Ison from the back. Jason Ison looked almost whimsical, confident, like he was sure he was being kidnapped for ransom. Everything would turn out OK. This was some big mistake. He didn't seem concerned, Katya thought. She knew that would change. Soon.

The Russians carried Jason effortlessly through the front door and then down into a basement that smelled of mildew, bad breath and urine. In the middle of the room, under a naked light, stood a chair, bolted to the floor, with a thin board rising above its back, like an electric chair.

That was the first time Jason really began to worry. Maybe something more than ransom was involved.

The Russians strapped Jason into a chair then wound duct tape around almost every inch of his body, from his legs to his upper torso. Then they wrapped the tape around Jason's forehead, immobilizing it. They wound the tape around him a second and third time, until the only things he could move were his eyes and his tongue. Jason could not help it. He felt bile rising, burning.

The Russians left him like that for an hour.

Muscle contractions began. Jason needed to stretch. Needed to breathe a little harder. Needed to get more blood to his legs.

Then, suddenly, there was a voice: "Hello, Jason," said a man. Where had he come from? Jason hadn't heard a thing.

The man walked from behind Jason's back. He was an older man, tall, gaunt, pale. White hair and dark eyes. He had an accent, somewhat British. And he was wearing a doctor's white gown.

"We don't know each other," the man said, "but that will change."

"Look," Jason said, "Just call New Company. They will pay you. You don't need to do all this."

"You don't seem to understand," the ghost-like man said. "We believe you killed a friend of ours, Boris Slavnik. You remember Boris?"

Jason felt a sharp fang of fear stab his heart. Shit, this was serious.

"I didn't kill anyone," he said.

"Think hard, Jason Ison. Try."

"You got the wrong guy."

"OK, Jason Ison. My name is Oleg Tsplyev, but in cases like this they sometimes call me Doctor Yes. And yes, it sounds a little too James Bondish to me, too, but it works. Do you know why they call me that?"

Jason didn't respond.

"It's because eventually everyone I see answers all my questions truthfully. Now, let's start with your name. What is it, really?"

"Jason Ison."

"Well, it seems we have a problem, Jason Ison. We need to find out why you killed Mr. Slavnik, and you don't seem eager to help."

"I didn't kill anybody."

"I'm afraid I'm not going to accept that, Jason Ison. Instead I'm going to make you more cooperative."

Jason had been trained for such encounters. The Agency's official rules called for holding out until death. But every operations agent knew that the real bar was to hold on until you couldn't any longer. Jason had played this out in his mind many times. He had always pictured that this would happen in Russia, and that he would win. The American embassy would save him. Now he was being held in his own country. And there was no one to contact. He was immensely frightened of this old, paper-white man.

"I was there. I went to get help," Jason blurted out.

"Ah, that's good," said Oleg Tsplyev. "A beginning."

Oleg Tsplyev brought out a large cage. He held it high.

"You see this, Jason Ison? It is a simple cage. See this hole in the bottom? That is to make room for your head. We built this chair so that this trick would work just right."

Then Tsplyev picked up another cage and held it up to Jason's eyes. In it was a huge rat, the biggest Jason had ever seen. Despite its size, the rat seemed strangely emaciated. Its ribs showed. It looked hungry. But it was its eyes that transfixed Jason. They looked angry.

"This rat," the doctor said, "was spoiled for three months. Given all the food it wanted. Then, four days ago, we cut it off. No food at all. Just water. His name is Rasputin, but we prefer Raspy. He is very hungry now and irritated."

"Look, there's been a mistake," Jason coughed.

"Yes, there has," Dr. Tsplyev said. "And tonight we are going to find out whose."

Jason didn't know where this was heading, but he knew he didn't like it. It was time to talk.

"I will tell you what I know," said Jason.

"Yes," said Dr. Tsplyev, "you will. You see, the trick that I am going to play on you, Jason Ison, was actually perfected by your CIA friends. Agents Terpil and Wilson later taught it to Idi Amin. We understand he used it for great entertainment. We are more prosaic. We use it for its utility."

Tsplyev put Jason's head inside the first half of the cage. Jason's eyes followed every move. He noticed the cramps were worsening, and spreading, but he couldn't stretch a single muscle in his body. His heart began to thunder, his vision dimmed. He heard blood roaring through his ears.

"Now, Jason Ison, do you see that slot in the cage just in front of your face. That's where we put this thin piece of plywood."

Tsplyev inserted the wood, which completely separated the back of the cage from Jason's face.

"Now I am going to put a very hungry and mean-spirited rat into the compartment separated by the wood. What Raspy will do, and we know this from experience, he will eat his way through the wood. It could take half an hour. Maybe more. But he will get through, because he is very, very hungry, Jason Ison. And he knows what he likes. Since you cannot move, Raspy's task will be simple. He will get through and then eat out your eyes to get to your brain."

Jason was breathing rapidly but he couldn't expand his lungs enough. There was a pain in his chest. Soon his whole body was one single unending spasm. The rules said he must try to hold out, to bargain.

"Look," he said. "I did nothing... to those two men... but... just before we dined... a man... a man... from the embassy... came... and asked about... them... maybe he did it... if you... let me out... I'll tell you... everything... everything."

"Excellent, Jason Ison," said Tsplyev.

Jason heard the doctor, if that's what he was, dropping the rat into the other side of the board. And then there came the scraping as the rat worked frantically on the wood, sounding like a hundred nails on a chalkboard. Jason's lungs and heart constricted and burned as if seared with a white-phosphorous poker. Jason thought he might explode. Sweat poured down his face. Cramps surged throughout his body. Wasn't the doctor listening?

Fifteen minutes later, the rat had made an opening. It watched Jason's eyes lustily. It was coming. It got a leg through. Jason heard it snorting in anticipation. It was then Jason Ison began to scream, a guttural, unearthly scream.

"Stop! Stop! I'll tell you...everything," he shouted.

Tsplyev had seen this before. Every time it happened. He could have stopped it then, but in a couple of cases his victims had regressed when the rat was removed too early. Tsplyev had had to start all over again. True, the men broke during the second round, but why waste time? Tsplyev prided himself on being efficient. So he ignored Jason Ison's screams.

Finally the rat was through, and Jason's screams increased a million decibels. Tsplyev let the rat tear off Jason's right eyelid and begin to eat away the cornea. Then he asked: "Will you now tell all?"

"Yes!" Jason screamed. The answer rocked the Ten Sleep house. Dr. Tsplyev was satisfied. He removed Raspy.

Jason, blood and membranes oozing down his face, did, in fact, tell everything he knew: his real name, his real job and all he knew of the real aim of Project Shutdown. The problem was, he only knew so much. He didn't know how many were involved, or even who gave the final orders. But he made deductions.

Wet jobs could only be approved at the highest level. The director, at least, had to know. But a murder in Putin's Russia? That call could only have been made one step higher. That could mean the president.

Jason Ison went on and on. He would have betrayed any trust. He would have betrayed his own mother. Anything to avoid the rat. Anything.

Tsplyev was satisfied he was getting the truth. After thirty minutes the Russians cut away the tape. Slowly, every muscle in Jason's body unwound. A wave like a warm waterfall cascaded over every inch, head to toe. Pain evaporated. Jason could not remember ever feeling such total relief. Everything was suddenly calm, dreamlike. He was free.

Katya came into the room then, aimed a gun at the back of his head and put a bullet into Jason Ison's brain. He never even knew it was coming.

They dumped the body in a remote cave near Thermopolis, some twenty miles away. They thought no one would find it for years, if ever.

But they would be wrong.

28. Cave Man

IT was break time at El Chapultepec, a smoky jazz joint near the Points. Lou was in a sport's coat and Sally a black evening dress. They had just seen a bad play at the Denver Performing Arts Complex and had decided to take in some tunes. Lou's ears were ringing.

"So," Sally said. Lou didn't really hear, but saw her lips move. "We know Dicerno must be good for Spilotro."

"Yes, but unfortunately the White House says otherwise."

"They know better."

Sally sipped her drink, a glass of white wine.

"And there's that detail called proof," Lou continued. "Brad broached the same theory."

"Did the jerk have anything working?"

"Sally," Lou pleaded with his eyes. "He's my friend."

"Oh, sorry."

"But, no," Lou said. "He didn't seem to have anything."

"What did he ask you?"

"To help."

"And you said?"

"No. Of course."

"Of course."

A no-nonsense waitress came by and looked Lou wordlessly in the eye. Did he want two refills? Lou just as wordlessly replied, yes. The waitress was off like a dust devil.

"I've been thinking about approaching it another way," Sally said.

"Mothers watch your children."

"Remember Bruno Palermo?" Sally asked.

Lou looked into the dark eddies where he knew her angel blues where housed.

"Sure, Sally. The killing at Maggie's Best?"

"He was also Dicerno's man."

The waitress was back with Lou's martini and Sally's wine, taking Lou's twenty dollar bill with a half wink. Still not a word spoken.

"You could probably forget Palermo."

"No, Lou. He may be the key."

"Sally. Palermo was no pro hit."

"How do you know?"

"Because who would use a pro to kill Palermo?"

"I believe they call that kind of reasoning tautological."

Lou nodded. "I believe you're right."

"Lou, two people who work for Dicerno are killed less than a month apart. There hadn't been a wise guy killed in Denver for years. Then suddenly two are dead."

"Spilotro wasn't in Denver."

"Pretty picky, Lou."

"Granted. But what connection could the killings have? Spilotro was a major threat to Dicerno. I can't see how Palermo was. How are they connected?"

"I don't know, but if we figure it out, we'll be way ahead of the game."

Lou had to admit Sally had a point. Yet he had no clue where it could lead. He took a long drink from his new martini. Then the saxophone began to play.

The waters of the Wind River plow through a canyon and emerge southeast of Thermopolis, where, due to a naming dispute between Native Americans and early explorers, they are changed into the Bighorn River and head north towards Montana, where they meet with a sibling river made famous by General Custer and Sitting Bull. Rocks painted on the side of a hill in Thermopolis declare the formations below to be the largest hot springs in the world.

The town is surrounded by undulating red stone hills. A little closer to the Bighorns, the area formed Bad Lands where almost nothing grew but for a few sagebrush plants. There was no water in sight. Nor visitors. Except this day a troop of cub scouts was out exploring. Mr. Anderson was in charge. It was hot. No clouds threatened to hide an angry sun. Mr. Anderson was sick of a few diehard lizards and lifeless ravines and empty crevices and caves. He was about to pull the troops out when one 9-year-old kid way out in front of the pack poked his head into a small cave. He darted back out, screaming and running towards the others, his hands covering his eyes. He tripped and fell and got up again, hands still over his eyes, and tripped again. There he sat, sobbing.

Jason Ison had been found.

The president was in the map room with Orvez, Strange and Hamilton.

"OK," the president said. "I want it all out on the table. What happened? Who are we dealing with? How do we respond?"

"What happened, sir," Orvez started, "is our agent was snatched away from Thompson Falls and tortured and killed."

"In what way?" the president asked.

"Larry…" She caught herself. "Mr. President, it's not pleasant. We had the body removed, quietly, to Bethesda. Something had happened to Jason's right eye. Something the pathologist had never seen. He had a hunch and called in a veterinarian. They got some DNA and processed it fast. It was a rat, sir. They had a rat eat Jason's eye."

The president turned pale, speechless. He sat down on the chair at the head of the table. All was silent but for the dull drone of air conditioning.

"These people are savages," said Naslund in a whisper.

Orvez lowered her head.

"Sir, you should know this. It was probably a persuasion technique perfected by a couple of our former agents, Terpil and Wilson."

The president acted as if he hadn't heard that last line.

"We must get these bastards," he said, regaining strength. "Who are they? Is it Ivanov?"

"Mr. President," said Orvez, "we do not know for sure. We are decoding some intercepted radio traffic now. But, yes. Ivanov. He had the motive. And means."

"Means?"

"Yes, sir. We just got a report from Moscow. Three members of Ivanov's organization were to try to slip into the country five days ago. We don't know names. Or plans. Or if they made it. But if they did, they probably were here long enough to team up and get to Montana."

"Then Ivanov has just declared war on the United States of America," said the president. "We pull out all the stops."

Michael Strange spoke: "There could be little we can do. Ivanov is in Moscow, and we can't send B-2 bombers to Moscow."

"We hit him everywhere. We will not use traditional means. Or rules. And when and if we do go back to Russia, it won't be to get a surrogate. We will kill Ivanov," said the president. "As far as I'm concerned, Project Shutdown has just become Project Ivanov.

"Any questions?"

No one said a word.

29. Double Act

DANNY Dicerno, at the bungalow, laid back in his hot tub drawing on a joint. Candy, one of the top strippers at "Secretaries," his high-test downtown club, stroked up his legs and took hold of his cock. When he was hard enough, she straddled him. At this, she was the best. Blonde, 23, firm and experimental, Candy was a rainmaker for Danny Dicerno. And she was now showing him exactly why. She was either the best faker in the business, or she really liked his machinery. He breathed hard and she grew more excited. He and she heaved, water cascading everywhere. Her nails dug into the back of his head just as his tongue found her hard brown nipple. She screamed suddenly, piercing and primordial. They came together.

Then the phone rang.

"Fuck ya want?" Dicerno panted. Candy dismounted and dried off. She seemed happy. Dicerno did not.

"Danny. Sorry," said Jimmy. "A guy from Chicago called. Someone saying he was important. He was rude. Wants to meet with you."

Candy had done much to salve Dicerno's disposition. Now this. It was like being awakened during a great dream.

"So fuckin' what?" roared Dicerno.

"He said he was with Vito Borelli," said Jimmy.

The change in Dicerno was instantaneous. The mention of Borelli galvanized him. Borelli was the boss of the Outfit. For Dicerno, that made him next to God.

"Do you have any idea who Vito Borelli is?" Dicerno said scrambling out of the tub and grabbing a towel.

"Some guy in Chicago."

"Some guy. Jimmy shit-for-brains. Someday your stupidity is goin' get me killed."

"So should I call him back?"

"No you shouldn't call him back."

The Outfit used to represent Denver at the national commission in the 60s and 70s. Danny dreamed that those days could return. The last thing Dicerno wanted was for Jimmy to fuck it up.

"OK, Jimmy. Think hard. What was the name of the guy who called?"

"He called himself Vinnie. Vinnie Terra-something."

"Vinnie Terranova!" shouted Dicerno, almost exploding.

"Yeah, that's it. Terranova."

"Motherfuckin' Mary," spluttered Dicerno. "What else did he say?"

"He said I should only talk about this to you in person."

"You idiot. You just mentioned it on the phone."

Silence.

Dicerno knew he could call himself an idiot too. He had asked the question. He was using a new smartphone that was in the name of one of his strippers, so he doubted the feds were listening. Still...Fuckin' Jimmy!

"OK, Jimmy, get your ass over here. I'll meet you outside."

"I'm coming."

Vinnie Terranova was the underboss of the Chicago Outfit, second only to Vito Borelli. Borelli wouldn't send the underboss on just any occasion, only on the most important, ones that needed to be perfectly secure. The permutations were blowing Dicerno's mind. Was this the day Danny Dicerno's luck changed?

When Jimmy arrived, Dicerno was already dressed and smoking outside. He would have liked to strangle Jimmy for being dumber than whale shit, but he told himself to be restrained. He might need Jimmy.

As Jimmy approached, Dicerno tossed down his cigarette and stomped it out, a substitute for stomping out Jimmy.

"OK," said Dicerno. "What did Terranova say?"

"He said he wanted to come here for a meeting, Danny. But he said it had to be in a totally safe place. He was pretty much a jerk, demanding, and I..."

"Shut up, Jimmy, shut up." Jimmy shut up. "What place?"

"Said you were to find it, give it to me and I was to go to Chicago and personally tell him. Like I say, a real demanding jerk, but I..."

Dicerno clenched his fist and landed a haymaker on Jimmy's jaw.

When Jimmy came to, he was hurting. The boss still had it, he thought helplessly.

The boss, looking down on him on the ground, said: "Jimmy, are you listening? This is what I want you to do..."

Jimmy listened.

30. Deep Cover

IT was a slow Sunday. The folks in Denver's Washington Park went about their strolls or just sat around soaking up sun. Tika was on a leash. No reason to take a chance here with another Chihuahua.

Lou and Sally found a shady spot where they sat, hauled out some El Dorado Springs water. Something had been bugging Sally. It was time to get it off her chest.

"OK, Lou. Time for the rest of the story."

"Story?"

"Becky Sue."

Lou shifted again, suddenly uncomfortable.

"That was a lifetime ago, Sally."

"Come on, Lou." Sally hit him in the arm.

"Sally, I'd rather talk about flamethrowers on Saipan."

She hit him again, put her hands on Lou's shoulders and looked into his eyes.

"Tell me," Sally urged.

Lou had space issues, even with Sally. And this had been the biggest one in Lou's life. For a long time, he had thought it would be impossible even to mention it, ever, to anyone. That prohibition even covered him. Lou had been keeping it buried inside, deep, at a place he didn't want to visit. Did Sally have a right to know?

"Tell me," Sally said again, but slower, gentler this time. It was enough. Lou took a deep breath, looked Sally in the eye, and then looked down.

"OK," he said. "Here goes: After the fight with my father, the 'My Little Nazi' fight, I left home, I drifted. I didn't know what I wanted, but whatever it was, it wasn't in Connecticut.

"Since I was a kid, I had read about the civilizations in Mexico and Central America – men who would stand on top of pyramids

113

and tear out the beating hearts of their enemies. Maybe that was it. But one way or another, I ended up in a pueblo near Santa Fe. I liked watching the Indians selling wares in the square and the artists selling godawful pictures. I liked how the adobe grew out of the earth, no boundaries. The people around me were dirt poor, but had deep souls. I signed up for a course in a junior college. That's where I met Becky Sue. We seemed to have a common heart. We fell madly in love."

Lou paused momentarily and looked at Sally's eyes fixed on him.

He continued: "Dad's private investigators tracked me down, of course, but I refused to return. I was working for a greasy spoon called the Casa Taco and sharing the rent with seven others in a rundown hovel on the outskirts of town.

"Then dad sent the papers, officially disinheriting me. I hadn't smoked much pot but thought this would be a proper occasion. A friend brought over some Jamaican and we rolled up part of the legal papers and made a fine marijuana stogie.

"That night I dreamed of a man in a beak-nosed red mask pounding out a crazy dance. He held a bloody heart over his head. My father's. The Nazi was dead."

"Oh, Lou." Sally said softly. "That must have hurt."

"No, not really. It just put me in my place. Suddenly as poor as all my friends, I worked my way through college and then, four years later, got a degree in anthropology from New Mexico State. After that, Becky Sue and I headed south."

Lou stopped.

"And then?"

"Not quite ready for that, Sally."

"Try."

Lou wished he could have one of Sally's cigars. Or a stiff belt of Wild Turkey. He tried.

"I was twenty three and she was twenty one," Lou said. "Both of us had just graduated. And we were going to live forever."

He fell silent. Sally didn't say a word.

"Well, Becky Sue, five-foot-two..."

"No way!"

"And she was the most alive thing I ever knew. A human hummingbird. We had saved up a little money and decided it was enough to live for eight or nine months in Latin America. We headed to the city of the Aztecs, Mexico City to you. From there, we headed to the Pyramid of the Sun at Teotihuacán. Becky Sue had scampered to the top like a feline with a meal in sight. I somehow managed to drag myself after her. And then it was off to the land of the Mayans in south Mexico, Guatemala and Belize."

"Lou, the wild adventurer," Sally smiled. Lou did not. He paused.

"One day in Belize, we were really down on funds. And for a two-dollar rent we got mats on the floor. Usually we drew the line before then. We would insist on real beds. But no more."

He paused again. Sally didn't have any idea what came next.

"When we woke up the next day, Becky Sue had some bites on her forearm. Bed bugs."

He couldn't go on.

"Bed bugs?" Sally asked.

When Lou turned to look at her he had something in his eyes that she had never seen before, and was certain she never wanted to see again.

"I intended to marry Becky Sue, to have a litter of children. But shortly after we got back to the States she began feeling ill. Her wings were clipped. And that wasn't like her.

"And then one day, while I was at Quantico, a greenhorn trainee at the Bureau, Becky Sue called to say she had just seen a doctor. There was a rare disease in certain parts of Latin America called Chagas Disease. It was a parasite. It destroyed muscles, including the heart. She had it."

Lou paused. Like something was caught in his throat.

"She said the disease was caused by a small bug that hit mostly the poor, people who slept on mats on floors."

Sally took Lou's hand and gently stroked it.

"You know, I could have asked my father for money. He would

have been glad to have his little rebel back. No need to sleep on mats. But I was too proud to ask. And too dumb."

"You didn't know."

"But no, we had to live as close to the natives as possible while on some foolish great adventure."

Sally waited. She knew the rest would come now.

"Chagas Disease can take years, or it can take months. With Becky Sue it took months. Eight to be exact. She died in my arms."

Lou hit his fist on the ground.

Sally knew she was seeing guilt as much as grief. The kind that never fully passes. The kind that causes depression. She hugged him, hard. There was still moisture in his eyes, but no tears. She figured he had cried out Becky Sue years before.

Sally recalled how Lou had been close at times to completely letting loose in their relationship. But then there had come tentativeness. Now she understood. Lou had demons just as she had demons, lodged far in the past. Lodged in death. She knew one day she would tell him about her demons as well.

That night, Sally took command of the lovemaking. She undressed Lou slowly, her tongue exploring every inch. And when she pushed him back on the bed it was like pushing over a pillow. He was helpless to resist.

When she mounted him he was as hard as anything she had ever imagined. She took it slow, and never changed. As she sensed he was near a climax she almost stopped completely, barely moving. Lou moaned, eyes closed. Sally moved again, up and down, faster this time, her whole body on fire. And then suddenly both she and Lou let out wild, untamed roars and she collapsed on him.

After a while she opened her eyes and saw that Lou's eyes remained closed. She wondered what he was thinking. And then she knew. And decided she didn't care.

31. Mob Meet

MR. COFFEE gave up his second cup of java to Sally who was sitting at the kitchen table, poring over the Denver Post. She was not happy.

Lou came in, scrubbed clean from the shower, feeling a full ten years younger than he had the day before. The joint powers of confession and good sex, he thought. No, he corrected himself, great sex. He went over to the coffee pot, poured a cup and noticed Sally pouting.

"What's up, Sal?" he asked. It was the first time he had ever used the name Sal.

"That asshole friend of yours, that's what's up."

She threw the Post at Lou. Lou looked at the headline: "Is the Feds' Spilotro Theory Bogus?" The subhead read: "Some Denver Cops Think So."

"Jesus, Sal. He can't base this on what some Denver cops think. It's a federal program."

"Think again."

Sally folded her arms across her chest, saying, "Try three – not one, not two, but three – anonymous sources in the DPD."

Then she grabbed the paper and read out the top of the story:

> While federal lawmen still hold to the theory that Felipe Spilotro was killed by a jealous husband, Denver police say they know better.
>
> "So far, no husband has turned up," said one Denver detective. "Ask yourself, 'Who benefits?' I know of one name: Danny Dicerno."
>
> If the Denver cops are right, then the very real possibility exists that there is a leak in the federal Witness Protection Program.

"They must be confiscating some pretty good dope these days," Lou said. "How can some unnamed Denver cops trump the FBI and the U.S. Marshals' office?"

"Brad is way out on a limb," agreed Sally. "It's a dangerous story."

"So why sweat it?"

"Because Brad is right."

Why is it, Lou thought, that great sex at night is not automatically followed by harmony and peace in the morning? He surveyed Sally's coffee mug with suspicion.

"True," he finally said. "But we've known that. Yet having three anonymous sources doesn't prove it."

"It's three better than my no anonymous sources."

"OK," he conceded.

"I'm going to have some pretty aggravated editors to deal with," Sally said. And she was right.

Mel Campbell called at noon.

"You see the Post story?" he asked Sally.

"Mel, I live in Denver, remember?"

"So there's nothing to it?"

"I don't know, Mel. Yet. But I do know this – Johnson's sources only have opinions, not facts. If that's the new standard I can get you all sorts of scoops."

Mel growled a little. Surrendering.

"So there's nothing to do?"

"Mel, there's a lot to do. I may be on to something."

"Anything you can share?"

"Not with some cranky old black guy."

"Sally, you know I wouldn't be on your case unless they were on mine."

"Then explain to them this opinion thing. They shouldn't go jumping out of windows because Brad Johnson went on a bender with three locals."

"OK, Sally, you're right. But..."

"But what?"

"Feel free to go on a bender of your own."
She smiled at that.

The early Colorado autumn was already turning the mountain slopes into a stunning blend of golds, rusts and yellows, showing the deference of trees to impending winter. Dicerno drank in the colors as he tooled alone up Floyd Hill just west of Denver, a big grueling slope that flatlanders would call a mountain. Then Dicerno dipped down to Idaho Springs, and up again to Georgetown.

As he approached the Eisenhower Tunnel, he did something he would never let any of his crew see. Alone and safe, he reached over and tuned the radio to KYGO, a country station. He secretly liked the tunes and all those Western oldies love-lyrics. He knew it was not music for a Mafia don. He told himself that he liked Sinatra just fine, but the Dixie Chicks were OK, too. He imagined them in a hot tub, with him. And there was Johnny Cash and the Folsom Prison Blues. And that crazy guy, Lyle Lovett, singing that dumb song about riding a pony on a boat on an ocean. Dicerno loved the image. He didn't know why.

After the tunnel, Dicerno blew past Dillon and Vail and found himself in Glenwood Canyon, which he thought must be the best stretch of interstate highway in America. Soon he emerged into Glenwood Springs, where he parked by the public pools and walked to what he considered the most private meeting place on planet Earth.

Dicerno had been here before, the first time with his wife. They were steered to the hot spring caves by an elderly man handing out flyers. Mr. and Mrs. Dicerno had walked down some 50 feet into the steaming caves, where wood planks led to even darker reaches. But for the artificial light, nothing could have been seen. Hot spring water gurgled up and there was a scent of sulfur. Dicerno felt it immediately. It was like being in the belly of a geological beast. There were caverns shooting off in every direction—small, private places where men, women and oftentimes both, could have private moments. And since one hundred and ten degrees is a bit much, there were garden hose hookups connected to city water, so bathers could cool off. Dicerno mouthed a term he had not used since the 70s: "Far out."

The caves not only instantly became Dicerno's favorite place, but they were practical as well. If he ever really needed a place to hold a secure meeting this was it. No FBI listening contraption ever discovered could penetrate these baths under 40 yards of solid stone.

For good measure, Dicerno had come early and paid the counter clerk a thousand bucks to close the caves down completely between 1 and 3 p.m. The young woman, maybe 19, kissed him on the cheek before she left. Dicerno thought fleetingly of her as dancing material but she wasn't much of a looker and he had more pressing issues in mind.

Vinnie Terranova arrived exactly at 1 p.m. in a Ford Expedition driven by a man with a huge head and tiny sunglasses.

Terranova thought, "What da fuck?" The signs said this was some sort of steam cave in the middle of a mountain.

"Fuck me," Terranova finally told his muscle man. "I guess we're not in Chicago anymore."

Ignoring the "Closed" sign, Terranova went inside and made his way to a dressing room. Dicerno was there, dressed only in a towel.

"This gotta be a joke, right?" Terranova said.

Dicerno rose and embraced Terranova in the don style.

"Just wait 'til we go down below," said Danny Dicerno.

"Down below? There's a below?"

"Yeah, the cave."

Terranova appraised the Denver don skeptically. But he had his orders. He would go along.

He undressed, toweled, made his way with Dicerno down into the cave. It was both dark and white with steam at the same time. Terranova had never seen such a place, never even imagined anything like this existed. There must have been some monster fire in the mountain, he thought. It made him feel strong and kind of insignificant at the same time. Magical.

They found a dark chamber that had a ledge to sit on and a bucket of water and hose.

Terranova took a deep breath in. His white-as-lint skin began to take on a ruby tone.

"This is fuckin' spectacular," were his first words. "Feds could never get down here. And it's kinda holistic."

Dicerno didn't know the word "holistic," but thought Terranova had probably meant to say "holy" and so he smiled.

"Yeah. No feds here, and, naturally, no body bugs, either."

That was a good one, Vinnie thought. No body bugs. We are almost naked. Who the fuck is this guy?

"OK," he said, "This man of yours that did Spilotro. We're impressed."

"He's my ace," said Dicerno, having no clue who his ace was.

Terranova turned to look directly into Dicerno's eyes.

Dicerno was not used to this. Most men turned away when he looked into their eyes. Now he was the one to turn.

"We need your man," Terranova said.

Dicerno splashed some of the cold water from the bucket over his back. The sentence – "We need your man" – kept resonating. Dicerno knew he was going to be asked a favor by the boss of The Outfit, and that he had no way of turning it down. That wouldn't be a problem, if he knew who Mr. Wood was. But he didn't.

"Look, Dan," Terranova continued, "Vito Borelli has a problem, just like you had with Spilotro."

Oh, fuck.

"And we need that problem gone."

Fuck. Fuck. Fuck.

"Tony Nails."

Fuck fuckin' fuck. Dicerno looked back at the bucket of cool water.

Tony Nails, also known as Anthony Frentis, was the most prolific hitman in America. His was a name so big that maybe even Jimmy knew of him. Tony Nails made Murder Inc. look like the ladies' bridge club. Frentis got his name because, during his coming-out years, he used a nail gun on his victims. Feet and hands first. Then one straight between the eyes.

"Tony has turned?" Dicerno asked.

"Yeah," Terranova said. "He was facing the Big Bitch."

The Big Bitch. Just like Spilotro.

How far in over my head have I gotten? Danny thought. And what should be the price of killing the murder machine?

"How much?" Terranova asked.

How should I know? Dicerno thought. He said: "That depends."

"Bullshit," thundered Terranova. "I'm not buying a used car. It's a simple turnkey operation. How much for the contract?"

Dicerno couldn't even keep up with his own thinking. He had no idea what to say and, recognizing this, he decided to say about the first thing that popped into his head, which he did: "Two million."

"Why are you low-balling me?" asked Vinnie, immediately on guard.

Dicerno realized he had made an error. Apparently The Outfit thought in numbers greater than he could ever imagine in his own business. Dicerno was not stupid, just uninformed. He quickly corrected his error.

"That would be his take," he said, "We'd want another two million."

Terranova was still not impressed. This was small change to eliminate Tony Nails. Vinnie had been authorized to agree up to eight million dollars, and he knew Vito Borelli would go for even more to save his skin. No one had ever killed a protected witness until Spilotro. Somehow, Dicerno had gotten to one. Why wasn't he asking for more?

But Terranova thought that if Dicerno could get it done for four million that would be fine. Dicerno was strange, he thought. Maybe he didn't understand the value of this hit to the Outfit.

"That would be fine," Vinnie Terranova finally said. "I will bring the money. This will be the spot. You will talk to no one about this," he said getting up. Dicerno also got up, held out his hand. Terranova took it, and with the deal sealed, headed up the stairs, showered and went on his way.

Dicerno thought, my God, four million dollars. He wondered if he could have asked for more, and immediately realized the answer was yes. Still...

On the way back to Denver, Dicerno hummed some Garth Brooks songs and thought of his wife. Then he thought of the 23-year-old stripper from Secretaries and felt something growing in his crotch.

Victory. That was the word he kept thinking.

When he got to Denver he went to the bungalow, not The Farm.

32. Bar Hopping

LOU slipped into the Gas Light Inn, a neighborhood joint on South Broadway. The booths along the walls were red vinyl – matching the short skirts of a couple of women talking at one end of the bar. Other regulars sat at tables sharing beer by the pitcher. Some wanted to whisper, others were getting rowdy. "On the Streets of Cheyenne" played on the Juke. Milo, a three hundred-pounder with an arm tattoo that said "MOM" minded shop.

Lou nodded at Milo as he entered and held up two fingers. Soon Milo deposited one bottle of Black Jack at Lou's table, and two shot glasses.

"Smiley?" Milo asked.

"If he shows," Lou said.

Ten minutes later, Smiley showed. With dark hair that was half braided and half just plain out of place, a faded Army jacket, camo pants and high-top sneakers, Smiley looked to be one short step away from sleeping on a grate. He also smelled the part, a sharp, acidic tang that could water eyes.

Lou had no idea how Smiley got his name because in the five years they had been meeting here irregularly, he had rarely seen Smiley smile. Maybe that was it: Irony.

If he cared, Smiley didn't show it. He figured no one worried about his looks or smell as long as he got them what they wanted, and he usually did. His specialty: first-rate information. Somehow, no one knew exactly, Smiley had near-perfect intelligence about much of the city's underbelly: rounders, hookers, dopers, burglars, fences, anybody on the come.

For a price Smiley also had a remarkable memory. When Lou needed to contact him he left a message at the store where Smiley got his wine.

Smiley picked up Lou's bottle and overfilled his shot glass.

Didn't apologize. Belted it back and poured himself another. Knew his value.

"So what's up," he said, wiping his mouth with his sleeve.

"You know that bouncer at the Lay Lady Lay that got whacked a while ago?

"Sure, yeah..."

"I need a lead on who killed him."

"Have you lost your mind? Palermo was as important as a fart." Smiley reached for the bottle. Lou grabbed his wrist. Not so fast.

"It's even worse than that, Smiley."

"What's worse than that?"

"I want to know if it's connected to Felipe Spilotro." Lou let Smiley's hand go.

Smiley used it to stuff a pinch of chewing tobacco in the corner of his mouth, considering.

"This ain't like you, Lou, chasing nobodies. You under the weather?"

"Smiley, I'm asking for a friend."

"She better be great in the sack to have Lou Elliott asking crazy questions like these."

"Smiley," Lou said, "I am going to get irritated with you pretty soon."

"Get irritated."

"Fine." Lou took his bottle and stood. It worked.

"Whoa, cowboy, sit down," said Smiley at once.

Lou sat but kept his hand on the bottle. Smiley watched Lou's hand.

"I ain't heard nothin' about who did Palermo. Figured it was kids."

"Ask around."

"I will, Lou. But life's been tough. My landlady says..."

Lou took out two $100 bills and slipped them under the bottle. Smiley smiled. Lou took one look at the war zone in his mouth and wished he hadn't.

Lou wasn't done bar hopping. Next stop was Sparky's. Sparky's was a lawman's dive, filled with detectives, assistant DAs and an occasional judge. Even a reporter who could be trusted could hang around. It was at Sparky's that Lou had met Brad Johnson. Lou was here to see Pat O'Dowd, chief of the criminal division of the Denver U.S. Attorney's office. O'Dowd was one of those big men who refused to shop in the "Big and Tall Men" store. As the years passed he had given up trying to close the top button on his shirt. His ties were always loosened, even before juries. That didn't seem to hurt him any. O'Dowd always seemed to win.

Lou and Pat went back a long ways. When Lou was with the Bureau they had gone to war together. Both had saved each other's skins more times than they cared to admit. Lou even played O'Dowd in chess. O'Dowd was ever aggressive, moving his queen out early, sacrificing with wanton abandon. None of that helped. He always lost – at least he did to Lou.

Lou saw O'Dowd enter. He nodded him over.

"So what's so important, Lou. Or are you just homesick for the old haunts?"

Lou bought Pat a drink and ordered another for himself.

"I'm trying to puzzle out this Dicerno thing," Lou said when he got down to the point. "For a friend."

"Friend?" repeated O'Dowd, his eyebrows raised.

"OK," said Lou, "Sally Will."

"Not bad!" O'Dowd said, almost a bit too loudly. Then he whispered: "Actually, Lou, word is out."

"Seems to be. Sally wanted to keep it quiet."

"In this town?"

"Right."

"So what does Sally want to know from anonymous sources?"

"Did you see Brad's story?"

"Amazingly, he got part of it right."

"That's news," Lou grinned. "Anyway, Sally wants to confirm it. And she's also spinning a new theory. You recall Bruno Palermo from the Lay Lady Lay?"

"Yeah, the guy popped at Maggie's Best."

"That's the one. Sally thinks they might be connected."

"I thought Sally was smart."

"She is."

"Palermo was a nobody."

"Sure, but Sally notes that he was a made-guy nobody. Old rules said that it takes a made-guy to take out a made-guy."

"That part of the Mafia is dead, Lou."

"Sally thinks Dicerno might be a traditionalist. Look, I warned her off. But I might as well warn a dog off a bone. Can't be done."

"Poor man."

"Sally is often right."

"Well, I grant her this. Her hunch on Spilotro is right on."

"Dicerno is good for Spilotro?"

"Undoubtedly."

"What about the jealous husband letter?"

"We think the killer wrote that letter. We may be dealing with a creative killer here, Lou."

"Mm, hate those."

"Not only can't we find the pissed off husband, our lab says it was a good bomb. Doesn't look heat-of-passion. Dicerno's good for it, but we'll probably never prove it."

"So why did the feds spin it otherwise?" asked Lou.

"Between us?"

"Of course."

"Would a presidential directive do?"

Lou cleared his throat.

"You didn't hear it here," said O'Dowd.

"OK, Pat, thanks. I owe you."

"And tell Sally to forget Palermo. Even if Dicerno ordered it, what does that prove?"

Lou shrugged.

33. Fly Fishing

THE creek wound its way through thick pines, tumbling, roaring, cascading its way down the mountainside. Then, just as suddenly, it smoothed out. The edge between the riot and the peace was Sally's secret place: The headwaters of the Colorado. She said the fish were here, and since she caught the limit almost every time she came, Lou believed her.

Sally, in green waders reaching to her chest, raised her rod in front of her with the grace of a fencer. She snapped it up and back as she teased the trout with one of her father's old handcrafted flies. A breeze danced through her hair.

"Come on, Lou," she said. "Just give it another go. You'll love it, really. It's relaxing."

"Sally, I'll get it someday."

He sought an excuse.

"I'm left handed. They don't make these things for us."

"Lou," Sally replied, "that is a special left-handed rod."

Lou conceded that he was fishing challenged. There were worse things to be. He tried a few casts and lost a few flies. He knew it all dated back to his growing up in Connecticut. There were just some things that you had to learn young. Like catching a New York cab.

He tossed the fly again and it more or less landed where he intended. A native trout made a run at it.

"Yank, yank," ordered Sally. "Yank!"

Lou yanked. But he had allowed too much slack in the line and the fish spit out the phony bug. Just then, Sally snagged a trout and began reeling it in with ease.

She was an artist, Lou decided. Every movement was precise, with an economy of motion, like Ju-Jitsu. Sally worked the fish slowly, letting it run out of steam, and then calmly reeled it in.

When she raised her net and turned to grin at Lou, he saw Sally had won a 14-inch Rainbow trout, about as large as they got here.

"Come on, Lou. They're all over the place," Sally encouraged.

Lou tried a few more casts, but soon resolved that fishing could be a spectator sport and he should prove it by becoming a spectator. He waded from the water, hauled a Coors out of his pack, popped it open, and laid back on a rock. As Tika ran wild after geese – at least, Lou thought, she wasn't afraid of birds – he sipped his beer and listened to the swish of Sally's rod.

Sally finally netted another rainbow, dehooked it, put it into her basket, and looked askance at Lou. "Kind of giving up?" she asked.

"Nope, only admitting a temporary setback," he said. He sought to change the subject.

"Sally, I got a whiff of something last night."

"That right?" She laid out a perfect cast near a small eddy, and waited.

"A good source says that you're right about Spilotro. The cuck-old-husband note was probably penned by the killer, who the feds believe is rather clever."

"Clever."

"And they believe Dicerno is behind it."

"Is Dicerno clever? I know he's not dumb, but to break into the Witness Protection Program?"

"I don't think they have any clue how he did it, just that Dicerno was behind it."

"And Palermo?"

"You're wrong there, Sal. Besides, they think, so what?"

"You know what I think?" asked Sally.

"What?"

"I think we're missing something."

Sally paused. Then she said: "Can you get the Denver PD's supplementals on Palermo?"

"Jesus, Sally. Everybody says you should give that one a rest."

"My dad said to watch out when everybody said the same thing. The opposite was usually right."

"So your dad was always right?"

"He taught me to fish, didn't he?"

And damn, if she didn't have another one.

On the way to the murder room, Lou walked toward the office of Steve Brandon, one of Sally's best sources. More than a source, perhaps. Lou had heard the rumors. Some people thought that Sally and Brandon had once been an item. To Lou, that would have been in another life. Didn't matter now. Still, he found it curious. Sally, he was hoping, had better taste.

As he passed, Lou saw that Brandon had his door open and his feet up on his desk. He was reading the Post. He appeared to be absorbed by some story and didn't look up. Just as well, Lou reasoned. He was here to see "the Young Turks." Brandon wouldn't like that.

On the wall outside the homicide room was a sign saying, "Our day begins when yours ends." Lou loved it. Inside was Young Turk number one, Scott Kirkpatrick. Lou and Scott had been friends ever since Lou, with the FBI at the time, had given Scott information about a series of bank robberies. The FBI seldom went out of its way to help the locals. Lou had. And Kirkpatrick made an important collar.

Even for a Young Turk, Kirkpatrick was just a babe. With a little work, he could pass as a 21-year-old college student. He had already used that ability several times while undercover. Scott looked up.

"Mr. Private I'm-in-the-Money Eye!" he exclaimed. "What has you slumming with us Plebs?"

"Some unimportant scut work," said Lou.

"Well, sit down. Scut is our specialty. Want coffee?"

"No thanks. This won't take long. I have a" – Lou searched for the right word – "client. She has an interest in the Bruno Palermo caper. I was wondering if I could have a peek at the supplementals."

Kirkpatrick's face changed.

"Curious case," Kirkpatrick said. "Why the interest in that dirt bag?"

"Scott, if this isn't Kosher..."

"No, no," said Kirkpatrick. "Wait."

Kirkpatrick pulled a file from a cabinet, made copies and handed them to Lou. There were only 14 pages, pretty slim for a homicide case, but about what Lou expected Bruno Palermo to be worth. Lou slipped them into a pocket.

"Who else, Scott, is concerned?" asked Lou.

"People around here are behaving a bit strange about this one, that's all."

"Who?"

"Brandon for one. He wants copies of everything having to do with it."

"Curious."

"Yes. And now you. So who is your client?"

"Can't say."

Scott grinned.

"So how is Sally?" he asked.

Mr. Wood had been driving past Capricio's every day for weeks. The southernmost window always contained the same thing. Nothing. But this day he saw a thin-necked vase holding what he had been looking for.

A yellow rose.

34. Green Eyes

DIMITRI Ivanov had first seen Katya when she was 13. She was dressed in a ragged dress, sitting on a curb in the part of Moscow where poor men from the provinces came to pick up teen whores. Ivanov, there to shake down the guy who ran that racket, noticed Katya and her incandescent green eyes.

Ivanov was not a man with a big heart, but he made an exception for Katya. He ordered an assistant to take the girl under his wing, get her some good clothes and hire a tutor.

"If the pimp gives you trouble shoot him," Ivanov said. That night, Moscow police found one more dead pimp in an alley.

Katya had never met her protector, but she knew he was the most important person in the world—a powerful man who had reached down and saved her when she had nothing at all to give, everything to lose, no place to go. He was, she knew, besieged by enemies, bad people with black souls. She would do whatever she could, anything at all, to help him. To her he was more than a father.

Katya got into a Moscow cab that was authorized to travel into a restricted district northwest of the city. It was a rainy morning, brisk and sunless. The cab sped by what once had been Stalin's inner dacha, a dark log building deep in the woods, then past those of the old Politburo members—Molotov, Beria and Kaganovich—and finally to the outer ring. The evergreen forests were thicker than Katya had imagined, and the dachas more spread out. She felt undeserving to be here amid all this greatness.

Just before the pavement ended, a man in a yellow rain jacket was standing at attention. He seemed to be a human signpost sent to mark the spot where the cab was to pull off the road and head onto a 150-yard drive deep into the forest. It opened into a meadow where a three-story monolith stood, a mix of Russian vastness with

American colonial. In front was what seemed to be an unending sea of flowers. Nearby, stood a sculpture that appeared to Katya to depict a Tsarina embracing an avalanche of entwined metal beams. It took Katya's breath away.

She was nervous, trembling. She had never imagined she would ever be invited here. She didn't really know how to act.

When she got out, she didn't need to tell the driver to stay. He knew who owned this home, what was expected. He lit a cigarette and unfolded a paper.

At the door someone who seemed to have stepped out of a foreign movie met Katya. Katya recalled the name these men had – butlers. She almost laughed. He seemed too oddly British to be found so deep inside Russia. But he welcomed her in good Russian. She entered a great room, warmly lit. There were murals on the walls depicting imperial times, an expressionist painting of the Winter Palace, and two works she recalled seeing in a book, painted by a man who called himself Picasso. There was no Socialist Realism to be found. A large fireplace, set into the far wall, held a crackling fire.

Ivanov, standing by a wet bar, glanced up. He was dressed in a dark sports coat over a white silk shirt. Katya noted his dark mane was combed straight back. He smiled, holding up a brandy glass.

"So you are Katya," he winked, "My sweet killer."

Katya blushed. It felt like her face was going to explode.

"Come here, my Katya. Have a drink."

She couldn't move. She was dizzy.

"Come on. Come, come."

She did, slowly, not looking up.

Ivanov handed her a small cognac. She took it and tried to put it to her mouth but she was shaking too much and some of it splashed over. Ivanov smiled and put his hand on hers. She calmed at his touch. Ivanov slowly brought the glass back to Katya's lips. This time she managed a small sip.

"Katya, dear, you are so pure," Ivanov said in a kindly voice, shaking his head. "Come, sit."

He took her arm and led her to a sofa. She sat. He did the same, in a nearby leather chair. Katya folded her fingers together, still looking down. She couldn't speak.

"Katya, you are so beautiful and so young. If I was young again I would take you straight away to Paris. Have you ever been to Paris?"

Ivanov's voice was smooth, reassuring. Katya managed to look up, briefly. She saw Ivanov's eyes and looked down again.

"No. Sir," she finally said. "I've never been to Paris, but...but... but I hope I will one day."

"Of course you will."

She blushed. The heat that was on her face spread throughout her body. Ivanov waited until she looked up again.

"Those eyes, Katya, are they from your father or mother?"

"Both, sir."

"Then that explains their depth."

Katya began to relax a bit. This man did not try to intimidate. He seemed like the men on newscasts, western businessmen or leaders. He had grace. She took another sip. Finally she tasted it. It was soft, like sheep's wool.

"So, Katya, what did Jason Ison tell you?"

He seemed to know when she was ready.

"Sir, he told us he was CIA. Some fifteen years. Always under cover. He had done business with Mr. Slavnik to get into what he called 'Ivanov's syndicate.' And then he got orders to do what he called a 'wet job.' That meant a killing. And so he killed Mr. Slavnik, then went off to Montana. He said he didn't like killing Mr. Slavnik, sir."

"Interesting, Katya. And who did he say ordered this killing?"

"He said he did not know."

"But you insisted..."

"Yes. When pressed he said it had to come from a director named Orvez."

Katya still remembered the screams.

"Linda Orvez?"

"Yes, sir. That was the name."

"And did you go deeper?"

"We did."

"And?"

"He said maybe there were to be more of these wet jobs. But he didn't know for sure."

"Who were to be the targets?"

"He said he didn't know."

"But again you insisted?"

"We did. Yes."

"And he said?"

Katya looked down into her brandy glass, and then met Ivanov's eyes. This time, she didn't look away.

"He said he didn't know."

"Yes?"

"But the name he said was being talked about was...yours. He said it was just talk, so far."

Ivanov nodded as though this concerned him not at all.

"Katya, you and Dr. Tsplyev have done a terrific job. First rate."

Ivanov rose. So did she.

"I'll have new orders sent."

He went to Katya, embraced her and kissed her on the cheek. He could have done with her whatever he pleased, as he could have with almost any woman in Russia. But that was not his object, or desire.

"You are one of a kind, sweet Katya," he said.

And she believed him.

35. No Tattooing

SALLY went back to the Tropical Conservatory, sat on a stone bench, closed her eyes and tried to remember the fourteen pages of police reports on the Palermo investigation that Lou had given her the night before, the ones from Scott Kirkpatrick. They seemed to be ordinary. The cops had put some effort into the investigation, but not much. They had recovered shell casings and a cigarette butt from where they figured the killer had stood.

A cop had also interviewed hookers at Maggie's Best. No one had heard a thing. In fact, no one acknowledged even being at work that night. The same went for employees at the porn arcade next door.

Maybe I should give it up, Sally thought. Lou and O'Dowd are probably right. Palermo was not a professional hit. But something was nagging her. Something didn't fit. Think, she told herself.

A moment later, something stirred. It was in the pathologist's report. Sally recalled it said that the bullets shot into Palermo's head had been fired from close range. You could tell that from the way the skull had splintered, it said. But someone, in a different handwriting, had stuck a Post-It note on the report. It read: "Then why no tattooing?" Below that, and on the same Post-It note, someone else had written: "Possible S?"

Sally had skipped right over that. How could something truly important be confined to a Post-It note? Still, it was curious. What did that mean? "S" for suicide perhaps? Impossible. Palermo had been shot five times. So what was it?

After a time thinking and failing to come up with a plausible solution Sally began to wonder if the Post-It note was crucial after all.

When Lou got home, Sally had the reports spread out on the

kitchen table. She was leaning over them as a cigar glowed from a nearby ashtray.

"Sal," Lou said, startling Sally.

She tried stubbing out the evidence.

"I thought..." Lou started.

"It was just one," she protested. "I've quit, for real."

"Sal."

She ignored him.

"I saw something in those reports Scott gave you," Sally said. "I want your opinion."

"OK, Sally. But give those things a rest, for Christ's sake."

"It was just a moment of weakness."

Lou snorted and threw up his hands, shaking his head, defeated.

"Come look," Sally said.

Lou put on his reading glasses and scanned the pages.

"It's this little thing over here," Sally pointed to the yellow note. "What does 'no tattooing' mean?"

Lou looked perplexed and reread the pathologist's report carefully.

"That's odd," he said.

"What?"

"Well, if the gun was fired from close range, as the pathologist says, there should have been tattooing around the entrance wounds, caused by gunpowder blowing out of the barrel."

"But if there was no tattooing?"

"Then it wasn't that close, I guess."

"So there's a contradiction?"

Lou scratched his head.

"I guess," he said.

"And, Lou, look at this on the note. The other handwriting. It says 'Possible S.' What does 'S' stand for?"

Lou looked again at the note, then put it back down on the table muttering a quiet "of course."

"Of course what, Lou?"

"The 'S' must stand for silencer. A silencer would absorb the gunpowder before it left the barrel. That way you could have a close shot without tattooing."

Sally put both her hands flat on the table and looked up.

"A silencer, Lou? What does that mean?"

"It means you were right, Sal."

"About what?"

"It was a professional hit, after all."

36. Team Blue

AFTER spotting the yellow rose, Mr. Wood put on dark glasses, a wig and a green windbreaker and headed to Boulder. He waited for night, for the crowds to thin. Checked for watchers. Found none. Went to the news box, reached in, grabbed the letter, stuffed it in his shirt. He almost ran back to his car and ripped the letter open. It read: "Mr. Wood. Anthony Frentis aka Tony Nails. $2 million. Reply."

Mr. Wood did not have to think long. Two million dollars did the talking. Of course he would take the contract. But who was Anthony Frentis?

When Mr. Wood got home he fired up Google. He liked what he saw. Anthony Frentis, aka Tony Nails, was interesting. The Chicago Sun Times said he was the number one contract killer in America. Yes, thought Mr. Wood! What could be better than killing the ultimate killer? Nothing.

Mr. Wood thought he might have been willing to kill Tony Nails without pay. It would be a happy crime. He was stoked. Mr. Wood wrote a note to Dicerno. It said: "Deal. $1 million down at the same place same time."

Linda Orvez sat behind an oak desk that seemed big enough to land F-14s on. Charles Ramson, deputy chief for covert operations, sat on the other side. His right eye twitched slightly.

"Charles," Orvez said, "you've followed what has been happening with the Russian Mafiya?"

"Yes." The twitch was still there.

"Well, Charles. The fight is going to pick up pace."

"Ma'am?"

"Charles, let me fill you in on what's been happening."

She did.

"Jesus," Ramson said. He threw his left ankle over his right knee. Orvez saw that he had a hole in the bottom of his shoe.

"So this is where you come in," she said. "I want you to form a new team. People who are discreet. Who we can count on in a pinch. It will work differently than in the past."

"How differently?"

Will you just shut up and listen, Orvez thought.

"I've just been studying a presidential directive. It gives us broad powers. Anything this team does will have the sanction of the President of the United States."

Orvez tapped a file on her desk with a knuckle. Ramson tugged his collar.

"You are to get ten of our best coverts." She continued. "Three should have top signals experience. They'll be assigned to the NSA. As far as the staff there goes these three will be just regular NSA people. Instead, they will work for you, gathering intelligence on Ivanov's U.S. operations."

"Eavesdropping in America?"

"Charles, maybe you weren't listening. I said we have a presidential directive." She again tapped the file.

Ramson nodded.

"Then I want you to gather seven others for field work. I'm thinking one of them should be Anne Burgess."

At the mention of Anne's name, the twitch got a little out of control. Ramson massaged his forehead. He hated Anne Burgess.

"Where are we going?" he asked.

"Charles, are you trying to be obtuse?"

"No."

"Then listen. This team isn't going anywhere. Not at first. It's going to stay right here. We are going to take out Ivanov's assets here, including the team that murdered Jason Ison. Questions?"

"What is this group called?"

"Christ, Charles, call it any fucking thing you want. How about Team Dog Shit?"

"OK."

"Charles, you and I are the only two people in the entire universe that will ever know about this conversation. You know what that means?"

"No."

"It means that if you even speak about this in your sleep to your wife, and we find out about it, you will spend your final days alone in some cave."

As he left, Ramson decided on the name for his team. Not Team Dog Shit. Where had she come up with that? From here on, he decided, it would be called Team Blue.

37. Steamed Up

VINNIE Terranova flew by private jet from a general aviation airport near Peoria to the Jefferson County Airport west of Denver. He was carrying a silver suitcase filled with $2 million, half the cost of the hit. Another $2 million would come if Dicerno's man delivered. At Jefferson Terranova rented a Cadillac and headed to Glenwood Springs.

Danny Dicerno had reserved the caves again. The counter girl remembered him. Once she let Dicerno down into the caves she waited for his friend to arrive. This whole exercise intrigued her. One old dude paid her a thousand dollars so another old dude could sweat with him for an hour or so. Pretty weird, she thought. She put out the "Closed" sign.

Soon Terranova arrived, dressed in a Hawaiian shirt under a down jacket and wearing dark glasses. He carried a silver suitcase. Terranova found Dicerno deep in the cave inside a long, dim chamber. He was engulfed in steam.

"Ah, there you are, Danny," he said. "We must make more business so I can come back here again. After the last time my wife said I fucked like a bull."

"It's the vapors," said Dicerno. "Holistic medicine." Danny had looked up the word.

Vinnie handed Dicerno the suitcase.

On his way back to Denver, Dicerno was happy. He tapped his fingers on the steering wheel. Then a tune from Patsy Cline came on KYGO. He knew it as her best: "Crazy."

Driving along, he laughed out loud: "Crazy? Right!"

38. Bum Tip

MR. Wood didn't think he had to do the guitar act on the Pearl Street Mall anymore. If the feds were onto him he should have been arrested by now. Since he was still free he felt safe. When he got to the mall it was blustery. The street actors had mostly gone. Didn't matter to Mr. Wood. He just sat on a bench down the block, obvious as a sitting duck, and waited, wondering how Jimmy would haul a million bucks to the Westword box. It would take a suitcase, he figured.

But when Jimmy rounded the corner Mr. Wood grew concerned. Jimmy wasn't carrying anything resembling a suitcase. In fact, he didn't seem to be carrying anything at all. Something was wrong. As Mr. Wood was considering making a dash for safety Jimmy marched double time right up to the box, opened it and deposited something small below the stack. Then he left.

What the hell, Mr. Wood thought. He found that Jimmy had left behind a single thin letter. It read:

"Dear Mr. Wood.

"The key here is to a safety deposit box at Wells Fargo on 17th Street. Your name is Daniel Fillmore. Your account number is 45DG92217FFT. Your first half is there.

"Good luck."

Mr. Wood smiled.

Lou and Sally got a table away from the crowd at Jazz@Jack's in the Denver Pavilions. They ordered wings.

Sally had been thinking about Dicerno and the Post-It note.

"So this is what we have," Sally said. "Spilotro was professional. No question. Dicerno did it. And Palermo was professional. Also Dicerno. So here's the question, Lou. Where's the connect?"

"Not a clue, Sally."

"Must be something we're not seeing," she said.

Then she noticed that Stan Markson, the attorney for the Hells Angels, had quietly taken a seat at a deserted corner of the bar, not ten feet away. He was nursing a glass of red wine. He appeared to be alone.

Small world, Sally thought. She lowered her voice.

"We must have overlooked something else in the police reports. Something like the Post-It note. Except less obvious."

She dipped into the barbecue sauce.

"There's not much to overlook, Sal. With Palermo, you have five .22 caliber slugs to the head. No spent shells. No tire marks. No prints. No witnesses. No nothing."

"That's it?"

"'Fraid so, Sal."

Sally poured herself some wine.

"This is depressing," she said.

She glanced at Markson. He hadn't touched his drink. Then she thought of something.

"Hey, there is something, Lou. Didn't the cops find a cigarette butt?"

Lou stopped to think. "You're right. They did."

Lou tried to visualize the report. Finally it came.

"Yeah, it was a filterless Dunhill."

"That's right, Lou. Dunhill. I don't recall a DNA report."

"Brandon probably didn't want to waste money on a DNA test for Palermo."

"Hmmph."

They ate in silence for a minute.

"Wait a minute," said Sally, louder than she wanted. "A filterless cigarette? I remember another case where the only thing left by a shooter was a cigarette butt. A recent case..."

"There're lots of smokers, Sal."

"...The biker shooting. Big Bow."

"Cigarette butt?"

"Yes. I remember Brad's story. He said the cops found a filterless cigarette butt right where the shooter had stood."

"A Dunhill?"

"Don't know."

"That would take the prize, Sal."

Sally looked at Markson. She was sure he was listening. "Tell me about it," she said.

The Commerce City police office was just 13 miles north of downtown Denver, near to the Rocky Mountain Arsenal. It was done in 1950s reformatory architecture: cement walls, blue-gray linoleum floors, and tiny windows. The Cajun Inn was just down the street.

Sally walked in like she owned the place and said she needed to talk to a homicide dick. A fat duty sergeant with an ersatz mustache and big ears was at the front desk. He examined Sally's ID, then Sally, and then buzzed her through.

"You will want Rick Sanchez," he said.

"My day is getting brighter by the moment," Sanchez said when Sally walked in. He was as big as Lou, with brown hair parted surfer-style and tight-in-the-crotch jeans. Sally showed him her press card.

"And I'm even more impressed, Miss Sally Will of the Chicago Tribune. I am at your service."

Sally smiled.

"Detective Sanchez, I'm interested in the murdered biker dude, Bow Hendricks."

"Mind telling Detective Sanchez why a Chicago fox is interested in a nothing Commerce City case?"

Sanchez winked.

Sally winked back.

"I got a tip that Hendricks was into white slavery," she said. "Shipping kidnapped girls all over the world."

It was an absurd lie. Always the best.

"Well," Sanchez said, "That does sound important."

"Further, this informant says you guys have all of that in your files but are covering it up. It's a conspiracy theory."

"Very good, Miss Sally Will. Guess you got us nailed."

"Humor me," said Sally.

Detective Sanchez flexed a bicep.

"Miss Sally Will. Bow was a meth man. He wouldn't know white slavery from white Christmas. You got a lousy source."

"So I'm a dumb broad," Sally persisted. "Disabuse me. Let me see the file."

Sanchez studied Sally.

"It's still an active case," he said.

"So you have an active suspect?"

Detective Sanchez pondered for a moment, studying her. There was no suspect, of course, not that he had actually looked for any. Still, the lady had a point.

"Maybe we could go through the reports after work," he said. "There's a bar just around..."

Before he could finish, Sally flashed him a large fake cubic zirconia diamond ring she kept on hand for just such occasions.

"Sorry, Rick," she said.

"Not half as sorry as me."

She almost felt sorry for him. "The reports?" she asked.

He hesitated, then said: "Oh OK. Since you ask so nicely."

Detective Sanchez brought Sally a thin folder and set her up in an interrogation room.

There was almost nothing inside the file: a two-page offense report, a couple of statements from the bikers who had called in the shooting, and an autopsy report. The evidence log listed a spent .30-06 cartridge, a couple of shell fragments from inside Bow's head and a cigarette butt.

Sally reached for one of the evidence packets, a small sealed paper bag. The wording on the tag said: "Cigarette butt at scene. NW by 12 inches from shell casing in 2-BB." The technician had not noted the brand. Too bad, thought Sally. She didn't often commit felonies while on the job but made room for exceptions. This would be one.

Sally slit the red paraffin seal with a small pocketknife she carried in her purse. She knew she could rub it shut afterwards. But she also knew that any serious examination would reveal her misdeed. She was betting that Detective Sanchez wouldn't be too fussy. She reached into the envelope with tweezers, grabbed the butt and brought it up to her face. It was filterless, just like Brad had reported. She could just make out a few small letters on the side that had not been obliterated by heat. They read: D-U-N-H-I... A Dunhill.

Sally felt a shiver.

"You were right," Sally told Detective Sanchez as she handed him back the file. "There's nothing in here about white slavery. Bum tip."

She allowed her hand to rest on his for just an extra moment.

"This was really nice of you," she said looking him in the eyes.

Detective Sanchez beamed. He didn't notice the seal.

Mr. Wood walked into the Wells Fargo bank dressed in a suit and dark glasses, carrying a large brief case. There was a danger that he would be recognized. But what would anyone really know? That he had a safe deposit box? Big deal.

He told the banker that he was Daniel Fillmore, with account number 45DG92217FFT. He showed his key.

Minutes later Mr. Wood was alone in a booth with a large box. His hands and back were damp. He loosened his tie. A few weeks ago he was just a guy with an imagination. Now he was not only a killer, but also perhaps a very rich killer.

He opened the brass box. Inside were stacks and stacks of hundred dollar bills, worn ones that would not attract attention.

Mr. Wood whistled.

39. No Witnesses

DIMITRI Ivanov trusted his new Korean-made smartphone. He had a three-step system. First, he used code. A contract was a fox, a kilo was a dime, a killing was a wedding, a million was a shoe. And so on.

Then he used digital scramblers with an encryption key. The person who had sold him the system said only someone who knew the cipher could unscramble messages. The salesman showed Ivanov how it worked. Ivanov thanked him, then killed him.

Finally, Ivanov built in redundancy. Every two weeks, he would have a man buy a phone, registered in the gofer's name. Once the gofer delivered the phone he would be killed. Tracing anything to Ivanov was difficult and as a consequence Ivanov felt secure. He remembered Stalin's saying: "You can't make an omelet without breaking eggs." It was a good system, but it was one that misjudged American technology.

It was after 2 a.m. and the NSA headquarters was quiet. Charles Ramson was in a room deep inside, insulated, electronically baffled and connected to the world's fastest super computer.

One of his three inside men sat with earphones on, adjusting a dial. He took the phones off and grinned.

"Do we have it?" asked Ramson.

"We do," the agent said.

Team Blue had tapped into the computers of Britain's Sky News. The computer contained a digitized recording of a five-year-old interview with Ivanov. Ivanov had a policy against giving interviews, having read that it was through such antics that the American criminal John Gotti had lost his empire. But on one occasion, in the presence of a striking redheaded correspondent, Ivanov forgot his rule, giving a short 20-second interview:

"They say you are the new Tsar of Russian crime," the reporter said, holding a mike to Ivanov's face. They were in Red Square.

"They say so many things that are so wrong," smiled Ivanov. "I am a copper wholesaler. You have them in your country. Germany has them. America has them. Are we all criminals?"

"But they are not talking about copper," the journalist said. "They are talking about drugs and weapons."

"Miss," Ivanov nodded, "when some people become rich in a country that has been so poor, there is going to be talk. And resentment. And exaggeration. And I have become rich."

Ivanov held out the palms of his hands. That was it. But it was enough.

The NSA computer broke down Ivanov's Sky News voice into a billion pieces and then reconstructed it until Ivanov's voice became like a fingerprint, unique to a single man. NSA computers could then compare the voiceprint to millions of others intercepted each day by U.S. satellites. Almost instantly, each conversation involving Ivanov was flagged, decrypted and sent to the team. It didn't matter how many men died getting Ivanov his phone, Team Blue knew what he was saying.

For two days the team listened as Ivanov ran his enterprise. He was sending guns to the Sudan, dope to Berlin, and money to Antigua. Then came a conversation about an American operation. It was what Team Blue had been waiting for.

Ramson marched into the director's office, excited. He had good news. Orvez shuffled some papers before looking up.

"I hear you've made progress," Orvez said.

Ramson had a hunch how she knew this already. Anne Burgess. The director's spy. But he kept his displeasure to himself.

"We have, Director. Ivanov is feeling pressure. He thinks the president is going to make a move. He's sending a lieutenant – name is Mika – to the States to meet with Ivanov's moneyman. We don't know who that is yet. We only have a name: Nikolai. Mika is to order Nikolai to send to the Caribbean any assets that aren't nailed down."

Orvez leaned back.

"Excellent. We're following this Mika?"

"Of course. He's booked to leave Moscow at 11:30 tomorrow. We will be on the plane. Another Team Blue crew will join in once he arrives at Kennedy."

"And what happens when you find Nikolai?"

"We make the arrests."

Ramson seemed self-satisfied. Orvez walked over and put a hand on Ramson's shoulder.

"I think we can do better than that," she said. "We don't need arrests."

Orvez sat down on a couch in front of a coffee table, motioning Ramson to join her. She crossed her legs.

"We need to destroy the man who tortured and killed Jason Ison."

That's exactly what Ramson thought he was doing. He looked confused.

"Charles, you arrest them and then they shut up. We learn nothing. Sure it will hurt Ivanov a little." Orvez held her thumb and index finger apart a couple centimeters, demonstrating. "But that's not what the president wants, demands. He wants Ivanov's heart on a platter."

Orvez saw that Ramson's annoying twitch had returned.

"You need to take this Nikolai and find out all he knows. We need the account numbers from all Ivanov's American and Caribbean banks. There will be a money transfer, except it won't be going to Ivanov."

Ramson stiffened. He brushed back his hair with his hand. Where was she going with this?

"Charles, you are going to have to be creative."

"Creative?"

Christ, Orvez thought, this is like speaking to an amoeba.

"Charles, you are going to force Nikolai to tell us everything."

"But I don't think he will just give us that," protested Ramson.

"Charles, you did training in intensified interrogation, did you not?" she said. "I read it in your reports."

Ramson was getting more uncomfortable.

"I did," he said.

"Well then, that's what we're talking about."

Ramson brushed back his hair again. He was a proud Army officer. He knew how to take orders. He would do anything for the president. But still...

"But, Director, we don't know yet who Nikolai is. What if he's an American citizen?"

"That bothers you?" Orvez asked. Her eyes were stone cold.

Ramson didn't answer.

"Charles, we are in a war. In wars, people die. We intend to make the right people die. These guys, Mika and Nikolai, are the right people."

Ramson studied the designs on the floor, stayed silent.

"Charles?"

"Director, the press will be all over this. It could make Snowden look small."

Orvez took a deep breath.

"Charles, listen and listen well. This is what they will think because this is what you will make them think. You will make it look like the Russian mob did it to their own. The locals, Charles, will be easily fooled."

"But Ivanov will know."

"Maybe," said Orvez. "Or maybe he will think he was betrayed. Maybe someone stabbed him in the back."

Ramson followed this fine. He just couldn't imagine how an American official could have said these words. And then it got worse.

"And Charles."

"Yes, Director?"

"You will leave no witnesses."

40. Devil's Island

MR. Wood had no idea where Tony Nails was, but he had private means and a special source. Within a day he found out part of the story: The feds had stashed Tony Nails somewhere on one of the Apostle Islands off the northwest Wisconsin coast of Lake Superior. His source didn't know which one.

Mr. Wood knew nothing about the Apostle Islands. But putting Tony there made intuitive sense. The feds had kept Felipe Spilotro in an urban setting, believing that no one could crack the program's veil. After Spilotro got blown apart, the U.S. Marshals could no longer make that assumption. For a witness as important as Tony Nails, they would need a place as far away from other humans as possible. Islands in Lake Superior sounded appropriate.

Mr. Wood got Google up and running and was quickly impressed. Lake Superior's 31,281 square miles contained ten percent of the world's fresh water. It was cold and deep – at times reaching down 1,300 feet. And it could get angry. Mr. Wood read about a ship called the Edmund Fitzgerald. The largest freighter on the lake, it sank during a terrible storm in 1975 with the loss of all 29 on board.

He zeroed in on the Apostles. There were twenty three of them, some inhabited and connected through ferries to Bayfield, Wisconsin. The furthest out was called Devil's Island. It was a strange name for an island in a chain called Apostles, Mr. Wood thought. He read that the island contained a lighthouse and a stone home, nothing else. A tourist boat went around the island but didn't dock. Instinct told him this was the place.

Mr. Wood wondered whether they would stash Tony in the lighthouse or the stone home. He couldn't decide. Finally, he felt it didn't matter. Tony was a state witness, not a prisoner. His minders would let him out, at least to exercise.

And that's when Tony Nails would die.

Sally rushed out of the Commerce City police office. She had to find Lou. Fast. She tried his cell. No luck. It was after 5 p.m. on a Friday, happy hour at the Denver Press Club. She figured Lou was there with that damnable Brad Johnson. She left some smoking rubber behind and headed into Denver where she double-parked outside the club.

The Press Club was already rocking when Sally ducked inside. Reporters, lawyers, editors, and assorted hangers-on were waging a war over who could be the loudest. Sally bumped into a backgammon table as she made her way to the rear, surveying for Lou. One player said, "Well, excuuse me." Sally ignored him.

She finally spotted Lou. Johnson was there too, drinking something fruity. She caught Lou's eye.

"Let's get some air," Sally said.

"What, no hello?" said Brad, his face flushed.

"Drinking to forget, Brad?"

"Hang in there. Sally. Someday you'll get a story, too."

He's such a jerk, thought Sally. She took Lou's hand and guided him through the kitchen and out into an alley.

"You're going to tell me it was a Dunhill," Lou said when they finally got stopped.

"It was."

Lou leaned back against a light post.

"Do you have one of those cigars?" he asked.

"Lou?"

"Just give me one."

Sally did, and gave him a light as well.

"This is voodoo," Lou said.

Lou knew what Sally had to do. And it was the last thing he wanted. Sally had to see Steve Brandon. Alone.

Lou had a reason for his reservation, a reason ancient as the hills. Steve and Sally had a past, something more than just professional. He didn't know the details. Never asked. Told himself he didn't care. He took a long drag on the black cigar to clear his mind.

"It's simple, Sally," he said at last.

"What?"

"You need Brandon."

Mr. Wood, in sunglasses, a five-day beard and a Banana Republic jacket, slipped inside the downtown federal building to get U.S. Geological Survey topographical maps of the Apostles. He had had a good look with Google Earth but he needed more precise contour information.

"The Apostle Islands," said a clerk. "We don't get much demand for those 'round here. They sound exotic."

"My firm mines them for bird dung," Mr. Wood said, deadpan. The clerk frowned.

Mr. Wood went home and spread the maps out on a basement office desk. How exactly was he going to kill Tony Nails? He took out a ruler and measured. Devil's Island was 20 miles off shore. Problem.

First, it was early autumn. Bad weather could come at any time. He could drown before a small craft even got close to Devil's Island. A 40-foot boat could make it easily, but would be spotted miles away. Then, there were dogs, and federal agents and electronic measures to consider. To Mr. Wood, it seemed he was in a chess game, where he had started with one rook down. The government had the advantage.

How could he kill Tony Nails on Devil's Island? For the moment Mr. Wood drew a blank.

41. Red Rocks

SALLY Will wanted to meet Steve Brandon someplace where they would not be seen together. She didn't need more rumors. Every female journalist had to put up with them, the whispers that she got her stories because she laid sources. Damned unfair, Sally thought. Especially as, in her case, the whispers were untrue.

Sally had never gone to bed with Steve Brandon. Not because it didn't cross her mind. It had. Many times. Maybe the attraction was because Steve was a strong man, tough, a bit like her father. Nothing to be ashamed of there, she thought. Then there was this: Men feared Brandon, serious men for whom fear was not a natural state. And he had a touch of the rogue, of the gambler. He was a presence. Whatever it was, Sally couldn't control it.

Months before she met Lou, Sally and Brandon had frequented clubs. Had been arm-in-arm. One evening, when Sally and Brandon were alone in a bar booth, loaded and unguarded, Brandon had tried to steer Sally's hand to his crotch. Sally put her hand above his, softly – then noticed the depression in his left ring-finger and felt a jolt. How had she missed that?

"You're married?" she asked.

"Doesn't mean a thing," Brandon said.

"It does to me," she said.

Sally didn't make a scene, but she left. She had felt miserable for a week, blaming herself mostly. What an idiot I am, she thought.

After that, Sally tried to put Steve Brandon out of her mind. It was not a badge of honor on her part. She still felt desire. But she never returned his calls. Since then, she had tried to avoid Steve Brandon. There were other sources in the DPD. She didn't need him. And she surely didn't need the temptation. Now this.

Sally had never been to Red Rocks, an amphitheater the jet-stream had sandblasted into the foothills west of Denver. She knew it would be a good, private place to meet. The concert season was over. The place was deserted.

On the phone, Brandon seemed anxious. All he asked was: "What time?"

When Sally arrived at 2 p.m. she realized how the place got its name. Three hundred-foot towering cliffs of red sandstone surrounded the stage below her. The seats in front seemed to be carved into the mountain. Sally had read that musicians had thought for decades that something mystical happened when their tunes played here. The cliffs didn't echo as much as they sculptured new harmonics.

Sally parked down below and climbed onto the stage. There had been no sign of Steve Brandon. Sally sat and leaned back on her elbows. She got a glimpse of an eagle perched a couple of hundred feet above, looking down.

A minute later, Sally heard a rustling behind and turned as a slightly winded Steve Brandon crested the final step leading to the stage.

"Sally, you could have picked an easier place," he said.

"A little out of shape, are we?"

"Not much."

He reached to touch Sally's cheek. She pushed his hand away.

"This is business, Steve."

"Come on, Sally. You still holding a grudge about the ring thing?"

"I've moved on."

"So I hear. Lou Elliott is a loser, Sally. Pissed his career away. Could have been the fuckin' director someday. You going for losers now?"

"You resent him?"

"Like almost getting killed for a billionaire is a badge of honor? Lou's got money, Sally. And the papers love him. But he ran away from real work."

Sally knew it wouldn't be easy. She could have almost predicted the cheek-touching routine. But she hadn't expected Brandon would be jealous. It almost was endearing. Almost.

"Sit down, Steve." Sally pointed to a bench. "Catch your breath."

They sat.

Brandon looked up and saw the eagle.

"What do you think that damned eagle is looking at?"

"A farce?"

Brandon laughed. That was a good one.

"OK," he said. "What murder business?"

"Spilotro."

"What's the mystery? Dicerno did it."

"Well, that was easy."

"But we can't prove it."

"Of course not. You're the police. What about Palermo?"

"Who?"

"Bruno Palermo. It was your case."

Brandon snorted.

"That's what this is about? Palermo? Sally, I thought you had a brain."

Brandon took out a cigarette. Lit it.

"I think they're connected," Sally said.

"My ass."

"But the trifecta, Steve, is a Commerce City case. Bow Hendricks."

"This is Area 54 stuff, Sally."

"Well, I was looking over the supplementals on Palermo..."

"Someone's leaked you the supplementals?"

Sally said nothing.

"Fine. Might as well put them online."

"Steve, there is a cigarette problem."

"A cigarette problem?"

Almost unconsciously, they stood and began walking on the stage.

"You guys found a filterless cigarette butt right where the shooter shot."

157

Brandon looked concerned.

"It was a rare brand," Sally said. "A Dunhill."

Brandon stopped walking.

"I didn't recall that."

"The killer dropped a Dunhill in Commerce City, as well."

Brandon looked up again. The eagle was still there. He exhaled, tossed his cigarette down and stepped on it. Sally watched his foot. The butt went between cracks in the staging.

"You're going to tell me it was filterless as well?"

"I am."

Brandon paced. He appeared to be thinking. Sally stood still, waiting.

"OK, Sally," Brandon finally said. "Here's what I think of your theory. Ready?"

"Ready."

"You're not all wrong. I'm with you that the Maggie's Best hit might be connected to Dicerno."

"What happened to 'my ass'?"

"Protecting an investigation. But since you're already on it... Look, I'll give you something as an unnamed source, OK?"

Sally nodded: "OK."

"We developed a suspect in the Palermo case early. Jimmy Fresno. He's a Dicerno sidekick. We haul Fresno in and, guess what, he doesn't have an alibi for the time Palermo went down. And a witness saw someone who looked pretty much like Fresno outside Maggie's Best not ten minutes before the shooting."

"Steve," Sally inserted, "if you're trying to drive a wedge between a reporter and a story, you're doing a miserable job."

"Write your story. But know this: Fresno says he had nothing to do with it, and even when we offered him a very good deal, he wouldn't budge."

Sally stayed silent.

"Here's what we hear," Brandon said. "Dicerno was under pressure because of Spilotro. Complained about all the jerks that were hurting him – and one of the jerks was Bruno Palermo. Anyway,

Fresno gets it in his mind to do Palermo. And he does. Dicerno wasn't even involved, and was pissed at Fresno when he found out what he had done. Cold cocked him, in fact."

"And Big Bow?"

"Forget it?"

"Two Dunhills, Steve?"

"Coincidence."

"Filterless?"

"Still coincidence."

"Jeez, Steve. I was expecting some high-octane insight here."

"Sally, you will find that Jimmy Fresno doesn't do outlaw bikers and he certainly doesn't do protected witnesses. So they're not connected."

"Maybe he got ambitious," said Sally.

"No way. If he did anyone, Palermo was it. And forget the cigarettes. You find all sorts of things around crime scenes: butts, bottles, balloons, and bullets, and those are just the Bs."

Sally shoved her hands into her parka.

"Sorry, Sally," Brandon said.

He stepped forward and lifted his hand to her cheek again.

Without saying another word Sally turned away and left.

42. Tough Shit

CHARLES Ramson stood in front of the mirror at his Silver Spring, Maryland, condo and wondered what was happening. I've done everything by the book, he thought. West Point, the infantry, a battalion leader. I've got medals, honors, commendations up the wazoo. Everyone knew I was fast track. Then in 2008 I got myself assigned to a desk job back in D.C. pushing pencils at the Pentagon. That's what did it, the nine-to-five tedium that brought on the nerves. Never had them during combat. Never. But in D.C. you had to suck up and I wasn't the suck up type. Then came a chance for real work with the CIA, an operations director, and I jumped at it. Back in the game. But the damn battle lines in this new world are fuzzy, the intent of orders so hard to decipher that sometimes I get headaches. And now I report to a boss who wants me to kill someone who might damn well be an American citizen for chrissake. What sort of job is that? "Intensive interrogation." "No witnesses." That was murder she was talking about. Is this what it has come to? And there was a new irritant. Anne Burgess. The director put her into Team Blue just in case I can't deliver. Hadn't fooled me. Anne practically advertised herself as a plant, barely thirty years old and a looker – another sassy Vassar chick who no doubt kissed the director's tight little fanny.

Jesus, Ramson thought, get a hold. All this pissing and moaning won't get the job done. Still, there was the damned twitch, getting worse. He took out two Xanax and threw them to the back of his throat. They sometimes worked. Ramson looked at his watch: Half past midnight. Mika Petrovich was just taking off from Moscow. It was Team Blue time.

I guess we'll see how Miss Kiss Ass Anne Burgess holds up, he thought. She's supposed to be on the plane. Ramson secretly hoped she would screw up. Just a little.

Mika Petrovich began drowning himself in booze the moment his plane lifted off. He never stopped. For a one-hour layover in Frankfurt he settled into an airport bar and chugged beer. Back in the air, he resumed drinking vodka. Anne Burgess, sitting three rows back, lost track of the number of little bottles that came his way.

Her alarms began to sound. She considered the possibility that Mika was bent on committing suicide through alcohol poisoning.

Petrovich caught United 247 out of Kennedy to Denver. Burgess called ahead to have an ambulance crew ready to sprint him to Denver General if needed. Anne was sure the whole mission was coming to a reckless end. But when the plane got to its gate, Mika Petrovich stood straight and steady, looked around and caught Anne's eye.

"Miss, please," he said, pointing to the luggage compartment above her. "My bag, please."

When Anne got it down, Mika said: "Thank you, Miss."

Perfect English. No accent. Mika's smile was large and his eyes perfectly clear. He then turned and opened his last Smirnoff bottle and drained it. And walked a straight line off the plane.

Christ, Anne thought, the man's liver must be the size of Nebraska.

The plan was simple. Team Blue would follow Mika until he rendezvoused with the mysterious Nikolai. The assumption was that the meeting would happen in some private place. Team Blue would then pounce, killing Mika and spiriting Nikolai away. The agency would get word out that it was a Red Mafiya hit. That was the plan. Ramson had drilled it into the heads of the team. No fuckups.

Mika rented an Accord at the Avis counter, and was soon streaking toward Denver on I-70. Anne Burgess followed in a Ford. Ramson commanded a disguised utility-company van, trailing behind. Above, George Phillips, the CIA man who had introduced

Jason to Montana, circled unobtrusively in a Piper. Mika exited at Colorado Boulevard and headed south.

"Looks like he's headed to Glendale," barked Ramson. "Let's not lose him."

"Roger," radioed Anne.

"I've got him, too," said George.

It seemed everything was going as planned when Mika turned his Honda into a parking garage. He appeared to be going to the top – a private space, again as planned. Anne swung her car onto the exit ramp and went up against the grain, tires squealing. Terrified drivers heading down honked, but some still got swiped. Anne sped to the top, her car looking like she had parked in Harlem for half an hour.

No Mika. Fuck.

"What's happening, Anne?" Ramson radioed.

"He's moved into a stairwell, probably heading for another vehicle."

"Fucking hell," said Ramson.

"I'm heading back down," Anne said.

"Come on guys. Talk to me," Ramson barked. "George, you see anything?"

"There's a pickup leaving the garage," George said. "Could be him."

"You sure? "

"No."

This is what he had trained for. Make a decision. Quick.

"Follow the pickup," Ramson said.

The pickup headed down Leetsdale Drive and into a residential area of upper-middle-class homes.

"OK. I see the driver getting out," said George. "I think it's him."

"What's the color of the pickup?"

"Green."

Anne saw it and pulled over. The man who got out was Mika. Yes! He walked into a two-story home with kids' bikes and toys scattered about.

"Problem, Charles," she radioed.

"What now?" Ramson said.

"It's a home."

"Damn."

"With lots of kid stuff."

There was no sound.

A minute later, Ramson's van pulled up behind Anne's battered car. Anne got out and climbed into the van.

"What now?" Anne asked.

Ramson's eyelid began to twitch. He didn't answer.

Then one kid ran out of the house, chased by another. They were laughing, yelling and wrestling about.

"Shit," said Ramson. Not good.

Anne repeated: "What now?"

"The wife's got to take the kids to school, right?"

"Maybe," Anne said.

"We wait for dawn. She takes them out, we move in."

Ramson dug out three Xanax pills from a shirt pocket.

Ten hours later, a woman came out of the home and fetched a paper. She went back inside. Minutes later, she emerged with two kids.

"Looks like you were right," Anne said.

"Thank God," said Ramson.

The grade schoolers, each wearing matching orange backpacks, were hyped – bumping, clutching, laughing. Then a big yellow school bus rounded the corner and the kids took off at a sprint. The woman waved to them.

"Shit," said Ramson again.

The kids boarded the bus and the woman turned and went back into the house.

"There goes plan A," said Anne.

Ramson did the calculus. The woman was a problem. If he went ahead she would have to be killed. He didn't like that. But this was war and in war there are casualties.

Then he decided: "OK, Plan B. Get Nikolai. Leave no witnesses." To himself he said another "shit".

Half of Team Blue, dressed as meter readers, went to the back yard while Ramson and the others rang the front door bell. The mom answered.

"Ma'am," said Ramson, "there is a gas leak in the neighborhood. Could we please inspect your furnace?"

"It's still warm," the woman answered. "We aren't using it."

"Still, please, we must check."

A man with a distinct Russian accent called out: "Who is it Pam?"

"They say they're from the energy company."

"And?"

"They want to check the furnace."

Team Blue heard Nikolai bolt for the back of the house. It was time to act.

Ramson shouted: "NOW!" lifted his gun and sent a bullet into Pam's head. She fell in the doorway like a sheet from a clothesline. Team Blue members crashed in over the top of her.

Anne found Mika cowering in a bedroom closet. He was covered with clothes that had fallen down. He held up his hands, eyes wide with fear. Trembling. Anne took aim and emptied an automatic into his chest.

Ramson tackled Nikolai as he tried to jump through a rear window. He yelled out Russian invectives, kicking and scratching. But Ramson was too strong. Another team member helped Ramson blindfold, gag, and handcuff Nikolai. Team Blue rolled him into a carpet, hauled him out to the van and sped away.

I-25 leaving Denver had never looked better. No jams. The air was clear. Wyoming was eighty minutes away. Ramson took two more tablets. As a reward. He thought he had won. Mika was dead. Nikolai was captured. Everything was just like the director wanted. Except for the wife.

Tough shit, he thought. Not for the last time.

43. Football Fans

IT WAS three games into the Denver Bronco season and Lou was a fan. He didn't paint himself orange and walk around in a barrel, but he got crazed in his own way. Sally didn't understand football. And she didn't come close to understanding its fans. Getting drunk and acting foolish she had insight into. She had been there. But doing so with seventy thousand others because some way-too-big big guys were bashing out each other's brains made no sense.

Lou, however, seemed oblivious to such reasoning. Worse, he had managed to garner tickets to the Oakland Raiders game, and those were the hardest tickets to get because Oakland was the baddest team of all.

Sally knew she was in trouble when an hour before they left for the stadium she caught Lou emptying a bottle of Johnny Walker Red into a plastic flask that he obviously and illegally was planning to sneak into the stadium. She didn't say anything. She went, as she did in every crisis, into observer mode.

Lou was hyped as they parked in the Auraria campus lot and joined an orange river of hooting fans approaching the stadium. Lou wasn't much of a hooter, but you could tell his heart joined in. Sally thought it was probably the right moment to tell him about Brandon. Catch him off guard.

She leaned into him, slowed his progress, and said: "Brandon thinks it was someone named Jimmy Fresno who did Palermo."

"What?"

A man dressed as a pumpkin passed by.

"I said that Steve thinks Palermo was killed by someone called Jimmy Fresno. And he dismissed the Dunhill findings out-of-hand."

Lou suddenly seemed concerned. He pulled himself and Sally out of the marching onslaught.

"You say Brandon said it could be Fresno?"

"He did. But Fresno did it on his own. Dicerno didn't know and got pissed at Fresno when he found out."

Lou thought about that for a moment, then asked: "And Brandon said the Dunhills mean nothing?"

"Yes."

Lou looked pensive.

"This could be a problem," he said.

"Why, Lou?"

"Brandon is a smart man and a good investigator. He would never, ordinarily, dismiss the Dunhills. That's way too much of a coincidence."

"So why does he?" asked Sally.

"Something's wrong," said Lou. "The Fresno thing is also absurd. Jimmy is not the hitman type."

The loudspeaker blared overhead and the crowd in the stadium erupted like the Space Shuttle at takeoff. The Broncos were taking the field.

"What?" Sally shouted. "WHAT DOES THIS MEAN?"

"I DON'T KNOW. SOMETHING'S WRONG," Lou shouted back.

As the roar evolved into an unnerving cacophony, Lou said: "Let me think on that, Sally."

He led her forward, at first slowly. Then, as he got his spirit back, quickening his pace.

Sally and Lou soon entered the stands. The game was indecipherable to Sally. The rules were riddles. But the fans were what most unsettled her. When a call went against the Broncos the crowd erupted into chants of "Fuck You. Fuck You," at the referees. Sally looked around. Some people had actually brought their kids here. Insane.

Then one woman responded to an onerous call by joining in the "Fuck You" cries by raising her sweatshirt to the beat: "Fuck," and her shirt came up, "You," and it went down. She had no bra. The crowd erupted. Sally did not understand why anyone would pay a hundred dollars a ticket and then loads more for food and drink to have their senses insulted. This was a part of Lou she knew she would never understand.

Lou apologized, kind of, after the game, and asked: "Tell me again about Steve Brandon."

To Sally, he seemed a changed man. No longer completely deranged. So she repeated her story, in depth.

Sally's iPhone rang. It was Brandon.

"Hey," he said. "If you want to tackle a crime that's real, why not wander off to 3276 Colorado Drive just southeast of Glendale. Some big-time Russian mobster got nailed this morning. It looks like a mob hit. A real one."

He clicked off.

"Hon, Brandon just called. About some mob killing in Glendale. He said 'this one' was real. I gotta go."

"Sally, Brandon is making me nervous."

"Me, too."

"Let me drive you."

"Are you kidding? You would blow .08 just walking into a room."

"No, Sal, I don't feel a thing."

"Exactly. Look, I'll hire a cab for a couple of hours. Paper's good for it."

Lou felt pacified and considered his options, He found one he liked.

"OK, Sal. I might angle over to the Wynkoop," said Lou, referring to his favorite watering hole where many would be celebrating the Bronco's great victory. From there it was a short walk home.

"Fine," Sally said. "Have one for me."

44. Stand Off

AN hour after the Team Blue van left with Nikolai, his wife, Pam, began to stir. The bullet that Ramson sent into her head had careened around the skull under her skin then exited from the occipital region, never having penetrated the brain. It had been enough to fracture her cranium and cause a concussion, but nothing worse. It was a freak wound, but experts testified every day to freak wounds. That's why assassins are told always to shoot twice. Ramson had either forgotten or something else was going on in his head.

There was still more potential bad news for Director Orvez. The funny bullet that had knocked Pam out had not wiped out her memory. Just the opposite. When she recovered an hour later, Pam remembered everything, in precise vivid detail. So she was able to tell the Arapahoe County Sheriff's deputies all about how the energy company terrorists – six men and one woman – had come to her house, shot her, then went to the back of the house and fired off more shots, before hauling away Nikolai. She described their clothes, their expressions, the smell of their breath, the color of their eyes. Everything.

Brad Johnson was standing outside the Boravick home when Sally's cab arrived.

"Not again," said Sally.

Looking peeved, Brad said: "Ditto."

They worked the scene and their phones hard. It was another tie. Each wrote almost identical stories. Sally's read: "A 32-year-old Glendale woman told police yesterday that an armed gang dressed as utility company workers shot her in the head, killed a Russian national and kidnapped her husband.

"Arapahoe County Sheriff's officials say they suspect the killers

168

left the woman, Pam Boravick, for dead. Sources said the woman's husband, Nikolai Boravick, has suspected ties to Russian organized crime.

"The identity of the dead Russian hasn't been established but authorities are checking into leads that he is an agent of Moscow-based mob boss Dimitri Ivanov.

"Pam Boravick described the man who shot her as 6 feet 2 inches, 220 pounds with brown hair and eyes.

"Meanwhile, authorities said the survival of Pam Boravick was a miracle..."

Lou got home about 11:30 p.m. He wasn't drunk, exactly. But he wasn't sober, either. Unsteady, Sally thought. And pleased with himself.

"So?" Sally asked, metaphorically folding her arms.

"Some guy at the Wynkoop challenged me to a game of chess."

"And?"

"I had a good night."

Lou flopped down on the couch. Sally knew that that was where he was going to stay.

Sally went out to the balcony, adrenaline easing away. There was a half-moon and Sally could see the dark shapes of the Front Range. She began to drift a bit. She sat down on a reclining chair. Within minutes she was out. Dreaming.

But you know why, don't you, Sally Will?

"No. Please."

Yeah, you know.

Then she's with her father and her father is driving a car, an old Buick. Sally is jumping up and down on the passenger seat. It is a bright, beautiful, warm day. Dad is happy, singing the University of Wyoming fight song about Ragtime Cowboy Joe. Then it is not so bright. Dad has stopped singing. Sally is worried. Something is very wrong. They are on a winding mountain road, now in Colorado. By Morrison. By Red Rocks. Rain is falling. The car is speeding up. Dad can't stop it. The brakes don't work. He is terrified. The car keeps hydroplaning. Suddenly, the car is spinning out of control. Dad is screaming as the car careens towards a wall of stone. The wall grows larger and larger. Then, suddenly, the car just stops. A policeman appears. He's leaning in the driver's window. He is shaking his head.

"So it's you, you old dead drunk," the policeman says to Sally's dad. The policeman blows smoke in his eyes. He snickers. Sally looks at dad. He has changed. He is shriveled. Dead. Now only a skull. The policeman walks away, but then looks back at little Sally. He has a plastic smile, evil. The policeman is Steve Brandon.

Sally awoke with a start, her heart racing. She is drenched. What was that, she thought? Where did that come from? She looked at her watch: 1 a.m. She had been here for an hour. She remembered Lou at the football stadium.

"SOMETHING WRONG," Lou had said. Think, Sally.

She thought, and recalled Brandon's reactions at Red Rocks. His inconsistency. His reaction at the mention of Palermo and Big Bow. His slipping her the bit about Jimmy Fresno.

"SOMETHING WRONG." What did Lou mean?

She remembered Brandon's reaction to the Dunhill cigarettes. Complete dismissal. She kept hearing Lou's voice. Something wrong. She remembered something she really didn't know she had seen at the time. It was the pack of cigarettes Brandon had taken out. She knew most of the American brands. And Brandon's didn't look familiar. Sally recalled Brandon stomping the cigarette out on the Red Rocks stage.

Was it a Dunhill? The thought hit like a revelation. Am I completely insane? No way it was a Dunhill, Sally thought. The world isn't that small. But then she remembered her dream. There, Brandon appeared capable of anything.

This is silly, Sally told herself. Sally-esk. It wasn't possible. But she couldn't help herself, now that the thought was out in the open. She had to see.

Sally considered waking Lou, but he was snoring softly and

looked pleased with whatever he was dreaming. So Sally wrote him a note explaining where she was going and why, just in case he awoke and got worried. Then she raced to Red Rocks.

She got there at 1:45. It was dark and moonless. She had to cross two "No Trespassing" signs even to get inside. She held a small directional flashlight that Lou had given her months before. He called it a burglar light, because it only lit up what it was aimed at, without spreading light around where it could be detected. But in a big, open space like Red Rocks, it was almost useless.

At night, in the dark, the park seemed to have different acoustics. There was a low moan from all directions bouncing off the huge dark walls, like the dying cry of a large animal. She knew it was the wind. Had to be the wind. But the noise and the darkness unsettled her. Suddenly, she heard a far off rustle and some small falling rocks. Sally looked up, alarmed. Then she recalled the eagle. Must have settled in for the night, she thought.

The moan picked up, and subtly changed. It now seemed lonely, guttural. And getting louder.

Steve Brandon doused the lights on his SUV when he saw Sally's Miata parked in the empty lot. He drove slowly, quietly, coasting to a stop. Feeling the gun secure under his left arm, he got out and closed the door softly, without a sound.

Sally stubbed her left toe twice trying to walk around the stage in search of her stupid, quixotic cigarette butt. Why am I here, scared out of my wits, she thought?

She shone the little light on the stage, following the path she thought she and Brandon had taken, looking for the dead cigarette. She saw nothing. She canvassed the area again, wondering if the eagle was watching. Still nothing.

Sally laughed silently at herself and turned to leave. She was loony. She knew it. There was no way Brandon had been smoking a Dunhill. It was just some American brand that she didn't recognize. Silly me, she thought. Seeing ghosts. Always seeing ghosts.

Then somewhere in the giant park she thought she heard a

noise, amplified by the walls, like a footstep on the stairs. Sally's pulse quickened, then she caught herself again. It was nothing, she told herself.

Brandon had tripped on a step. To him it seemed to echo like a firecracker. Then he saw Sally's silhouette, motionless, on the stage. Had he given himself away? He waited.

Sally got over her surge of nerves, and started to walk back towards the steps. Towards Brandon.

Just then, her flashlight lit up something on the stage. Something small and off-white. She wondered if she should go and examine it. She decided what the hell. Lou would get a good laugh out of this tale when she got home. As she neared the object – it would probably be just a piece of paper, she told herself – she heard something flying overhead. The eagle, she thought.

Brandon now began to move slowly up the final steps to the stage. Sally's back was turned to him. He knew exactly why Sally was here and what she was doing. I should have come back here myself first, he chastised himself thinking. Now it was a problem, a big problem.

When Sally was six feet away from the white reflection she realized it was a cigarette butt. And she knew it was Brandon's. Then she had the same sensation she had had in Commerce City. There was no way this was going to be a Dunhill. She thought to herself: Sally you should walk away. But she couldn't.

She dug into her purse for tweezers. She had watched too many TV detective shows, she laughed to herself. She reached down and picked up the butt with the tweezers.

Brandon inched closer. He was now only ten feet away. Sally raised the butt and aimed her spotlight. It was a Dunhill. She felt as if the eagle's claw was at her neck.

"Sally," said Brandon, low, like the moaning cliffs.

The claw tightened and Sally lunged forward as if pushed by an unseen force, propelling her away from the sound. She fell. She could feel the pulse of her aorta, something she had never sensed before. Her burglar light fell away, spinning. She thought something insane, like she had read sometimes happens before you die. She thought of a Beatles' tune: Maxwell's Silver Hammer.

She turned back to where the voice had been. The spinning light had spun just right. It clearly showed his shoes, and then, in increasingly darker shades of gray, the rest of him. Sally could barely make out any more than a rough outline of his face. But there was no doubt. It was Brandon.

"What the hell are you doing here, Sally?" asked Brandon.

Sally couldn't answer.

"Do you have suspicions, Sally?" Brandon continued. Brandon seemed to move his right hand into his coat.

Sally, thinking she had only a moment left to live, backed away and tried to think of a prayer. "Now that I walk through the valley of the shadow of death...now that I walk through..." She couldn't remember the line.

Damn it, Sally, at least die well, she thought. She rose, glaring into Brandon's faint eyes. She was ready to charge.

Brandon smiled as his hand began to emerge from inside his jacket. Sally remembered the line.

"Stop!" A shout shattered the tension and a man came into the dim light behind Brandon. It was Lou. He held a gun. Hearing Lou, Brandon whirled around and then back at Sally, who now looked fierce and dangerous. He shook his head.

"You guys are crazy," he said. "You're in way over your heads."

"You're the one out of his depth," said Lou. "Why did you do it?"

"I thought you were smarter than this, Elliott," snorted Brandon. And he turned to walk away.

"One more step and you're a dead man, Brandon," Lou shouted.

Brandon continued to take small steps.

"I will shoot," barked Lou. "Don't move another step."

Brandon paused, briefly, and then resumed walking, his chin up. Lou felt his left index finger begin to press on the trigger. He was aiming at the back of Brandon's neck. But Brandon continued walking and Lou relaxed his pressure on the trigger. Brandon had wagered correctly. A private eye would not shoot a Denver homicide lieutenant in the back. Brandon reached the stairs, and disappeared quickly into the night.

Neither moved for a while, and then Sally came to Lou and rested her head on his shoulder, just barely holding in a sob.

"How did you know?"

"I didn't. I saw your note and thought I would come. It's a nice night. Then I saw his car and knew he had followed you."

"I thought that was it, Lou." Sally said, clutching his arm. "I was prepared to die."

"Yes," Lou said, hugging Sally, "and so was he."

45. Thumb Screw

TEAM Blue took Nikolai to a cabin in the Snowy Range west of Laramie. All around were glaciers and lakes and streams caught between seasons. Ice crystals bobbed on top of the water reflecting tiny rainbows of light. In ordinary circumstances it could have seemed enchanted. But not now.

Charles Ramson had prepared for this. Didn't like it, wouldn't have done it on his own. Wouldn't have even thought of it. But he had his orders.

The method called for a mix of science and art. Part of the science came in the form of synthetic adrenaline and acetylcholine. The adrenaline could make the heart pump hard and fast and flood the brain with fear. Acetylcholine did the opposite. It could stop the heart dead if an operator didn't know what he was doing. The procedure was to alternate the two. Hit the subject with severe pain, multiply it with the adrenaline, and press forward until the subject was close to passing out. Then use the acetylcholine to bring him back for another round. A vasodilator was injected to insure that spiking blood pressure didn't blow a cerebral vessel and kill the subject prematurely.

The instrument that caused the pain wasn't nearly as modern. A thumbscrew. Ramson imagined that it was just like a mousetrap, perfect for the job.

After team members strapped Nikolai to a chair, Ramson rolled up his sleeves, inserted needles. A couple drops of blood bubbled up. For a man about to face a brutal test, Nikolai seemed detached.

"What, no truth serum?" he asked.

"Be quiet," Ramson commanded.

The manual said the operator was to stay in control of the conversation at all times. Never answer questions.

"Come on, mister. You must have truth serum," Nikolai said. He was actually smiling.

"Be quiet!"

That's all I need, Ramson thought A chatterbox, Subjects frequently try to divert the operator from performing his necessary tasks in correct order by engaging in irrelevant conversation. Avoid this.

"Mister, what's wrong with your eyelid?" Nikolai asked.

Ramson felt like belting Nikolai but decided that would be undisciplined and unprofessional. Nikolai knew exactly what was about to happen and what Ramson wanted of him – names and places – and Ramson knew he knew.

This was not going to be easy, thought Ramson. He gobbled some more Xanax.

"Can I have one of those?" Nikolai laughed.

Think you're funny, huh? Ramson thought. Just wait.

Ramson took out the thumbscrew and for the first time thought he might just enjoy this after all. Nikolai was a prick. Fuck him. Ramson began twisting. Nikolai flinched just a bit but didn't pull his hand away, as the manual said he would.

A big prick, thought Ramson. He pumped in a little adrenaline that should have boiled Nikolai's brain. The manual said this should result in "patterned screaming" that was to be ignored. Wait for the subject to plead for you to stop. But there were no screams. Nikolai's brow furrowed, eyes closed. But he didn't scream.

Ramson twisted more. Twisted until it was hard to twist with only one hand. Twisted with both hands until there was a loud crack as Nikolai's nail split. Specks of blood flew at Ramson's face. He blinked and kept turning.

No screams. Just a low rumbling groan, and clenched teeth.

These fuckers must have some pretty good training, Ramson thought. Ramson put his full weight into the next couple of twists. Nikolai passed out. That, the manual said, was not supposed to happen. Wrecked the timing. Ramson brought him back with some acetylcholine, but Nikolai just seemed more resolved.

And so it went for an hour. Nikolai went in and out of consciousness without ever pleading for mercy. About all that was being accomplished was the total destruction of Nikolai's thumb. Bone had shattered as Ramson pancaked it into the shape of a teaspoon. But it didn't help. Ramson was both frustrated and in awe. Nikolai was a solider. An honorable opponent. A fighter.

Ramson moved the screw to Nikolai's other thumb. If he had to, he would slowly break every bone in Nikolai's body, screw the chemicals. This was a test of wills. It was at just that moment of resolve that Nikolai said:

"Ah, hell. This isn't working."

Ramson stepped back, hoping he hadn't shown his surprise. He decided to listen.

"You guys are going to kill me anyway. Why continue this?"

This was nowhere in the manual. But West Point taught you to think on your feet, and that's what Ramson decided to do. Had somehow this torture worked?

"Will you give us names and numbers?" Ramson asked.

"Of course I'll give you names and numbers. And places. But why wait all night? I'll tell you this: we have a perfectionist at what you are trying to do. He can break anyone in 30 minutes."

Yeah, right, Ramson thought. Thirty minutes. Fat chance. Still, it was time to test the Russian.

"OK, let's start with the American banks. Which ones do you use?"

"No," said Nikolai, "Let's start with some scotch."

Ramson reached down to the thumbscrew, prepared to carry on against this crazy Russian. But Anne Burgess touched Ramson's arm.

"Do we have any scotch?" she asked.

"No we don't have any scotch," Ramson barked. "We're in the middle of a fucking interrogation."

"There's a liquor store down in Centennial. You can get a bottle there."

"You're fucking kidding!" shouted Ramson.

"What's the down side?" asked Anne.

Ramson returned from the liquor store to find Nikolai and Anne sitting on a couch, laughing and sharing the best dirty jokes they had ever heard. There were no cuffs in sight. Other agents stood around, holding weapons, but otherwise seeming relaxed. One was grinning. Ramson was appalled. How did this help? He could see the Russian getting really drunk, if that was possible for a Russian, and then what? It would be 24 hours before Nikolai would feel any pain again.

"Oh," Anne said, seeing Ramson. "There you are!"

"Come, Mr. Bond, sit down," cried Nikolai.

Both Anne and Nikolai laughed unrestrained at Ramson's puzzled look. This was the most unprofessional sight Ramson had ever seen. Still, he handed Anne the quart of scotch.

Nikolai downed most of it before dawn. By then, he had put on a performance. He listed every Ivanov account he laundered in America, named the funds that went to B banks in St. Martin, Guadalupe, the Isle of Jersey, and Nigeria. Between jokes, Nikolai revealed 17 shell companies that traded the funds back and forth until the funds became fresh and clean and ended up in Switzerland. Nikolai would halt only long enough to refresh his glass and exchange a joke. He did it all from memory. He finished as a glimmer of morning light appeared. Anne was holding his hand.

"Now it ends," he said.

Anne squeezed his arm softly.

"Yes," she said. "I'm sorry."

"Don't be sorry," Nikolai said. "I'm not. You killed Pam. I'm dead already."

Anne and Ramson exchanged glances. Nikolai looked at Anne.

"I want this done right," said Nikolai. "Please, Anne, you do it."

He stood and walked to the door and opened it. Rays from the sun peeked over the evergreens. A few shards of light erupted from the crystals on a glacier lake. Anne came up behind him softly. She cocked the gun, put it to the base of Nikolai's skull and pulled the trigger. Just like Katya.

Team Blue put Nikolai's body into a pre-dug grave. Anne didn't help in any of it. She sat against a tree, head on her knees. She appeared shaken.

Then the team headed east towards Laramie where they planned to send a coded fax containing the account numbers Nikolai had given them to D.C. From there they planned to head for Fort Collins, then drive to Denver International.

Ramson turned on the radio to KOA. A news bulletin came on. They had picked up Sally's story.

"...Police say one Russian, perhaps a major crime figure is dead, and his U.S.-based counterpart is missing.

"But police did get a break. The wife of the missing man survived. She was able to give investigators detailed descriptions of the assailants. She said they appeared to be Americans." Ramson nearly lost control of the van.

"Alive! How?" Ramson shouted. He knew he had shot her. She had to be dead. The newsreader continued:

"Police are looking for a blue van, believed to have been rented at the airport. There are six people involved, five men and a woman..."

"Holy Christ," said Ramson.

"Charles, I thought you shot her," Anne said sharply.

"I did."

"Twice?"

Ramson ignored the question. He knew she knew he hadn't.

"We must split, right now," Ramson said. "Lose contact. Make our way back to D.C. We can't afford to be caught together."

"And how do you propose we do that?" asked Anne.

"There'll be rental car places in Cheyenne and Fort Collins. I'll drop each of you off. You're on your own."

46. Trail Blazing

TEAM Blue had survived, somehow, and was again assembled in the CIA situation room with Director Orvez. She was angrier than a smoking volcano.

"OK, geniuses," she said, "Who is going to explain how this happened?"

The crew was bedraggled. There had not been a good night's sleep amongst them. They slumped in the chairs, looked to the floor, anxious and miserable.

"Charles," said Orvez. "Why don't you begin?"

"Ah, Linda..." he began.

"It's director, buddy," Orvez snapped. She could be a bitch, he thought. Then he corrected himself. She could be a wounded badger. Be careful.

"The woman wasn't supposed to be there," he said dumbly.

"The woman wasn't supposed to be there," Director Orvez mocked back. "What do we pay secret agents for, to be slow on their feet? And they want to put more of you out in the world. God have mercy on this country."

"That's damned unfair," cried Ramson.

"I'll tell you what will be unfair, Mr. Ramson. Unfair will be when you get convicted of murder, sent to Leavenworth to live out the rest of your wretched life as Bubba's prom queen."

The image got to Ramson. He frowned. Orvez calmed. She needed Ramson, even though, right then, she hated him with every molecule in her body.

"OK. Fresh start," she said. "What went wrong?"

"I shot her," Ramson said. "Must have been a bad round."

"Did you ever think of shooting her twice? And, if not, why not?" the director asked, and then paused.

"No. Let's not go there. Answer this one: She is saying you guys were Americans. It was supposed to look like a Russian hit team. What do we do now?"

Ramson looked stumped. Anne spoke up. She was the freshest looking of the crew. Amber eyes, auburn hair, a work-at-it-hard toned body. She actually had some color in her cheeks.

"No reason it still can't be like we planned," Anne said. "We let the press know that the Russians are trained to act like that, Americans with a southern accent. Director Hamilton has already started speculating about that without any prodding on our part. If he's that dense, why not others?"

Orvez steepled her fingers. Said nothing.

"Look, Director, the agency should leak some information that just such a group entered the U.S., say last week," Anne said.

Orvez looked up, still frowning, but not so severely.

"Maybe, Anne," she said.

"Let's firm up what the FBI already believes," said Anne. "Let's leak something hard. With any luck, the press will buy it. Looked at another way, this mission was a success. We got all the bank numbers, passwords and history. We got more than we expected. Let's start draining the accounts. Actually, we really have only a few problems to iron out."

Orvez looked up. She was beginning to think of her coming talk with the president. Maybe she wouldn't be bringing her resignation, after all.

Dimitri Ivanov was sitting in the lounge of the Moscow Marriott, sipping Glenlivet with a Duma delegate when an associate sat down. The associate seemed troubled.

"Sir, I'm sorry, but could you give us a moment?" Ivanov asked the politician.

"Sure, Dimitri. I'll be at the bar."

After the delegate had moved away, Ivanov asked:

"What?"

"Mika is dead, sir. Killed shortly after he got to Colorado."

"How?"

"Don't know. News reports say a team of assassins invaded Nikolai's home, kidnapped him, and killed Mika. Tried to kill Nikolai's wife."

Ivanov reached for a pipe, lit it.

"Is that all?" he asked.

"No, sir. Some of the accounts Nikolai controlled have been invaded."

"Close every one."

"We have. But in some cases, we've been too late."

Ivanov took a sip of scotch.

"How late?"

The aide's hand was shaking.

"We believe half the Caribbean has been rolled up."

Two billion dollars. Ivanov took another sip, this one larger.

Detective Scott Kirkpatrick knocked on Lt. Brandon's door, waited a second and then opened it. Brandon looked up.

"Just got these from Arapahoe County. It's their reports about the Russian shootings," Kirkpatrick said.

He tossed a file on Brandon's desk.

"That's fine," said Brandon. He went back to reading the Denver Post. Uninterested.

Kirkpatrick shrugged and turned to leave. But when he got to the door, Brandon spoke up.

"We got anything new on Big Bow and the loser Palermo?"

"Big who?" asked Kirkpatrick.

"He's that biker killed in Commerce City. You don't read the papers?"

"Guess I missed that one."

"OK," said Brandon, dismissing him.

As Mr. Wood's plane approached Minneapolis International the deep woods below were putting on a show. Shades of red and orange and yellow seemed to envelop everything. Then Lake Minnetonka came into view, weaving its 110 miles of shoreline through dozens of western suburbs. There were piers and boats everywhere. Mr. Wood always thought of Minneapolis as cold and barren. This was very different.

For his scouting recce to Devil's Island he rented a car at the airport, headed north on I-35 for Duluth, turned east and hugged the belly of Lake Superior until he got to Bayfield, Wisconsin.

Bayfield is a small town built on some hills and surrounded by woods. Small paved roads fan out to dozens of berry farms. On his way in, Mr. Wood bought jars of raspberry jam. Later, after checking into a bed and breakfast, Mr. Wood walked to the town's commercial fishing pier, dined on fish boil, drank beer and then watched the distant lights of Madeline Island.

The next morning, Mr. Wood boarded a tourist boat for a trip around the Apostles. The season didn't officially end until mid-October but there were only a couple dozen tourists on board, mostly gathered down in the warm, enclosed lower deck. Mr. Wood pretty much had the run of the upper level to himself.

The boat churned past Madeline Island and headed to Oak Island. The PA system informed the guests that hundreds of black bear roam Oak Island. Other islands of the archipelago came and went until, 20 miles out, the boat approached Devil's Island. Mr. Wood attached a telephoto to his Nikon and got busy.

There was nothing ordinary about Devil's Island. Fully three-quarters of it rested atop red cliffs, 15 to 30 feet high. The stone was weathered from a million years of Superior gales. Crevices and caves were everywhere. Above the cliffs there was a flat expanse of pines.

Mr. Wood listened as the tour guide gave the details. The white lighthouse he was shooting with the Nikon had been built in 1891, together with the adjacent stone cottage. In 1928, President Calvin Coolidge had spread out a blanket on the rock ledges and, together with Mrs. Coolidge, had had a fine picnic. Mr. Wood filled a four-gigabyte memory card with pictures until he thought he had captured it all.

As the boat turned back to Bayfield, Mr. Wood was depressed.

How was he ever going to kill anyone on Devil's Island? The problems were clear: First there was the lake, which behaved more like an ocean than a lake. No small boat could get there. Then there were the cliffs. If you did manage to get to Devil's Island how did you scale the cliffs? How, and where, did you hide the boat? There could be dogs. There certainly would be spotters.

And then there was an even bigger question: How could he escape? By the time a boat made it back to the mainland, an army of troopers would be waiting. The feds had picked a great place for Tony Nails, Mr. Wood decided. Maybe too damn great.

Mr. Wood sped back to Minneapolis, caught a late afternoon flight to Denver and landed at DIA at 7 p.m.

Think, he told himself. Think.

47. Lucky Shot

LOU walked with Sally along Cherry Creek, holding her hand like some high school fool. He wanted to be an anchor. Lou knew Brandon had scared Sally. What he didn't want Sally to know was how much Brandon had scared him as well. Steve Brandon, he thought, was a very dangerous man.

"Sal, you should just drop this," he said.

"Yeah, and maybe I should turn into a grape," she replied defiantly without feeling it.

"No, no. Listen. This isn't worth it."

"It's worth it to me. I need to write this story. It's the only way."

"Is it worth your life?" He emphasized the word "life".

Sally stopped, locked her eyes into Lou's.

"It won't come to that."

"It almost just did."

Sally looked down. Watched the water flow.

"Look, we just need to be careful," she said.

"It might take more than that."

Lou didn't know what to do. He had already lost one woman by being stupid. Would he lose another?

"Sally, promise me you will reconsider."

"No, Lou," Sally said. "I promise you I won't."

A day later Lou and Brad Johnson met at the DAC for another racquetball game. Lou thought he needed the diversion. Otherwise, he feared he would just go flat-out nuts. He saw that Brad had a new racquet, but one less expensive-looking than the last.

On the court Brad scampered about like a teen, swatting volleys like he was in one of those Mayan games where losers were put to the sword. Brad conceded not a single point. He was everywhere. Blew Lou out in the first game to zero.

"Putting on a little weight, are we?" Brad asked, grinning broadly.

Lou smiled weakly and shook his head. The truth was he was preoccupied, thinking of Sally and Brandon and the stupid newspaper story Sally felt she had to write. His head was just not in this game at all.

Brad, pumped up with his singular victory, did not give an inch, pounding the ball around as if on automatic overdrive, moving now almost with a grace and an athleticism Lou had only suspected he possessed.

Lou's head was in a deep fog, barely tallying the score. It wouldn't have been hard. Brad wiped him out. Two nil. It was the most one-sided game Brad had ever experienced against Lou.

Brad looked suspicious, like he was being sandbagged. But that wasn't the case. Lou's mind just kept coming back to the image of Steve Brandon on the stage at Red Rocks, and the grit in Sally's voice, and the dead certainty that Sally was in danger. Sally could get hurt. Sally could die.

At the end of the last game he had just stood on the court and lost track completely of one of Brad's shots.

"Just tell me if you don't want to play," Brad said, sounding irritated. "It happens when you get older."

That rang Lou's bell. It wasn't enough that he had to worry himself sick about Sally, now he had this irritant on his hands. He began to play, and the more he played the harder he worked, until he, too, was in a sweat, running from one end of the court to the other, slamming the ball harder and harder like a man possessed. He was unstoppable.

Lou won the third game, and then the fourth. During the rubber match, Brad fought back, the competition affecting him like a contagion. Both men were a blur of motion all over the court, grunting and shouting as they laid into the ball, both sweating, both, in the end, grasping their sides. The score was finally tied twenty all. But Lou had the serve.

"Are you expecting my one good shot?" Lou wheezed, both

hands on his knees, looking back at Brad, who was in an identical position.

"Just hit the damn ball," said Brad unsmiling and taking a step back.

When Lou served it was not his drop-dead slow shot, the one Brad had seen a million times, the one he was ready for. Instead, it was a rocket, faster than any of the others, like a comet blasting through the court. Brad ducked. He didn't even make an attempt to score. Game over.

"What was that?" he said, sucking air, looking around like maybe he expected the ball to have blasted itself through the cement wall.

"I've changed my spots," said Lou, also gasping.

"Shit ," said Brad. "I prefer the slow one. You on meth?"

Finally, Lou laughed.

"No, man. It's my new magic racquet."

This time they both laughed. For Lou, it was a like a tight spring unwinding. He almost forgot about Sally. Almost.

Later, in the shower, they talked about the Broncos, a police shooting and the weather. Anything but work. But on the way out Brad turned to Lou.

"Hey, do you remember the case involving that biker. Big Bow?"

Lou was jarred. As far as he knew, Sally was the only one poking around Bow Hendricks.

"Big who?" Play dumb.

"The biker guy, up in Commerce City."

"You lost me there, Brad."

"You ever hear of Dicerno having a beef with the Sons?"

Christ, thought Lou. Steer clear of this.

"I think Dicerno uses some as bouncers, but I have never heard of any trouble."

Brad shrugged.

"Oh, well," he said smiling. "Next game, I expect you to be back to your one lucky shot."

Damn, Lou thought as he smiled back, how was Brad onto this? Was he that good?

That evening Lou took Sally to a joint on 32nd Avenue for burgers, beer and folk songs. At first, he thought it might be just the atmosphere needed to try again to talk Sally into forgetting Steve Brandon. But the chances of that were now gone. When Sally learned of Brad's question, she would be on the warpath for sure. There was no way she was going to lose this story to Brad Johnson. And Lou had to tell her, he thought. He had no choice.

After half an hour, Sally seemed to be getting into the music. A baby-boomer sang an almost perfect Neil Young rendition of "Harvest Moon."

During "Lyin' Eyes," Sally kept time with her foot, didn't smoke her cigars, sipped a Pepsi. Lou wished it could stay just like that. But he knew it couldn't.

At the next break, Lou described the game with Brad, and told the tale of the final shot and Brad's startled look. Sally got a kick out of that.

"You have such bad choices in friends, Lou. I can't get over it."

"Probably. And you're soon going to hate him even more."

Sally didn't have to say a word. She gave Lou a you-don't-say look and waited for him to explain himself.

"Sally, Brad asked a strange question."

"That's not news, silly man."

"He asked me about Big Bow."

Sally froze, blinked once, and then threw down her napkin.

"What! That jerk must have us bugged."

"Sal, it's probably just some weird coincidence."

"No. He's onto it. Somehow. That bastard wants to bury me."

Sally's eyes had become blue darts.

"I have got to prove to Mel that what we saw up there at Red Rocks was the truth. Got to move on this."

Sally got up and marched to the door, Lou being swept up in her wake. The two walked down Lowell Boulevard, Sally with her hands clasped behind her back.

"How do we prove it? Maybe the Dunhills are enough. They are to me."

"You know Mel will want more to name a top cop like Brandon, a lot more. And so will your lawyers."

"Yes, I know. Dammit."

Sally and Lou walked along for a minute in silence.

"Well," Lou finally said, "I can check with Scott. Maybe he knows something new about Big Bow. And there's Savannah. If Brandon did that he would have had to take time off. Maybe we can find out if he was gone last July."

Sally bumped Lou with her hip, knocking him slightly off balance.

"That's a start."

She walked on for another half a block in silence.

"OK," Sally finally said. "I can dig into Brandon's background. Put the Trib's databases to work. I bet the S-O-B is broke. You want to wager?"

"With you? I would rather bet the winner of the Kentucky Derby."

They returned to the tavern to listen to more from Neil Young.

A slender young woman in shiny black hair came by and took their orders. Lou, distracted, gave her a twenty dollar bill and told her to keep the change.

Sally's foot no longer kept time to the music.

48. Innocent Suspect

LOU set up a meeting with Scott for the next afternoon at Writer's Square, a LoDo walkway with million-dollar town homes, expensive restaurants, and pricy boutiques – the last place in the world you would expect to find a cop. Lou had given Scott the name of a new gallery.

"This is kind of bizarre, don't you think?" Scott said as he slid next to Lou who was looking at a painting. Lou hadn't even heard him enter.

"No," Lou said, not missing a beat. "Consider the structure and content of the piece, and the delicate play of the pastels. In its own way it's bold yet elegant, don't you think?"

Scott choked off a laugh.

There was a mousey, 6oish woman standing behind a far counter. She was looking over her glasses at Lou and Scott. Lou realized she must be the manager.

"Yes, quite impressive," Scott said. "You think we could split for a bar?"

"Your friends are in bars, Scott. That's why we're here."

"OK," said Scott. "Time to elucidate me."

"I have some problems with Brandon," Lou said.

"Take a number."

"It might be a serious problem, Scott."

That got Scott's attention.

"What do you need?"

"Has he been acting strange about any case?"

Scott thought for a moment, then said: "I told you about Palermo."

"Any updates?"

"On one hand he wants everything. On the other he insists some kid did it. Weird."

"Any besides Palermo?"

"Is this still for Sally?"

"Yes, but now it's also for me."

Scott examined his older friend, and then shook his head.

"I should probably ask why you want to know," Scott said.

"You should, but you won't." Lou looked straight at him.

"Right... OK, well, there's Spilotro. Brandon ordered us to stay away from Dicerno. We wanted to go down to Capricio's and express our displeasure with the demise of our witness. Brandon put that off limits."

"Isn't that odd?"

"Yes. And he's rummaging around everything. Can't keep his hands off cases. Even asked about a case that's not in his jurisdiction. Commerce City, for Christ sake."

"Commerce City?"

"Bow Hendricks."

Of course Brandon would ask about Big Bow, thought Lou. He probably killed him.

The mousey lady took off her reading glasses and scowled.

"Scott, I'm starting to have some dark thoughts."

With that, the mousey woman came over.

"Are you two gentlemen here to buy something or just to get out of the rain?" she asked.

"It isn't raining, ma'am," Kirkpatrick answered.

"Yes," the lady said. "I just thought I would point that out." She folded her arms to indicate she wasn't going to go away.

Lou and Scott left and found a bench outside the gallery to sit. Pigeons came their way, then left, disappointed.

"Scott," Lou said, "I need something."

Kirkpatrick was silent.

"I need Brandon's vacation schedule."

"What sort of question is that, Lou?"

"The innocent sort?"

"I bet. Anyway, I don't know his schedule. He doesn't advertise."

"When does he take his vacations?"

"He doesn't. He's a workaholic. The only one I remember was earlier this year."

"When, exactly?"

"Don't remember, exactly."

"Try."

"In the summer. June or July. He took three weeks."

"OK, Scott."

"You going to fill me in?"

"No."

"Hope you know what you're doing."

"Me too."

They stood to leave. Then Lou thought of one more question. "Oh Scott, was Jimmy Fresno ever a suspect in Palermo?"

"Jimmy Fresno? You got to be kidding me, right?"

"Right."

When Lou got to the balcony Sally was already there, scribbling on a yellow legal pad. She barely acknowledged his presence.

"Sit down. I've got news." She said without looking up.

Lou sat. Sally flipped through some pages, said: "I went to the Clerk and Recorder's office. On paper, Brandon was financially screwed. He had a $280,000 first mortgage on his home and took out a $55,000 second a year ago. His oldest daughter is a freshman at the university. It takes bucks."

"And he makes?" Lou asked.

"$91,370. Not bad. But not great."

"So maybe it's a close shave."

"Very close," Sally said. "Listen to this. Brandon's son is a senior at Arvada West. Made the honor roll. That's another college ticket to punch."

"Sport's scholarship?"

Sally removed something that she had clipped to the side of the legal pad and pushed it across the table. It was a picture from a high school annual, ripped out.

"Sally, you've got to stop doing these things."

"Just look."

The picture was of a nerdy kid in thick glasses. The inscription read: "Most likely to die a virgin." Ruthless. Lou winced.

"Well, scratch that," he said, handing back the photo. "Perhaps his wife is a stock broker?"

"Try substitute teacher."

Lou scratched an ear.

"And there's this," Sally said. "He has managed to recently pay off the house and the second mortgage, support his three kids, and pay college tuition, while buying a new SUV and a boat. Twin 350 Mercs on the boat, no less. Nothing cheap."

"Well, Sal, that tightens the noose."

"I thought you'd think so. What did Scott have to say?"

"Paints an ugly picture. After Spilotro got blown up, Scott wanted to roust Dicerno, let him know that the arm of the law wasn't getting any shorter. But Brandon wouldn't have it."

"Why bother the boss?"

"Apparently. And I guess we shouldn't be surprised that Brandon wants updates on Big Bow?"

"Big Bow?"

"That's right."

Sally was speechless. Then she shrugged.

"And what about Palermo?"

"Same. Wants updates."

"And I suppose Scott backed up the story about Jimmy Fresno being the shooter."

Lou laughed. "Of course not. Jimmy was never a suspect."

Sally furiously drew several boxes on the yellow pad and then connected them with arrows.

"Vacations?"

"Scott says he never takes them, with one exception. He took three weeks off sometime this summer."

Sally eyes darted into Lou's, computing.

"I'm calling Mel," she said.

"Sal, wait until we get those dates."

"Why?"

"Mel will want them."

Sally pondered this for a second. "You're right. Any ideas?"

"Not yet."

In the morning, Sally was up first, a rarity. She ground up some Kenyan beans and heaped extra tablespoons into a French press. Then she sat down with the yellow pad, made notes, connecting more boxes. The aroma got to Lou. He soon came into the kitchen in flip-flops and pajamas, sporting a nascent beard, disheveled hair and drowsy eyes.

"Sally, it's 7 a.m.," he said, looking concerned. "Are you sick?"

"Lou, I have an idea how to get those vacation dates."

Lou poured himself a cup.

"OK," he said. "How?" He creamed his coffee.

"I'll go to the source."

Lou seemed to awaken slightly.

"Jesus, Sally. You can't go to Brandon."

"I know," Sally said. "I'll go the chief."

This was too much, too early. Lou took some purposeful gulps of coffee.

"Wouldn't that be like blowing a bugle?" he said.

"Honey, I won't say I'm after Brandon. I'll make something up."

"It better be good."

"I'll say we're looking at double-dipping Denver detectives. You know, officers working for strip-joints while on duty. That was a scam in Chicago. The chief will check into it, and, hopefully, will find that it's not true in Denver. He'll try to kill the story by forking over the records. With any luck, the reports will include vacation time."

That's a damn good idea, Lou thought. And it could work.

49. Wasp Sting

MR. WOOD was troubled looking at photos on his computer screen. Devil's Island looked impregnable. The cliffs made it impossible to get off a shot from a low-lying boat, and a big enough boat could be seen for miles. Worse, even if he did manage to kill Tony Nails, Mr. Wood still hadn't figured out how to get back to Wisconsin before every lawman in the state was on his tail. He didn't like it, didn't like it at all.

He worked on the puzzle all night, learning everything he could about the island, the currents on Lake Superior and even the number of sheriff's officers operating out of Bayfield. Everything he looked up spelled trouble. He was desperate, thinking maybe he should return the money. Then he thought that maybe he was looking at it backwards, that Tony Nails, not Devil's Island, was the key. Maybe. Most likely, that was just wishful thinking.

Without much optimism, Mr. Wood fired up Google. Sure enough, there was no shortage of clips on Tony Nails, one of the finest killing machines that ever graduated from Sam Giancana's Outfit.

Mr. Wood learned that Tony had begun as a small-time burglar and thief and slowly morphed into a big-time burglar and thief. Later, he did five years for a series of jewel heists. The New Yorker reported that Tony got made in the early 1980s, and soon was running Cicero strip joints. In all, Tony Nails was suspected of personally killing 25 men over the years and being indirectly responsible for dozens more. He had made it all the way to the Outfit's third position and one of Vito Borelli's right-hand men. Everybody in Chicago knew what he did, but the feds and cops could never seem to catch him. But then his luck ran out. So he cut a deal.

Mr. Wood downloaded pictures of Tony Nails at his daughter's wedding – cutting the very portrait of a proud father, dressed in a black tie with his coat off, rosy cheeked and apparently tipsy drunk. Mr. Wood logged onto the archives of the Chicago Tribune. Reporters, he found, seemed to love Tony Nails because they could use all their favorite clichés without any threat of being sued: Tony was an "alleged racketeer," a "suspected mob boss," and their favorite: a "hitman."

Then Mr. Wood caught something that had not been in the cutline of the picture of Tony Nails at his daughter's wedding. It was a story that ran two days later. Tony Nails, it read, had become violently ill while at the wedding. He had been rushed to a hospital. The Tribune had then begun reports on Tony's health for each edition. Early on, a hospital spokesman told the media that Tony's condition was extremely critical: he was on life support, a priest had been called. Chicago was at risk of losing a celebrity.

But then, Tony began to make a slow recovery. Two weeks after he entered the hospital, the Trib got a picture of Tony being rolled out in a wheelchair. He looked good for a man who had just escaped death, but it was obviously going to be a long rehab. The spokesmen refused to discuss details, or to say precisely what illness had befallen Tony Nails.

Now that's interesting, thought Mr. Wood. He logged onto a highly secured medical database, one that ordinary people had no access to. He checked out all the spellings of Tony's real last name against databases for the year when the sickness struck. Soon he found it.

Tony Nails had been taken to the University of Chicago hospital in convulsions. There was a severe pulmonary edema, high fever and a peculiar rash. Doctors suspected an allergic reaction and administered steroids and antihistamines. That helped. Tony's vital signs began to stabilize.

A day later, disease detectives went on a hunt to find what had caused Tony's reaction. At the scene of the wedding, they found a dead wasp. They suspected it had bitten Tony and sent him headlong into anaphylactic shock.

Mr. Wood discovered that the medical sleuthing did not end

there, not with a victim of the stature of Tony Nails. An entomologist from the Smithsonian Institute was called in to do a consult, and he solved the case. His findings made it into a footnote in the New England Journal of Medicine, with Tony's name omitted. The wasp that almost killed Tony Nails was of a rare line *Vespa mandarinia ceylonica*, discovered in 1992 and found mostly in Sri Lanka. Investigators discovered that several had escaped from a Northwestern University lab. One, apparently, had found its way five miles south to the wedding reception.

Tony Nails, the medical chart noted, was highly allergic to *Vespa mandarinia ceylonica*. Another bite would kill him. No question. But researchers thought there was little chance of that – unless Tony visited Sri Lanka. The species did not naturally live in the United States.

For the second time in his new profession, Mr. Wood could think of only one word: Bingo.

50. Double Bluff

SALLY sat in the small office the Tribune rented in LoDo when the phone rang. A young woman who sounded about Sally's age said her name was Jan.

"There's something going on with the Pam Boravick situation that needs to be known," Jan whispered. "I saw you were on the story. I don't know any press people. But I'm sure the Tribune Company could get the word out."

"Shoot," said Sally.

"I can't do it on the phone, even this one, which I'm pretty sure is secure," Jan continued. Sally thought she heard some traffic in the background. Pay phone, she thought.

"I can only talk in person, here in D.C."

Fine, Sally thought. I'm close to breaking the story about Steve Brandon and the leak in the Witness Protection Program, and some woman who won't give her name wants me to fly to Washington.

"Look," Sally said. "One, I have other things going on. Two, I've got to know if this is serious. And three, even if it is serious, I think it's something our D.C. bureau should handle."

Sally had dealt with her share of psychos. Sometimes they started out sounding as sane as Jan – who sounded very sane – only to go downhill fast.

"OK, listen," said Jan. "Do you have ways to get police reports?"

"Maybe."

"Well, if you can check, you will find that the gun that killed Mika Petrovich at Nikolai Boravick's home fired nine millimeter rounds manufactured in the Czech Republic. The local cops were told that information but not the press. I will call tomorrow. Same time."

"OK," said Sally, "I..."

But Jan had already hung up. Sally put down her phone. She thought her life was getting complicated. First Lou, then Brandon, and now this. Then a better word than complicated occurred to her: Interesting.

Sally asked Lou to call Scott.

"Someday, Lou, this one-way street has to end," Kirkpatrick said, sounding peeved.

"Dream on," said Lou.

"Hmm, OK, just this one. Tell Sally that the bullets that killed Petrovich were Czech-made nine millimeters, just like her source says. The FBI didn't put that out in a bulletin. I found out about it in-house. Her source must be pretty good."

"Thanks, Scott, truly."

"Lou, buddy, just a hint. How does she get her sources?"

"In this case, Scott, she doesn't even know."

The phone rang in Sally's office right on schedule. It was Jan.

"You convinced?" Jan asked.

"I'm convinced."

"Good. Let's do it this way..."

Sally caught the first United flight to D.C. She was not happy to leave the Brandon investigation. But Chicago said to jump on the Russian mob story, drain Jan of her information, and then get back to Denver. So OK.

Approaching Reagan International, Sally could not believe after 9/11 how close big jets could still get to major targets. As United Airlines 762 approached touchdown she clearly made out the White House and Capitol, no more than five miles away.

As instructed, Sally took a cab to DuPont Circle, and then walked a block to a gay bar named Adventure. It was just early evening, but the music was booming and the guys were already glistening sweat. Sally didn't see another female in the place, though she detected a couple of men clearly in drag.

As she sat down on a bar stool, Sally thought this whole thing was perhaps a gag. Her next thought was that Steve Brandon was behind it. Maybe he had friends in Washington. Maybe, in fact, she should get the hell out. Just then, a woman sat down beside her.

"I assume you are Sally Will," the woman said, brushing back her auburn hair. Her voice was rich, with some rumbling Southern harmonics.

"You got it," said Sally.

A bartender in a wife-beater t-shirt came to take their orders.

"Ladies, you have chosen the safest bar in town. What do you want?"

Sally ordered a white wine. Jan went serious with a martini.

"Interesting place to meet," observed Sally.

"Like the man said, safe."

Jan had dark eyes to match her hair. And she was dressed well, but conservatively. A suit and teal blouse. Sally wondered if all intelligence agents – she had made that assumption about Jan in the first few seconds – dressed like this.

"OK," Jan said, "You don't know me."

"You have that right."

"I mean, we never met."

"OK, we never met."

Jan leaned forward, lowered her voice an octave.

"I work for the NSA. And I could get fired for talking with you."

"So why are you?"

Though it sounded abrupt, Sally had in the past found this was often the perfect approach. It appeared it was again.

"Because the public should know about what was behind the Pam Boravick shooting. The old farts in NSA never want anything released, even when it could not possibly harm the United States. They're career stiffs, nothing more."

Jan ordered another martini. Sally waved the bartender off. She needed to stay sharp.

"What don't they want released?"

"Russia – the 'new' Russia, our good friend – has some bad actors. A team of Russians has entered the U.S. with instructions to kill not only Russian nationals, but Americans, as well. Pam was not their first American casualty."

"Is the Russian government involved?"

Jan leaned back and took a gulp.

"My girl, you are direct."

Jan wasn't whispering anymore and seemed a tad off-balance, thought Sally.

"Directly involved? Probably not," Jan continued. "But do they know what these gangsters are doing? You can bet on it, honey."

Jan looked disgusted or was a very good actress.

"The best we know," she continued, "there are six men involved in the team, and maybe a woman. Some or all of the members were in Denver for the Petrovich-Boravick hit. We even have some of their pictures taken when they used ATMs."

Jan handed Sally an envelope.

"They're in there," she said. "We believe this is a group operating against the interests of Dimitri Ivanov, a *vor v zakone*."

"A vor a what?"

"*Vor v zakone*. In Russian it means mob boss."

"Oh."

"There's more." Jan nodded to the door. Sally got the message: time to go. Jan and Sally walked around DuPont Circle at 9 p.m. It seemed that every car around had some driver dying on the horn.

"Sally," Jan said, "there was a killing earlier this year in Wyoming. The victim's name was Jason Ison. He was one of ours. CIA. The squad that killed Ison, we believe, is the same one that did Petrovich in Denver. This is a bad bunch."

"Why would a team working for a Russian mobster kill an American secret agent? Wouldn't that mean Russian government involvement?"

Jan looked at Sally but didn't answer. Instead she stomped out her cigarette and immediately fished out another. A cab came forward and Jan held up her hand. The cab stopped. Sally was still waiting for her answer.

"Gotta go," said Jan.

"Hold it a minute," cried Sally. "How do we stay in touch?"

"We don't."

"But I need a name or a number."

Jan slipped into the taxi and rolled down the window.

"I'm sure you'll do what's right for America," she said.

The cab sped away.

Sally raced to the Chicago Tribune's Washington office and dialed Mel. He didn't sound too thrilled to be disturbed. Sally thought he had probably just gotten back from Mike's Pub. But he became instantly alert when Sally told him what she had.

"Get Jerry to scan those pictures to us right away," Mel told Sally. "You must call the CIA on this. Ask to speak with Linda Orvez, herself. Get back to me afterwards. This could be a pretty good scoop."

Pretty good scoop, snorted Sally when she put the phone down. Mel and his understatements. She wrote a note for Jerry Roth, the bureau chief, typed her notes and emailed them to the Trib, and then left for an overnight at the Grand Hyatt Washington. Mel would not like the five hundred dollar hotel bill but he would approve it.

The next day Sally called the CIA and got the press office. Go to the top, Mel had said, just like Lou would have.

"Let me get this straight," a press officer said. "You want to speak with the director?"

"Right."

"And who is this, again?"

"Sally Will. Chicago Tribune."

"I'm sorry, the director doesn't take calls from reporters, especially ones she doesn't know."

"That's fine," said Sally, "Then I'll just say she had no comment about the Russian gang here killing Americans or about the three pictures I have of its members – pictures that we're running in tomorrow's Chicago Tribune and LA Times. And I will also report that she had no comment about one of the dead Americans being CIA."

There was a pause. Then the voice on the other end said, "Ah, could you hold on a minute?"

It was ten minutes, but when the phone rang through it was Linda Orvez.

"I hope you know, young lady, that publishing those pictures and talking about the group affects a very sensitive operation involving national security," Orvez lectured.

Yes, thought Sally triumphantly. Confirmation.

"It also means there is a leak here and we will do an investigation," Orvez continued. Better still, thought Sally. The director is launching a probe.

"But do you have a comment on anything to do with this?" asked Sally.

"Absolutely not." Orvez hung up.

Sally was smiling. Mel would melt over this.

What Sally didn't know, nor could imagine, was that Linda Orvez was also smiling. Her agent Anne Burgess, playing the role of Jan, had handled Sally Will expertly, Orvez thought. And so have I. Team Dog Shit would soon be off the hook.

As she rested on the plane headed back to Denver, a couple of things bugged Sally, almost subconsciously. First, she didn't know Jan's last name and had no idea how to contact her. Also, hovering just outside the subconscious, was the ease with which the director of Central Intelligence had been tricked into confirming everything. Didn't these old Washington hands know how the game was played?

The doubt, though, didn't linger. Sally was soon asleep.

51. Flight Plan

MR. WOOD's plan would work only if Tony Nails took regular walks on Devil's Island. Mr. Wood guessed that he did but had to find out for sure. The cost of failure would be too great.

On a Friday evening he flew commercial to Minnesota, drove to Duluth and rented a room in a Motel 6. He soon regretted that decision. The walls were thin and the couple in the next room had little interest in sleep. He turned on Fox. Geraldo was on again, wearing a safari outfit and red bandana, a gun strapped to his side. He was in a war zone. There was incoming. It was nip and tuck. Mr. Wood finally drifted off.

Saturday morning he drove the short distance across the bridge into Wisconsin. At Superior Airstrip he rented a Cessna, showing the young blonde woman phony everything: driver's license, pilot's certificate, credit cards. She looked down at the ID for Tennessee Walker, and then up at Mr. Wood with false mustache and goatee and smiled. The label on her shirt showed her name was Amber.

Amber handed him the keys.

Mr. Wood had memorized the Apostle Islands and, taking off, knew exactly where to head. As he neared Devil's Island, he banked into lazy arches four thousand feet up and three miles away. There was a chance the marshals below would spot him but not much. He wasn't threatening. He was just a hobbyist taking in Superior.

He had figured the single engine plane could stay airborne for five hours. He also figured that Tony would take his walks in the afternoon. He was a gangster. He wouldn't get up early.

At 2:30 p.m., Mr. Wood, using binoculars, saw two men emerge from the stone house. They had that lawmen look, paced, observant, checking things out. Then a single man bounded through the door, quickly followed by two others. The marshals were making a sandwich of Tony Nails. Mr. Wood watched them for some minutes and then flew back. He repeated the steps the next day, staying even further away and a thousand feet higher. Again, at exactly 2:30 p.m., two men emerged from the stone house, then Tony, then two others.

Perfect, Mr. Wood thought. It can be done.

When Dimitri Ivanov first saw Sally Will's story, he was intrigued. Her intelligence sources claimed that a Russian team, headed by Nikolai Boravick, was working against him. Miss Will had somehow even acquired pictures of Nikolai and two of his alleged confederates.

Miss Will reported that when Mika came to Denver to seize control of Ivanov's accounts, Nikolai and his partners killed him, and tried to kill Nikolai's wife. But Pam Boravick had survived, and muddied the waters by saying at least one American was on the team. Ivanov smiled. Just one? He continued reading.

According to the report, Nikolai and his renegades had commenced to pilfer Ivanov's Caribbean accounts, garnering over a billion dollars of his ill-gotten funds. Then came the coup de grace. Miss Will revealed that members of the same pirate team had earlier in the year tracked down and killed a CIA agent named Jason Ison who had double-crossed them in Moscow.

Ivanov chuckled. He was the one who had killed Mr. Ison, not this imaginary hit team. This was all smoke and mirrors. Clearly, the CIA was playing games and had enlisted the help of this Sally Will. The agency had taken Nikolai, forced him to reveal the account numbers and then stolen his money. He was sure of that. Was Miss Will one of them? Ivanov believed that was a good possibility. But always careful, he would check it out. No need to take unnecessary chances, he told himself.

Putting on heavy gloves and grabbing pruning shears, Ivanov headed for the greenhouse. It was his wife's name day, and he wanted to harvest for her a dozen red roses. There were ten rows of roses, twenty feet long and four feet wide. Ivanov carefully checked each one, taking his time, selecting only the very best flowers, even those that were hard to reach. He nicked himself on a thorn doing so. A drop of blood bubbled to the surface of his skin.

Back inside, Ivanov arranged the flowers in a new crystal vase and put them on the dinner table, together with a half a million dollar Faberge egg. He signed a card and pushed a buzzer. He retrieved Sally's article and the pictures that had appeared in the Chicago Tribune, and spread them out on a table beside the flowers and the egg.

Gregory, his top associate, appeared. Gregory was a bull of a man, six-four, two hundred eighty pounds, little piggy eyes and a little piggy snout. He sat down across from Ivanov.

"Gregory," Ivanov said, "an American journalist says these men are working against me."

Ivanov slid the pictures across the table.

"Find them for me," Ivanov said. "I want to know what they say."

Gregory emailed the pictures to every Russian cell that Ivanov controlled. The first to report in was a small band of thieves in Las Vegas. One of the pictures, they said, was of a man named Rubol, a card dealer at the Tropicana. Gregory dispatched a team to question Rubol.

When police found Rubol's body in the desert three days later they determined he had not died of a thousand cuts but of many more. Every possible brutality had been done to the man's teeth, eyes, nails, tongue and genitals. The first cop on the scene vomited.

During the torture, Rubol had confessed to everything, real and imagined. None of it checked out. From what Gregory could tell, Rubol was just a typical expat in America, staying away from the Red Mafiya, living in the suburbs with his wife and daughter, making a new life. Gregory reported back to Ivanov that Rubol was not involved. Ivanov agreed, but told him to continue searching for the other man.

Soon, a Kiev cell identified the second man as Youssef Albridi, a Muslim with suspected extremist ties. Gregory hated the Muslims and would have very much liked to get his hands on Youssef. But Youssef was beyond his reach. He had died three years before in Chechnya after stepping on a mine.

Ivanov was watching Casablanca – his favorite American movie – in a theater room in his house when Gregory slipped in beside him. Ivanov motioned to have the movie paused. Gregory explained about the dead Albridi.

"What now?" Gregory asked. "Should I continue searching for Nikolai?"

"I doubt that will be useful," Ivanov said. He shook his head at the absurdity, now one hundred percent sure that Nikolai was dead at the hands of the Americans. But exactly which ones? And what was their ultimate aim?

"Gregory, I think it would be more useful right now to talk to Nikolai's wife, this American woman named Pam," said Ivanov. "She is probably in better condition."

"And Gregory, could you tell Katya that I need her."

52. Insect Deal

MR.WOOD knew that buying wasps wouldn't be easy, especially when they were rare and from Sri Lanka. He had no idea what red tape he would have to hurdle if he tried to import them into the United States. At the minimum, he was sure he would need to fill out a mountain of forms, any one of which could trip him up. And how exactly do you ship wasps across an ocean while keeping them alive? Mr. Wood had no idea. He went to bed believing that it might be hopeless.

At 2 a.m., still sleepless, he hauled himself out of bed, made himself some tea, settled down in front of his computer monitor and started Googling "*Vespa mandarinia ceylonica.*"

The hit told him that in St. Augustine, Florida, a Dr. Jesus Fernando had imported *Vespa mandarinia ceylonica* because of the unusual characteristics of the wasp's venom. Dr. Fernando, according to a research abstract, had discovered the venom had an effect on the blood in mouse tumors. Mr. Wood learned a new term "antiangiogenesis." Tumors need blood to grow. *Vespa mandarinia ceylonica* venom stopped capillaries from forming in mouse tumors. It beat cancer in mice. Neat.

Unfortunately for Dr. Fernando, what worked in mice didn't appear to work in humans. This involved a second experiment involving something called transgenic mice. Mr. Wood followed part of the science involved before his eyes and his mind glazed over. But he understood this: the second experiment had busted Dr. Jesus Fernando. Mr. Wood learned that Dr. Fernando's grant from the National Institutes of Health had not been renewed. Using private databases, he also learned that Dr. Fernando was going broke. Dr. Fernando, Mr. Wood reasoned, might want to make a deal.

The next morning, acting as a representative for the University of Colorado, Mr. Wood called Dr. Fernando. There was a team in Boulder doing some very quiet research on capillary formation in tumors, he told Dr. Fernando. Members had learned through the scientific grapevine about Dr. Fernando's work, and had some ideas of their own. He said they needed some of his wasps, maybe a thousand, for further tests.

"Our team is very impressed with your research," Mr. Wood said. "And would agree in writing to put your name first on any research paper that we might publish."

"And what would you pay for these rare wasps?" Dr. Fernando asked.

Mr. Wood was prepared for this inevitability.

"Yes, Dr. Fernando," Mr. Wood said. "The university realizes you don't run a charity down there and must have paid a lot to get those wasps from Sri Lanka. The budget here is tight but we have squeezed out an extra $20,000 for the venture. Would that do?"

Would it do? Hell, yes it would do, Dr. Fernando told himself, spirits rocketing.

"I think it could all be arranged," he said dryly.

"And the transport?"

"I developed some large humidors to bring them to Florida from Sri Lanka. One of them could hold a thousand wasps."

Mr. Wood arranged for the wasps to be shipped to a mail drop in Boulder in two days. He warned the manager that an unusual package would be arriving. The manager just shrugged. Boulder.

While Sally waited in the reception room to see Denver Police Chief Walter Henry, she flipped through the magazines he kept on a coffee table. All had to do with police or corrections work, and all advertised products for sale. Sally went immediately to the back pages of the journal, because that's where she found entertaining ads. She had found a magazine in the Public Works department that told of a special digging tool designed to "quickly and efficiently remove antique human remains" found at construction sites. In the chief's journals were ads for mace, handcuffs, badges, body armor, and, interestingly, body armor-piercing bullets. She wondered how many cop-wannabes or crooks ordered this stuff.

She was finally ushered into the chief's voluminous office. After some chitchat she got down to business.

"Sir," Sally said, "I want to spot-check the vacation records of all the detectives and commanders in the homicide bureau for the past three years. I thought I'd ask the man who could push the button."

The chief had so far tried but failed to keep his eyes off of Sally's legs, but now he looked straight into her eyes.

"Is there a problem?"

"Probably not. You know how it is. Ninety percent of tips are flaky."

The chief eyed her suspiciously.

"Flaky?"

"Yes," she said. "But we all live for the exception."

"Ten percent?"

How had this one floated to the top, Sally wondered.

"Chief, I could go ask the city attorney for the records under public records laws, and I might actually get them in five months. I mean they are public records. But you could help me so much, and I would owe you a favor."

"I don't know, Ms. Will. I'll have to think about this and get back to you."

"That would be so kind."

Sally thought it could work. The chief would have auditors look over the records. If nothing was irregular she would get them fast. If not, she would get the stonewall treatment. Sally was hoping Steve Brandon ran a tight ship.

Three days later, the chief left a message on her machine. "Ms. Will, Chief Henry here," he said. "We have those records and you can come by anytime. Public Information Officer Stimson will help you."

When Sally arrived, she found that PIO Stimson had arranged a room for Sally to use to examine the records.

"The chief said to help anyway I can," Stimson said. He looked about twenty four years old, with a thin mustache to match his toothpick-thin frame. He looked eager.

"That's very nice of the chief," Sally said.

Sally sat down to begin looking at the records. Stimson stayed in the room, hands behind his back.

"Officer Stimson?"

"Yes ma'am."

"What are you doing?"

"I'm staying to help."

"This will go so much faster if you aren't here. I won't steal anything. Promise. You can body search me." Sally winked, and Stimson went red. He left immediately.

Sally looked at the stack of records covering vacations and comp time for the homicide bureau. Sally only wanted to know one thing: was Lt. Brandon on vacation on July 22 when Felipe Spilotro was blown away? She took a deep breath and went for the kill. And there it was. Brandon returned to work on Monday, July 27 after a three-week vacation. Sally felt her temperature rise. She clenched her teeth.

Sally stayed awhile to give the impression that she was rummaging through all the records. But she was lost in thought. How could he do this? Money problems make people crazy. But to kill? And do it in a way that could destroy a program that meant so much to the law?

Sally had once trusted Brandon. Now she feared him more than anyone she had ever feared. He was a sociopath, she decided, that was now clear. She chastised herself for being a fool, for not seeing it. Once, he had seemed to be the perfect cop. Sally told herself her father would have known. He would not have been taken in by the bluster of this cop.

When the time seemed finally right for her to leave, Officer Stimson was sitting just on the other side of the door.

"No copies?" he asked.

"No, officer. Tell the chief everything was in order."

53. Test Run

KATYA entered Ivanov's greenhouse. She was only a little less nervous than the last time. Ivanov was tending some tulip bulbs. Katya cleared her throat to announce her presence.

"Ah, yes," Ivanov said, turning. "My Katya." He dispatched a trowel into a flowerpot and took off his gloves. "As usual, Katya, you are looking criminally beautiful."

Katya looked to the side, embarrassed. Ivanov raised her chin with a bent finger.

"Come, let's go inside," he said. "I have a mission for you."

As before, Ivanov poured Katya and himself a drink of brandy. They sat, he in a chair and she on the nearby couch. Ivanov took out a picture of Pam Boravick and handed it to Katya.

"This woman, an American, may know a great deal about a group that is out to destroy our family," Ivanov said. He paused while Katya memorized the photo. "Gregory will give you the background. But I need for you and the doctor to find out everything she knows."

"Yes, sir. I understand," said Katya, still absorbing Pam Boravick.

Ivanov took out another picture: Sally Will's.

"This woman is an American journalist. She is also trying to hurt our family. We must find out who she is really working for."

Katya looked at the photo, then looked up, resolute.

"Understood," she said.

"Katya, in America they protect their journalists more than here. It could create an incident. So, for right now, just check her out. Nothing more."

"Yes, sir."

Katya tried to put on a brave face, but inside she was shaking. This man was placing into her heart a trust and responsibility she had never known. She hoped she deserved it. She knew the mission would be difficult, but she would give it everything she had.

Ivanov rose slowly. Katya followed. He walked her to the door with a hand on her shoulder. At the door, Katya turned to him, shaking slightly, and in a barely audible voice asked: "Sir, why are you so kind to me?"

Ivanov laughed: "Because, my dear Katya, you are an angel" and bent and kissed her cheek. He held her shoulders in his hands and stepped back while Katya slowly looked up. "An angel," he repeated.

Outside the dacha, after the door closed, Katya could not control her tears. She had never been so happy in her life. But why did he not want to touch her like other men did? He was a god, she decided. Her god.

Mr. Wood was planning to drop the wasps on Devil's Island in a three-gallon canning jar. He didn't know much about wasp psychology but he figured that after they found themselves rudely flung to earth they would be pissed. And would take it out on Tony Nails. That was the plan at any rate. What he didn't know was how fast to drop them, or from what altitude. But Colorado offered a great laboratory for such an experiment.

Mr. Wood took three three-gallon jars to the bridge over the Royal Gorge near Canon City, 1,053 feet above the Arkansas River. It was night, but with a full moon, he could see into the gorge. He had designed separate parachutes for each jar, from small to very small. He didn't want the jar to hang in the air or be blown away by the wind. He wanted fast but not too fast. He had no time to do the test with real wasps because he didn't have any real wasps to waste. He was gambling.

He dropped all three, one after the other. They all broke on the boulders below. With a stopwatch he calculated that the smallest parachute slowed the jar to twenty-five feet per second, while the largest brought the speed down to five feet per second. He chose the one in the middle, the one that descended at ten feet per second. It would have to do.

Lou was sitting in his office, wadding up paper sheets and throwing them into a distant basket, thinking about Sally and Brandon and how Sally almost got herself killed. Lou had long since known that he was in love with Sally Will but hadn't told her that. He had only said it to one person before and she was dead and he didn't know if he could do it again.

How was it that life could end? It was one of those questions that Lou knew he could never answer. Becky Sue had been real, not just a collection of atoms and laws of chemistry and physics. She laughed, cried, made up silly tales. And then she had stopped living. Although the molecules were all still there, as Lou watched Becky Sue's last breath she was suddenly as far away from him as the edge of the universe. It was as though she had never been.

Lou tossed another errant shot at the basket and wiped some dampness from his right eye. How could that be? And now Sally. Would there be two bad ends?

The phone rang. Lou lobbed the wad toward the basket. It went in. The phone rang again. Lou pondered it. Should he answer? On the fifth ring, he did. It was Smiley. He had something. They had to meet.

The Orange Buck was a mountain tavern located at the end of a dirt road eight miles off U.S. 285 near Turkey Creek Canyon, the canyon where Lou had talked the kidnapper into giving up his hostage. A log building, the bar must have been around when Jesse James roamed the West. The only thing that warmed the place was an ancient wood-burning stove set in the middle. When they said it was red hot, that's exactly what they meant. It glowed. The owner, a leftover from the days of purple haze and free love, played guitar and sang country music anthems and the ballads of folk heroes: Pete Seeger, Joni Mitchell and Bob Dylan. Patrons, rich and poor, from the city and the high country, played tambourines and makeshift drums, danced, wrote their names on the walls and defaced one-dollar bills with messages and then stapled them on the ceiling. There were toddlers, young adults and old folks clapping and stomping and drinking. Often drinking a bit too much.

It was raining lightly and dark and Lou made two wrong turns, but finally he found the joint. Smiley was not in the main room where the pandemonium was unfolding, but in an almost empty poolroom.

"How did you find this place?" Lou asked. He shook off some raindrops. Smiley thought he looked like a big dog trying to get dry.

"Ended up here drunk one night," said Smiley. "It's a good place."

"Where haven't you ended up drunk, Smiley?" Lou smiled.

"Don't know. There must be someplace." True to form, Smiley didn't smile.

"OK. I'm here. You're here. What do you have?" Lou asked.

"I get to go first?" said Smiley. "I ask: what do you have?"

Smiley meant money.

"You know," said Lou, "you can be damn irritating, Smiley. I've never shorted you. Have you got something for me or not?"

A waitress with a neckline falling nearly to her navel passed through. She was dressed in black silk like a beautiful witch. The owner was on an electric mandolin playing "Tequila Sunrise". Everyone joined in. The place vibrated.

"This is worth a lot, Lou," said Smiley. "I could get killed for it."

"No one is going to know anything."

"You say that but who pays for the funeral if you're wrong?"

"That would be the state, Smiley."

Smiley shook his head.

"Seven hundred dollars," he said.

"You been doing crack again, my friend?"

"Six hundred."

"Two hundred," Lou countered.

"Ah, Lou. You're busting my chops here. My landlady is into S&M. She'd love to see me under some bridge."

"Three hundred and fifty, Smiley. That's it."

Smiley appeared to do some mental calculations.

"OK, that works. Here's the skinny. The talk is that Dicerno met with the killer at the Italian June Festival," said Smiley. "That's where it was all set up. Dicerno had Palermo killed by the guy he met there. Then the guy killed Spilotro."

There was a pause while Smiley looked at Lou.

"I'm waiting for the punch line, Smiley. Who's the guy?"

"I dunno."

"You want three hundred and fifty dollars for 'don't know'?"

"Whoever it was he had on some sort of stupid mask."

"Smiley, the festival is a masquerade party."

"OK. It was the mask of some modern guy. Not Frankenfuckingstein or anything. Dark hair. Creepy."

"You got this from someone first hand?"

"Are you crazy? I don't run in that crowd. Some guy called Fresno got shit-faced one night with a gal at Maggie's Best. And after the third or fourth bang he kinda ran his mouth. Probably doesn't even remember."

Lou was impressed. Jimmy Fresno. Maybe this was worth three hundred and fifty dollars.

"So you got this directly from that hooker?"

"Yep. Best sources in the world."

"Good work," Lou said. He peeled off four Franklins.

Smiley almost raised a smile when he saw he was getting a tip. But all he managed was to get his mouth into a straight line.

"And Smiley?" Lou said.

"What?"

"Cheer up."

It was after 2 a.m. when Lou got home. Sally had fallen asleep on the couch. Lou decided this was too hot to wait. He nudged her awake and told her Smiley's story.

"Arranged at the Italian June Festival?" she protested. "But Big Bow was killed before the Festival."

"Maybe Brandon was working for somebody else before the Festival. Maybe the Hells Angels."

"Lou," Sally said, "the Angels have their own killers."

"Probably, but Smiley never gets these things wrong. He says the leak is Jimmy Fresno, something Fresno said to a hooker when he was zoned out. What we need, Sal, is a list of the attendees at the festival. Was Brandon even there?"

Sally hauled herself off the couch, went over to the computer and began pecking at the keyboard.

"I think there was a list on the Web," she explained. "The local papers maybe ran something on it."

Within seconds, a list came up.

"Jesus, Lou, here it is." Sally had gone from foggy to pulse-pounding awake in an instant.

Under the Bs was the name that mattered: "Brandon, Lt. Steven."

"We got it nailed, Lou."

"It looks great," Lou nodded. Lou's heart was racing, too. That son-of-a-bitch.

"No, I mean we have it."

"Right, Sal. But we still need to ask him about the July vacation. Will he alibi it? I think the bastard will try."

"I'll do that as soon as possible, by the end of tomorrow evening," said Sally.

"Not alone, you won't."

Sally paused.

"No," she finally said, "not alone."

54. Bomb Run

THIS time Mr. Wood drove from Denver to Duluth in a rented SUV, the wasps in the rear, their jar swaddled in a blanket to keep them warm. Only about a hundred had died since he got them from Dr. Fernando. The ones that were left had to stay alive. He fed them some concoction he had read about on the Net: lots of sugar and nectar and caterpillar juice. He could hear them humming. They seemed pleased.

He drove straight through, stopping only for gas, candy bars, and an occasional snooze. At a filling station in Duluth, he pasted on the fake goatee and mustache. He would rent the Cessna, using the same phony name, ID and credit cards he had the last time. Again, he was Tennessee Walker.

The Superior airstrip was private, isolated and in need of care, but perfect for his needs. In what looked like an old wooden shed Mr. Wood found the same young blonde woman, behind a counter reading a magazine and listening to music on an iPod. She pushed paperwork across the desk without even looking up.

"Hi there, Amber," Mr. Wood said in a lazy Southern accent.

"Hi again," she said, perking up. "Same as last time?"

"Same."

She again gave him the keys.

"Thanks Amber. See you when I get back maybe?"

"I'll be here," Amber smiled.

Striding out into the autumn sunlight Mr. Wood took in the plane and smiled. It was the same Cessna 172 known and loved by countless amateur pilots the world over he had used last time. He knew it well. But he also knew this takeoff would be a little more complicated than normal. He breathed in, then released slowly. Time to focus.

Going back to the SUV, he took out a large rolled-up banner

and attached it to the back of the fuselage with a thick leather strap. Mr. Wood was being creative. This was the trick he had bet on to calm the suspicions of the federal agents watching over Tony Nails.

He knew that taking off with the banner unfolded was a risk but it was one he had to take. It would work if he managed it carefully. And if he managed it, he thought, today would be a good day. It would be a triumph – bigger, much bigger, than Bow Hendricks or Bruno Palermo or even Felipe Spilotro. It would be huge. If Tony Nails died, the feds would stop at nothing to find him. And if Tony Nails didn't die, the Outfit would come after him just as hard. This was the point of no return.

Mr. Wood took another deep breath and tried to push doubts out of his mind. Best not to think about it, he decided. Just do it in the same way as he had started with Bow Hendricks. With no regret. He just had to have faith.

Mr. Wood unfurled the banner carefully behind the plane, then returned to the SUV to get his jar of little assassins. He placed the jar on the passenger seat, using the seat belt to secure it, and climbed in. For a moment he hesitated. He could see Amber watching him from the office door and hoped his cover story was good enough. Probably she was just curious, he decided. He breathed in and out slowly, paced himself, feeling the adrenaline rise.

Easing out the throttle gently, the little Cessna moved forward slowly. There were no other planes landing, taxiing or taking off. Thank God for rundown private airstrips, he thought. No attention.

He eased onto the battered old runway, hoping there would be nothing to snag the banner as he accelerated for takeoff. He pushed the throttle forward and felt the craft pick up speed. He could hear the metal bridle-assembly pole of the banner scraping the tarmac behind him.

As soon as the speedometer hit sixty five knots he pulled back on the yoke and the shabby little Cessna did its job. He was airborne. Better still, the banner was trailing behind him, intact.

As he turned east, trying for a bee-line to Devil's Island, a calm washed over Mr. Wood, the sort that comes after making an irreversible choice. Nothing mattered now but to get the job done.

Thirty minutes later Devil's Island came into view. Mr. Wood put the plane into a slow turn. It was 1:45 p.m. Tony Nails should take his walk in about half an hour. With binoculars, Mr. Wood watched the island from less than a mile away as he circled.

At 2:15, a Coast Guard boat arrived. A man in a business suit got off and marched to the gray stone house.

What the hell?

Below on Devil's Island Tony Nails' lawyer entered the stone house. He had a testy client to try to mollify. Tony was upset because he thought the government was trying to stab him in the back. The feds were insisting he spend at least five years in protective custody in some prison somewhere for his 25 murders.

Tony railed: "Where the fuck do they get off? Didn't the lawyers for Sammy 'The fuckin' Bull' Gravano get him no time, zero, when he turned on Gotti. Bet your sweet ass they did."

"No," the lawyer said, "Sammy also went down for five."

"The fuck he did, asshole," yelled Tony Nails. "You're my lawyer. I pay you to keep me the fuck outa the joint, fuckhead."

Tony's lawyer tried to explain the government's position, but Tony was in no mood to listen. He vented, spewed, raged, threw things with venom. His handlers stayed in the next room, playing poker. To them, Tony was a riot.

"It was spelled out in court," the lawyer said. "You told the judge you understood."

"Whaddaya mean, spelled out?" he fumed. "Spelled out my ass. Zero, that's what was spelled out. Zero, zero, fuckin zero!"

And so it went.

2:30 p.m. came and went with no sign of Tony Nails and his handlers. Nothing moved on Devil's Island. Mr. Wood was not overly concerned. It was a minor delay. But Mr. Wood's back already hurt and he was tired. He wondered how long it would be.

An hour later Mr. Wood had begun to worry considerably. He had used up over half his fuel and still no Tony Nails. He thought maybe he should go back and try for another weekend. But there was an insurmountable problem with that: Wasps don't have a long shelf life. It had to happen today.

Where was Tony? Mr. Wood stared out with the binoculars. Still nothing. This was getting serious. Whatever was wrong it was something to do with the man in the business suit.

Mr. Wood couldn't help himself. Goaded by the anxiety of the brilliant plan falling apart because of something as stupid as running out of fuel he decided to get in a bit closer, to make sure he wasn't missing anything.

As Tony Nails and his lawyer continued to argue, Jim Black, a deputy U.S. Marshal put down his cards.

"Do you hear that?" he asked agent Richard Cohn.

"What?"

"That plane."

"No."

"It's been here for a while," Black said.

They went to a window to look. The plane appeared to be carrying a tail.

"Give me the glasses," Cohn said.

Through the binoculars he saw a lone pilot in a single propeller Cessna trailing a banner. The pilot seemed to be bearded. The banner read: "Welcome to the Apostle Islands."

"It's a tourist advertising plane," said Cohn.

By 4:30 p.m. the sun was dropping fast. But not as fast as the fuel meter in the Cessna. Mr. Wood had to return soon or he would run dry. He was feeling steadily more desperate. It was no longer just an issue of killing Tony Nails. This was also becoming about his own survival. It was decision time again.

Just then, the lawyer left the house and stormed toward the

Coast Guard boat. Two minutes later, the boat pulled away from the dock. But still no Tony Nails.

Down below Tony Nails tapped the door, told Agent Black: "Gotta take a walk." It was nearly 4:40 p.m.

"Tony, it's too late. It's getting dark," Black said.

"You just want to play that fuckin' game, Black. Don't give me this 'it's too dark' bullshit. If I don't walk I'm going to explode. You try talking sense into a fuckin' lawyer for three hours."

Black laughed. Sure, Tony Nails could have his walk. There was just that one small plane around. That was all. It wasn't going to bomb Devil's Island. It was a harmless-looking advertising plane. Hardly Top Gun. Even so, Black raised the alarm a notch. Other agents were alerted. Just as a precaution.

Mr. Wood banked west, readying for his return to the mainland. He felt he might still just make Duluth. But he was growing fearful and depressed. That damn man in the boat. Whoever he was he had really fucked this whole thing up. Then he saw them: first the two marshals, then Tony, and finally the two rearguards. Tony Nails was finally going for a walk.

Mr. Wood tried to calm his shaking. He had never been to this point in life where he had to will himself out of a rising panic. He didn't know if he could.

But then something began to change. The panic turned to anger. And determination. Suddenly Mr. Wood was furious. Furious at that son-of-a-bitch down there who had caused this. Fucking Tony Nails! Mr. Wood was going to get Tony Nails – even if it was the last thing he ever did.

Any thought of turning for home now had gone.

Mr. Wood gripped the steering yoke and pushed forward. The plane lurched, then fell rapidly. The altimeter reading spun downwards. Within seconds he was at 500 feet. The men were only a quarter mile away, coming up in a ground rush. Mr. Wood lifted the jar of wasps into his lap and pushed on the cockpit door. It didn't budge. He tried again, flexing every one of his muscles. Still nothing. He was nearly at drop height.

"Open damn you," he yelled, loosening his seat straps at the same time. Finally, with one superhuman effort that only adrenaline can produce, he rammed the door open with his shoulder.

The men on the ground had turned and were looking up. Some were already grabbing for guns.

Mr. Wood looked down through the door buffeted by slipstream. He was at 200 feet. This was it. Mr. Wood, sweating and taut as a piano wire, lifted the buzzing jar and, pushing the door open with his foot, hurled the container with full force at the ground.

"Banzai Motherfucker!" He yelled at the top of his voice.

At that precise moment gunfire opened up.

As soon as the marshals heard the plane coming they realized it was flying too low, moving too fast and getting too close to be an advertising plane.

"Assassin!" cried Black. "Open fire!"

All four agents pulled their triggers at once. Three of them had Uzis and sent a hundred bullets toward the plane in a single second and kept firing. They saw a man in a goatee beard and a fraction of a second later a small dark object fall from the plane, quickly getting bigger.

A jar shattered at their feet.

Tony Nails bent down slightly for a closer look at the strange contents. They moved like boiling black treacle and made a buzzing noise. An instant later he realized what it was and, with a strangled cry of fear, turned to run for his life. Too late. A swarm of the surviving and now very angry wasps had already settled on his head and face in a thick black mat as if they wanted to suffocate him.

"Run for it!" Cohn shouted, swatting as many insects as he could off Tony Nails' head with one hand and grabbing him by the arm with the other. With the help of another agent he half dragged and half carried Tony to the stone house. Agents and their ward crashed open the door and fell inside.

"Fuck, I thought he was going to strafe us or something at first," said Black, half-laughing half angry, as he continued to swat insects off both Tony Nails and himself. "But bombing us with fucking wasps!"

He looked for some reaction from the ward he had just rescued. But then he saw that Tony Nails was neither angry nor laughing. In fact, Tony Nails looked very far from well indeed. He was wheezing and sweating and his eyes were bulging.

"Tony?" Cohn said. "Oh shit, no. He's going into shock!"

But Tony Nails had already gone beyond the point of no return. He had fallen to the floor shaking uncontrollably, foam dripping from his mouth and down his chin, his wheeze turning into a terrible rumble as he struggled for air, his bulging eyes focused on something in the distance. His heart gave out long before anyone had time to pump in enough antihistamine.

Black got on an immediate secure line to D.C.

"Somemadmaninadinkyplanbombedus," he said.

"Take it easy," said the agent on the other end. "Slow down."

Agent Black caught his breath and tried again: "Some guy in a small plane threw a wasp bomb at us. Tony Nails is dead."

There was a pause. Then: "Say again?"

Finally Agent Black got his story told. The agent on the other end – who at first thought it was some kind of joke – was finally persuaded.

"Tony Nails is dead?"

"Yes."

"Fuck us all."

Washington reacted swiftly. Agents called the Wisconsin National Guard, the state police, the Federal Aviation Authority, and the FBI. The message was they had to find a Cessna 172 riddled with bullets that had left Devil's Island smoking badly. Likely as not it was already in the lake, they thought. The guy with a goatee flying it must have got shot up pretty bad.

55. Land Fall

ABOVE Lake Superior, flying south, Mr. Wood was now struggling for his own survival. Despite the fusillade of bullets aimed at him he had escaped almost unscathed. Two bullets had ripped through the cockpit, one coming up between Mr. Wood's legs, missing the femoral artery by an inch but a nasty gash was oozing blood. His plane had not been quite so lucky.

Craning his head back to check the scene behind him, Mr. Wood was dismayed to see his view obscured by smoke coming from somewhere under him. But he was certain his aim had been good and he could only hope the insects had done their stuff. The other good news was that the trailing banner had caught the top of a pine tree and torn away making the plane lighter and easier to fly. But that was the only good news.

Falling back into his seat he saw that the plane was on an impact course with the darkened waters. He had three seconds. He pulled back on the steering yoke with all his strength. The plane responded but the water kept coming up at him. He said a quick prayer and prepared for the impact.

But it didn't come. Instead he felt a slight shudder as the plane's wheels skimmed the lake and then left it and began to climb. Slowly but inexorably the plane gained altitude. And it was no longer billowing smoke.

Mr. Wood began to breathe properly again. He checked the dials. He was two hundred feet above the water and still heading south, toward the dark land mass ahead.

He made good distance before he noticed the engine temperature was rising rapidly and oil pressure was dropping. Something must have been severed. At this rate, the pistons would bake shut and might even explode. He estimated he was still about two miles out and he didn't have a lot of time left.

"Come on, come on, give me altitude," Mr. Wood shouted at the engine as he pulled back on the yoke. The plane climbed a little and then began to vibrate uncontrollably. Mr. Wood was tossed violently to one side despite having strapped himself back in, hitting his head hard on the cockpit edge and almost losing consciousness. He thought the wings would rip off. But they held. He throttled back and the vibration stopped.

A second later the shoreline came into view about a mile ahead. Then another thought struck him: where to land? Northern Wisconsin was filled with hills and forests, it was now dark, and there was no way he would make any landing strip even if he knew where one was. And with little doubt that most of the country's considerable law enforcement agencies would now be out looking for him he was just as sure he didn't want to.

Mr. Wood made a quick decision. He would ditch as close to the shore as he could and hope to make it to land intact. If not at least the end would be quick.

A piston blew, shooting a piece of shrapnel right through Mr. Wood's jacket but miraculously missing him. Just as miraculously, the entire engine didn't immediately seize up. But he knew that at any moment the engine would lock and he would go down. Hard. He thought the only good thing was that there was practically no fuel left to catch fire.

He looked again at the Wisconsin hills, black in the gloom. From here they looked like the Rocky Mountains. Ditching was the only option and it was now or never. Just then the last pistons locked and suddenly Mr. Wood heard only the roar of the wind. He put the plane into a glide, hoping against hope that he could judge the descent well enough to bellyflop safely and give himself enough time to get out before the thing sank. If he got lucky he would hit at about fifty miles an hour. He could do it, he said to himself.

Checking his seatbelt he steered the plane so the glide was taking him more or less parallel with the shoreline to his left and only about a hundred yards out. A slight headwind helped him keep direction. He glimpsed what appeared to be a small campsite near the water's edge, with a light showing, but anyone not looking up would not have noticed the small dark shape gliding silently by. The water drew closer and darker. He was just feet above the surface, This is going to need split-second timing but it's going to be OK, Mr. Wood thought. Just believe.

Then suddenly ahead he saw what appeared to be a small wooded headland jutting out right in his path. Hitting that is going to be sayonara. It's now or never. He edged the flaps down, saw a faint metal reflection off the ruffled water and pulled the nose of the plane up sharply, hitting the water tail first. The rest of the plane followed, pancaking forward so heavily water quickly began filling the cockpit. The impact broke off the tail and half tore off one of the wings and the plane began to turn turtle, its shabby underside showing. Mr. Wood threw off his seatbelt and more or less swam out of the cockpit just as the small craft did a final roll and sank beneath him, belly up.

The swim to the shore was harder than he thought and the water colder and when he finally stood on dry land he was exhausted and frozen. But the bleeding had stopped, the goatee and mustache had gone, and he was intact. By the time he had got his breath back he was even beginning to feel exhilerated. Lucky old me, he thought. He was lucky with the weather too. It was a relatively warm autumn evening, with only a slight westerly wind.

Looking back at the lake Mr. Wood was satisfied to see that nothing of the plane remained on the surface. His sense of satisfaction increased. He had some time to regroup.

He decided to walk to the camping ground by the shore he had seen from the air and test his luck again. The way it seemed to be going with him right now it was worth a try.

Mr. Wood stumbled into the campground half an hour later. His jacket was torn, he was wet and bruised – and the bleeding in his thigh had started up again. He was depending on the unorthodox ethics of outdoors types to get him out of this mess.

The campground seemed to be deserted but for one old-timer

staring at embers inside a ring of stones. He looked up when Mr. Wood walked over. Mr. Wood was too tired to try anything clever. He went to a log opposite the embers and just sat. The old man looked at him closely.

"You look pretty busted up," the old man said eventually, seemingly unfazed that a stranger had entered his camp looking like he had just wrestled with a grizzly bear.

"Ain't too good," Mr. Wood agreed.

The old man lit up a joint, took a hit and passed it to Mr. Wood.

"You on the run, son?" the old man asked.

Mr. Wood nodded and sucked in some marijuana. It felt good.

"I'm on the run from some pretty angry dudes," he said. He passed the joint back. The old man, who said his name was Orville, got up and rummaged in a tent, emerging with some coveralls, a flannel shirt and a sleeping bag and gave him a dressing for his wound.

"Stay here," he said. "We'll get you out in the morning."

Mr. Wood wasn't sure who "we" was but nodded in thanks. He dressed his thigh and changed into the dry clothes and after a couple more tokes the old man went into his tent. Mr. Wood crawled into the sleeping bag and fell asleep almost immediately to the sound of the wind in the trees.

He slept dreamlessly, like the dead. In the morning, Mr. Wood's savior made them bacon and eggs with instant coffee. It was damn near the best meal he'd ever had. Added to that the weather was spectacular – dry and sunny, crisp but not cold. Orville asked Mr. Wood who was after him. Seeing no percentage in lying, and feeling on a lucky streak, Mr. Wood said "the feds."

Orville nodded, seeming to know about such things.

"OK," he said finally as he stood and stretched, "let's get you on the road."

At the first bend in the road after they had pulled out of the camping ground Mr. Wood thought his luck might just have run out. A county sheriff's checkpoint pulled them over and asked for ID. But Mr. Wood had prepared for this. He pulled out backup

ID he had not used before. He'd kept it, with cards and cash, in a waterproof pocket in the cargo trousers he'd worn for the flight. All had survived the ditching.

"You two see any strangers around?" the deputy asked, ducking his head in, examining the occupants. "Looking for someone who might be injured? Might have a goatee?"

Orville and Mr. Wood looked at each other and then at the agent. They both shrugged and shook their heads no.

The deputy didn't appear that interested. He checked their IDs and waved them through. Orville then took dirt back roads all the way to Duluth to avoid any more roadblocks and they were not bothered again. In Duluth, after handing Orville a hundred dollars and thanks, Mr. Wood rented a car and drove slowly to Minneapolis, bought a paper, and caught a plane for Denver.

When the stewardess with the drink cart came by he asked for a scotch and ice. The drink warmed his mind and his aching body. At thirty three thousand feet he reminded himself he had survived. It was against the odds but he had survived. And even more pleasingly, he said to himself, it was likely Tony Nails had not.

56. Closing In

THE STORY of Tony Nails' death exploded on the all-news networks at the same time as Katya and Vitali checked into a suite at the Oxford Hotel in Denver's LoDo. Ostensibly, they were man and wife. And since they never came out of their room for the first 24 hours, ordering room service, the hotel staff assumed they had just wed. But what they were doing was waiting.

A day later, a tall gaunt man with a paper-white complexion also signed in at the Oxford. He was polite and spoke with a slight accent. A little British, some thought. A real gentleman. He carried three bags and what appeared to be a covered cage. The staff thought it held a bird. How endearing. When the bellman came to take his luggage, the old gentleman insisted on carrying the cage himself. Dr. Tsplyev was now in Denver, five blocks from Lou's condo. And he had the rat.

The killing of Tony Nails was the biggest news event since the fall of Lehman Brothers. It was as if the Witness Protection Program had never existed. Cons all over America called their attorneys to get out of deals. Scores of wise guys, bikers, and Mexican mafia thugs were just let go. There was no one to testify against them.

Even some Al Qaeda associates were sprung. One, Mohammed Hijazi, smiled at the cameras as he walked from the prison gate to freedom and held out five fingers.

"What are these?" he asked winking at reporters. When reporters said they didn't know, Mohammed turned his fist around and gave the audience the finger, saying: "It's a bouquet of these."

There was little but Devil's Island on talk radio. Callers wanted blood vengeance. No one any longer believed that a jealous husband had blown Felipe Spilotro to pieces so why had the government fed us that line? Callers asked. Who was behind the cover-up? How had the government failed to stop the madman in the plane?

Many thought both the protected witnesses and the cons they were going to testify against deserved summary execution. Why are we letting them go free?

Comedians had a field day. David Letterman drew up a list on "The top ten ways a protected witness knows his cover has been blown?" The top answer: "He opens the door and there's a singing messenger dressed as a wasp." Grade schoolers were using the term "*Vespa mandarinia.*"

It seemed everybody was launching an investigation: three congressional committees, the FBI, the government Accountability Office, the Inspector General. The U.S. Marshals' Service was investigating itself. Newspapers and networks assigned teams of reporters to the story. The image of the Al Qaeda man flipping off the nation was played over and over.

America was angry.

Before Tony Nails, the president's administration had been seen as winning the war on organized crime. The Mexican, Colombian and Italian syndicates were on the run, as were the Russians. Now this. If nothing was done, the president could kiss his second term goodbye. The president had to crush those behind the conspiracy. Had to crush them right away.

It had been years since the president was a prosecutor but he remembered his first lesson as an assistant DA trying to figure out a homicide. An old investigator had told him: "First, find who benefits." That answer was easy: Vito Borelli. The president called in his Lilliputian FBI director, Roger Hamilton.

"Roger, who did this?" he asked.

Hamilton was on the edge of his chair, his knees unsteady.

"We don't know, Mr. President. It appears to be a hired hitman."

"That's really good work Roger. Just great," the president said sarcastically. "Now for the big one, Roger: who is the man?"

Hamilton seemed almost in tears.

"Best guess, sir. He works for the Italians. Or that might be worked. We haven't been able to find any trace of him or the plane he flew. We think he might have crashed into Superior. We think he might have been a kind of mafia suicide bomber."

The president threw up his hands.

"Think? Think? Is that the best you can do? Next time you come here, Roger," he said, "you better bring more."

The national media made the same assumption as Roger Hamilton. The crazy man in the plane had died in the lake. But his actions spelled the revival of the Italian La Cosa Nostra.

Reporters had no doubt about the epicenter: Denver. Spilotro was a Denver man, the wasps that killed Tony Nails had been sent to a Denver-area address, and Denver mafia don Danny Dicerno was the first known beneficiary of the attacks. Media vans with their satellite antennas camped outside Capricio's.

The feds placed Dr. Fernando, the man who supplied the wasps, under arrest. He was interrogated round the clock without an opportunity to see a lawyer. Patriot Act rules. But the FBI couldn't shake his story. He said he had bought the wasps for cancer research and had subsequently sent one thousand of them in a humidor to a man in Boulder calling himself Douglas Applegate. Applegate said he was with a team of scientists at the University of Colorado and had paid him in good order. How was I to know it was a conspiracy? Asked Dr. Fernando.

Agents confirmed the broad outline of his statement. Dr. Fernando had sent his humidor to a mail drop in Boulder. But there was no Douglas Applegate. No research team. No trace.

Mel Campbell seemed to be calling Sally every fifteen minutes.

"Sally, how is that theory of yours working out?"

"Mel, you asked me that the last time."

"But I can't remember the answer."

"Mel, I said in time."

"Sally, the time is now."

In the condo Lou's first instinct was to find out exactly where Steve Brandon had been over the weekend. Was he on duty or out of town. In Wisconsin perhaps? He called Kirkpatrick.

"We need to meet," Lou said.

"I know," said Kirkpatrick.

"Let's make it the same place."

"Fine. I'll wear my dinner jacket."

The gallery was again deserted but for the mousey manager. Lou and Scott ignored her and moved to a corner as far away from her as possible.

"Where was Brandon last weekend?" Lou asked after almost no preliminaries.

Scott looked almost persecuted. He didn't need to be told what this was about. He seemed to know.

"Don't know where exactly but he wasn't in town. He took Friday off as a floating holiday. On Saturday we had a double homicide that looked particularly bad. Someone called Brandon's house. His wife was there but she said she didn't know how to contact her husband. He was somewhere in Wisconsin."

"OK," Lou said, and took a step toward the door. Scott held back.

"Don't hurry, Lou."

Lou turned.

"There's more?"

"There's more," Scott said. "Brandon called in sick on Monday. Like maybe he had been delayed in getting back from wherever he was? Like Wisconsin maybe?"

"Jesus."

Scott walked right beside Lou, so that they both were looking straight ahead.

"Lou, level with me. Is Brandon the son of a bitch?"

Lou looked over at the manager, who hadn't moved. He lowered his voice even more.

"We think so, yes."

There was a pause. Then Scott said: "What can I do?"

He looked like he was going to cry. He was young. He looked like he had been betrayed, hurt to the core.

Lou had been thinking of an extra step they could take. It wasn't needed, he told himself. The interview with Brandon would probably settle things. Still, there was something. Something a lawman would think of.

"I could use a piece of the Palermo cigarette butt. Check the DNA."

Scott did not hesitate.

"You got it," he said.

"And after that," Scott said, "tell Sally this: Write it."

The FBI ran Amber, the clerk in Superior, through the wringer. They had a million questions. She had one answer: "I fucked up."

Agents found no fingerprints on the flight contract Mr. Wood had signed. And when they finally traced Tennessee Walker down they found him in an Arizona nursing home. He couldn't remember his own name, much less who had stolen his identity.

All surveillance video cameras in Duluth and Superior were checked for any sign of a man in a goatee and mustache. No luck.

The investigation was going nowhere.

Ivanov's team left the Oxford and rented an isolated farmhouse in Last Chance, Colorado, a desolate town out on the eastern plains. They buried chemical waste at Last Chance. Who there would care about a few eccentrics?

Dr. Tsplyev was to stay there with Raspy as Katya and Vitali were to go back to Denver to snare their prey.

Lou called Sally. "We have to talk."

"Where?"

"Either the condo or The Shamrock?"

"The Shamrock."

Lou slid into a booth at The Shamrock – an Irish bar downtown known for dark corners. He told Sally about Scott.

"Damn, Lou. That settles it. We do the interview. If he has no alibi, which he won't, I'll have it in the paper in two days."

Lou blinked, took a drink of Fat Tire. Sally could tell he was holding something back.

"What is it, Lou?"

"Two days, Sal? Isn't that a bit optimistic?"

"What do we need besides the interview? We know the answer. If we wait more people could die."

Lou had dreaded this moment. He knew he was just being fussy. But he couldn't help himself.

"Maybe there's something," Lou said.

"Why are you getting cold feet?" Sally said, exasperated. "Lou, it's so clear."

Lou babied his beer. "One thing," he said.

"Que, mi hombre?"

"I wish we had Brandon's DNA on all the Dunhills."

Sally smiled and shook her head. Negative.

"Sally," Lou said, "Scott is getting me a snippet of the one from Palermo. And you seem pretty able to handle a certain detective in Commerce City. Between them, we ought to be able to get a usable sample. And then we compare them to Brandon's DNA from the butt he left at Red Rocks."

"Lou, sweetheart," Sally said, deliberately condescendingly, "The whole world is crashing down on this. And we got it. Right?

"DNA would be nice."

"Fine," Sally said. "And do we do the genetic sequencing in your lab or mine?"

"I think maybe I could get O'Dowd to do it."

"Are you joking? It could take weeks."

"No, a quick test doesn't. And it's pretty good. Enough to tell us if we're on the wrong track."

"*Wrong* track?"

"I didn't mean that. Bad choice. DNA is just something I would do if I was a detective on the case. That's all."

"I'm not going to lose this scoop, Lou."

"I know."

In the morning, Sally headed to Commerce City. Detective Rick Sanchez still appeared interested when Sally arrived. She knew he would be, and this time she didn't discourage him. She was desperate. She had a Lou problem to get off her back.

"Detective Sanchez, nice of you to see me," she beamed.

Detective Sanchez looked Sally over. He noticed the absence of a big, sparkly rock. He nodded at it. "Problems, Sally Will?"

"A little choppy water," Sally said. "It'll pass."

"How can I help?" Sanchez said. He actually flexed a bicep in one arm and then the other, as if by habit.

"You know that stupid white-slavery tip I got awhile back?"

"Would never forget that," Rick Sanchez winked.

"Well, I have an editor who just asked about it again. Wanted some detail from my notes. A real nerd," Sally put out her hands.

"What can I do?" he said.

"Well, I don't have any notes because I threw the notebook away. There was no story. Rick, I need to see the file again."

Sally didn't know if Detective Sanchez was buying any of this bullshit but she was sure he was interested in something else.

"Sure, Sally. Maybe we could talk about it after work?"

"I'd love to, detective, but not today. I've got editors breathing down my neck."

Sanchez considered the image, smiled, then rose to get the evidence.

Lou had O'Dowd over to the condo and filled him in.

"That sonofabitch," O'Dowd said afterwards.

"So you'll help with the DNA?"

"Of course. I want to personally cuff the motherfucker."

"Thanks, Pat."

"No, Lou. You thank Sally for me. Tell her to write the hell out of it."

57. Interview Time

SALLY and Lou parked in front of Brandon's two-story 1970s home. There was a brick chimney. A cord of wood was stacked irregularly outside. A basketball hoop was nailed above the garage. The backyard was cheaply fenced. Sharon Brandon's beaten Subaru and Brandon's shiny new SUV were in the driveway. An old Civic was parked along the curb. Lou figured Brandon's son used it. Then there was the boat. Sally thought it looked big enough for Noah.

Sally and Lou walked up the steps, knocked on the door. A cute five-year-old girl in blond ponytails answered. Sally asked to speak to her father. She said "OK," and went inside. Two minutes later, nothing. Sally rang again.

It took another minute, but Brandon appeared. He was in a black shirt and blue jeans. He had an amber-colored drink in his hand.

"Time to talk, Steve," Sally said.

Brandon looked at Lou. He looked weary.

"I knew you were a loser, Elliott. But, Sally, you had class." He was slurring his words slightly. Lou noticed his eyes were bloodshot.

Sally stepped up, until she was just below Brandon.

"Tell us about Spilotro," she said.

Brandon took a small step back.

"You guys are crazy."

Sally took no notice. "You were one of a handful of people who knew where Spilotro was," she said. "After he died, you blocked your men from pressing Dicerno. Why?"

"That's an issue of how I run my team. I don't talk about that."

"Where were you when he was shot?" Sally asked.

"That's my business."

Lou had had enough. He came up to Brandon, grabbed his shirt and pushed him against a house wall. Brandon dropped his drink. The glass smashed on the flagstone.

"You fucked up, Steve," Lou hissed at him. "We have your vacation records. We know where you were."

"You know I can have you arrested for this, Elliott," he said.

Still holding him with one hand, Lou took out his iPhone with the other.

"Here, Steve. Make the call."

Lou released his grip and held the phone out for Brandon. Brandon did nothing. He suddenly seemed lost. Old even.

"You know the routine, Steve," Lou said. "You need an alibi. What is it?"

Brandon was taking short breaths. He didn't say a word.

"Last chance, Steve," said Lou. "Where were you last weekend?"

"Away," Brandon said.

"We know that. Where?"

"I had nothing to do with any of it," Brandon said. He looked cornered.

"OK, so you didn't," said Sally. "But where were you?"

Brandon shook his head, turned toward the door.

"The Dunhills, Brandon," Sally said. "How long have you been smoking them?"

Brandon took a step to go inside.

"Brandon," Sally asked, "what did you say to Dicerno at the Italian June Festival?"

That one seemed to get to Steve Brandon more than the others. He stopped.

"We have a picture of you two chatting," Sally fibbed. "What was that about?"

Brandon stayed still. He still had his back to them.

"How much money is he paying you, you sonofabitch?"

If rage had been the only issue, Sally could have torn Brandon apart right there. Brandon turned, his eyes vacant. Sally didn't understand why the man was not at least trying to defend himself.

"Don't do this, Sally," Brandon said. He was plaintive. Weak. Not at all like she knew him, like he had been at Red Rocks. Lou stayed in his face.

"Then tell us," he demanded.

"I can't," Brandon said and reached for the door. Lou didn't stop him. But just before entering his home, Brandon turned again. He looked at Lou.

"You were at the festival, Lou," he said. "Maybe you could help Sally."

There was a hint of a smile on his face. Then he disappeared inside.

"You were at the festival?" Sally asked after they got in the car.

"Yeah," Lou said, turning his head to the rear before pulling out.

"The festival is a society event, Lou. Why were you there?"

"It's not important," said Lou with a tinge of annoyance.

"Yes it is. The festival is key, dammit, Lou."

Lou said nothing.

"And why didn't you tell me?"

"There was nothing to tell."

"Did you see Dicerno?"

"Yes."

"Talk to him?"

"Briefly."

"Jesus, Lou. Who else was he talking with?"

"Couldn't tell. They wore masks."

"Jesus."

Sally crossed her arms over her chest and felt a knot begin to tighten in her stomach. Jesus.

58. Fresh Start

KATYA and Vitali followed Pam Boravick to King Soopers. Pam got out of her Escalade and went inside. Vitali parked his pickup nearby, got out, walked to the side of the Cadillac and appeared to drop something. When he knelt down to retrieve it, he took out an ice pick and punctured Pam's left rear tire. Then he followed Pam into the store.

Since Nikolai had disappeared Pam Boravick had been in what she could only describe to herself as hell. She had never been interested in politics, or the Russian Mafiya, or even what her husband did for a living. What she did care about was Nikolai. To her he was the center of her soul, a good man. Sure, she wondered why Nikolai spent weeks on end in the Caribbean. But so did a million other wives, she believed. The point was this: Nikolai had called home every night he was away, saying sweet things to her and always gentle things to the kids. He never complained. He was always there. Always did his best. But now he was gone. Simply vanished. Despite what the government was telling her she was sure he was dead and her life had been one long torment ever since,

Pam Boravick had been a Cherry Creek High School pom-pom girl, daughter of a Realtor, a swimmer who had taken third in a district swimming meet. She had gone to Denver University and majored in psychology. She met Nikolai when she was 21. He was so handsome and self-assured. They fitted together, and soon settled in together.

All Pam ever really wanted was to be a great mom. She had stumbled now and then, she knew, but really, no more than others. The kids had a large wonderful home in Denver, with a backyard Jungle Gym, a pool and toys that when stacked end-to-end could have rounded the moon. Sure, Pam had wanted more of Nikolai. She had wanted him to tell his boss that enough was enough.

Take a hike. But Nikolai would never have done that. He needed the income – not for himself but for his family.

What Pam remembered most were the moments after they made love, when both were drained, quiet, and without pretense. She could talk to Nikolai then about anything that came into her mind – her mother, her exercise class, the situation with Iran. And Nikolai would just lie back and run his hand through her hair, listening, and smiling, and agreeing. He would sometimes kiss her just above her eyes. She never knew anyone who had done that. It was his special signature just for her. Then all this nightmare thing had happened.

They came to her door, rushed in, and destroyed everything. Everything. Nikolai had vanished and the kids had fallen apart.

Like almost everyone facing an absolute loss Pam Boravick tried at times to pretend that it had all been a dream. That she would one day wake up. But she never did. She didn't understand why the government had put out a phony story that Russians had done it, members of Ivanov's gang. Who were they kidding? Pam had a Polaroid of the killer in her mind. The man she saw – the man who shot her – had a southern accent. He was not Russian. He didn't look it, didn't act it, didn't sound like it. He was as American as she.

She had insisted on a funeral, even though Nikolai's body had never been found and the U.S. government would not admit he was dead. The government was saying he might be in South America. No way, Pam believed. Nikolai would never have left her like that. A few close friends showed up in the mortuary chapel. There was the scent of incense and formaldehyde. A CD by Judy Collins played Both Sides Now.

After that, Pam determined to mask it all. Get the kids settled again, go on with life, look forward. She tried to immerse herself in routine things: do the laundry, read a book, shop. She wanted to survive. She was thirty-two years old and still trim.

Men liked her, she knew. Maybe one day, she told herself, she could get over Nikolai. Find someone new. Start again. Maybe.

241

Lou and Sally drove home from Brandon's house in silence. Sally was upset at Lou for not telling her about the festival. What had he been thinking? What new quirk was this? She wondered. But the more important thing, she told herself, was to stay focused.

She recalled how her father had told her about a fighter who, after he had a man on the ropes, backed off. The nearly beaten fighter then rallied and won. In fact, he had more than won. He had hit his opponent so hard about the head the man suffered brain damage and later died. Never relent, her father had said. Never be a sucker.

Sally had no intention of relenting, of letting Brandon off the ropes. To her, Steve Brandon was the face of evil. Focusing again, she soon forgot Lou's odd behavior.

Pam, dressed in blue jeans and a yellow v-neck sweater, took her cart through the store like everyone else. No one knew her loss, just as she didn't know their life stories. Shopping was an equalizer. Pam gathered corn, milk, trail mix and rib-eye steaks. She was relaxed. She rounded a corner and squeezed the melons, trying to find the ripe ones. A well-built young man with an innocent face came up beside her.

"The ones in the next bin are probably better, ma'am," he said. He had a baseball cap on backwards and a Colorado Avalanche t-shirt. He shuffled his feet and appeared harmless.

"At least that's what my wife tells me," he said. He looked embarrassed. Pam liked him straight away.

Finishing her shopping, she walked back to the Escalade, popped open the rear gate and deposited the groceries. The Escalade was listing. Pam looked down and discovered the flat tire. The young man from inside King Soopers, walked by.

"Ma'am," Vitali said, "Looks like you have a problem."

"Just my luck," said Pam.

"Kids around here have been vandalizing cars, ma'am," Vitali said. "Sorry."

Pam pushed herself up.

"I'll call Triple A," she said.

"That could take all day," Vitali said. "I've got a friend who owns a service station on Leetsdale. Let me take off your flat. We can get it fixed in no time."

Pam noticed his smile. What a charmer.

"Well...," said Pam.

"Well nothing," Vitali said. "It won't take long. I'll get the jack."

Vitali had the tire off in sixty seconds. He threw it into the bed of the extended cab pickup he had rented. He opened the front passenger door.

"Hop on in," Vitali said.

Pam hesitated for a moment and then got in. Vitali smiled. Such a friendly face, Pam thought.

Vitali headed down Leetsdale Drive, passing several service stations along the way. Pam began to get concerned.

"Where's the station?" Pam asked with a nervous laugh.

Vitali said nothing, just reached over and turned the stereo up high. Reba McEntire was singing about being five hundred miles from her home. At the corner of Leetsdale and Colorado Boulevard Vitali turned north. Pam knew there were no service stations in that direction and no tire shops. Her heart began to drum.

"Where are we going?" she demanded.

Vitali stayed mute. At a stoplight Pam tried to open the door to get out. But the handle was missing. She was trapped.

She began to scream and beat on the window. Katya sat up from the back seat and placed a gun to Pam's temple.

"No more noise and no more questions," she said coldly.

Pam was suddenly too afraid to scream but Katya taped Pam's mouth shut anyway.

In the house near Last Chance, Dr. Tsplyev sat in a rocking chair humming English nursery tunes to his rat. Raspy associated the tunes with meals:

"Mary had a little lamb, little lamb, little lamb. Mary had a little lamb. Her fleece was white as snow," crooned Tsplyev.

The rat squirmed. A dot of foam dropped from its lips. It was really hungry now.

"Ah, there you are," said Dr. Tsplyev as Vitali pulled up to the house and Pam's captors led her in.

Inside the house Dr. Tsplyev turned to Pam and patted the sofa. Apart from the worn leatherette sofa the room was empty but for two wooden chairs. In the corner was some object covered in a red sheet.

"Come here, Pam, sit."

It was not a request. Pam was frozen, and not just because this lanky pale man who looked like the grim reaper knew her name.

"Come now. Come, come," Dr. Tsplyev repeated.

Vitali pushed Pam forward. Pam quivered as she sat next to Dr. Tsplyev.

"I want to introduce you to a friend," said Dr. Tsplyev.

"Katya, could you bring Raspy over here?"

Katya lifted the red sheet and slowly brought the cage to Dr. Tsplyev. Dr. Tsplyev smiled warmly as he lifted the rat from the cage by its tail. Raspy's eyes darted around him, then settled on Pam's. Pam had feared rats all of her life. Nothing was worse, not even snakes. The rat was salivating as it watched her. It seemed eager for something. The fear Pam now felt was a hundred times greater than the fear she had felt in Denver.

"This is my friend Raspy," Dr. Tsplyev said holding the rat close to Pam. Raspy bared his teeth and hissed. Pam began shaking uncontrollably.

"Unfortunately Raspy has no manners," Dr. Tsplyev said. "He makes his desires very plain. He is saying he wants you. And what he wants to do to you, Pam, is this...."

Dr. Tsplyev explained in vivid detail. Pam vomited less than halfway through the description. Dr. Tsplyev took out a handkerchief and handed it to her.

"However," he said, "It doesn't have to come to that."

Half fainting Pam wiped the mess from her chin and sobbed: "No, please God, no."

"I have some questions," Tsplyev said. "And I believe you have the answers. You give me the truth, and we'll let Raspy have his regular meal. You can return to Denver."

Pam nodded her head violently to make it clear she understood. Her shivering lessened.

"But if you lie, Pam, things could turn very unpleasant." Dr. Tsplyev said it like a father gently chiding a child.

Dr. Tsplyev did not consider himself a particularly cruel man, only an efficient interrogator. He suspected that Pam was already broken, and that she would do anything to avoid the rat. She wasn't, after all, a trained CIA operative.

"Now, Pam. Let's begin that day you got shot. Who was it that shot you, what was he like?"

Within half an hour Dr. Tsplyev had all his answers. Pam told him everything she knew. The team that killed Mika and took Nikolai consisted of six men and a woman. The leader was American. Pam didn't know why all the leaks out of Washington pointed towards a Russian squad. Dr. Tsplyev didn't push. When he was confident he had the truth he stopped.

"Thank you, Pam," he said. "You have been very helpful."

"Can they take me back to Denver now?" asked Pam.

"Of course," said the doctor.

Pam felt so relieved she almost hugged Dr. Tsplyev. She got to her feet and looked at the door that would lead to freedom. The feeling of relief was so great she did not hear Katya come up behind her, nor sense the gun being raised to her head.

Immediately after burying Pam's body, Katya and Vitali headed back to Denver.

Dr. Tsplyev knew Ivanov would not be happy to learn that the U.S. government was behind the attack, that it had thrown out the rulebook. But he knew Ivanov would strike back. But where? Against whom? Dr. Tsplyev didn't know. It was not his job to know.

His job was to stay in Last Chance and prepare for Sally Will.

59. Race Relations

DIMITRI Ivanov sat in his great room with a fire roaring. There was a foot of snow outside, but inside it was warm. The brandy he sipped helped keep it that way. He indulged in a Cuban cigar.

Several American newspapers lay around the floor. He had had them translated into Russian so he could read a most fantastic story. The Italian mob had gotten its hands on an amazing and resourceful killer, someone who had assassinated two star witnesses in the vaunted U.S. Witness Protection Program. The program was now in disarray and several of his Russian confederates from Brighton Beach had already been freed from jail because witnesses were suffering sudden-onset amnesia.

He read and reread the story about the attack plane and the killer wasps. He told himself that he wouldn't have thought of that in a million years. This killer was a genius.

He read, too, about the man who most benefited from the hit on Tony Nails: Vito Borelli, head of something called the Chicago Outfit. The word "Outfit" had no exact parallel in Russian but the translator had gotten the point across. Borelli was a crime boss, just like him.

Ivanov smiled and picked up an encrypted email. It was from Katya:

"Dear Mr. Ivanov – Mrs. Boravick certain the hit team American. The stories put out in Washington meant to confuse you and the American public. Mrs. Boravick disposed of. Waiting for word on Sally Will.

"Your devoted servant,

"Katya."

Ivanov called for Gregory. He handed him a glass of brandy. The two drank in Russian fashion: one long, continuous swallow until all the liquor was gone. Then Ivanov told Gregory he was to go to Chicago and deliver a message to Vito Borelli and the Outfit. Ivanov was growing convinced he might soon have a need for a very special killer for a very special mission. It was one he hoped to avoid. But he had to make plans nevertheless.

Linda Orvez hopped off the presidential chopper and headed to the private rooms at Camp David. The First Lady was away at a World Hunger fundraiser in New York.

"Linda, so glad you could make it," Naslund said more than warmly.

"Mr. President, so nice of you to ask me." She winked at the President of the United States.

They embraced, and then kissed. It was a kiss that hid no secrets.

"Mm yes, Linda," the president said, pulling away at last and becoming suddenly matter-of-fact. "But business first."

"Larry, I...," Orvez began, but her protest tailed off.

They sat down on a western style couch made out of pine and wool.

"Linda, just when we make progress against one problem – Ivanov and his gang – something else hits us. You helped me with Ivanov. Got hold of two billion dollars of his money. Exceptional."

Orvez reached over and touched the president's hand: "So what's the problem?"

"The problem is the Witness Protection Program," said Naslund unmoved. "If we can't stop the leak in the program, I could be a one-termer. And so will you. I told Roger to fix this. But sometimes he is not as aggressive as I would like."

"Mr. President," Orvez said, moving closer. "You know I'll do whatever is necessary."

The president smiled. He was pleased. He always knew he could rely on Orvez. He took Orvez's hand and led her further into the house.

Interpol picked up a new face traveling from Moscow to Frankfurt. The man had a fresh passport and an apparently solid cover story. Gregory Serov said he was traveling from Russia to Miami via Frankfurt and New York for a symposium on the Latin American textile industry. Unfortunately for him, his documents also said he worked for a St. Petersburg company called Simmex LLC. Only days before, the FBI had sent out bulletins that Simmex LLC was an Ivanov front. When the computer brought up the Simmex LLC name, it was in orange – elevated alert. Interpol took Serov's photo.

Serov acquired an FBI tail before he left Frankfurt. To FBI agent David Cane the mission was routine: to make sure the subject went to where he said he was going. He was to land in New York and catch a Delta flight to Miami. Easy one, Cane thought.

At Langley a CIA analyst caught the problem right after the Russian's Interpol picture was emailed through. The man in the picture was not a low-level Simmex LLC flunky, Gregory Serov was Ivanov's second-in-command.

"Abby," the analyst said on a secure line, "Could you patch me through to the director's office?"

"I could but it would do you no good. She's not there."

"Can you patch me through to wherever she is then?" the analyst said testily.

"She's at Camp David, Morris. And has a 'Do not disturb' sign on the door knob."

Morris had heard the rumors just like everyone else.

"Even so, I think we should knock."

"Morris, this better be good."

"This better be good," an angry director of Central Intelligence almost snarled on the phone when someone finally had the balls to disturb her. Hell hath rather less fury than a frustrated Linda Orvez.

"Director, Gregory Serov, number two in Ivanov's operation, has entered the United States. This man knows all Ivanov's secrets. We think Ivanov wouldn't have risked sending him here unless there was something big afoot."

"Where is he now?" Orvez asked, cooling down rapidly.

"From what we know, Director, he should still be at Kennedy International."

"Are we there?"

"No. But an FBI man is."

"Are we in contact with him?"

"No."

"Dig up that shrimp Hamilton. Get him on the line. And call Ramson. Now."

Ramson's voice came on a moment later: "Director."

"Charles, we've got another Russian roaming the land, this one far more important than the last. Do you think you can get Team Dog Shit on it right away?"

"Of course."

"The analyst will fill you in. And Charles, no fuckups."

As Serov walked down the Kennedy concourse carrying his hand luggage, agent Cane was close behind. Serov had spotted him much earlier. He seemed to Serov like a pleasant enough American, in his 50s and coasting toward a Florida retirement. No problem. Except the man had no hand luggage. Serov ducked into a restroom. Cane ambled in behind him. Serov went into a stall, locked the door and opened up his bag. Two minutes later a man emerged four stalls further along looking nothing like Serov and left.

Agent Cane suspected nothing at first. He settled in front of a urinal and pretended to pee. But after five minutes Cane became concerned. A minute later he was down on all fours looking under the stalls. No legs. Shit. The mystery man had given him the slip.

He was just about to shoot out of the restroom in search when his scrambled phone rang. It was Director Hamilton himself. Cane had never spoken to the director, never imagined that he would. He felt a sudden pain in his lower back, the kind his chiropractor said came from stress.

"Are you on your mark?" Hamilton asked.

"Ah, no sir. Not right this minute."

"Well where is he?"

"He seems to have disappeared, sir."

"What!"

"He was in a stall in a restroom. And then he wasn't."

Agent Cane knew it sounded feeble.

"Did anyone else leave a stall while you were there?"

"Yeah, but it wasn't him." Agent Cane was already having doubts.

The director let out a long exasperated breath.

"Are you dead certain?"

"I think." The penny was dropping.

"How many others left the restroom?"

Cane suddenly knew he had screwed up, big time. He couldn't say a word. To himself he said: Fuck. Hamilton broke the silence.

"OK, agent Cane, do your best to find him. And then call this number."

The number was Team Blue's.

Ramson scrambled. There was no doubt that Ivanov's top man visiting the United States was bad news. Ramson called Anne Burgess and the other Team Blue members and ordered them to get to Langley, pronto. Then Ramson called the NYPD's anti-terror team. Soon, its agents were all over Kennedy.

Cane hoped that Serov would show up at the connecting Delta gate, that his slipping out of the restroom was some sort of aberration. He wanted badly to get off the director's shit list, knowing that he had just advanced to its top. Cane and his wife were already talking Florida. All he had to do was this stupid assignment of tailing low-level bad guys. Now this.

First he went back into the restroom. The stall door where he had seen his mark go in was still locked. Ignoring onlookers, he hauled himself up to look over the partition. Nobody. All he could see was a bag sitting on the toilet tank and some clothes lying untidily on top. But they were not the clothes the man was wearing when he went in. Fuck and double fuck, he said to himself. What's he done? He's changed his disguise but how and to what?

Sprinting out of the restroom, agent Cane headed for the Delta gate. When he rounded the corner near the gate he saw a man in the clothes Serov had been wearing surrounded by black-uniformed NYPD SWAT officers wearing helmets and toting machine guns.

Thank God they got him, Cane thought with relief. His retirement plans could proceed unhindered. When he got up to the officers, the man, cuffed and bruised, turned to face him. But it wasn't Gregory Serov.

"Hold it," Cane said to the lieutenant heading the operation, showing him his FBI card. "Who is this man?"

"Gregory Serov," the lieutenant said. He showed Cane Serov's ticket and passport. Cane looked from the documents to the suspect and then back to the documents again.

"This is not right," Cane said. "This man is not Serov. There must have been a switch."

Agent Cane frantically called headquarters and got Hamilton.
"A switch?"

"Looks that way, Director."

"You're not sure?"

"I'm sure", Cane said, not feeling at all sure. He had really screwed up this time.

"Agent Cane, listen," Hamilton finally said. "We need to be absolutely sure. Find a place RIGHT NOW where you can receive secure email. We'll get you Serov's picture."

"Roger that," was all Agent Cane could utter.

The email arrived minutes later at a United Airlines computer. It confirmed what Cane already knew. The man arrested was not Gregory Serov. Cane had color copies made and soon the New York officers blanketed Kennedy Airport with copies, asking ticket agents if they had seen Serov. No one had seen anyone remotely resembling Serov's photo.

Cane filled Hamilton in. There wasn't anything left to do, Cane said. Serov had escaped. Hamilton was not convinced. He told Cane to go back over the entire terminal again.

"But, Director, the New York team says it's no use. The guy left in a disguise. They are standing down."

"Listen, Agent Cane" – the emphasis was on the word "agent" – "you personally do this or I will have your ass fired for dereliction of duty. Do you understand?"

"Yes sir," said Agent Cane. Deflated by the certainty that his was now an impossible task, he went through the airport, but didn't hurry. He was calculating how he could survive if Director Hamilton carried through with his threat. Finding Serov now, he was certain, was a hapless task.

But an hour later Cane happened upon a United Airlines employee – an art student working for her tuition – who said she had seen a man who looked a bit like the photo, except the man she saw had a goatee beard and wasn't balding. But he did have an accent and she was certain it was Russian. He had checked in for a flight to Indianapolis.

Cane checked the flight manifest. The man the employee said she had seen was named Felix Mueller. It wasn't much, Cane feared, but it was something. He called the director.

Hamilton alerted the Indianapolis field office and agents there went Code 10 – sirens and lights – to the airport. The director had a rush job of Serov's picture emailed to Indy – composed of Serov's photo with Bureau artists adding a goatee and bushy black hair.

The problem was that by the time the Indianapolis agents got to the airport with the new rendition, Gregory Serov's plane had been on the ground for 30 minutes. Gregory Serov, in his new disguise and using a Felix Mueller ID, had rented a car at the airport and already left for Chicago before the FBI agents arrived.

Eventually, the FBI agents who smothered the airport found an Avis agent who was almost certain that the sketch depicted a man she had rented a car to. The customer's name was Felix Mueller.

Vito Borelli was in Club Classico on Lake Shore Drive, sipping a scotch and talking to the boys. The Club was new to Chicago, catering mostly to new money, adventurous women and crooks. Borelli's kind of place. He had signed up the day before because he needed a place too new for the feds to have bugged yet. There was to be a meeting. An important one.

It was long before the nightclub would open, so Borelli and his crew had the run of the place. Borelli's stock had rallied considerably since Tony Nails' death. That was cause alone for celebration. Borelli knew the feds would be watching every move he made, but nothing would come of that. No one could connect him to the wasp man. Hell, he couldn't even do it.

In a car outside the club sat two federal agents watching. They had the routine task of following Borelli. After a while an unknown man drove up to the Club Classico, gave a valet his keys, and headed in. One agent made a note of the car, the other took photos of the man. Otherwise, they did nothing. All they knew was some stranger was in the same building as Borelli. Big deal. That list was growing. The agents wished that Club Classico was bugged, but it hadn't happened yet.

Borelli greeted Serov with a hug, kissed his cheek, handed him a glass of scotch and led him to a secluded room furnished like a study. It was comfortable enough with a few bits of office equipment. They were now alone.

Borelli began to talk about how fine it was that the Russians and Italians were getting along so well when Serov put his finger to his lips to signal silence. Borelli nodded. He was a bit offended at the brusqueness but let it pass.

Both men sat down on facing chairs. Serov, looking about with his little piggy eyes, loosened his tie and then took out a photo. He studied it for a moment, seemingly uncertain. Then, without a word, he slowly handed it over.

Borelli looked at the photo and his mouth opened. He glanced up at Serov and then down at the photo again, shaking his head.

Serov took out a notebook and pen, scribbled something and

handed it to Borelli. The note said: "$300,000,000. For the use of wasp man."

There was a long pause. Borelli broke out in a cold sweat. He, too, loosened his tie. It was suddenly hard to breathe.

Serov whispered: "Half now, half later."

Borelli's hand shook as he put down his scotch. Gregory Serov wrote on another piece of paper: "No middlemen."

No middlemen. Borelli thought that was a laugh. The only way he could take the contract was through Danny Dicerno. Might as well spell that out, he thought. No choice.

He whispered, "There has to be one middleman."

Serov absorbed the information and understood. Borelli was dealing with the assassin through a cutout. Not a problem. Serov took out another piece of paper and wrote: "No middlemen means no surviving middlemen. We can help you there. We have a team."

Borelli smiled and nodded. That was his solution as well. Only Borelli and the button man would know anything. And the button man – the killing genius – would not know who hired him. Even if the Bureau caught him, all he could give them was Dicerno. Perfect. Danny Dicerno was history.

Serov wrote out the word: "Deal?"

Borelli gave one, almost imperceptible, nod. Deal. The two men shook hands.

Serov wrote out the name of a bank in Antigua, an account number and a code word. One hundred fifty million dollars was already in the bank. Ivanov was sure Borelli would not rip him off because if he did even Borelli's grandchildren would pay the price. Borelli knew that as well as anyone.

Borelli took one last look at the photo. Then going over to a shredder he shredded the picture of Lawrence Naslund, President of the United States of America.

When no more trace turned up of Gregory Serov, Ramson finally issued an all-points bulletin. It was a risky move. Word could get out. The media might get involved.

Forty minutes after Serov left Club Classico, the FBI crew tailing Borelli received the APB. The description of Gregory Serov matched closely that of Borelli's visitor. The agents called headquarters. A clerk there took his time in notifying some new outfit called Team Blue. Team Blue, in turn, asked the agents to upload their photos.

By then, Serov had picked up a new car and was heading for Kansas City, the first step on his way back to Moscow.

60. Cave Men

VINNIE Terranova had told Vito Borelli about the magical caves at Glenwood Springs. Borelli was fascinated, thinking it would be just the place for a quick meeting. He punched quarters into a pay phone and called Jimmy Fresno.

"Jimmy, this is a friend of yours."

"A friend of mine?"

Was this guy stupid? Borelli thought.

"Yes, Jimmy. Your friend."

"Oh, OK."

"Look, Jimmy. Don't think. Listen."

There was silence on the other end. Jimmy was listening.

"Jimmy, I want you to tell your boss to meet me at that special place at 8 p.m."

"Well, he's plenty busy."

"Jimmy, tell him Vito wants it."

"OK."

Borelli doubted this was getting through. He decided to be more direct.

"You remember Vinnie?"

"Yeah, sure." Suddenly Jimmy's radar was engaged.

"Tell your boss it should be just like before."

"Like before."

"Yes, tell him that."

He was hoping Jimmy Fresno would do as he was told. There was no way he was going to be more explicit on the phone.

Borelli left Club Classico and ordered a driver to take him to a regional airport west of the city. He boarded a private plane and flew directly to Aspen. From Aspen he rented a car and drove himself to Glenwood Springs. He was alone. No middlemen. No witnesses.

"FUCK!" roared Ramson when he saw the photos. He recalled the recent headlines about the wasp man and Borelli. Now this. The president's two major concerns – the witness programs and the Russians – had maybe just merged. Did this mean the Russians had been involved in the Tony Nails attack? Or did it mean the Russians needed Borelli's hitman? If so, who might be the target? Ramson shuddered.

He called Chicago's FBI SAC, learning that agents had followed Borelli to a regional airport where he boarded a plane. The pilot did not file a flight plan.

"Call the FAA," Ramson ordered Team Blue. "We need a fix on that plane."

It took only moments for Ramson to get the bad news. The transponder on Borelli's plane had been shut off. All that the flight controllers knew was that the plane had headed west.

Ramson paced. Anne Burgess looked on. She loved to see this man riled up. It was entertaining. Finally, Ramson fathered an idea.

"Send every airport in that direction Borelli's photo. We need to know where he's going. ASAP!" shouted Ramson.

They were in a small room. He didn't need to shout, thought Anne. But that was Ramson's way. He was a classic type A, she thought. Would have a heart attack at 50.

"How can we do that?" Anne asked.

More pacing.

"There's just too much area, too many airports," Ramson shrugged.

"Charles, maybe we could limit the search."

"I'm listening, Anne."

"The first protected witness killing involved some mobster in Colorado. That's probably where the killer is. Two plus two. Why not just stick with Colorado?"

"Correct, right," said Ramson.

He issued orders. Officers throughout Colorado were sent Borelli's photo. They were asked to check local airports for the

Chicago plane. Ramson and Team Blue then sat back and waited for the phone to ring. Ramson paced. His eye twitched.

An hour and a half later, a call came in. A sleepy clerk at Aspen's airport recalled that a man who looked "one hell of a lot" like Borelli had landed there.

Jimmy Fresno had got the message right. Dicerno pulled into the parking lot near the caves fifteen minutes earlier than agreed. He wanted to be first, show he was running his home turf. He was sure he had managed to evade his tail. He had hidden in the trunk of Jimmy Fresno's PT Cruiser and, only when it was clear no one had followed, did he get out. Then he drove a Taurus to Glenwood Springs.

Dicerno was feeling particularly good. For the second time, Chicago was coming to him. He would get a big suitcase full of money from Vinnie Terranova. Bringing the Witness Protection Program to its knees was a momentous achievement, bigger than anything he had ever imagined. He was proud. It put his gang back on the map.

The girl at the counter smiled as he approached. But as he pulled out his wallet she held up her hand.

"Sir," she said, "the other gentleman already got that. Didn't you see the 'closed' sign out front?"

What the hell? Dicerno thought. He wondered if this was a set up. Then quickly decided it wasn't. If they were going to kill him they would have killed the girl first. He relaxed. The hit on Tony Nails had established his position, he told himself. Vinnie had arrived early to meet The Man. Dicerno undressed, wrapped on a towel and headed down.

Vinnie wasn't in the customary place. Dicerno didn't like that. Why the change? He began to have dark thoughts. Had the girl been paid off? Was she one of them? He took a few steps before stopping. Was he now a witness to be eliminated? Dead meat? He weighed the risks. He had assumed Vinnie was bringing the other half of the money he was owed, and Dicerno didn't want to give that up. Then he thought: If I'm wrong, I'm dead. After a couple of yards Dicerno decided he had had enough. Vinnie would understand. You just didn't change protocol like this. He should have been where he had always been. It was his fault that this deal didn't go down. Dicerno turned to walk out.

"Danny, would you get your fat ass in here," a voice called out. "Getting boiled like a fuckin' lobster ain't my idea of a pleasant evening."

Dicerno knew the voice was not Terranova's. He looked down an alcove he had never seen before. He could see plump white legs but nothing above the man's ample belly. The rest was in the shadows. Dicerno felt the tingling down his arms and back as adrenaline said hello. But he was too afraid to move.

Finally, Borelli said, "Danny, it's Vito Borelli. Come here."

Dicerno's legs almost gave way. Borelli rose and his face came into view. Dicerno approached slowly. Borelli extended his hand. The two shook.

"You had me guessing there for a moment," Danny said, faking a light-heartedness he didn't feel.

He looked for a silver suitcase, but there wasn't one. The two sat down and Dicerno showed Borelli how to cool down with cold water from a hose. Borelli was relieved. He relaxed. So did Dicerno.

"Danny," said Borelli, "you really did me a fuckin' favor. I owe you."

Dicerno cleared his throat. He wanted to be appreciative, but he also didn't want to appear a fool. He said the first thing that popped into his head:

"Yeah, I believe you owe me two million dollars."

Borelli laughed. "That I do. I almost forgot."

Dicerno thought: How could you almost forget two million dollars?

"Danny," Borelli continued, "we have another project for your man, and the sum we will pay can't be carried in any suitcase. We got an account set up for you in Antigua. I'll send the two million there today. But if you agree to take the new hit that account will grow."

Dicerno was interested. "Grow how much?"

"Danny, slow down," said Borelli. "It will take balls as big as Jupiter to carry out this hit."

Dicerno tried to remember how big Jupiter was. For a moment he pictured the guy in the funny mask with planet-sized balls.

"Well?" Borelli interrupted Dicerno's daydream.

"My man did Tony Nails," said Dicerno. "He can do anything."

"Fine, Danny. I want your man to do the president."

Deadpan. Kill the president. Go to a movie.

"Da fuck..." Dicerno's heart almost stopped. "Mr. Borelli?"

"Please Danny. Call me Vito."

"Mr. Borelli." Long pause, then: "Maybe the man can do it, but maybe he can't. It is the president."

He wanted to ask why the president but knew that was a question you never ask, especially of someone like Borelli.

"Understood. Of course. But we want him to try. We want him to try real hard."

"I don't think..."

"Dicerno," Borelli interrupted. "We want you to try. Understood?"

Dicerno did. He knew he had no choice.

"It will be worth your effort," Borelli smiled. "You take the contract, that Antigua account grows by fifty million. Right away. And another fifty million after. You don't take it, I guess the money goes elsewhere."

And that means I go elsewhere too, thought Dicerno.

"OK, sure. My man will do his best," Dicerno said suddenly. It was a deal.

"Yes, Danny," he said. "That's all we expect. His best."

Borelli stood, then looked down at Dicerno: "You're taking precautions, aren't you? You don't actually meet with this guy in person, do you?"

"Of course not," Dicerno said. "We have a system."

"That's good," said Borelli. "How does it work?"

Dicerno was surprised to be asked and didn't particularly want to answer. But this was the head of the Outfit, a man who had just given him fifty million dollars. Dicerno decided this was some sort of test that he better not fail. So he told Borelli about the yellow rose and the Westword box.

"That's great. That's perfect," said Borelli.

Borelli handed Dicerno a damp piece of paper. Dicerno looked puzzled.

"It's the account number, Danny," Borelli said. "For the bank. Antigua. Better not lose it!"

Dicerno smiled. "Sure," he said. The two men shook hands.

"I'll leave first," said Borelli.

When Dicerno got to the dressing room five minutes later the Chicago boss had gone. Back in his car, Dicerno wondered what he had gotten himself into. He liked the sound of fifty million bucks, just as he liked the sound of a hundred million if Mr. Wood actually succeeded. But killing the president was nuts. Dicerno even quite liked the guy. Then he reminded himself of his choices: None.

Agents took Borelli's picture to every public place in Pitkin County. No one had seen Borelli or his rented Land Cruiser. The next logical place to look was Glenwood Springs. An agent got to the caves just as the girl there was closing up.

"Sure," she said. "I seen the guy. Let me tell you there's something weird going on. He was here to meet with another guy. Perverts, I think. That's why you're after them, right?"

"Can you describe the other guy?" an agent asked. She did.

61. Scoop Time

AN UNEXPECTED Indian summer had hit Denver, the temperature hovering near 73 degrees. Every bit of snow from a few days before had gone, the sun was warm and some shorts and t-shirts made an appearance at the Civic Center Park between the Capitol and the City and County Building. Sally was heading to the C&C Building to check over search warrants. Maybe there was something there on Dicerno. Sally didn't know.

Just as she was about to cross Bannock Street she spotted Steve Brandon and Brad Johnson on the steps. They were facing each other and Brandon appeared upset. Then another man appeared at the top of the steps and both Johnson and Brandon stopped their argument and turned to look. Sally thought she recognized him but couldn't put it together at first. Then she did. It was Stan Markson, the Angels' lawyer.

At 11:30 p.m., after a meaningless correspondents' dinner that Lou had found an excuse to skip, Sally took a detour on her way home. She shot her Miata through two yellow lights and slowed as she approached the employee parking lot of the Denver Post. There were only a few vehicles around, probably belonging to the late-night copy editors and police reporters. But there was one vehicle that didn't fit. Brad Johnson's. There was only one reason for Brad to be there at that hour. He was working on something very, very hot.

Sally thought briefly about getting out and cutting Brad's tires.

About the same time Danny Dicerno sent word to Capricio's to have a yellow rose put in a vase behind a certain drape.

Linda Orvez slipped into the Oval Office via a hallway that another, younger, woman once made famous.

"Linda, you look your radiant best," Lawrence Naslund said

beaming, putting down his reading glasses and rising to embrace her. She held the embrace, but not quite with her usual enthusiasm.

"What's wrong?" he asked.

"Mr. President," Orvez said, sweeping back her hair. "The Russia problem and the witness protection problem have dovetailed."

The president blinked a couple times and frowned.

"Dovetailed? I don't understand."

Orvez took both his hands, said: "Sir, you should sit for this."

The president took his hands away and remained standing.

"Ivanov sent his top man, Gregory Serov, here Tuesday to meet with Vito Borelli. We believe Borelli may have then met with Danny Dicerno."

The president walked towards the grenade-proof windows of the Oval Office.

"Did we manage to arrest the Russian?"

"No, sir. He slipped in and out again like lightning. He's gone. If the FBI had been on its game we would have gotten him. They had a physical tail from Frankfurt but they lost him when he slipped out of a john at JFK."

"And then?"

"He slipped through their hands in Chicago and Aspen.

So you're telling me Hamilton is an incompetent," said the president harshly.

"Well, Larry, what do you expect from a state college grad from North Dakota?" Linda Orvez smiled in silent triumph.

The president merely grunted. Then: "So what does this mean?"

"My analysts are saying it could involve the killer, the guy we're calling Wasp Man."

"Who might this killer – this Wasp Man – be after next?"

Orvez knew the answer but didn't say.

"Mr. President," she said. "There's one more thing to consider."

"Linda?"

"Immediately after Gregory Serov returned to Moscow Ivanov had him killed."

Now the president knew. There was only one reason to get rid of a witness of Serov's stature.

"Jesus Christ," the president said. "They're after me."

"I'm sorry, Larry."

The president sat down at his desk and put his head in his hands. Orvez scarcely dared even breathe. Then Naslund looked up.

"No, Linda. Don't be sorry," he said. "We are the United States of America. Ivanov will be the one who will be sorry. Get that team of yours ready."

"Sir?"

The president got up and went to the window.

"Linda, get Team Blue packed. You're sending them to Moscow."

"Larry, what about Putin?"

"Putin will understand. He'll even thank me."

The president thought for a moment before adding grimly: "After it's done."

When she looked at the Post in the morning, Sally's heart nearly stopped. The screaming front-page headline read: "Borelli, Dicerno Linked." It was a Brad Johnson piece quoting police sources. They said that Vinnie Terranova had come to Colorado to meet Danny Dicerno weeks before the wasp attack. Police did not know where the two had met but underworld sources said it was unlikely it happened in the city. Authorities believed the meeting was held to arrange the killing of Tony Nails. Terranova, Brad had reported, had been subpoenaed before a federal grand jury sitting in Denver.

"Goddammit," cursed Sally, throwing the paper down.

The phone rang. It was Mel Campbell. He had seen the story too, and he wasn't happy.

"Sally, this Johnson story hurts. It's the Chicago connection. Where's your story?"

Sally protested that the Johnson scoop only amounted to blatant speculation and nothing more.

"The cops have no evidence," she said.

"Sally, there are parts here that are not speculation. Terranova coming to Colorado isn't speculation. And that a grand jury has been impaneled to hear evidence is news to me."

"OK, Mel. It's news to me, too."

"What are we going to do?"

"What I'm going to do, Mel, is give you a real story with real facts."

"You got something in mind?"

"Yes."

"You going to keep me guessing?"

"Yes."

"When will I see something?"

"Tonight."

"Wonderful."

Sally poured herself a glass of Chablis and sat down at the laptop. She was going to write the Steve Brandon story, and she knew just how to do it. It wouldn't be an indictment, something in black and white, with a bill of particulars written out at the top. That's how a traditional investigative piece was done. Sally's piece would not be traditional. Her case was circumstantial. That did not mean it was weak. Fingerprints were circumstantial. But to make the case, Sally needed space. Needed chronology. Needed context. She knew Mel would give her that.

Sally began the story in the only way she could – on a dark night on the stage at Red Rocks. It was in the first person, hardly ever used in investigative pieces. But it was perfect for this one. She was part of the story.

She wrote about finding the Dunhill. About Brandon coming up behind her. About Lou, "an investigator and close personal friend," getting the drop on Brandon. The words were haunting. The reader would feel the tension, Sally was sure. Would get involved.

"I thought that in a second I would be dead. I said a prayer. I waited," Sally wrote.

Then Sally shifted to a more conventional voice and presented accounts of the various homicides, starting with Big Bow, then Palermo, then Spilotro, and finally Tony Nails. She told of the other Dunhills, those found at murder scenes. Like the one at Red Rocks they were all filterless. The same man.

For the Felipe Spilotro killing, Sally reported that Brandon was one of only five people in the universe who knew where he lived. She wrote about Brandon's absence for the days leading up to his killing, and about Brandon's refusal to offer an alibi.

Lack of alibi also featured in the Tony Nails killing. Brandon could not explain where he had been when Tony was killed. But sources, she reported, said he had been away.

Sally also had high-ranking sources in the Denver police department who said that Brandon had ordered them off promising leads in the Dicerno investigation. Those same sources also said that the lieutenant had taken an interest in the Big Bow killing, even though that happened in Commerce City, outside his beat.

And there were issues over Steve Brandon's finances. He was in a hole. Sally had asked an accountant to look at the records she had gathered. The accountant thought Brandon was facing bankruptcy. He had one kid in college and another headed that way. He was mortgaged to the max. Had limited income. Still, somehow, Brandon had recently found money to pay off his house and to buy a new $34,000 SUV and a very large boat, with two 350hp Merc engines.

Sally wrote on. She weaved the story together like a master. She didn't accuse Brandon of being the witness protection killer. Not directly. She always said there might be an out. But as the reader learned more of the details there was little room left for innocence.

Sally ended her piece with a series of questions: "Why won't Steve Brandon tell us where he was last July? Why won't he tell us where he was last month?

"Only one man knows the answers," she concluded. "And he isn't talking."

When Lou read the story later he thought it was great too. She had convinced him. He felt foolish for wanting the DNA tests. But only for a moment. The next moment he wished he had them. Being picky, he told himself.

Mel Campbell looked at Sally's story. It was strong. Made a case. In the parlance of the trade it was a good yarn and it hung together. Libel lawyers lived by the phrase "Reckless disregard for the truth" but he considered Sally had passed the test. She hadn't been reckless. She had gathered her facts carefully, and presented them to Brandon. He had decided not to respond. Further, there wasn't a thing she had written that was untrue.

Managing editor Ed Wilson decided the piece should run as Sunday's page one lead.

Mr. Wood was in his car. He was bushed. And a little drunk. It had been a hell of a run, he told himself. First class. But was it over? He was having nagging, unwelcome doubts.

He remembered the prayer he had said on the plane, when he thought his time was up. He marveled at that. Prayer had been absent in his life for so many years. Then, at the ultimate moment, it had blurted itself back into existence.

Mr. Wood tossed an empty can out the window and grabbed another. He pulled into a lot beside a church on 29th Avenue. He sat there. Downed another beer. Then he decided to go inside.

Inside he felt like a burglar. What was he doing here? Some candles flickered and a small light was aimed at the cross and the Christ. Otherwise, it was black as death. Unseen hands were playing Bach.

Mr. Wood was unsettled. He sat in the back pew with his head down. He had to get a grip. He took measured breaths, tried to empty his mind. After twenty minutes his shoulders relaxed and his back unwound. He lifted his head and studied the Christ figure on the cross in front of him. Who was he really? Mr. Wood asked himself. A god? A man? Or just a magician? For years now he had imagined it was probably the latter.

Back in his car, Mr. Wood turned on talk radio and listened to a political rant. He liked the lady host. She was so sure of herself. He was not. It was something about the church. His doubts were growing. He admitted it to himself. But could he go back to living like he had before, before he became Mr. Wood?

Yes, he thought. Then maybe. Then maybe not. He thought maybe what he had done was just inside a wrinkle in time, a quantum phase change or some such phrase he had picked up somewhere. Then he remembered he was out of beer.

He swung down 32nd toward Speer Boulevard, found a 7-11, darted in, and bought a new six-pack. He drove around drinking, and thinking, and tossing the empties out the window. He didn't care about the cops. How could he? By the fourth beer he was fully loaded, the lines in the road seeming to crawl around like white worms. What the hell? He decided he would go past Capricio's, for nostalgia's sake. Maybe even go inside. Yes, go inside and see Danny Dicerno. Why not roll the dice?

He drove down 38th Avenue well below the speed limit. A couple of drivers behind honked to get the jackass off the road. Mr. Wood gave them a lazy finger. He slowed to a crawl as he got to Capricio's. He checked the windows and thought he saw something, something he remembered. What was that? He drove around the block and saw it again on his second pass. He could scarcely believe his eyes. He sobered up immediately. It had not been the booze.

In the window was a yellow rose.

62. Party Time

SALLY's story shook not only Denver and Chicago but also the whole nation. A respected homicide lieutenant was a suspect in the destruction of the U.S. Witness Protection Program. Because of him, hundreds of criminals were being let go. Other cases were being appealed. People were afraid to testify. Talk radio was abuzz with almost nothing else. All the national networks asked Sally to appear. And one editorial said Sally was a "slam dunk for a Pulitzer."

Lou led the parade. He was so proud of Sally he thought he could explode. She had done it. It was like a work of art.

To honor Sally he arranged a surprise party at the condo. It was a wild affair. The condo could contain maybe fifty people. Three hundred appeared. They flooded over into the halls. The neighbors didn't care. They joined in. Lou must have bought a thousand dollars' worth of booze but it was soon clear it wasn't enough. Lou had to make several trips to the liquor store. And the cigars: Everyone wanted to smoke one of Sally's. Before long, Lou's condo smelled exactly like a Turkish whorehouse.

Local writers from both Denver papers showed up, as did the editor of Westword. And the editor of the Post, Stan Church, made an appearance. Lou only knew him by reputation, someone who hopped around the newsroom like a kangaroo on steroids. He was doing the same at Lou's, bopping around nervously. There were even politicians. Three state senators showed up whom Sally had never spoken to. That didn't slow them down. They acted like they had known her as a baby. Then came a real surprise.

Brad Johnson arrived. Lou hadn't expected that. Sally's story must have killed Brad. She had taken over something on his turf. But Brad was gracious – in his own way. He took Sally by the arm and led her to the balcony, where words could actually be heard.

"I was only a day late," he told Sally. "I could have had that story first."

Sally smiled. It was a sweet moment.

"Maybe next time," Sally said. She patted Brad's arm. Sally's eyes got tablespoon-sized when Brad leaned over and kissed her on the cheek.

"You're good, Sally," he whispered. "But I'll get you back."

Sally laughed. No point in rubbing it in.

Some officers from the DPD also showed up, Scott Kirkpatrick among them. Pat O'Dowd was also beaming for Sally. No honest law officer likes crooked ones and O'Dowd was certain that Brandon was more than crooked. He was broken.

Lou and Sally did not clean up after the party wound up in the early hours but fell arm-in-arm onto the sofa. They sat there without saying a word until they lost track of time. It was around 4 a.m. that anyone spoke. Then Lou whispered into Sally's ear, for the first time: "I love you."

Four hours later, at around 8 a.m., Mr. Wood marched down the Pearl Street Mall. It was a Sunday and few people were about. He hadn't disguised himself this time and he didn't look for Jimmy. Revved, he went straight to the Westword box and flung it open.

A single note was under the papers. Taped to it was a gold locket. The note read: "Mr. Wood, We have deposited $25 mill in the account listed below with the $1 mill for the work from before. You will get another $25 mill when done. If you don't do the job there will be problems."

That was it. No name. No directions.

Mr. Wood looked down at the locket. It was small, the kind his grandmother once had. He reached down and picked it up. It wasn't very fancy and he doubted it was even real gold. He opened it up. The photo inside made him stagger. He plopped down in front of the Westward box. He felt he needed a little more oxygen. After he collected his senses he opened the locket again and stared at the picture. When his thinking cells had finally reassembled he thought, well, this is certainly interesting. They want me to kill the President of the United States. Some pigeons gathered around as if picking up his thoughts.

A teenage girl, a lost soul with a pierced nose and orange hair, came by, looked down at the pigeons and asked Mr. Wood for a dollar. Tucking away the locket, Mr. Wood gave her a twenty.

"Shit, mister, thank you," she said.

"No, thank you," said Mr. Wood. He pulled out another twenty and pressed it into her hand. She looked down in awe.

"Buy some great weed," Mr. Wood said.

He had made his decision.

63. Love Child

THE NEXT morning, Sally got word that a quickly arranged news conference had been called at Steve Brandon's house. The scene outside the house was the proverbial mayhem. You couldn't have squeezed in another TV satellite truck. Reporters, photographers, camera crews, and producers were crushed together to get a look. Locals showed up for the same reason. People were shouting. Four network helicopters flew overhead. Cops were out in force, radios crackling. An enterprising young man had shown up with a hotdog cart. He was doing bumper-to-bumper business. And somewhere in the maze of people, a baby cried.

Sally had gotten word when Mel Campbell called from Chicago.

"Sally, I don't want to be alarmist but the news release says Chief Walter Henry will be there too. What's going on?"

"Jesus, Mel. The chief is going to be there? You sure?"

"That's what is says."

Sally didn't like the sound of this at all. She called Lou. They met and headed for the press conference, managing to park two blocks away.

As they approached the roaring horde, someone shouted: "There she is!"

The crowd turned. The noise stopped. Everybody watched as Sally approached. Even the baby stopped crying. Sally felt as though she was approaching the gallows. She knew she was in some trouble when the journalists let her drift unopposed to the front, the most fought-after position. They wanted her on camera.

A podium had been set up at the top of the steps to the porch. The paint Lou had once observed peeling from the clapboards was still there. The beat-up cars were there. The new boat and SUV were missing. Steve Brandon was trying to look poor.

Almost immediately Sally and Lou took up position the front door opened, as if they had been expected, and a stone-faced Steve Brandon emerged, followed by the chief, a red-eyed Sharon Brandon and a girl, about five, who was sobbing and looking down. Sally could almost hear the tears pelting the ground. Brandon's teenage son and older daughter stood stoically behind their mother. And there was another person in the background. A young woman with black hair holding a baby. Her eyes were awash in red and she looked unsteady. Lou thought she looked familiar.

Brandon walked to the podium. He was in his police dress uniform. His hair was trimmed, in perfect place.

"Thank you for coming," he said. He nodded but didn't smile.

"I intend to get straight to the point. Some of you know me," he nodded in the direction of Brad Johnson. "And some of you think you know me based on recent reports in the Chicago Tribune. That's a Steve Brandon that doesn't exist. Never has. I have been accused by a young and inexperienced reporter of being an assassin. It isn't true," Brandon said, as he appeared to wipe a tear from his eye.

Sharon Brandon pressed her despondent daughter's face to her hip, as though the most important thing in the world right then was to stop her kid from seeing her dad cry.

"That reporter's name is Sally Will. And I see that she is here. Central to Ms. Will's case is that I haven't been able to explain my whereabouts on the dates of the killing of Mr. Spilotro and the man known as Tony Nails."

Brandon turned to the mystery woman who stood, facing down, to his left. She held a baby with a pink face inside a blue blanket.

"This lady is the mother of one of my children, three months old. She is not my wife. And that is my shame. I made a mistake, and tried to hide it from my wife and kids. On the date of the Spilotro killing, I was with my new son's mother. She was not my wife and so I disguised it as a vacation."

Brandon, pale and stony-faced, went on: "When the Chicago paper asked me about this I decided, wrongly, to cover it up. When the man known as Tony Nails was killed I was with my new son. Sally Will took my silence about these two dates as an admission. I don't blame her for that. Perhaps I should have told her everything. But it was personal and embarrassing and I couldn't do it.

"To you all and to Sally Will I declare I am not the killer. To prove it I have collected credit card receipts and eyewitness accounts to show where I was during both the Spilotro and Tony Nails killings. You will see that I was thousands of miles away on both occasions.

"That is all I have to say. Thank you."

Steve Brandon stepped aside, taking his wife's hand. Police Chief Henry then stepped to the podium.

"We have completed DNA analysis on the cigarettes found at the Big Bow and Palermo killings, the ones mentioned in Ms. Will's report."

From the press pool, there was a rapidly rising crescendo.

"Neither matches the DNA of Steve Brandon."

The crescendo exploded into uproar as print reporters yelled the findings into a variety of smartphones and TV reporters sought for open space to give a live report. The man the whole world was calling Wasp Man was innocent. And a huge journalism scandal was erupting.

Just then a voice popped up from the back. It was Brad Johnson.

"Was the DNA from the Big Bow hit the same as that from Palermo?"

It was a solid question. Chief Henry cleared his throat.

"Yes it was," Chief Henry said. "I guess Ms. Will got one thing right."

Questions filled the air in an instant and they were all directed at Sally. Several of her fellow reporters were sticking mikes in her face as she tried to crawl out of the news conference. Sally felt her life draining out of her.

"Sally, are you going to do a retraction?"

"Do you have any more evidence, Ms. Will?"

"Were you set up, Sally?"

"Are you resigning?"

"Does Lou Elliott believe you?"

The last question rocked both Lou and Sally. Lou's instinct was to put his arm around Sally and usher her out. But that would not be good. Sally would look too much like a defendant. So Lou kept his distance.

A thousand times she had been on the other end of such spectacles. What was it that she was supposed to do? Be strong, defiant? Or would that just make matters worse? In the end, Sally decided to do nothing. Just march through. She noticed that several of the reporters were making sniggering comments to each other.

When they were finally alone, Sally turned to Lou. In a shaky voice, she said: "The man is lying, Lou. He must be."

"I know," said Lou. He was not sure he did but he didn't know what else to say.

"What do we do?" Sally said.

"Prove him wrong."

"How?"

Lou thought for a moment. Then said: "I need to talk with Pat O'Dowd. Maybe they're lying about the DNA."

"OK."

"Sal, did you recognize the woman with the baby?"

"No."

"I think I've seen her somewhere. But I can't place it."

Sally buried her head in Lou's chest. She began to sob. Lou knew it was only going to get worse.

President Lawrence Naslund watched the news conference in his private study. He was amazed. A day before he had thought an arrest was about to be made, the Witness Protection Program restored, and the political hemorrhage stapled shut. And now this spectacle.

How on earth had a paper like the Chicago Tribune made such an error? Hadn't he heard of this Sally Will before, maybe from Linda? He couldn't quite recall.

Whatever, he had had enough. He had to act like he was doing something, was in control. Heads had to roll. He could decapitate Linda. Her Team Dog Shit had made blunders all along. He got out a yellow pad and listed all the ways the CIA had screwed up the Ivanov probe, and how Ivanov was now in contact with this son-of-a-bitch who had ruined the Witness Protection Program. But he quickly realized there was no way he was going to pin this on Linda. No way. He buzzed his PA.

"Charlie, get Roger Hamilton. I want him here in person, right now."

The president rose as the FBI director walked into the Oval Office. He looked like a dwarf, the president thought. A frightened dwarf.

The president balled his fists and punched them down on his desk, leaning slightly forward. He did not offer to shake hands. He did not make small talk.

"OK, if this Steve Brandon guy didn't do it, who did?"

"We don't know," was Hamilton's honest reply.

"That is not good enough!" Naslund barked.

The president was wound tighter than Hamilton had ever seen him. He was seething.

"Sir..."

"No, you listen and listen well! You mean, as director of the FBI, that we have some madman flying about and ripping apart the Witness Protection Program and you have no clue who he is? Not one?"

"A clue, maybe. But no suspect."

Naslund carried on speaking over him: "And when Ivanov's man comes to the United States to meet with Borelli you lose track of him, and he gets away?"

"Other agencies are also responsible."

"And then Borelli meets with Dicerno?"

"Yes."

The president took out a chronology of Hamilton's various failings, real and imagined, that had been prepared for this occasion by Linda Orvez. He handed it to Hamilton who studied it briefly before the president retrieved it.

"Roger," the president said looking directly into the director's eyes, "I'm sorry but I want your resignation on my desk in two hours."

"Sir, did you have Linda prepare this?"

"Two hours."

Hamilton stood for a moment staring, and then lowered his head, realizing there was nothing he could do.

"Yes, sir. Two hours," he said. And he walked out of the Oval Office for the last time.

The president punched a number on his phone. Linda Orvez answered.

"Linda, it's done. I'll have a press conference before the evening newscasts."

Lou met Pat O'Dowd at a Starbucks near the Cherry Creek Mall. Pat spotted him as he entered, but he looked down immediately. No smile. No greeting. Nothing.

Lou bought a cup. He was dreading what was coming.

"Not good, huh?" Lou said, sitting down.

"I'm sorry, Lou, they weren't lying," O'Dowd said, and he really did look sorry. "The DNA was not Brandon's. It's got to be terrible for Sally. I can't imagine."

Lou took a small sip.

"I don't know if Sally can survive this, Pat."

"Ah, come on, Lou. Sally's a fighter."

Lou closed his eyes.

"Unfortunately, there's another side. It's a Daddy thing, Pat. A dark pit with no bottom."

He could not go on. He hefted himself up and left his coffee on the table.

Lou arrived back at the condo half an hour later even more concerned.

"Sally, why didn't you answer the phone?" he asked her anxiously. He had found her on his condo's balcony. She turned. Her eyes were ruby red and had dark shadows under them.

"I didn't want to know."

Lou put his hand on her shoulder.

"It's true, isn't it?" she said at last. It was not so much a question as it was a concession to the inevitable.

"Yes, I'm afraid it's true."

Naslund's press conference was held in the Jefferson Map Room in the East Wing. Just as in Denver, the press corps had a buzz on. The president's approval ratings had dropped from the mid-sixties to the high forties since the destruction of the Witness Protection Program had hit the front pages. Although the president had made strides against the Russian mob, those were now being blocked out by dark shadows cast by the Wasp Man.

Something in the nation seemed out-of-control and a law-and-order politician didn't seem to be fixing it.

At 7 p.m. the networks interrupted programming. Almost immediately the president's face came into view. The makeup people had managed to hide most of the bags under his eyes, but they had done nothing for the weariness they expressed. No longer was Naslund the cock-sure guy of the first year.

"My fellow Americans," he started. "I want tonight to speak with you about two recent events in our war on America's new criminal syndicates – but first let me tell you about the great inroads we have made against one of the most pernicious organizations in the world: that of Dimitri Ivanov of Russia.

"The other item I want to discuss is my great disappointment with your federal government's handling of the Witness Protection Program debacle. Recently we had news that a man named Gregory Serov – the second most powerful crime boss in the world – met a well-deserved fate on the streets of Moscow. I cannot give details, but rest assured that our intelligence services, and I particularly want to single out CIA Director Linda Orvez, played a key role in neutralizing this foe of the United States and friend of Ivanov."

That the president was lying - Ivanov killed Gregory Serov, not Orvez - was undetectable. The president was good, thought Linda Orvez watching.

"But even with these gains I know that in another sector there are a lot of concerns. There is an obvious leak in our country's valued Witness Protection Program. And recently many suspects, some associated with Ivanov, others with terrorism, have been released because protected witnesses are now refusing to testify.

"In July, after a protected witness in Savannah was killed in a car bombing, I asked FBI Director Roger Hamilton to take over the case personally. Now we've had yet another killing of a top informant. A recent report in a major American newspaper seemed to solve the matter. But that report appears to have been fabricated.

"Roger Hamilton has served his country well. The White House is passing out a press release chronicling his amazing achievements for which I am grateful and this country is grateful. But in the situation we find ourselves in Roger Hamilton has felt obliged to submit his resignation and I have felt obliged to accept it. We will begin the search for a replacement immediately."

Linda Orvez, standing behind the president, looked like a tiger just before its final killing lunge.

64. Last Write

FABRICATED. The word rang in Sally's head. She waited a long time before she said anything. Everything she had wanted to be, and everything she wanted to show her father she could be, was over. Her future was flushed away. She was ruined. She could go on to sell real estate, billboard advertising, cars, whatever, but she couldn't stay in journalism. She was out. She would have to be like everybody else, only less so.

Sally grabbed onto Lou's shoulders to steady herself.

"It wasn't fabricated, Lou," she said as tears poured down her cheeks. "It was all real. You saw it in his eyes."

"You'll get past this, Sal," Lou lied.

"What went wrong?" Sally said, barely able to stand.

"We'll figure it out."

"And then there's Mel," Sally said.

"What about Mel?"

"He'll be ruined, too."

"Why?"

"Because he was too close to the snake that bit the Trib."

As if on cue, the phone rang. It was Mel. She was to be in Chicago ASAP.

Sally caught a flight from DIA and landed at O'Hare at 6 a.m. She got a cup of coffee and donut, caught a cab and went directly to the Trib. The guard on the first floor examined her employee card, and then took a careful look. Yes, that's her, he seemed to be thinking. The embarrassment to a famous newspaper. The fabricator. He gave Sally a disapproving look before finally letting her pass.

It was 7:30. Hardly anyone was in the city room. Row after row of lonely computers displayed blank monitors or crazy screensavers. One PC periodically popped up a new instrument of the death penalty: a noose, an electric chair, a guillotine, a gurney and some contraptions Sally didn't recognize. It was a police reporter's desk. Nice touch, she thought. Beside the desk a police scanner blared out the day's early crimes. Things were hopping. Two homicide dicks were being summoned to the South Side. Another up north. There was a suspicious suitcase at Midway. The anti-terrorism squad was on its way. This was the life Sally had thought she wanted. But it was her life no longer.

Sally wondered where her own execution should take place.

Then she realized the perfect spot. She eased into the office of managing editor Ed Wilson. It was dark. She sat on a sofa and waited. Soon she drifted off...

Her family had a cabin in Wyoming's Bighorn Mountains. In grade school and middle school she spent at least five weeks each summer there. She now remembered a bend in the Upper Ten Sleep Creek where her father first taught her to fly cast. The boulders were slippery and she had found herself slipping and falling before dad showed her how to stand against the current.

"Sally, the current can take you down, or support you. Always position yourself where it can support. Like this rock over here." She recalled her father stepping into a current. And sure enough, she was stable.

"Work with the current," he said...

Sally was coaxed out of her daydream by a faint rustling noise. Wilson had arrived. He took off his coat and was briefly startled.

"Sally," he said when he made out who it was.

"Ed," Sally said, "you better call in Mel."

As Wilson listened to Sally's story, he rose and put his hands in his pockets. He went over to his windows and looked out. It was a gray, cold and miserable day. Even for Chicago.

When she finished her story thirty minutes later, Sally said:

"Ed, I could have waited for the DNA. But I was sure. And I thought Brad Johnson was going to scoop us."

Wilson had still not turned around from his window.

"Did you tell Mel about the DNA tests?" He said talking to her reflection in the plate glass. It was the first time Sally had thought of that. She should have done so but it hadn't occurred to her. It was the final, fatal blow.

"No," she said quietly.

"Why not?"

"I don't know. I guess I didn't think DNA would be an issue. I thought the story held up without it."

Ed Wilson turned around and faced her.

"Sally," he said, "I want you to write this up, straight. No excuses. And that will be the last thing you ever write for the Chicago Tribune. Do you understand?"

She understood. It is what she had expected.

After turning in her final story Sally walked out of the Tribune, past the sneering guard and out onto a drizzly street with its snarling honking traffic and harried pedestrians. She made it to Mike's Pub. It was 10:30 in the morning and already a few regulars were having beers. Sally sat down alone.

Mike, the octogenarian owner, came over. He was all of five feet five, with a shiny hairless head and tattoos of women in bikinis down both arms. He had on a greasy-spoon apron, already dirty. He remembered Sally alright.

"Sally," he said, "don't let the bastards get you down."

Sally looked up, as if just then realizing where she was.

"Mike," she said. "Sit with me for a bit will you?"

Mike settled down opposite Sally. He looked worried. He cupped her hand in his.

"Mike, they don't just have me down. They have me out. Mel too."

"Now, don't go saying that, Sally. You'll bounce back. And I've known Mel since the old days. No one ever knocked him down so that he couldn't get back up."

"Those times are over, Mike." Then: "Mike, I need a drink."

"I got that white wine you always liked."

"Something stronger. And a cigarette."

"Now, Sally."

"A gin and tonic, Mike. And a pack of Marlboros."

He hesitated. "You gave both those up, Sally."

"Please."

Mike tried to make sure Sally didn't overdo it but lost the test of wills. He did the next best thing: he got her a cab for the airport and watched in the drizzle as it left the curb.

"What a damn shame," he said under his breath.

The next morning Sally's story played on the front page, along with a long editor's note that said the Tribune had launched an internal investigation into the most egregious error the paper had ever made. The paper's lawyers were already in Denver discussing with Lt. Steve Brandon an appropriate settlement. The note explained that Sally Will had been fired outright. Mel Campbell had been suspended pending further investigation.

Sally had scored only one point. The paper was calling it an error, not a fabrication. But that was only the Chicago Tribune. The tabloids and journalism mags were beside themselves in their condemnation of her. The American Journalism Review called it "the most embarrassing moment in American Journalism since Jayson Blair." Another compared her to Janet Cooke, the Washington Post reporter who fabricated a story that won a Pulitzer. The Poynter Institute called it a "case study of gotcha journalism gone mad."

65. Gin Swing

WHEN Sally landed at DIA it was clear she had been drinking during the flight. She was unsteady, her hair tangled, eyes gone pink. Lou had to grip her arm to keep her from falling.

On the ride back to the condo Sally didn't lean toward him as she usually did. She didn't run her hand along his arm. She didn't talk. She sat with her head pressed against the passenger-side window, facing out, a dead look in her eyes.

"Sal, honey, these storms pass," Lou offered. He kept glancing at her, worried. She said nothing. Closed her eyes. She didn't move.

At home, Sally went straight for the balcony, a bottle of gin in hand, a cigarette in her mouth. She sat looking at the last vestige of a sunset. Then it was just dark and gray. The Front Range looked to Sally like giant tombstones.

Lou paced in the living room, watching Sally as she pondered the deepening night, hoping he would have time to act before she could hurl herself to the ground. He would not sleep tonight, he knew. He was wondering how much he would ever sleep again.

In the weeks that passed, with Sally no better, Lou developed deep bags under his eyes. He grew a stubbly beard. Businesswise he was turning clients away. He had time for only one thing: Saving Sally.

He had taken money out of his retirement account. He would take it all if he needed to. He didn't care about the money. He cared only that the woman he wanted more than anything was missing. The fire was gone. The witty, fierce, hard-as-steel Sal was locked away someplace in a bell jar.

He worried so much that he took to hiding his guns. He was no psychiatrist, but he knew what he was seeing was the return of Sally's depression. He was desperate to find a way for Sally to recover but she didn't seem to want to. She refused to go to El Chapultepec. Washington Park didn't interest her. When it was warm enough she sat out on the balcony with gin. When it was too cold she sat in the living room, avoiding newspapers and watching senseless television. And always the gin.

The gloom even enveloped Tika, who took to following Sally around but with her head down. Akitas are famous for their beautiful tails that arch proudly in the air before curling towards the head. But not Tika, not any more. Her tail was down and her legendary appetite nonexistent. When someone came to the door she was indifferent.

One of the first stories Sally covered as a cub reporter was that of a man who had jumped to his death from a seven-story parking garage. He had been a broker who had helped to underwrite bonds for a Chicago port expansion. There had been kickbacks. The mob was involved and a federal grand jury convened. The man had left behind a darling little girl and her devastated mom. Sally had wanted to see what the broker would have seen just before he died. She wanted context. So she had taken the elevator to the top of the garage and looked down. A cop friend said that the man's right eye had never been recovered. Things happen when you hit hard, he had said.

Sally imagined falling, knowing that in three seconds you would be dead. She wondered how long that would last in psychological time. Did your life actually pass before you? Sally now recalled that Denver had such a garage on Tremont Place and she suddenly had an overwhelming desire to go there. Maybe find out what happens in those three seconds.

It was cold as she made it to the 16th Street Mall, dressed in a Columbia parka and Reeboks, sleet pelting her face. She didn't get on the Mall Shuttle. She didn't want to be around anyone. She walked the 10 blocks and then took the elevator to the top floor. Only a few cars were that far up, and no humans. The wind made a lonely whistle. A newspaper page caught a gust, took flight. Sally went over to the railing and looked down. She saw concrete. It offered a sure and welcome death.

Yes, that would be the easy way, she told herself. And so what? She was ready for easy.

Sally climbed over the railing and onto a thin ledge. A panhandler on the other side of the street paused to watch. Sally inched forward. A gust of wind was all it would take. Sally took out a flask and drank some gin. Then her father's image came suddenly to mind. Lester Will was sitting at the kitchen table. He had a lost blank look in his eyes. Before him were bacon and eggs. But he didn't eat. He didn't read the paper as he normally would have. He didn't talk to mom or Sally. Then, without saying a word, he stood straight up and walked towards the door. Sally remembered the sound the door made that day, when her father left.

A sudden gust pushed her forward. Sally slipped. A shot of adrenaline went through her like a .38. She overreacted and started to fall.

Maybe if she had had just one more drink she couldn't have done it. But out of sheer reflex Sally managed to swing her arm back, catching the railing at the last moment. But her grip was weak. It started slipping. It was giving out just as she got her other hand to the railing.

Sally was dangling eight stories up. The wind moaned. A few people gathered below.

Should she just let go? She closed her eyes. She could only think of one reason not to: It would be unfair to Lou. Still... She began to wrestle her way up, slowly. Then she was over the railing, on her back, looking up at angry clouds. Sally could taste fear. She sank to the floor and waited for her heart to slow, the world to stop spinning. Eventually she got to her feet and looked back at the elevator door. She remembered she had seen a bar nearby.

66. Bar Brawl

SALLY would have normally avoided going into a bar where the jukebox was playing Folsom Prison Blues. But not today. She sat on a lonely stool as a bartender wearing the nametag "Bruce" approached.

"Lady, maybe you ought to rethink things. This is not a place for you," were the first words Bruce said. But Sally knew she could have been dead right now if the breeze had been a little stronger. She didn't care where she got hammered.

"You got any gin worth a damn?" she asked.

"Nope. Just well gin."

Bruce looked nervously over at the pool table. Two bikers had put down their cues and were eyeing the lady with the blonde hair. They whispered to each other.

"Well gin it will be," Sally said. She lit a cigarette.

"Lady..."

"What do I have to do to get drunk around here, Bartender Bruce?"

"It's your life," Bruce shrugged, pouring her a drink.

Two other men had also stopped their conversation and were staring at Sally. George Phillips, the head of New Company Logging in Montana, and Stan Markson, the Hells Angels lawyer, were drinking in a back booth.

"I met her at the toughest bar in town," said Markson. "Up in Commerce City. She had protection then."

"She's had a fall," said Phillips.

The two bikers at the pool table decided that their eight ball game was over, and started walking towards Sally.

The smaller of the two had a buzz cut, a ragged goatee and a bouncing gut. The taller man looked solid with bad prison tattooing on his neck.

"Miss, go now," Bruce told Sally under his breath. Instead, Sally pushed her glass towards him.

"Fill it up," she said.

At the condo Lou wondered where Sally was. It was dark and she was supposed to have met him an hour earlier. She hadn't been the model of reliability lately but she hadn't been this late either. As he paced the apartment Lou knew things were terribly broken. He had even entertained the thought that maybe they would remain that way. Maybe Sally was going away forever. He had secretly braced himself for that. Then his iPhone rang.

"Mr. Elliott, you don't know me," said a voice. "Your lady is at the Triangle, off 15th. There's trouble."

Then the line went dead.

Lou exploded out into the street and sprinted toward the Triangle. Crowds tried to get out of the big man's path. Some failed and went down. Lou could not be slowed.

When he got to the Triangle and threw open the bar's door, the fat biker had Sally's left hand pinned to the bar while his tall partner was nudging her legs apart with his pelvis. The bartender had backed out of sight and the rest of the place seemed deserted. Folsom Prison was still playing in an endless loop. Lou moved so fast that the bikers didn't have time to consider options.

"Who the fuck..." said the fat biker.

Just then, Lou hit him with an uppercut and he went down like a spent shell. The larger man was backing away when Lou grabbed his crotch in a vice grip and squeezed. The biker's eyes bulged and he screamed. Lou put his other hand to his throat and hurled him over the bar like a bale of hay, smashing glass and sending half the liquor on the back wall crashing.

Both downed bikers were groaning. Neither appeared anxious to get up. The bartender must have hit the fire alarm because it started blaring out. Then, in the distance, came sirens.

Lou put his arm around Sally and hurried her outside. George Phillips, in the shadows, left through a side door.

"Suppose you're a hero, right?" Sally said when they got to an alley two blocks away. She stuffed her hands in her parka. She refused to look into Lou's eyes and pulled away whenever he got close.

The alley was dark. Spilled garbage was everywhere. A drunk who was either dead or passed out was propped up near a door that had "No Entrance" stenciled on it in yellow. A river of his urine snaked towards a drain. The cops had arrived at the bar, followed by an ambulance. Sally tried to steady herself.

"I can get home from here," she said.

She pushed off but stumbled, twisting an ankle, and found herself on the ground, looking up. She sat with her head down and hugged her knees. Lou crouched down in front of her.

"Go away," Sally said. She wouldn't look at Lou. "I want you to go away."

"Why?" Lou demanded. "So you can return to those two assholes?"

"They're what I deserve."

"Sally," Lou said, "Don't be ridiculous. Don't you see it? You're killing yourself."

"I see it fine. I was this close. But I was a coward."

She held her thumb and index finger a quarter inch apart. She didn't tell Lou about the parking garage but he seemed to understand.

It was time for Lou to gamble, he thought. Push hard.

"So you are going to check out, is that it? And take me with you?"

Sally brushed back her hair and finally looked at Lou.

"That's so unfair."

Something moved in the garbage. A cat's green eyes appeared, shining, frozen.

"No," Lou said. "You care only about Sally Will."

"I am the one with a ruined life!" shouted Sally, throwing her fists against Lou's chest.

"Dammit, Sally. My clients are leaving the sinking ship. Because of Brandon my reputation is crap. And what about Mel?

289

He's hung out to dry. You've got three lives at stake here, not one. And you don't care."

Sally looked devastated. This was one area she had refused to contemplate. It was too terrible. The abyss.

"Why...?" Sally managed, before breaking down totally.

"Because, Sally, goddammit, you owe it to us. We must figure it out."

Sally went still. If she was breathing Lou couldn't detect it.

"Figure what out?" Sally asked finally. "You're not making sense."

"Brandon," Lou said. "What we missed."

"Simple, Lou. We missed that he was not the killer."

"You're wrong."

Sally didn't respond for a while. She was looking down. At last she looked up.

"Wrong?" she asked.

"Wrong," said Lou.

"But the receipts, Lou. The phone records. He wasn't there. I blew it."

"We're missing something, Sally. We must be."

"Yeah. Facts."

"I think we have facts, Sally. We just need more."

"So we're just to branch out on our own. Solve the caper?"

"Yes. We have to solve it."

"Don't be ridiculous," Sally said.

"Don't be a quitter," Lou shot back.

Sally again made eye contact with Lou. Don't be a quitter was the phrase her father used to tell her. She had never told Lou about that. How did he know to push that button? The dizzy world in the alley got a bit steadier.

Sally tried to get to her feet. It wasn't pretty.

"You know, Lou. I think I'm drunk."

For the first time in days, Lou laughed.

"I don't know, Sally. Drunk is a pretty big word."

Sally finally stood erect and dusted off her jeans. Lou got up too. Sally took his hand.

"Jesus, Lou, you really creamed those guys. Your fist is bleed-ing."

Lou looked at his hand. He hadn't known he was injured.

"Sal, I'm way too old for stunts like that."

Sally laughed. Something she hadn't done in a month.

"I thought the big guy was going to eat me," Lou smiled.

"No, Lou. I've seen that look in eyes before. Tika, you know. Scared to death. Believe me, Lou, that guy had a heart attack when you lifted him like a forklift. He'll never walk or talk normally again."

"Guess I was a little pumped."

Sally came close and held Lou around the waist.

It wasn't eureka. Sally didn't snap out of it. But there was a little stirring at the back of Sally's head. She was starting to find her legs.

"So we solve it?" said Sally.

"Yes," Lou said. "We solve it."

67. Dancing Dogs

THE next day Sally slept in until noon, then made herself some coffee, and sat down to read the Post. It was the first newspaper she had looked at since the Brandon press conference. It felt good reading news, Sally thought. It felt good being alive. Something was changing. Solve it, Lou had said.

She shook her head and smiled. Sure. An army of FBI agents was on the trail of Wasp Man and they couldn't find a thing. Now Lou was saying she could do it. She laughed out loud. Absurd. But instead of hitting the gin now Sally went to work. What had she missed? Besides everything that is?

She got up and went to the den, rifled through the files. Everything was still there. She borrowed Lou's reading glasses, sat down on the balcony, and took out a yellow legal pad. She lit a cigar.

Two hours later, Sally had a pad full of items, ranked in importance. The Dunhills topped the list, just like before. Then came the chronology of the killings and Brandon's vacations. And there was the Italian June Festival. Everything was the same. Everything led to the same conclusion. Everything was wrong.

What had she missed? She couldn't figure it out. She was on the point of giving up when, almost as an afterthought, she remembered the one thing that she and Lou had that the FBI didn't. Smiley.

Smiley had told Lou it was a guy at the Italian June Festival who was the killer. Sally had pretty much stopped thinking about that after she found Brandon's name on the list. But what if it was someone else?

Sally headed to the den, fired up Google, got to the festival's home page and located the list of attendees. Brandon came up first. Sally jotted the name down on her pad and continued on down the list.

When she got to the Es she had a little jolt. "Elliott, Louis" it read. That's right, she recalled. Lou was there. And didn't he tell her that he had talked to Dicerno? No, she thought, it couldn't be Lou. But then she corrected herself. Making assumptions is what got you into trouble, girl. Lou had told her he was there...but only after Brandon said it first. And Lou hadn't looked too pleased with the subject. She wrote down Lou's name.

The Js brought another surprise: Brad Johnson. Why would he have been at the festival? Well, he was a local investigative reporter at an occasion that attracted a lot of power brokers and hoods. Sally wrote down Brad's name.

When she got to the Ms, Sally saw a name that gave her pause: Stan Markson, the lawyer for the Hells Angels. Could he have been involved with the Big Bow slaying? He knew the territory. Was it the Angels after all? Sally wrote down his name.

Most of the other names on the list meant little to Sally. They had no known connections to the witness slayings. But there was one she wondered about: George Phillips. Sally didn't know who he was at first, but a search revealed that he was CEO of some company in Thompson Falls, Montana, named New Company Mining. Why would an executive in a Montana mining firm attend the Italian June Festival? For the moment Sally had no idea.

So five names: Lou, Brad, Brandon, Markson, and Phillips. What do I do now? Sally thought. Tell Lou he's a suspect?

Danny Dicerno spotted it when he left his bungalow, a blue Lexus with dark windows up the street. It didn't belong. He knew, somehow, that there was more than one person inside. He got into his Caddy and headed toward 38th Ave. When he glanced in the rear view mirror, he saw the Lexus pull away from the curb. Trouble. And not the usual kind. Feds didn't drive Japanese cars.

As he approached the on-ramp to I-25, the car was three vehicles back. Dicerno took Park Avenue into downtown, parked, and darted inside the Bronco Café.

"Jimmy, I gotta problem," Dicerno barked into his smart phone. "Listen."

Jimmy listened.

The manager of the restaurant guided Dicerno through the kitchen to a back entrance. Jimmy showed up ten minutes later. Danny slipped into the PT Cruiser.

"We need to lose some assholes following me in the Lexus," he said. "Get to 17th and turn south on Glenarm."

Danny Dicerno was slumping down as they passed the Lexus. Who were they? What did they want?

"Jimmy," he said, "go to Capricio's. Pronto."

When Lou got home, Sally was at the desk, going over old files, smoking a cigar and drinking a little white wine. It was the best thing Lou had seen in ages.

"Hon, this detective bullshit seems to be working," Sally said. She got up and gave Lou a reasonably good kiss.

"Care to share?"

"Later, big guy. Now I intend to celebrate."

"You'll give the track owners a stroke."

"Their tough luck."

Sally grabbed a jacket and winked at Lou.

"Mas tarde, amigo," she said as she swept out the door.

When she was gone, Lou pumped his fist, like Tiger Woods.

"Miss Sally, you be back!" shouted Andy as Sally walked in.

"Yeah, Andy, I'm back."

"You goin' be quinellin'? Ya betta be, 'cause last time you made me four hundred dollars. You did, Miss Sally. Mama was sure pleased with that. Oh, brother."

"Andy, there's a dog racing in the fifth. Rainbow. I saw her run last year. I'm going to box her. Let me see the sheet."

Andy handed her one. Sally took out her calculator.

"OK, Andy, try two, three and seven in the fifth."

Danny Dicerno dashed into Capricio's office, retrieved a Mach 10 machine gun, then darted out and jumped into Jimmy's car. There was no Lexus. The followers were probably still downtown, he thought, waiting at the café.

"Jimmy, go to the racetrack in Commerce City," he ordered.

The track owner had invited Dicerno to watch a new guaranteed-to-win dog named Purple Dancer. Purple Dancer, the owner said, was doped. Dicerno hadn't planned to attend but the Lexus changed his mind. He wanted to get lost in a crowd. Things were fuckin' screwy, he thought. Things had been easier before Mr. Wood showed up. Who was that guy?

He lit up a Cuban, blew a little smoke into Jimmy's face, trying to forget his problems.

"Boss," said Jimmy.

"Yeah, I know. You can't stand that."

"No, boss."

Jimmy was glancing at the rear view mirror. Dicerno snapped his head around. Three cars back, there lurked the Lexus.

"Who are those fuckers?" Dicerno said.

"You want me to lose them?"

"They're not losable."

"What then?"

"Get me to the track and then call Big Red."

Big Red, whose name stemmed from his days as right offensive tackle for Nebraska, was Danny's enforcer.

"I want Red and his crew to follow that Lexus and find out who those assholes are," Dicerno said. "If he's sure they're not feds dust 'em."

Jimmy looked into the rear view mirror. He no longer saw the Lexus.

Sally bought a hundred dollars' worth of quinella tickets on dogs two, three and seven. Number seven was Rainbow. There were drunks and cons and loan sharks milling about, mixed in with college kids chugging beer, businessmen looking self-assured, and expressionless middle-aged women lining up at the two dollar show window.

"I got fifty dollars on this one Miss Sally," Andy said with big appreciative eyes.

"Rainbow is going to rock, Andy. You'll see."

"Mama's goin' to be happy agin."

As race time approached, Sally left the stands and got onto the blacktop area near the finish line. When the announcer said "Post time in one minute," Sally managed to push herself to the very front. It was a tight squeeze, hip to hip.

"And they're off!" said the announcer. The crowd exploded.

Rainbow, a svelte female smaller than the others, got crowded right out of the gate and fell into last place. Sally shouted encouragement.

"You can do it, girl. You can do it! Go. Go. Go!"

Rainbow passed one dog, and then another. But she was still far from the leaders. The other two dogs Sally had chosen were in the middle, with one greyhound named Purple Dancer way out in front, chasing the phony rabbit.

"Go, Rainbow! Go!" Sally shouted as the dogs raced in front of her on their way to the first turn. Purple Dancer was running far too fast, too early. He would burn himself out by the halfway point, Sally figured.

Past the first turn, Rainbow had passed two more dogs. Sally helped all she could.

"You can do it, Rainbow. You can do it!" Sally shouted.

Rainbow was halfway up the pack in the backstretch and moving up. Sally's other two picks were running two and three. Sally couldn't believe it: Purple Dancer had widened his lead!

"Rainbow, go! Rainbow! Go!" Sally screamed. She said it with such force that many other bettors were turning to watch.

"Go! Go! Go! Rainbow, Go!" Sally was now almost shrieking as the dog rounded the turn. Rainbow had finally made it to second place, with Sally's other picks in positions three and four. But still, somehow, Purple Dancer maintained his lead. Impossible.

"Rainbow! Rainbow! Rainbow!" Sally continued shouting, but she saw no way for Rainbow, much less the other two dogs, to overtake Purple Dancer as the dogs entered the home stretch.

"Go, Rainbow..." Sally said. But it was no longer a shout.

She turned to leave, not wanting to see the finish. But just before she threw her tickets to the ground she heard a collective groan from the fans. She turned to look. Purple Dancer had pulled up and decided it was time to poop. He made quite a show of it as enraged fans screamed bloody murder. Sometimes juiced dogs did this, Sally knew.

An instant later, Rainbow crossed the finish line, a nose in front of her number three dog. Sally had won.

"Yes! Rainbow! Rules!" Sally shouted, triumphant.

Even more eyes fell on Sally. She didn't notice. God, it felt good. Not long ago, she had stared down at the hard concrete on Tremont Place. Sally didn't even care about the purse. It would be big. Andy and his wife would be very happy. But it was Rainbow that had done it. She had beaten that badass, juiced-up Purple Dancer.

As she lazily walked towards the cashier's booth, a man tapped Sally on her shoulder. Sally's blood was still pumping and she didn't notice. He tapped her again. She turned, expecting to see Andy with a wide smile. Instead, she saw a strange apparition. Jimmy Fresno looked embarrassed.

"Ms. Will," he said. "I'm Jimmy Fresno."

After that, Jimmy locked up. If hired killers worried Jimmy beautiful women terrified him.

"Yes," Sally said, with just a hint of encouragement. "I know who you are Jimmy."

"Ms. Will?"

"Jimmy? What?"

Jimmy seemed to take a deep breath: "Ms. Will, Mr. Dicerno saw you down here. I guess everybody did. Ah, he's up there in the owner's suite. He wondered, ah, if you might want to watch a race or two from there."

Danny Dicerno wants to see me? Sally thought looking up. A disgraced journalist who had told the world that Dicerno had hired Steve Brandon to kill the Witness Protection Program?

"Is this a joke, Jimmy?"

"No ma'am. He saw you jumpin' up and down. And he said to go get you if you wanted to get got."

Sally thought for a moment, then said: "I want to get got, Jimmy."

"Ah," Dicerno exclaimed as Sally entered the booth. "If it ain't the lovely correspondent from the Chicago Tribune!"

Dicerno got up to shake Sally's hand. Sally had imagined that Dicerno's hands would be pudgy and soft. But they were sleek and strong. And warm.

"I think it is former correspondent," Sally said.

"Yes," Dicerno said. "I heard about that. You should have let me take care of them editors when I offered."

"You mean, I don't have a rain check?"

Dicerno didn't laugh so much as he roared.

"Rain check! Jeez, Sally Will, you take the cake."

He poured Sally a glass of Merlot. In the distance, another race was being announced. The tote board still had not tallied the value of Sally's winning tickets. It didn't matter. She had forgotten them.

"Mr. Dicerno," Sally said, as she set the wine aside, "these are strange times."

For an instant, Dicerno softly squeezed Sally's palm between his thumb and forefinger. Sally did not pull away. Dicerno quickly let go, reddening a bit.

"They are, Sally Will. These times are very, very strange. I saw you down there. You picked that race?" Dicerno asked. "You must have. Everybody in the entire stadium is jealous-mad at you. But don't worry. My boys can keep them at bay."

Turning a bit red, herself, Sally said: "Got lucky this time."

"Everybody here said Purple Dancer was a lock," Dicerno said. He didn't mention the two thousand dollars he had just lost on a doped-up dog. As he looked out on the track, a man with a shovel was cleaning up Purple Dancer's error.

"And everybody was right until near the end, when everybody was wrong," said Sally.

"Damn, Sally, that sounds good. I have a business partner right now behavin' just like Purple Dancer."

The next race was off and either Dicerno didn't have any money on it or didn't care. Sally didn't either.

"How come a big city reporter like you comes to a rat-hole race track?" Dicerno asked. "I wouldn't think that stud boyfriend of yours would let you come here alone."

"He doesn't know I'm attracted to long shots," said Sally, not at all surprised that Dicerno knew something about her domestic relations. She knew about his.

"You win?" enquired Dicerno. "I mean, most of the time?"

"I'm lucky with dice and dogs," said Sally. "But my luck with men is spotty."

"That's good, Sally Will, spotty." Dicerno gulped down some Wild Turkey without once glancing towards the track where the race was just finishing.

"And I guess I also pick dogs better than I pick murder suspects," Sally said, finishing the thought.

Dicerno thought about that as he sipped the Kentucky whisky. He then looked back at Sally as if he wanted to say something about her comment. Apparently deciding otherwise he turned.

"Sally," he said at last, "it's not wise to wait too long to collect your winnings."

Sally took the hint and started to leave.

"I'm glad you won," Dicerno said, with suddenly soft eyes. "Kid, you're going to be OK. Maybe you will get the – how do you guys call it? – 'the scoop' after all."

"That might be better for me than it is for you," she said.

Dicerno raised his glass and smiled: "Go get your money, Sally Will. Spend it on somethin' stupid. And take care now."

As Sally opened the door a tall man with a blond ponytail brushed by her heading in. He didn't say a word but he tried to distance himself from Sally – as if he didn't want her to recognize him. But she did. It was Stan Markson.

Instead of running back to her car, Sally put her hand out just in time to stop the door to the luxury box from closing. She silently slipped back in. The rear of the box had only enough light for people to find liquor and snacks. The front of the box was almost completely dark. Sally poured herself a small glass of white wine and watched the silhouettes at the front of the box: Markson and Dicerno. They were laughing and toasting and doing anything but watching the race.

Sally heard Markson talking. She couldn't make out much but she did hear him use one phrase: "Sally Will."

68. Sally's Secret

BIG Red and his crew followed the Lexus as it headed down Colorado Boulevard. It turned down Louisiana and into the parking lot of a club called Moscow Nights. Big Red had heard of it. It was supposed to be mobbed-up big-time with a rough bunch of Russians. The boss always railed against the Russians, Big Red recalled. This was going to be a blast.

A massive Russian emerged from the Lexus just as Big Red's van was pulling into the lot. Then out popped a petite woman. Even from 30 feet away, Big Red could see that she had dazzling green eyes. Big Red couldn't believe his luck. His targets were a large Russian and a tiny gal. No contest.

Big Red and three shooters stepped out of the van with their weapons. A driver stayed behind for the getaway. The four men sauntered towards the tall Russian, thinking he was dead meat. The Russian's eyes opened wide when he saw the group approach. He showed them the palms of his hands to say he was unarmed and wanted no trouble. Big Red smiled at him. This was too easy. Then suddenly the two men beside Big Red crumbled to the ground. Big Red looked back to see his third man begin to bleed out. In front of him, the giant Russian still stood with his hands palms out. But the petite green-eyed woman with him was holding something silver in her hand and it was pointed right at him.

The last words that played in Big Red's mind were "Oh shit" as Katya's bullet hit his forehead dead center.

At the first sign of gunplay, Big Red's driver peeled away and roared off. He had no intention of going to Capricio's. He was intent only on saving his own life. People were killing Danny Dicerno's boys. Instead, he called Jimmy Fresno.

Dicerno had every rounder and made guy he could muster meet at Capricio's after leaving the track. Something was wrong. They were grouped in the back when Jimmy's old cellphone rang. Jimmy looked frozen as he took the call. Danny put his hand up to quiet everyone. Then Jimmy clicked off.

"Boss," Jimmy said. "Trouble. Big trouble."

"Don't need more of that," Dicerno said. He was watching Jimmy's eyes.

"Big Red and three of the guys are dead," Jimmy continued. "In the parking lot of Moscow Nights. The driver got away. That's him who just called. There was a big Russian and a small woman. The woman was the shooter."

"What you mean they're dead?"

"Dead as in dead, boss. No more."

Dicerno could not imagine four members of his already shrinking crew shot dead in a Glendale nightclub parking lot. Who are these guys? Then the answer came to him. It was the hit on the president. Had to be. After Mr. Wood took the contract Dicerno only had one role left – as a potential witness. Whoever was following him and killing his men wanted to shorten the witness list. If he was to survive, Dicerno knew he had to somehow break the contract. And for that, he needed help.

It was near midnight before Sally got back to the condo but she wasn't surprised to find Lou up reading the latest issue of Scientific American. Two nights earlier, Sally had seen him reading an article about the universe actually being a hologram, some sort of grand illusion. He was reading it again. Although Lou usually read very fast he appeared to be going over it very slowly. He was moving his lips.

"Lou?"

Lou startled briefly, then pushed his reading glasses over his head.

"Sal, I didn't hear you."

"You big lunk. The universe got you snookered again?" Sally said as she slid in beside him.

"It's got me snookered, checkmated and deep-sixed, Sal. Nothing changes."

"Not true. I've been changing."

Lou let the magazine drop. This was serious.

"Two stories, Lou," Sally said. "Ready?"

Lou straightened. Sally began. She had been thinking in the car home.

"Lou, I've told you little about my father, right??

"True."

"He killed himself."

Lou couldn't think of anything to say. Sally took his hand.

"He was a great man," she said. "It was a waste. He was a cuddly smiling giant when I was little. His waders were taller than I was when he first taught me to fish. He took me along with him to Hyattsville, east of Worland on the lower Tensleep. It was lures at first, but when I got a smidgen older he graduated me to flies. I loved our time alone together, the water twinkling with sunshine, the breeze scattering the scent of sage and pine.

"He was a natural rodsman. And when he finally had me arching a perfect line I felt like I ruled the world. Afterwards, we would sit creekside and clean the fish. I thought that was yucky so he did most of it.

"That's when he talked about the people of Greybull. He taught me a new word. Foibles. Dad was the town banker, so he knew everyone. And he knew all their secrets. He told me the people of our tiny town had plenty of them. There was the undertaker named Hitchcock – this is true, Lou – who would circle the hearse waiting for an unfortunate to die. There was a postmaster named Ranger who may have been the only Democrat in town. And there was a lawyer who lived under giant cottonwoods who may or may not have killed his wife. The inquest said he accidentally backed over her in his driveway. Others reported hearing loud arguments.

"Foibles, Lou. He taught me about those. And I was mesmerized. I wanted to learn all about them. But not only in Greybull. On a bigger scale. But there was one foible he never talked about – his own. My father, you see, suffered depression, terrible dark bouts of it."

Lou had seen those dark bouts in Sally. Now he knew.

"He self-medicated himself by taking time off and going fishing," Sally said. "One time I saw him removing a flask out of his jacket and taking a swig. And he caught me spying. After that we didn't go fishing together as often."

Lou shifted slightly and held Sally's hand a mite tighter. This was hard.

"He had a problem, Lou. Fishing was enough to medicate it for a while, but then it wasn't enough. He went to hard liquor. In a town the size of Greybull, you couldn't exactly go to the doctor with something like that. The whole town would know you were wigged out.

"The drinking escalated. He tried to hide it from us, so he must have been terribly ashamed. But it was the only thing that helped him. When he didn't drink, he couldn't sleep and when he couldn't sleep, he couldn't work. It's hard to keep this from your family. And it's particularly hard to keep it from your wife. But he tried and tried."

Sally touched Lou's cheek.

"And then he couldn't hide it anymore. And the whole self-medication routine stopped working. It was only making things worse. And it was killing him to know that I knew and mom knew. I was pretty confused and pretty angry with him, and I suppose it showed. And that also didn't help."

Sally paused, and the pause seemed to last forever.

"One day I asked him to stop drinking. Didn't he know that he was hurting his family? I asked. Why was he being so selfish? He reached over and kissed me on the temple. He said, 'Honey, if I could stop I would.' I said, 'You can!' Real loud. Real angry. Too angry. Fourteen years old. He cupped my face in his hands and said 'I will'. And his eyes said he meant it. He was going to beat his demon.

"I didn't tell my mom what I had done but she seemed to sense it. For a week, dad rose early – he never did that. And everything seemed OK. Then one day he said he was heading for Hyattsville, to go fishing."

Tears were rolling down Sally's face now.

"On the way back home he hit a cement abutment at ninety miles an hour."

Sally brought her right hand to her mouth and she closed her eyes.

"Sal, don't," Lou said.

"No, Lou, it's alright."

Sally gathered herself.

"There were no skid marks, Lou. When they tested his blood he was sober. Everybody in town knew what that meant. No one said a thing.

"He killed himself, Lou. Because of something I said."

Lou remembered that the last time he cried was when Becky Sue died. He was trying not to do so now. But a tear was welling.

"It took me quite a while to get over my guilt and anger. I don't know which was greater. When I got to college, I read about the problem. Then in this past month I tasted the sickness myself. Now I've gotten control, and I never want to lose it again. I won't give up a little wine. But when I self-medicate it won't be on whisky."

She leaned over and kissed Lou. Lou's one tear ran down his cheek. Then Sally changed. She had told a story she had never told to anyone before. And now it was behind her. She sat up and wiped Lou's tear away. Then she began her second story, the one concerning Stan Markson.

69. Steamboat Springs

LOU had never before heard of Stan Markson. He didn't know that he was at the Commerce City biker's bar when Sally interviewed the Sons and Angels. He had never heard of the incident outside the courthouse, nor that Markson was at the Italian June Festival, nor that he met with Dicerno at the racetrack.

"Lots of coincidences," was Lou's verdict.

"Lots," said Sally.

"Let's run it down."

"Yeah, and this time," said Sally, "No assumptions."

Sally began hitting the databases. There was the usual: Markson's mortgage, driving record, press clips. He had been a mouthpiece for some bad actors. Nothing surprising there. But at one point Markson had been trapped in a big mess. Markson, according to an account in the Post, had once had his law license suspended for subornation of perjury. The case involved a professional killer named Tiny Samuelson, a biker with an arrest record that could fill the Atlantic. Tiny was on trial in Adams County for the murder of another biker named Tex Anderson. The only reason anyone knew Tex was dead was that his head showed up on the median line of northbound Highway 85 heading to Greeley. An old-style cellphone was wedged in his mouth. That's all of Tex that was ever recovered. The cops said his killer had placed his head on the road as a form of humiliation, and as a warning for snitches to keep off their phones.

It had been a routine murder case until the day Markson had his client take the stand. That was almost unheard of. A client with as dubious a past as Tiny's should go on the stand only if he had a rock-hard alibi. Otherwise, the DA would churn him into mush. What was worse for Markson was the law that said a lawyer cannot knowingly have a client testify falsely. An attorney can do everything else for a guilty client – distort, obfuscate, dance on his head. But he cannot have his client perjure himself. But, according to the article, that's exactly what Markson did when he had Tiny testify that he was in South Carolina when some other dude placed Tex's head on the highway. Records Markson produced backed up the tale and Tiny was acquitted.

Later, those records were shown to be counterfeit. Tiny could not be retried. That was the law. So the DA's vengeance came down on Markson. Right or wrong, Markson was out of the law business for 365 days for suborning perjury.

Two words germinated in Sally's mind: Hitman and Biker. Maybe Tiny was the killer. Maybe Markson pulled the strings. Sally checked other records. Markson was doing well since returning to practice. He had a new cabin in Winter Park worth $470,000. And he had topped that off with a new $60,000 Hummer. Money from somewhere special, Sally reasoned. She set out to try to find Tiny Samuelson.

Tiny, she discovered, had been busy. Since his acquittal for the Tex murder he had been convicted, sentenced and paroled for a liquor store robbery. Other than that, Sally hit a brick wall. Tiny apparently no longer existed in Colorado or any other state. Databases showed he didn't own property or cars, didn't have a driver's license, hadn't been ticketed, arrested, sued, divorced or married, and his social security number hadn't been used in a debt transaction. The only good news: Tiny was apparently alive, since he didn't show up in the Social Security Death Index.

Sally called Tiny's parole officer. Tiny had checked in once, the first week after he got out. After that nothing. There were warrants out for his arrest.

"If he's not in Mexico, he's dead," said the parole officer.

Danny Dicerno was desperate. He knew he was way in over his head. Mr. Wood was on the loose. Maybe he could stop him. If the president wasn't killed maybe the Russian bastards would get off his case. No need to eliminate witnesses if there was no crime.

Dicerno went into a North Denver florist and bought one yellow rose. A clerk looked at him like he was crazy. At Capricio's he placed the rose in the window, and centered it. He hoped Mr. Wood was still checking. Dicerno sent Jimmy to Boulder to leave a desperate message in the Westword box. It read: "Mr. Wood, The contract has been canceled. Please, please call real soon or leave message here. Again – No contract." But no calls came. When Jimmy returned to the Westword box, there was nothing there. After taking a fifty million dollar contract on Lawrence Naslund, Mr. Wood apparently had more important things to consider.

Dicerno reached out. He decided to call Vinnie Terranova. Dicerno thought there had been chemistry there, some bond down in the steam caves. Maybe Vinnie owed him one. Dicerno went to a pay phone and called Vinnie's house. A woman answered.

"Ma'am," Dicerno said. "I'm calling for Vinnie. Tell him it's Danny."

He heard the woman exhale, then gulp, then sigh.

"Ma'am," Dicerno said, "have I caught you at a bad time? I'm sorry."

"Mister," the woman said in a barely audible choke, "Whoever you are, Vinnie, my husband, died last night."

Terranova, it turned out, had died in a steak and seafood restaurant in the Loop at 7:27 p.m. the night before. He had dined with a tall gaunt man with a paper-white complexion, someone who spoke with an accent. Terranova, who had been eating oysters, seized up and died on the spot. His dinner companion disappeared. Dr. Tsplyev had learned the trick from Jason Ison. Borelli was leaving no middlemen.

Dicerno looked out through his blinds. In one direction there was parked a dark Lexus. Panic time. Stacy was in a back booth waiting for him. Dicerno ignored her.

Michael Strange, head of the Secret Service, was not pleased. The president, under the possible threat of assassination from a Russian gangster, was insisting that he keep his schedule intact.

He wasn't going to let Ivanov upset his cart. That meant Lawrence Naslund and his family would be making their annual foray to Steamboat Springs, staying in the ski lodge of a Detroit automobile CEO. Strange would have preferred the president to stay in D.C. where he would have a steel wall of protection. There was a lot that could go wrong in a small place like Steamboat Springs, all of them Strange's responsibility.

Strange came to Colorado a week early to prepare. He walked around the CEO's chalet with his tactical squad chief, Jeff Arnold. The house was on a hill, eleven thousand square feet with vaulted ceilings and windows everywhere. It sat on five acres of pine and brush. As is the Colorado custom, there was no lawn. Neighbors didn't appear to be candidates for food stamps either. All the homes were huge.

"You know the routine," Strange explained. "We need motion sensors around everything."

He brought his hand to his face, looking pensive.

"Make that two loops of sensors, all around," he said. "If anyone even has an evil thought, we want to see it."

"We've never done two loops," Arnold noted.

"You're right," said Strange. "Make that three loops."

Arnold looked stunned. Three loops of motion detectors would task his team to the extreme.

"And we need the dogs here," Strange insisted. Bomb-sniffing dogs are much better at detecting nitrates than any human-built machine.

"They've already been through the paces," Arnold noted.

"Do it again."

Do it again. Arnold thought this bordered on the insane. But all he said was: "OK."

"And recheck the neighbors." He was referring to computer checks that went far beyond those available to private citizens.

"Sir, the neighbors haven't changed since last year."

"Recheck them all," said Strange. "Maybe one has become a paid member of Al Qaeda."

"Got it," Arnold said. "And what about Rendezvous Park?"

"Same old problems." Arnold shrugged.

Rendezvous Park. The president absolutely loved it. He had gone there every year, religiously. Seven miles from Steamboat and high into the Rockies between Copper Ridge and Rocky Peak, Rendezvous Park consisted of three hot spring pools formed by 150-degree mineral water that burst out of the earth two hundred feet above. Rolling plumes of vapor rose above the ribbon of water as it cascaded down. Since its 150 degrees would cook humans, colder water from a nearby creek was diverted to the pools, bringing temperatures down to 104 degrees. But that didn't stop the steam. A band of white cotton always covered the pools.

Some locals liked to experience the pools in the buff. The president had discovered this aspect when, as a college kid, he and a girlfriend had stumbled upon the park. The only thing that had changed since was that the president now kept his swimsuit on.

"Two ways he can get the First Family to Rendezvous Park," Arnold said. "Helicopter or snowmobile."

"Snowmobile?"

"That's how we got there last year," said Arnold.

"No," said Strange, "that opens miles of territory we have to neutralize. We'll chopper them in."

"What about the cross-country skiers?"

The president enjoyed meeting hearty young people who skied into Rendezvous Park.

"Not this time," said Strange. "Keep 'em out."

"Anything else?"

"Yes. Put motion detectors in all areas where there should not be motion. And build two 12-foot-high blinds at both ends."

Arnold thought Michael Strange had gone way over the top but what was he to do? He issued orders.

70. Markson Marked

SALLY had looked up the Mark "Tiny" Samuelson case on the net and learned that Scott Kirkpatrick had been one of the detectives. She headed to the DPD central office on Cherokee Street.

She had no current press credentials but the sergeant at the front desk was too involved reading The Sporting News to let any unnecessary synapses fire when Sally showed him an outdated Illinois Press Association card. She got a green tag, saying she could visit the third floor. The desk sergeant took another sip of coffee and returned to his paper.

To get to the homicide room, Sally would have to pass Steve Brandon's office. She prayed that he would not be there. But her prayer wasn't answered.

"Ms. Will, what are you doing here?" Brandon barked as he pushed his way from his desk and surged out. "You're not working press anymore."

"I'm working for Lou."

"What case?" Brandon was in Sally's face.

"You know the case."

"Are you possessed, woman? Even the President of the United States says you're a liar."

"The President of the United States is wrong."

They were toe to toe. Sally didn't give an inch. The men in the homicide room had all stopped what they were doing and were listening.

"You should have come here to apologize," Brandon said. His eyes bore right through Sally's head.

"Never," Sally said through a clenched jaw.

"OK, Sally. Go on. In-Ves-Ti-Gate," Brandon mocked. He put his hand on Sally's shoulder. She turned to stone.

"I guarantee that one day you will apologize." Brandon took a step back. He looked sure of himself. "You're not a liar. But you were wrong. This was madness, Sally. We could have talked it out."

Sally didn't budge. Every muscle in her body was coiled.

"And I hope, Sally," Brandon continued, "that your investigation ends before some other poor schmuck's name gets dragged through the mud." Brandon turned on his heel and went back into his office.

"Jeez, Sally, that took some balls," Kirkpatrick said quietly when Sally entered the homicide room. He was shaking his head and smiling.

"Scott!" Sally brightened seeing him. She sat down on the edge of Kirkpatrick's desk. "Just the man I hoped I would find. I want to ask about an old case."

What Scott told Sally about Tiny Samuelson didn't help her theory one bit. Sure, Tiny was good for the homicide he had been charged with, but the evidence that finally got into court wasn't great. Even before Markson introduced the phony alibi evidence he was not giving the state's chances at over 50-50.

"Sally, Tiny only did grade-B hits. Bikers that ripped off meth. Mid-level guys facing too much time and knowing too much. That sort of thing. I mean, don't get me wrong, Tiny is a bad dude. But he probably couldn't tell you who Vito Borelli is, much less Tony Nails. The only way Tiny Samuelson could get close to the Witness Protection Program would be if he was going into it."

As Sally left headquarters she flipped her green pass to the desk sergeant. One of his eyelids twitched up, but only briefly. Bye lady, it said.

Sally got in her Miata and gunned it up Floyd Hill on I-70 west of Denver. She needed to assimilate what Scott had said. She figured the best way to do that was by reaching 100-miles-an-hour while climbing an eight-percent grade. As she passed the exits for Golden she began to relax. OK, she thought, so Tiny was too dumb to be the man. Could have Markson done it himself? Possibly, she considered.

Sally slowed to eighty miles per hour at the Genesee exit and finally turned around at the Chief Hosa Camp Ground. She had made a decision. If she wanted to know if it was Markson she would observe him. That's what Lou would do. He called it getting inside a suspect's skin. Seeing what they saw, feeling what they felt.

She called Lou's iPhone to tell him to meet her at Markson's Broomfield home, but Lou didn't pick up. She remembered that this was racquetball day. She decided to go it alone.

Markson lived in an area built in the 40s and 50s when residents thought they lived in a small town with a lot of empty space between them and the dangerous city. Now Broomfield was part of one single metroplex, sprouting its own ring of wealthy subdivisions and swanky malls. But old Broomfield seemed stuck in time, sporting mostly ranch homes with single-car garages and well-maintained lawns. Most of the homes in the old part of town sold for $220,000 or less, which in the Denver area meant they were dirt-cheap.

It wasn't easy for a red Miata with a blonde driver to just blend in but Sally tried. She drove slowly by Markson's home. But for the shiny new Hummer parked outside it would have seemed a humble dwelling. The Hummer was out of place, she thought. Definitely out of place.

Sally parked a block down the street, behind a van. She had a clear view of Markson's front yard but doubted anyone going into or out of the house would make her. Sally thought of popping the top. But in the interest of stealth she merely rolled down the windows.

For two hours nothing happened at the Markson home, and Sally's attention drifted. She watched girls across the street playing hopscotch while some nearby boys were wrestling and chasing. A few dogs romped with the kids and an unlikely ice-cream truck came by playing Disney music. Play stopped while some of the kids bought ice cream. Ice cream in December, grimaced Sally with a slight shiver.

Any idea that Sally might get lulled to sleep in bucolic Broomfield was aborted when one boy, a cute freckled-faced kid no older than 11, suddenly shouted out "You jive-ass motherfucker" as he tackled another similarly aged kid and began beating his nose in. The girls stopped hopscotching and gathered round cheering. The dogs growled and bared their teeth. The ice-cream truck rolled away. The heartland is changing, Sally thought, alertness recovering a tad.

Just then a car she hadn't detected sped by. Sally caught the plate. It was Markson. Sally knew Lou would have spotted it in the rear view mirror long before it got near, and by then Lou would have slipped down, out of sight. Too late, girl, Sally thought. She watched Markson park a hundred yards away and go inside his home, nonchalant. If he had detected her, he gave no hint. The kids and dogs dispersed and Sally was suddenly alone on the street, and on edge. She rediscovered her rear view mirror.

An hour passed. No kids. No dogs. No Markson. Sally began to relax again. She knew some loon would soon come on the radio to talk about space aliens or witches or some crazy thing. She loved late night loons. Perhaps, she thought, she could play the radio very quietly. But just as she reached for the knob she heard something. It was like a scuff on pavement. She looked in the rear view. Nothing. But she had heard something. She knew it. She tried calling Lou again, still no answer. She slid down in her seat. Night was approaching. Another twenty minutes passed. Then she saw him.

Markson furtively left the cover of a tree and was slowly approaching, hunched down. Something was in his hand. Sally reached into her glovebox for the .38 snubnose that Lou had given her despite her protest. Sally had skipped the training session, thinking having a gun was absurd. She was now surprised by the heft of the weapon. She looked back. Markson was ten yards away, slouching more but somehow appearing to grow. Sally thought she should have waited for Lou before she ever came here. Girl, you did it again, she thought.

Markson crept forward. Sally felt she could soon be history. She had to act. She remembered a scene from a Hollywood flick where the blonde rolls out of the car and caps the bad guy. Might as well, she figured. Nothing to lose.

Just as Markson began to rise at the rear of the car Sally flung open the door and rolled out. She ended on her belly with the gun pointed squarely between Markson's eyes. But unlike the movies, Sally didn't shoot. Even if she had tried it wouldn't have worked. She had forgotten to take the safety catch off. Markson didn't know this of course and the gun was enough for him. He froze, his eyes wide, plaintive, scared. When the blast didn't come he let his hands drop to the side and the pipe wrench he was carrying clattered to the ground.

"Sally!" He exclaimed, holding his arms up as Sally kept the gun trained on his head. "I didn't know it was you."

"You're just a team leader in Neighborhood Watch?"

Sally had used one hand to get to her knees while the other held the gun straight and steady.

"I have some strange clients," Markson explained. "I saw someone here so I came to investigate."

"Your clients always send women to case you?"

"My clients could do anything."

"Clients like Tiny."

"Tiny Samuelson?"

Sally nodded: "Yes, like him."

"Tiny is in Mexico," Markson said. "Has been for six months. His decision, not mine."

"You're blowing smoke, Markson."

Finally Markson allowed himself a thin smile, the only kind you can muster with a .38 is pointed at your head: "So you thought Tiny might have been the killer?"

"I'm sort of leaning towards you at the moment?"

"Me?"

"I'm an egalitarian accuser."

"Sally, my neighbors..."

"I don't give a fuck about your neighbors."

"Look, I wasn't anywhere near Savannah when Spilotro was hit. And I've never been to Wisconsin. Tiny was gone, too."

"Prove it."

Markson thought for a moment, then said: "I have telephone records for Tiny, receipts for air tickets."

"Good job, counselor. Client services?"

Markson let his arms down slowly and opened his palms. "Tiny got a subpoena about an escort service Danny Dicerno controls. Danny wanted Tiny to get lost. So I helped. That's all. I represent some bad actors and they sometimes lean on me a little. I've got a wife and kids. I can't be choosey."

"And a new Hummer."

"Occasionally, a client pays," Markson said ruefully.

Sally stood upright and lowered the gun.

"I want to see the records, Stan. For Tiny and you. Now."

"They're at my office."

"OK, let's go," Sally said, motioning towards the open door. "Get in. You drive."

Once Markson got the car rolling Sally asked: "Was that why you were at the track the other day with Dicerno?"

"Uhuh, I nearly dropped dead when I saw you. No way I wanted a reporter to associate me with the mob."

"Outlaw bikers are just fine though?"

"You're considered a criminal defense attorney if you represent bikers. You are considered a *consigliere* if you lawyer for the mob."

"Why the meet with Dicerno?"

"Tiny wanted a raise for keeping lost."

"Did he get one?"

"Hell no!" He laughed.

Markson's office could not have been mistaken for one of Denver's powerful 17th Street firms. It was a second story walk-up near 32nd and Federal. Sally saw that it had a window air conditioner and an old rusting hot water radiator that rattled. The office smelled of too much Pine Sol mixed with the stale stink of a chain-smoker the freshener couldn't conceal. Markson fluttered around, looking in this file and that until he had assembled his evidence.

For a second-rate lawyer he made a pretty good case. He had receipts and telephone records showing Tiny in Cozumel when Spilotro was hit. And he had records showing Tiny was there two days before Tony Nails died. He had similar records for himself. According to the receipts he'd been in neither Georgia nor Wisconsin on the required dates. He had been home.

Sally was not quite convinced but held her gun loosely in her lap as she drove back.

71. Guilty Secret

DICERNO had one hope left: Borelli. He was weaving in and out of traffic as he made frantic calls to Borelli front companies. A receptionist at Dandy Dan's said Mr. Borelli was out and would not return soon. Other Borelli fronts said the same. The man was out of touch. After each call, Dicerno noticed the Lexus following. Dicerno pulled over a curb at Capricio's and rushed in. He didn't think the Russians would follow, but they were Russians. Who knew?

"Jimmy, I got a problem," he said.

"I know."

"This is real important. I need you to go to Chicago and meet this man."

He handed Jimmy a piece of paper with Vito Borelli's name written in block letters. It also had Dandy Dan's address and some of the other fronts. Jimmy stiffened when he saw the name. Though he hadn't at first known Terranova he now knew who Vito Borelli was. He ran the Outfit.

"You want me to meet him?"

"Yes, Jimmy, you have to. Or else both of us are dead." Dicerno dug out eight hundred dollar bills and pushed them into Jimmy's hand. "Get the first plane out."

Jimmy didn't like it, didn't like it at all.

"You must tell him, Jimmy, that two can play the game. Back off now or you pay, too."

"I'm supposed to tell Vito Borelli that?"

"You must."

With a rare flicker of defiance, Jimmy chanced an opinion: "This is nuts, boss."

"Jimmy, listen to me," Dicerno grabbed Jimmy's shoulders and forced him to look into his eyes. "This is your only chance to live, get it?"

Jimmy Fresno fared badly in Chicago. No one at Dandy Dan's Gentlemen's Club said they knew anything about the man called Vito Borelli.

"Who wants to know?" spat the bouncer. He had arms as big as Jimmy's thighs, a mustache and laser eyes with a yellow glow. A nude stripper worked on a pole, zonked. Some guys sitting in front of her seemed to Jimmy to be drooling.

"I represent Danny Dicerno," said Jimmy. The bouncer got a laugh out of that.

"Never heard of him," he said. "Now get lost."

Jimmy went to another club and asked for Borelli. This time the bouncers didn't laugh. One got Jimmy in a headlock and the other started kicking his legs. They wrestled Jimmy through the club and towards an alley. Patrons watched and didn't interfere. The women didn't seem to give it any attention at all.

The guy who had had Jimmy in a headhold was tattooed from his hairless head to his ankles, with big Dumbo ears and a nose that must have been broken a dozen times. Jimmy saw something in his hands.

"You want Vito Borelli, you punk. Here's Borelli." He swung a chain at Jimmy's head. The first swing caught Jimmy on the face. Jimmy fell and went fetal. The tattooed bouncer swung again. By the time it was over the beating had lasted ten minutes and didn't spare any part of Jimmy Fresno. He was a bloody pulp when the bouncers went back inside.

A day later, Jimmy awoke in a hospital with morphine pumping into his arm. His front teeth were gone along with a chunk of his tongue. Despite the drugs, it felt like his skin was being ripped away when he reached for a phone. Still, Jimmy managed to call Dicerno.

"No Borelli," Jimmy managed to spit out. It sounded more like "No-well-he."

"Who the fuck is this?" Dicerno demanded.

"Me, boss, Jimmy." It sounded like "Me-bob-Any."

"Get the fuck..." Dicerno said, then reversed course as realization dawned.

"Jimmy is that you?"

"Yesh boss." Dicerno was just able to make that out. "You sound bad Jimmy. What happened?"

"Beat me. Beat me bad."

Dicerno understood. It was over. Time to bail.

With over fifty million dollars in an Antigua account, Dicerno felt he could live the rest of his life in Costa Rica in a mansion on the beach and still have money left over. Fuck the Outfit. Fuck Borelli. Fuck the president. Fuck this life. Dicerno was retiring. He called his Antigua bank, gave his account number and codeword and asked to have two million dollars wired to Costa Rica.

Dicerno was put on hold several times before, finally, the bank president came on the line.

"There must be some mistake, 1880465," said the bank president, referring to him only by his client account number. "You transferred everything to the Isle of Jersey on Monday and closed your account."

Dicerno didn't answer. He looked at the phone as he sank into his chair. He was finished. There was no way out. It had been a mistake to have accepted a contract on the President. Too big a job. Out of his league. If he had had the chance to get the money and run he would. Fuck the fucking president. But now he was alone, powerless. He only hoped the Russians wouldn't shoot him before he made it back to his wife and kids for one last hug.

Then he thought of something.

Markson had pretty much convinced Sally. Sally now thought: If not Markson and Tiny, then who? When Sally pulled her Miata up in front of Markson's house she said: "OK, Stan. What dickhead client paid you off so you could afford that new Hummer?"

Markson didn't seem in any rush to explain but he saw Sally still touching the gun, fingering the trigger. The lady was crazy.

"I don't know," he said.

"Stan, you're really starting to piss me off." She lifted the gun.

"Sally, it was someone from Chicago, wanted some information. I got it for him. Information on Dicerno."

"So much for loyalty, Stan."

"It was just some bullshit. Properties he had, places he went. Bullshit."

"Get out, Stan."

As Lou, Sally and Tika walked along the Marshal Mesa Trail in Boulder County, it was sixty-five degrees. After a mile, Sally was down to a t-shirt, her coat wound around her waist.

"So if it's not Markson, who's left?" said Lou.

"No idea," said Sally.

Tika smelled every interesting thing along the trail and there must have been thousands. Occasionally, when another hiker walked by with a loose dog, Tika came close to Lou and Sally.

"Let's keep with the Italian June Festival. Someone must stand out." Lou bent down and scratched Tika's ears fondly.

"How about you?" Sally was smiling but it was forced. It was something she had dreaded asking but it was something she could no longer ignore. There had been a little cloud in the back of her mind that had grown and spread. She loved the man. But maybe she was a fool. Some men lived double lives. Another man she had loved had tried to do the same.

"If you want to waste your time," Lou said, "go for it."

"OK, I'll go for it."

Lou paused.

"Well?"

Lou looked down and frowned. Then made up his mind.

"When I met you a couple of months before the festival," he said, "I was involved with another woman."

Sally shot him a quizzical look. Was this ominous cloud simply about sex?

"I tried to break it off after we met..."

"Tried?"

"Yes, tried. But I didn't entirely. We sometimes had lunch. The sex part stopped, and she knew I was with someone new."

"And she still wanted to have lunch?"

"She's a hard person to turn down."

Lou was busted.

"Anyway, she had tickets for us for the festival. I tried to beg off but she was insistent and so I decided to go."

Lou couldn't tell how Sally was taking this. He hadn't actually cheated on Sally. But he hadn't been upfront either. He wished there was a hole to crawl into.

To Sally, it felt like the weight of all the Rocky Mountains had been lifted from her shoulders. She was not overjoyed that Lou had seen the other woman. But she didn't consider it the crime of the century either, even if, as seemed likely, he had probably slept with both women simultaneously for a brief period. She understood the pull and push of relationships. She had done it herself in the past. What she liked most was that maybe now she could finally banish her secret cloud. She pushed on.

"And who is the mystery lady?" Sally asked.

Lou stuffed his hands in his pockets and shook his head. He didn't really want to go there. But one look at Sally convinced him that he had no choice. He took a deep breath.

"Andrea Anastas," Lou said, chagrined, helpless.

That stopped Sally. Andrea Anastas was the 30-year-old daughter of Denver's biggest billionaire, an oil tycoon who had drifted into telecommunications. Sally looked at Lou in genuine surprise.

"Andrea Anastas?"

"She's not like the tabs say," Lou said defensively. He looked embarrassed, and guilty. Sally took his hand and patted it.

"OK, big guy, you're off the list."

"The list?" asked Lou.

"Yeah, Lou. The shit list."

That's when Lou put it together. He really had been a suspect. Sally can be a hard lady, he thought.

They walked a ways without talking, Lou thinking he had somehow dodged a bullet, Sally knowing she had found her final man.

The next morning Lou was up early. He dripped hot water through Café Verona, took out a yellow legal and began to write. Sally, never an early riser, slumbered on. On the yellow pad, Lou noted a few facts:

The killer had been in Georgia in July and Wisconsin in October. Not Markson.

He had been in Denver on a date certain to receive the wasps.

He had been able to hide his identity, forge or receive counterfeit documents and handle cash. That means he is smart. Not Tiny.

To get his information the man must have needed connections. Brandon?

And he had been at the Italian festival.

Lou jotted down "6" – but didn't put anything after it. He was missing something. As usual, the coffee aroma got to Sally and she wandered over to the table. She leaned over, gave Lou's cheek a kiss and said, "You cramming for an exam?"

"No," Lou said, "It's time to find a solution to a chess problem. But there's no Bobby Fischer to help. Something is missing."

Sally went to the fridge to pull out a carton of milk. With glass in hand she sat next to Lou, examining his five points. She liked Lou's method but agreed: something was missing. And then it occurred to Lou. Maybe it wasn't yet a Sherlock insight but it was something. How had they neglected it?

"OK, Sally. I thought of something."

Sally waited expectantly.

"We know he can fly a plane."

Sally's head shot up, sharing the thought. "That's it," she said. "He must have a pilot's license."

"Or had one."

"Damn Lou, how did we miss it?"

"The funk I guess," said Lou. "Or just plain native stupidity."

"The feds are bound to have thought of this," said Sally.

Lou sat, looking at the list. "I'm sure they have, and all their super computers working on it too," he said. "But we have something they don't have."

Sally cocked her head, waiting.

"The feds don't know he was at the festival. We do."

Sally perked up. "I'll cross-reference every male at the party with the FAA's pilot's list. I can do it fast."

Lou was pleased that Sally offered. She was much better at that stuff than he was. If pushed he would have to admit she was a bit of a master at it in fact.

"Sal," he said, "maybe we are a step ahead after all."

72. Pizza Delivery

MR. WOOD entered the U.S. Geological Survey offices, wearing dark wool slacks, a light Nautica sports jacket, a button-down eggshell shirt and a Jerry Garcia tie. He had on sunglasses.

A man behind the desk said, "What do you need, sir?"

"I'm looking for topographical maps for the Steamboat Springs area," Mr. Wood told him.

At home, Mr. Wood spread the maps out on the floor in his den. He got down on all fours to study the contours of the maps of the terrains around Rendezvous Park, and backwoods ways to get there. He didn't have a plan just yet. But he was thinking.

Danny Dicerno was cloistered at his Capricio's table, looking at news clippings from a scrapbook. He had ordered everyone to stay away. A song by Willie Nelson played in the background – a song about lawmen hanging bad guys and then getting their horses drunk. Danny Dicerno loved that one. "Whisky for my Men, and Beer for my Horses." Danny Dicerno wished he had met Willie Nelson, and that other guy, the one with the pony on the boat. Lyle Lovett.

He flipped through the pages of the scrapbook. There was the story from the Denver Post about his first arrest at age 21 for selling illegal weapons. There were clips about his associates' arrests, particularly when they said something about the associates' "alleged connections to reputed underworld figure Daniel Dicerno." He loved reading the word "reputed" as much as the press loved using it. It seemed so sophisticated. He loved the words "mob," and "Mafia," and "underworld." It had been his life. Nearly every moment. He was particularly proud of a Brad Johnson exposé. It used all the catchwords, even referring to him as "Don Dicerno." There was a special section reserved for pictures of Dicerno.

Not mugshots, but high-class happenings: Dicerno at a wedding, Dicerno at a wake, Dicerno walking out of court, acquitted, Dicerno with Sinatra. But the picture he was looking for now was Dicerno at the Italian June Festival.

He recalled the photo in the Post because it was so strange. There was a man appearing to be the Marquis de Sade, there was another dressed as Bin Laden, and then there was a man wearing a Wheaties box. Cereal Killer. But it was the other guy in the picture that Dicerno recognized. The guy who looked like a lawyer. Mr. Wood. He found it toward the back of the scrapbook. He took it out and circled Mr. Wood with a red marker.

Dicerno had thought for a moment about telling the feds about the plot but he hated the feds. Dicerno had another plan.

Jimmy walked into Capricio's on crutches, with casts on his arms and bandages all over. Both eyes were nearly closed, his nose was bent down, and part of his left ear was missing. Jimmy had managed to put on a tie, a thin red thing a billion years out-of-date. Dicerno thought he looked like a fuckin' Egyptian mummy or something. But whoever worked Jimmy over had missed vital organs. Jimmy was hobbled but not worthless.

Jimmy came up to the back booth, spilling a crutch along the way. Danny actually got up and bent down to retrieve it, then stayed standing to meet Jimmy. Never before had Dicerno done that. He never stood for anyone in Denver. Everyone in the bar turned to watch.

Danny came up to Jimmy, gave him the crutch and then bearhugged him. It was a long embrace, not a formality. Jimmy was almost in tears from the pain of it as much as the unexpected emotion.

"Jimmy, come and sit," said Dicerno gently. "There's something I need to talk to you about, something only you can do."

"Anything, boss." Dicerno knew the words by watching Jimmy's lips. The actual sound was almost foreign.

"It's Danny, Jimmy. Just Danny from now on."

Jimmy looked concerned. He twisted slightly to sit and mostly fell into the booth with a thud.

"You OK, boss? Er, Danny?" Jimmy asked as he recovered. Jimmy was fumbling for his words.

"I'll be OK if you listen to me one last time."

"Shoot," said Jimmy, not taking in the significance of the "one last time" bit.

"Jimmy, I made a mistake." Dicerno was looking at his hands. "I did something stupid. Got in way too deep."

Jimmy looked at Dicerno, nodding, trying to follow.

"Boss, whatever it was, it can be fixed."

"We've done a lot of fixing over the years, right Jimmy?"

"Yeah, boss. Everything can be worked out, right?"

Dicerno reached over the table and placed his two hands on Jimmy's two hands.

"This time it's different." Dicerno looked resigned. "This can't be fixed, Jimmy."

"No, boss. No." Jimmy was getting agitated, or as agitated as the pain throughout his body would let him.

"Jimmy, listen carefully." Dicerno still kept his hands on Jimmy's. "You know that woman from the Chicago paper, the one at the track?"

Jimmy nodded. "Yeah, Sally Will?"

"Yeah, her." Dicerno was looking straight into Jimmy's eyes. "This is what I want. If something happens to me, I want you to take this to her. Tell her it is the man in the red circle."

Dicerno handed Jimmy the picture. Jimmy fingered it like it might explode.

"What do you mean 'if anything happens to me'?" Jimmy said. He shifted again. He didn't like how this one was going.

"Happens to me means if I get killed, Jimmy."

"Oh, boss..."

"Now listen, Jimmy." Danny added pressure to Jimmy's hands and Jimmy tried not to wince. "If that happens, if those guys out there get me, getting this to Sally Will ain't going to save my life,

OK? It'll be too late for that. But getting it to Miss Will could save your life. And others. Understand?"

"Boss," Jimmy slurred, "ain't nothin' goin' happen to you." Dicerno took a toothpick he had been chewing out of his mouth.

"Listen, Jimmy. The people we're against apparently want no middlemen alive."

Jimmy looked confounded.

"You, Jimmy, are a middleman."

A flicker of understanding found Jimmy's blood-red eyes.

"And Jimmy, I also want you to give her this?" Dicerno said, handing Jimmy a locket. He remembered the locket.

"You understand?" Dicerno asked.

"This is fuckin' serious, ain't it, boss?"

"It will be the most important thing you ever do, my friend."

Dicerno had never called Jimmy Fresno a friend. It would have been something so absurd to be out of the question. It couldn't happen. But it just had. Jimmy didn't know what to do. He put his hands to his face and closed his eyes. He took a deep breath.

"OK, Danny," he said softly. "OK."

Tika stood straight up and wagged her tail furiously as Sally downloaded the FAA's database. There were more than a hundred thousand names in the file, which Sally converted into an Excel spreadsheet. Tika knew something was up. Sally was radiating excitement.

When the twenty-megabyte file was loaded and all the columns properly delineated, Sally sat back. She lit a cigar and allowed herself to breathe it in. Soon she would have her answer. Or she wouldn't. Tika began to pace. Somehow, she sensed something important was underfoot. Sally then loaded in the names of all the attendees at the Italian June Festival. She blew a ring. Then another. She reached back and scratched Tika's ears.

It was 3 a.m. and she really didn't want to disturb Lou but she didn't want to be alone when she pushed "Enter." She went into the bedroom and nudged Lou. He groaned and grabbed a pillow to hug. Lou Elliott was a big time pillow-hugger. Sally nudged him again. Lou stirred.

"Lou, come on," said Sally. "There's something on the computer you really need to see."

Lou groaned, threw off the sheets and followed Sally to the computer.

"OK, let's see this computer trick of yours," Lou said.

"It hasn't happened yet," said Sally. "Push 'Enter' and let's see."

Lou hit "Enter" and the computer responded in a microsecond. Suddenly not one name appeared on the screen but two.

"Brad Johnson has a pilot's license?" asked Sally.

"News to me," said Lou. "Hope he's better at it than racquetball."

"And who is George Phillips?"

"It says something about New Company Mining. Ever hear of it?"

"No." Sally looked puzzled.

Danny Dicerno was at his home when the doorbell rang. It was 6 p.m. and already dark. The Farm was a gated subdivision. Guards usually didn't let strangers in unless they had been cleared. That gave everybody a sense of security. Dicerno had that sense when he went to the door. But he also had a sense of caution. He got out his Glock and stuffed it in his pants. The doorbell rang again. Dicerno recalled the scene with little Johnny outside the bungalow. He would not make that mistake again. He turned on the porch light and looked through the peephole.

A woman stood there in a dark coat with a white fur hood that accented a striking face. She held something in her left hand: A pizza box. Dicerno's first thought she was a delivery woman at the wrong address, but what a woman. Then he thought again. No one who looked like that delivered pizza.

Dicerno backed quickly away and reached for the Glock at exactly the same moment Katya raised her right arm. Her .44 magnum sent two shots through the door and directly into Dicerno's chest. Dicerno fell back against a wall and then slowly collapsed to the floor, his face a picture of disbelief, blood smearing the wall in a broad macabre brushstroke.

What Danny Dicerno thought was so remarkable was that he felt no pain. He was outside his body, looking down. I am dying dammit, he thought. But this is not so bad. That was some lady out there. She might be a match for Mr. Wood. Then he felt himself moving further and further out of his body, drifting into a white warm light. He felt peace. He said a final prayer for his soul. And for Jimmy, to get his message to Sally Will.

73. Rendezvous Park

LAWRENCE Naslund was reluctant to hit the world's biggest mobster right under President Putin's nose, particularly when Putin might have had an understanding with Ivanov. But Ivanov was not in Moscow. He was in Uzbekistan, negotiating an oil deal that could make him $60 million richer.

Charles Ramson, Anne Burgess and the rest of Team Blue were at an airfield in Mazar-e Sharif, Afghanistan. Other American agents had readied a drone. Ramson was in full combat gear, out on the runway, pacing about and speaking into a walkie-talkie radio. He looked at his watch. He was waiting for confirmation that Ivanov was where Team Blue thought he was. He was worried about the time. He didn't want to try to track Ivanov in the dark, infrared equipment or not. Finally word came.

"Are you quite sure?" Ramson asked. He listened and then turned and keyed his radio.

"Go for launch," he said.

The Predator drone lurched down the runway.

Ramson returned to a situation room where most of the team sat looking at flat screen monitors. He saw that the drone was right on track. Ramson sat down and opened up a Mars bar. He looked relaxed. The twitch was gone.

An hour later, Predator was over the Uzbek presidential palace. It started to make lazy circles a mile up. It met no antiaircraft fire, no planes were sent to intercept. That was perfect, Ramson thought, except for one thing. There was also no Ivanov.

Anne Burgess leaned closer to a screen. It was getting dark. Pretty soon, the visible light camera would be no use.

"You sure the sonofabitch is there, Charles?" she asked. She was thinking back to the day Ramson was sure he had killed Pam Boravick.

"Sure, it's solid."

Just then something began to stir. Anne moved some dials and zeroed in.

"They're coming out," she said.

Ramson jumped up and started manipulating a dial of his own.

"I got 'em," he shouted at last, taking control of the drone and zooming in and activating a laser sight that would guide the Hell-Fire missiles.

Below the drone Ivanov walked slowly to a black Mercedes with three men in dark suits. He shook their hands and lingered with one man, talking.

"Should we shoot?" asked Anne.

"For chrissakes Anne, I'm not going to kill the President of Uzbekistan."

"Your call."

Ramson's eye began to twitch, just as Anne knew it would.

Finally, Ivanov patted his host on the back and turned to get in the Mercedes.

"Now?" asked Anne.

"No not now. They've got to get some distance."

Five minutes passed. They switched over to infrared as the darkness intensified but they had trouble following the car as it darted in and out of woods.

"You're going to have to scrub it." Anne's voice had gone up a pitch.

"Wait, there they are." Ramson leaned closer to his screen. The Mercedes emerged, a block of orange moving fast.

"I'm locking in." Ramson shouted. "I got it!"

A red dot appeared on the top of Ivanov's car.

"Ready?" Ramson asked.

"It's our only chance," said Anne.

"OK. Three, two, one." Ramson hit the fire key.

The Hell-Fire streaked towards the Mercedes. When it exploded, the infrared monitor lit up like a flash bulb. There was so much fire that the visual light cameras easily caught the scene. Cars that had been near Ivanov's were still exploding. Nothing but a pile of black twisted metal was left of Ivanov's Mercedes. Everyone in the lead Mercedes was dead. They had to be. Ramson stood up quickly, knocking off his earphones.

"Yes!" he shouted. "The sonofabitch is dead."

He turned to give high fives and Anne slammed her palms against Ramson's.

Mr. Wood walked near the perimeter of the president's Steamboat vacation chalet, trying to figure out a point where the president might be vulnerable. The main problem was access. None appeared possible. The house sat alone on a hill surrounded by five acres of land, much of it forested. Mr. Wood would need to get through the forest to get a chance, and he was sure the Secret Service would have the place draped with motion detectors. Even if he got around them, and Mr. Wood didn't see how that was possible, there was no guarantee that the president would oblige and come to a nearby window to be shot. Mr. Wood turned his attention to another spot local reports said the president intended to visit: Rendezvous Park. According to the Steamboat Springs Pilot, Lawrence Naslund had been visiting the park even before he became president.

Mr. Wood rented a snowmobile and drove the ten miles up the mountain to Rendezvous Park. He paid five dollars to get in. Above the pools were cabins where people, mostly cross-country skiers, could stay overnight. Nearby was a changing room. Mr. Wood went in and changed into a swimsuit. Halfway down a path leading to the pools he came across a country sauna, a small log structure with an exterior cove oven. Interested, Mr. Wood opened the door to go in – and stopped dead in his tracks.

Inside, looking out at him with welcoming smiles he thought, were three very attractive young women. He guessed them in their early twenties, possibly coeds. But the item that most got his attention was that they were naked. From top to toe there was not a thin thread on any of them.

"Excuse me," Mr. Wood said, and began to close the door.

"No. No," said a strawberry blonde with a girl-next-door smile and the devil in her eyes. "Come 'n' join us. And take off those silly trunks."

Mr. Wood blinked in the low light. He wondered if a porn movie was being filmed nearby. He stood there for a moment with a jaw slacker than he would have liked, and certainly slacker than another part of him, and then shook his head, decision made.

"Sorry, ladies," he said. "Next time."

He closed the door quickly and wondered how long this had been going on. Wondered why the papers hadn't mentioned it. He rather regretted that he had work to do at that moment but still, he continued down to the upper pool.

When he got there he couldn't see it. The pool was completely engulfed in steam. He walked slowly forward, watching each step, trying not to fall in. Finally, he got close enough so that he could see the first pool. There were bathers there, some floating on their backs, and some drinking from plastic cups.

Ages ranged from eighteen to eighty. There were twenty or so bathers, both men and women. Half of them were naked. A sign read: "Adult swim today. Bathing suits optional." The times they are a-changing, Mr. Wood thought approvingly.

He went around the other two pools. They, too, had visitors. Most were dressed in swimsuits but, again, not all. Mr. Wood was in love with the place. But that didn't solve his immediate problem. He had a contract to fulfill.

He walked around the pools again, seeking an idea. Certainly, he reasoned, the Secret Service would have Rendezvous Park surrounded by motion detectors, just like up at the house. The service would have dozens of agents deployed along with a host of state and local officers. Rendezvous Park was open and not fenced off. That would make agents nervous and extra vigilant.

Openness might provide Mr. Wood a way in but there was a larger problem: Steam. You had almost to be on top of the pools to see them. No remote shot would be possible. On a third pass

Mr. Wood noticed the ribbon of hot spring water tumbling down the mountain. This was the super-hot water that had to be merged with cold creek water before it hit the pools. Without it, bathers would be cooked.

He watched the stream for some time and then walked up the mountainside to the point where it emerged. And an idea formed. Yes, he told himself, this is how it would work.

After a moment's pause he followed the ribbon of hot spring water back down the mountain. By the time he reached the pools the plan was there. He knew what he would do and how he would do it. Looking briefly around he turned toward the sauna. Arriving at the cabin he stopped. He thought for a moment and then swiftly took off his trunks and went inside.

Sally and Lou rode her Miata to Estes Park, a summer tourist attraction that was dead in the winter. Sally knew you could find great deals on jade jewelry in the off-season. Lou was listening to KOA radio's afternoon sport's talk program when a news bulletin interrupted.

A reporter read the story: "Daniel Dicerno, the local mob boss believed to be behind the killing of two top federal protected witnesses, was gunned down at his home earlier today, police said."

Sally gasped involuntarily.

"Police are looking for a female believed to be in her mid to late twenties who may have posed as a pizza delivery person to gain access to Dicerno's home in The Farm.

"Police say Dicerno was shot multiple times and died at the scene.

"Dicerno, known as Danny by his friends, had recently..."

Sally turned off the radio and glided the Miata to the side of the road. Her reaction even surprised herself, as one tear after another cascaded down her cheek. Lou looked alarmed and confused. Dicerno, ultimately, was a criminal and a killer who had cost Sally her career. Why this?

"Sally?"

"I know, Lou, I know. He was a wretched man. He killed people. And I was out to get him."

"OK, so?"

"Dammit, Lou. I don't know. For some reason I liked the guy. It shouldn't have ended like this."

"You liked him?" To Lou, Sally was a puzzle more difficult to solve than Bobby Fischer.

"Yeah, Lou, I did. He was a teddy bear with a Tommy gun. It's silly I know. I can't explain it but he had a certain twinkle in his eyes. There was something there, Lou. He wasn't just human waste."

Lou could think of nothing to say. So he did the next best thing and got hold of Sally's hand. It took Sally several minutes to recover. But when she did it was back to business.

"Who would do this, Lou?"

"He was dealing with tall timber. It doesn't get much taller than Vito Borelli."

"Yeah, but he had just saved Borelli."

"Maybe Vito Borelli isn't the grateful type."

"And maybe we still don't know what's really going on," Sally said, lowering the boom on the accelerator.

In Estes Park, they found a beautiful jade and turquoise necklace for two hundred dollars. It would be over a thousand next summer.

As they rode back to Denver, Sally wondered: "What's next?"

"We've got two names. One of them has to be right."

"Yeah, shithead Brad Johnson or some guy named George Phillips. My money's on shithead."

"Why, Sally?"

"Because he's a shithead."

"Sally!"

A blizzard roared outside Ivanov's greenhouse, but inside the mob boss paid it no heed as he tended tulips. He was making a bouquet of yellow ones for his wife. He had the chorale from Beethoven's ninth piped in. Ivanov had survived Team Blue's attack because he was a very careful man. Ever since the Slavnik assassination Ivanov had recruited two men to act as his doubles. With a little help from plastic surgeons and a Bolshoi Ballet makeup artist, the doubles looked just like Ivanov. They took it in turns always to travel in front in the Mercedes while Ivanov traveled behind in a Ford. He paid the men well. In return, one of them had paid him back, with his life.

As he trimmed another tulip Ivanov wondered if he had overstretched. He had ordered a hit on the President of the United States, a man who was proving a resourceful adversary. Maybe he should have tried negotiations. Maybe he should call Borelli and have the whole thing called off. Then he recalled that angel child Katya had just killed Dicerno. Wasp Man was on the loose. There was no going back.

As Ivanov arranged the tulips in a vase he decided it was too late to second guess. Soon the president would be dead and the Americans would launch a merciless investigation. What did it matter? He wondered if he could survive. But then he smiled to himself as he went inside. Sure he could, he told himself. Sure he could. Always.

As soon as Team Blue left Afghanistan, Ramson started to drink. He had killed Dimitri Ivanov. The president couldn't begrudge him a little celebration. Russian newspapers were filled with details of the "car bomb" that had killed Ivanov. How stupid are these people, Ramson thought.

Team Blue flew commercially to Islamabad and then to New York where they caught the shuttle to D.C.

The next day they assembled again in the office of Director Orvez. Ramson was smiling broadly when Linda Orvez walked in. It didn't last long. Orvez fixed Ramson with an eye so cold it could have frozen a continent.

"Care to tell me how you fucked up this time?" she spat.

74. Jimmy Visits

IT WAS mid-afternoon on December 23. A good solid snowstorm had hit Denver and blanketed the mountains. Sally sat on the sofa reading Lou's Scientific American. It was the article that Lou had lip-synched. She saw why he had. Reality was two dimensional not four, and what we thought as real was an illusion, Sally read. She knew that Lou had likely made it to the end. But there was no way she was going to get there. Why did Lou even attempt these things? She had no idea.

There was a knock at the door. Sally stiffened. How had anyone gotten through security? The doorman should have called from the entry and asked her if she wanted a visitor to come up. Having read the details of what happened with Danny Dicerno, Sally was on edge. Someone had gotten into The Farm by pretending what she was not. There was another knock.

She edged herself closer to the door, trying not to make a sound. Just as she was about to look out the peephole the person on the other side of the door knocked again. Louder. Sally's heart nearly exploded out of her chest. She put her back up against the wall and made an unintended noise.

"Miss Will?" she heard a voice. It seemed distorted but vaguely familiar.

"Miss Sally Will?"

Sally unplastered herself from the wall and inched over to the peephole. Half expecting to be blown away she looked out and blinked. It was Jimmy Fresno. He looked like a truck had run him down. She looked again. Jimmy seemed anxious, his head bounding from side to side to see if anyone was coming. He also had bandages all over his face, and his eyes were seas of blood above dark crevices. His black hair looked almost spiked.

"Mish Sally Will. Pleesh," Sally heard Jimmy say.

Sally opened the door. Jimmy Fresno stood there in a too-long overcoat and cowboy boots that Dicerno must have given him. And something bad had happened to his voice. Sally had no idea why he had come. Jimmy stepped inside and quickly closed the door. He looked drawn and confused. He had some flakes of snow on his head.

"Jimmy, what happened?" Sally was shocked.

"Looong stooory," said Jimmy morosely.

"Well, come sit down, Jimmy."

Sally led Jimmy toward the sofa. But Jimmy didn't sit. Sally asked if he wanted a drink. He shook his head.

"What is it, Jimmy?" Sally asked. "I heard about Danny. I'm sorry, sorry for you."

Jimmy looked down, a mix of fear and embarrassment.

"I shun't be here," he said. "This can get me dead."

"What, Jimmy?"

"Mish Will," Jimmy stammered, "Mr. Dish...Dicerno ashed me to ta...talk with you if anything, you know, whas to hap... happen to him. He want me chew gib you shomethin'."

Was he drunk? Sally wondered. He could hardly speak.

"Msh Will," he said, "Mr. Disherno ashed me da give you disjust before..." Jimmy choked a bit. "Jus before..." He tailed off, handing Sally an envelope.

Inside was a faded photo on newsprint depicting several of the participants at the Italian June Festival. Dicerno was there, without a costume. There was someone in a Bin Laden mask, a guy dressed as a box of cereal, and a fellow pretending to be Ted Bundy. Someone had drawn a red circle around the man in the Bundy mask. Sally didn't understand.

"What is this, Jimmy?" she asked.

"Mr. Disherno vanted you to have dish."

"Why, Jimmy?"

After a pause, Jimmy gathered himself a bit and said: "He shay da man in da circle ish da man you vant."

Sally looked down at the photo. She still didn't get it.

"The man I want...?" Sally repeated.

"Msh Will," Jimmy said looking down at his boots, "Itch da man. Da man you're lookingsh for."

Sally's knees fell victim as she finally got it.

"Who is it? Give me his name?" she finally asked.

"I don' sink Mr. Dicherno knew hish name. But da man in da masck had a code name."

"Jimmy, what was it? Don't play games."

"I only knew lashed name. It vas Mr. Wood."

Sally plopped down on the sofa, unable to stand any longer. Jesus Christ, she thought. Mr. Wood. Danny Dicerno had apparently hired someone he didn't know to do a dandy job at wrecking the Witness Protection Program. She didn't know if she believed that but why else would Jimmy Fresno, just after Dicerno's death, be handing her a faded photo and looking so miserable at doing so?

"OK, Jimmy." She looked up. Jimmy looked away. "Did he say anything else. This is important."

Jimmy was having a hard time getting it out but Sally sensed there was something more. She waited.

"Mish Will," Jimmy finally said. "Chis didn't come from me. Promish?"

"I promise."

"I will dany I vas ever here."

"And I will swear you weren't."

Jimmy again examined his boots. Sally waited. Then Jimmy spoke.

"He shed he had shtarted shumething terrible. I don' have any details. I vas not involved. He shed he vants you to shtop it."

"Stop what?"

"He din' shay. I think he vas 'fraid even stelling me. He shed you vere schmart. You would figure itsh out."

He turned to leave, then stopped.

"Oh ves," he said, "Mr. Dicerno shed to tell you it involved Mr. Wood and to give vou this."

Jimmy struggled with something in his pocket and pulled out the heart-shaped gold locket on a chain.

"It meansh nothin' to me," said Jimmy. He handed her the locket and left.

Sally stared at the closed door for some time wondering if there was something more she should have asked Jimmy Fresno.

When she finally opened the locket she felt a stab in her chest that buckled her knees again and propelled her back onto the sofa. She thought for a moment she might be having a heart attack. Inside the locket was a picture of the President of the United States of America. Sally knew immediately what it meant.

Mr. Wood, already suddenly rich, wondered at the meaning of Danny Dicerno's death. Would it mean he wouldn't collect the second half? Maybe. But Mr. Wood seemed to know that wouldn't be the case. He always doubted that Dicerno was the heavy behind his new assignment. Probably someone much bigger had hired him. Maybe even the Russians. In his mind it came down to this: Mr. Wood had been given a contract. He would complete the terms. The men who ordered it would probably pay. Mr. Wood had grown quite a reputation after all. Besides he was getting into it.

Thinking about it some more, he felt killing the president would be amusing.

75. Big Trouble

"OK. I'll tell you how you fucked up," Linda Orvez thundered at Charles Ramson. "You blew up the wrong fucking sonofabitch, that's how. You managed to kill an Ivanov double. And now the Russian president is screaming bloody murder."

"But he was a dead ringer," Ramson protested.

"And dead is a word that succinctly describes your career with the United States government. I will send your ass to someplace where even you can do no more damage."

"Linda...," Ramson almost pleaded.

"You're done Charles. Get out of here. And if any of this leaks I will personally introduce you to the devil. Scram."

Ramson stood erect and hesitated. His military instincts welled. Finally he turned, clicked his heels, and walked out of the room, his career over.

The other members of Team Blue were wide-eyed, wondering how many of them, if not all of them, would meet similar fates. But after Ramson left, Orvez sat back down at her desk and said, calmly, "Well, then. It's on to 'Plan B.' Anne here is the new leader of Team Dog...Team Blue. I am tasking her with the job of getting rid of Ivanov. The president wants this done and you are to do it."

"Rules of engagement?" asked Anne.

"There are none."

Orvez dismissed everyone but Anne.

In a hushed voice, she told Anne: "Ivanov will not venture back to a handy country like Uzbekistan again. He'll stay near Moscow. The president has authorized an operation there."

Anne wasn't shocked. But she was concerned. This was extremely dangerous. Ivanov was no Boris Slavnik. President Putin would not be happy. This was the big leagues. Anne had come from a small Midwestern town and had managed to get a scholarship to Vassar. Pure drive and smarts had put her there. Now she was rising fast in the agency. She could even picture herself someday in Linda Orvez's place. She knew this would be her biggest challenge yet but she was ready.

Orvez outlined her preliminary thinking. The plan would involve the oldest trick in the book: a honey trap. The agency knew that Ivanov frequented the Moscow Marriott. Often his eyes wandered. Anne would be there for him and with any luck...

Sally called Lou at his office. He rushed home. Sally had laid out the newspaper photo and the locket on the kitchen table.

"This is trouble big time," Lou said almost breathlessly as he studied the evidence.

"What can we do?"

"Don't take this wrong, Sal, but we can't go to the police. The president himself said you were a liar. What would they say if you told them that a man in a Ted Bundy mask named Mr. Wood was an assassin? Or that the man who told you this appeared too busted up to talk? Dicerno's man revealing his secrets? On Dicerno's orders? They would split a gut."

"I know. Maybe you could give it a shot."

"No, I don't think it would work, Sal."

Sally understood and nodded, grim-faced.

"I guess we need to find who was behind the Bundy mask," she said finally.

"Well," Lou said. "We have two names and we know the drill."

"I'll take Brad," Sally suggested, "since you two are such good buddies."

"So I have to do the hard work," Lou deadpanned. "Do we know anything about George Phillips?"

"No," said Sally.

"That's just great. Where do I start?"

"That's *terra incognita* Lou. You're the agent. Get whatever you can. And where should I begin?"

"Datelines would be a start, Sal. If Brad wrote anything from

Denver just before or during either Spilotro or Tony Nails, he's off the hook."

"And if he didn't?"

"Not so clear. You don't need me to tell you investigative reporters don't turn out copy every day. Sometimes they don't write every week."

"But it would be a sign," Sally agreed.

Over the next day Sally searched online for any articles Brad Johnson had written during July, just before Felipe Spilotro had been hit in Savannah. There were none. She searched for the time before the Tony Nails wasp murder. Again nothing. There were plenty of articles after the killings. None immediately before.

Sally dug deeper. Something in the post-murder stories caught her eye. In his first Tony Nails article, Brad had reported that the wasps used in the attack were from the species *Vespa mandarinia ceylonica*. No one else in the media had that information. Was Brad that good? Or was this part of a game?

Then Sally found an article Brad did on the killing of Big Bow. Brad had not only reported that the cops had found a cigarette butt at the scene of the crime but he had also written that it was filterless. As she knew, the cops had been keeping that secret. So how had Brad known? From sources, or because he was there?

Lou had less luck with George Phillips. Lou hunkered down with Scott Kirkpatrick at Scott's home computer. Scott had access passwords to a vast amount of data. Together they did checks on credit, property, professional licenses, criminal and civil records, and even medical records. Nothing. George Phillips didn't seem to exist before his sudden appearance as chief of sales of New Company Mining three years earlier.

Lou had seen this pattern before. It usually meant that George Phillips was a phony name carried by a con or, and far less commonly, by a spook. Lou also knew this: in either case, George Phillips could and should be considered a suspect. Lou called Pat O'Dowd, his friend in the U.S. Attorney's office. Pat said he would check on New Company Mining and George Phillips and get back.

76. Pillow Talk

ANNE looked like a successful American businesswoman as she sipped a purple martini at the bar inside the Moscow Marriott. A little thigh showed from her short blue skirt. And she seemed unoccupied.

A Russian who had come in with a large entourage glanced at her. She held his eyes only a moment, smiled briefly and then turned away, apparently disinterested. Dimitri Ivanov, however, was very interested. He asked an aide to check Anne out.

Pat O'Dowd called Lou back within an hour. He sounded concerned. Lou could tell from the street sounds in the background he was in a public booth.

"You've caused a firestorm," he said.

"I seem to have the knack."

"Washington called. It was the assistant director. He wanted to know why I was nosing around after George Phillips."

"And you said?"

"I used the old line about getting an anonymous tip that something was amiss."

"Did he believe it?"

"Of course not. He's used the trick himself. He probably taught it. He warned me off in no uncertain terms. Said New Company Mining is a government operation but not the Bureau's."

"CIA?"

"You were always too smart to be a fed, Lou. Of course CIA. How's Sally doing?"

"She's stitching herself together, one body part at a time."

"Tell her hi."

"I will."

"And, Lou, be careful. I'm slipping you something I got on the sly. Phillips was in covert operations. He did wet work."

O'Dowd broke the connection.

Lou stared at the phone. As a spook, George Phillips could have had access to protected witness lists. He lived in Denver, had a pilot's license and had been at the festival. He looked good as a suspect. But why would the CIA want to bring down the U.S. Marshals' program? Then again, why would Brad?

When Lou and Sally compared notes later they were perplexed.

"We can't eliminate either one," Lou said.

"I like your guy Phillips more and more," said Sally.

"And I'm taking a shine to Brad," replied Lou. "Maybe he makes up as a killer what he lacks in racquetball."

"So what next?"

"I suppose Brad will be easier to check out than some spook who probably has seventeen identities and a whole government to hide behind," Lou said.

"For sure."

"I know Brad's wife, Carla," Lou said. "Maybe I can call and poke around."

"Maybe even ask about a mask?"

"That's good, Sal."

"Hi, Carla, this is Lou," Lou said on his mobile a few minutes later. "Have I caught you at a bad time?"

"No, Lou. What's up?"

"Hey, do you remember when Brad went to the Italian June Festival last spring?

"Faintly."

"Did he have a costume?"

"Beats me."

"Maybe just a mask?"

"Don't know," Carla said. "Why do you need to know?

"Oh, it's OK, I..."

"No, wait," Carla interrupted. "I did find a mask. We had a crawl space disaster in the spring. A little flooding. When we hauled the junk out we put some of it in the garage. Most of it got tossed. But

I think Brad did keep a mask. Why don't you just call him?"

"I tried," Lou lied. "But he wasn't in."

"You need this mask?"

"Well, I'm going to this masquerade party and I wanted to go as Ted Bundy. Weird right? But I think that's the mask Brad had and I can't find it anyplace in town."

"Well, you're welcome to come by and look."

"Fine, thanks, I'll be over."

An aide told Ivanov he had found nothing suspicious about Anne. As far as he could tell she was a mid-level executive at an American telecommunications giant. That was enough for Ivanov. He was entranced. The honey trap was working.

A day later, Anne was again alone at the bar, showing even more leg, when Ivanov went in alone. He sat at a nearby table. Waiters started towards him in a rush but he waved them off. With his finger, he motioned one over.

"Buy that lady a purple martini." He told the waiter.

When the waiter brought the drink to Anne she first seemed embarrassed. Recovering, she turned to Ivanov and raised her glass. Then she took a drink and smiled. Ivanov raised his own glass but didn't drink. Instead he got up and came over.

"I see you are alone," he said in British-accented English. "Is your husband crazy?"

Anne smiled and pointed to her bare left ring finger.

"He was crazy," she said. "Fortunately for me, he was also rich."

Ivanov was aroused. The lady with the red silk lips was small but toned, she had great blonde hair and a quick mind. She was perfect.

Lou and Sally got to Brad Johnson's house fifteen minutes after Lou's call. Carla greeted Lou with a kiss on the cheek. She had long auburn hair and was in spandex shorts and top and looked like she could lift a ton. She looked over to Sally.

"You made it sound like this would be our secret rendezvous.

Who's this witness you brought?"

"Sally, Carla," Lou said smiling. "Carla, Sally."

They both smiled and shook hands.

"Brad told me you were dating Sally. Is this the lady who has stolen your heart?"

"She is the larcenous one," said Lou.

"You don't know how many hearts you are breaking, Sally." Sally blushed a bit. "Mine included of course!"

"I heard about your troubles," Carla continued. "A bum break. Even Brad said so. He really respects you."

She patted Sally's arm before turning suddenly business-like: "Now, what about this silly mask?"

"Where would Brad have left it?" Lou asked.

"After things dried out, he put what he wanted to save in a chest. It's just over there." Carla pointed to a corner of the garage and led them to it.

"It might be in here. Take what you want. I'm sure Brad won't mind. I'll be inside if you want me. Just yell."

Anne and Ivanov hit it off immediately. So she invited him up to her room after the second martini and he didn't decline. Once there he slowly turned her towards him and softly kissed her lips. Ivanov did not act like a boorish Russian thug, as she had imagined. Instead, the most feared gangster in the world was delicate as he removed her blouse and bra, far more delicate than she was in getting off his shirt. This had always been a fantasy for Anne, screwing professionally. And to have her first time to be with such a powerful and evil man excited her even more. Knowing that Team Blue was listening was icing.

The rest of their clothes flew off as if they were part of a David Copperfield illusion and they tumbled to the bed. Anne was ready to take him inside her right away. Although he was quite ready he was also in no hurry. He savored her body, talked to her. He told her he could not believe how firm her breasts were and how sweet they tasted as he went gently from one to the other, increasing

Anne's desire in spite of herself. His tongue continued down her belly, slowly, methodically, tantalizingly. He continued talking to her gently, praising her. Anne's excitement was mounting to fever pitch and really getting the better of her. When Ivanov's tongue arrived at her pussy and began slowly licking her clit Anne could no longer control herself. She grabbed the bedposts behind her head and arched her back as if an electric jolt had gone through her. The orgasm overwhelmed her completely.

Ivanov could have stopped there, and Anne would have sworn she had found the perfect lover. But Ivanov didn't stop. He entered her, moving slowly, gently back and forth, in perfect rhythm with her thrusts, just as she liked it. He was a master. He was a dream. Jeez, she had never had a man like him. Suddenly Ivanov moved harder, faster. And Anne moved harder, faster. And now she couldn't get enough of him. Suddenly she was consumed. She came again, stronger than before, crying out in abandoned ecstasy. But Ivanov still wasn't finished. He kept thrusting. Who had created such a man? Ann marveled, just before reaching another crescendo, even more massive than the one before. She could not believe how hard and big this old Russian was. She knew there were drugs but who cared? This was on another planet.

Anne came three more times, maybe more. She lost count. And still Ivanov kept going. How did we ever beat these guys? When Ivanov finally came, with a roar she thought could lift the top off a mountain, she was utterly spent. Ivanov too. After lying exhausted for a while Ivanov got up and poured them both a brandy. He raised his glass to her and drank it in one swallow.

In the shower, as Anne scrubbed Ivanov's back, she thought: Ivanov, you are the greatest lover in the world, the best I may ever have. I had to fake nothing. But tomorrow I must kill you.

When it was Ivanov's turn to rub Anne's back, he thought: Anne is perfect. Then he thought: Yes, maybe too perfect.

Lou opened the chest and both he and Sally dug in. It was filled with discarded shirts and bedding and some antiquated board games. Sally put aside Risk and Life and Clue Master Detective, which appeared to have gotten a lot of use. Right below those they saw it, a mask, facing down.

Lou and Sally paused and looked at each other. They both thought they knew what it would be. Sally reached in and turned it over. Ted Bundy.

Lou immediately took out his phone and called the city desk at the Post. He asked to speak to Brad Johnson. He didn't want to speak to him but he needed to know where he was.

"He'll be in later today," said a city desk clerk. "Want to leave a message?"

"No, that's fine," said Lou.

"You better leave a message if you want to talk to him. After he gets back here he's going to leave town for the next few days."

"Oh really. Where's he going?"

"Search me."

Lou clicked off.

Sally knocked on the door to the house from the garage.

"Oh, so you found it," Carla said, looking at the Bundy mask. "I remember. Brad was very proud of that."

"I really need to talk to Brad about it. There are some parts of the costume missing. When will he be home?"

"I don't know if he's coming home," said Carla.

"I hear he's on some important assignment," Sally said.

Carla touched Sally's arm again. "Don't worry, Miss Will. This doesn't concern anything you had been doing, before..." Her voice faded.

"It's OK," said Sally.

"He's going up to Steamboat Springs to cover the presidential visit," Carla said.

Lou caught Sally out of the corner of his eye.

"Isn't that a bit off his beat?" asked Lou.

"I know. He usually steers clear of pack journalism, as he calls it. But he was very excited about this visit. He's even gone up there to figure out the best spots to get views, and he did it on his own time."

Sally tried not to show surprise.

Lou prodded. "Carla, I'm trying to remember the date of the ball. It was a month or so before you guys went to Georgia on vacation, wasn't it?"

"No," said Carla.

"Oh, no vacation in Georgia."

"No."

Lou decided to drop the subject, but Carla didn't. "Brad went to Georgia but it wasn't a vacation, and I didn't go."

"Don't mean to pry," Lou somehow managed to say.

"No, that's OK. Brad had a problem with a relative. He went down there and fixed it."

Lou pressed again. "Savannah, right?"

"How did you know?"

"Oh, I remember now Brad mentioned something about it."

Sally suddenly grabbed Lou's arm to steady herself. She thought it was time to leave. What more could they get? What more did they need? But as they turned to leave the garage something caught Lou's eye. There were a couple of cans in a corner with Hazmat written on them and skull-and-cross bones poison sign.

"What are those, Carla?" Lou asked.

"Just something Brad got for insects."

"You have a bug problem?"

"Not a big one. But Brad says we will if he doesn't act. You know him."

"You mind?" said Lou, nodding towards the cans.

"Brad said to be careful handling those cans."

"Oh, I will be."

Lou didn't need to read the label after he caught the scent.

Almonds.

Cyanide.

77. Deep Satisfaction

LOU and Sally rushed to the Post's parking lot. They had to be there when Brad left for Steamboat. They would tail him, and, hopefully, somehow, some way, come up with a plan.

"How is he going to use the cyanide?" Sally wondered.

"No clue," Lou said. "But he is."

"Lou, look! It's him."

Brad was walking toward the parking lot. He had a driven expression on his face, the kind big running backs have when they decide not to sidestep the linebacker, but to plow right through. He jumped in the Liberty and began speeding away. Lou followed. He was not happy to be pursuing in a red Miata. Good tail cars were dark and ordinary. But he and Sally had no choice. Brad went west on Speer Boulevard and then north on I-25. He took the I-70 exit and headed west.

"He's going to Steamboat," Sally said.

"He must have a way to get the cyanide into a ventilation system, or something," said Lou.

"Lou, he's murdered in stranger ways than that."

"Whatever the plan we can't let him get close to the president. I'll kill him myself if I have to."

Sally looked hard at Lou. Could he really kill his friend? The look in Lou's expression left no question. He could.

"Lou, I may have to be the one to do the killing."

Lou looked puzzled.

"I'm the one with current Secret Service credentials they have yet to cancel. I could maybe get close."

Lou nodded.

Up ahead, Brad Johnson had spotted the red sports car in the rear view mirror almost immediately. It was hanging far back but there was no mistaking it. He laughed to himself that a famous private detective was following him in a cherry-red Miata. Ridiculous.

Brad already knew the score. He had been expecting them. Carla had called, told him about Sally and Lou dropping by and taking the Bundy mask, and also about how Lou was interested in the poison. Brad had shrugged it off. Carla suspected nothing. But Brad knew that Lou and Sally were making a key mistake. They were assuming something that wasn't true. If he played it right, Brad believed he could turn the discoveries into a blessing. He planned a feint and he hoped they would bite.

Steve Brandon and his team had worked with the Secret Service to get the president from Denver International to Steamboat and from Steamboat to Rendezvous Park. With a possible assassin on the loose they took a plane to Steamboat while a phony presidential limo drove up on I-70. It was routine duty for Brandon. Nearly every time the president had come to Colorado, Brandon and his team had been on the security detail. The president even called Brandon by his first name.

Once the president was settled in the contributor's chalet Brandon went to inspect security at Rendezvous Park. There, he shook hands with an old friend who was in the secret world. Brandon called the man Jake. It was not his real name.

"You're looking good, Jake," Brandon said. The two hugged.

"Steve, I followed it in the press," Jake said. "The business with the Chicago Tribune. It was terrible."

"That's what the press is down to nowadays. I'll get by. What's happening here?"

"We're kind of on edge. You know the rumors. This damn place has too many trees. And way too much steam."

"Steam could be an asset," Brandon said.

"Only when the president is in it," Jake said. "The danger zone is just before he gets there."

"I see what you mean," Brandon said, looking out at the steam above the pools.

"But I don't see any real danger here that you can't handle," Brandon said.

"Hope you're right," said Jake.

Brandon smiled. He knew he couldn't call him by his real name. That was classified. But he knew what it was: It was George Phillips.

Brad Johnson stopped at a Radisson, took a bag from the Liberty and went to check in. Lou and Sally pulled into a filling station down the block.

"What's he doing?" Sally asked.

"I guess he wants to take his time."

Sally moved the Miata next to a stone wall. From there, they could watch the front of the hotel. But just as they settled in for a long wait, Brad reemerged. He was wearing a bright yellow coat, blue jeans and pointed brown cowboy boots. Lou had never seen him in boots.

"What the hell? Is he John Wayne?" Lou said.

"The yellow coat helps. Can't lose track of him while he's wearing that."

"But why does he want to call attention to himself?" Lou asked.

Sally shrugged. No clue.

Brad ambled down toward the town center, with a lift in his step. It looked to Sally that he was whistling.

"Should we tail him on foot?" Sally asked.

At first Lou thought that would be a good idea. But then he reconsidered.

"No, Sally, I don't think so. It doesn't look like he is carrying anything. He doesn't have the cyanide. Better to wait."

"I don't know, Lou."

"Without him having the cyanide we have nothing."

"OK, we wait." But she had a question in her eyes. Sally took out a cigar. Lou didn't stop her.

In town, Brad went to the Café Colorado, got a table by the window, ordered Eggs Benedict, and settled in. Ski bunnies walked by, laughing, investigating the landscape for men. A couple of women caught Brad's eye and smiled. Brad smiled back. Men followed the women, their attention glued to their back-sides. This was the place, Brad told himself again. When this business was over, this is where he would settle.

A young waitress with both dimples and freckles came by. She, too, smiled. What a town, Brad thought. He ordered a large glass of Colorado Plum Creek Merlot.

By now Lou was regretting his decision not to follow Brad. Brad had seemed to disappear. Had he somehow pre-positioned the cyanide? Had he fooled them? Two hours passed. No Brad.

Sally had tried almost all the dials on the radio but couldn't settle in to listen to any of them for more than five minutes. Lou was growing irritated by the constant station changes. Lou and Sally were hungry, thirsty, and concerned. Their tempers grew short. They stopped talking to each other. Lou looked out of the window in one direction, Sally in the other. Another half an hour passed.

Suddenly Sally grabbed Lou's hand and shouted: "Lou! I think that's him." She pointed. Far down the street Lou saw a yellow dot.

"I think you're right," said Lou.

Minutes later, the shape of Brad Johnson came into focus walking slowly towards them. He was taking his time. A Sunday stroll. Again, Sally thought he was whistling. When he got to the Radisson he turned and walked in.

Team Blue met at a Moscow safehouse. Richard, the young Team Blue member who had been tasked with listening in on Anne's hidden mike, came shyly up to Anne.

"You could be an actress," he said.

"You thought I was acting, huh?" Anne smiled.

Richard turned red. Although in his late twenties with, he believed, reasonable looks, a good head of soft brown hair and doe-brown eyes, he was aware, at just five feet four inches in elevator shoes, of his physical inadequacies in the face of the passion of a woman like Anne. He couldn't bring himself to look at her.

"OK, guys," Anne told Team Blue. "I'm going to get Dimitri into the sack again." She winked at Richard who flushed again. "And then, when we are finished, he will want a little brandy. We will have a surprise for him. Formula J."

Formula J was a special concoction the Agency had created to spike blood pressure so high that vessels in the brain explode. If pathologists looked carefully enough they would see it but the bet was that no one would look too closely.

"And you guys will be right there in case anything goes wrong," continued Anne. "Which it won't. When Ivanov's dead I will call the police. When they get there I think I can make them understand what was going on. Overexertion leading to cardiac arrest. I don't anticipate too many questions."

"Remember," Richard said, looking anxious. "We're in the room above. We can't get to you instantly."

"Don't worry your sweet little bippy about that," Anne said "This will be pretty smooth sailing, I'm sure of it. And besides, you will be listening to every little sound, won't you Richard? So you'll know everything that's going on all the time." She said it almost tauntingly. Richard lowered his head. To Anne, Richard was almost like a puppy dog.

"After that, Richard, you and the team get me out and we go home."

That evening, Anne had on a red dress that came a good two inches above her knees. She ordered a Tom Collins and waited at the hotel bar. Ivanov walked in alone. He saw Anne, smiled, walked up and gave her a kiss on both cheeks followed by a bracelet covered in what looked like diamonds. From behind his back he also produced a bouquet of tulips.

Anne took both with a profusion of thanks. The diamonds must have cost a fortune, she thought. They were so bright Anne was sure they could blind. The tulips wouldn't have cost much but they were special. Thoughtful. Unexpected. A mob boss bearing flowers. For a brief moment Anne wished she didn't have to kill this man. But the thought passed. Anne took Ivanov's hand and led him toward the elevator.

Richard was both relieved and apprehensive as he listened in to Anne's mike. He was relieved that Ivanov had fallen into the trap. But now came the hard part. They were heading to the room. And he was going to have to listen.

Anne's mike was small, and well disguised. It looked like nothing more than a lipstick tube. There was no chance, Team Blue believed, that anyone could detect it. No chance.

The elevator stopped on the seventeenth floor where Anne and Ivanov got out and walked down the hall. Halfway along a bellboy wearing a red cap emerged from a room and brushed by.

"Ma'am," he said as he passed and tipped his hat. Anne did not yet know it but the red cap meant more than she ever could have imagined. A year before, Ivanov had purchased the best anti-bugging equipment the Russian secret services possessed. The Russians had always been ahead of their American adversaries in this technology throughout the Cold War. They had not slackened off since. The red cap signaled Ivanov that Anne was wearing a bug. She was not who she pretended to be. She was a spy.

In her room Anne did not waste much time in undressing and getting Ivanov in the same state.

"Dimitri," Anne breathed as Ivanov slipped his fingers between her legs, "you are a master." She ran her hand up his thigh and felt him expanding.

In the room above Richard briefly took his headphones off.

"Here we go again," he told Team Blue. He hit a switch so that they could all listen.

"Take it slow," Anne told Ivanov. "Slow."

In another minute she said: "Slower. Slower."

Anne pushed her fingers into Invanov's back.

"There," she said. "Yes, there. Oh Fucking God!"

Ivanov's breathing grew heavy, like a regular drum beat. Anne's vaginal muscles were working overtime on Ivanov's erection and Ivanov began to go faster.

"Oh. Oh. Oh." Anne cried. Then she screamed as a flood of juices poured from her and she climaxed as never before. But Ivanov didn't stop. He was remorseless. Unstoppable. Finally Anne's screams increased until they seemed loud enough to lift the roof off the hotel. Behind them came Ivanov's roar. The harmonics seemed to sway the world. And then it was over. And there was silence.

Team Blue was silent. The listeners themselves looked exhausted. Richard was embarrassed he had grown an erection. There had been a moment when he thought Anne's screams might be pain and they should carry out a crash attack but it soon became obvious that pain was the very last thing she was experiencing. Richard took short breaths and started to listen again.

He heard Anne tell Ivanov: "You are the best."

"No, Anne," Ivanov said, his voice a satisfied rumble, "that honor goes to you."

The agents heard the glasses clink. Formula J should be flowing. Suddenly, the connection broke.

78. Baby Face

BRAD Johnson came out of the Radisson hotel and walked towards his Jeep.

"This is it, Lou," Sally said. "He's going to make his move."

If it was his move it was starting out slowly. Brad walked around the Liberty with the deliberation of a pilot checking a plane before a flight. He then yawned, and finally got in. Lou and Sally were prepared to follow him to the chalet. If he rented a snowmobile for Rendezvous Park they would follow him there as well. Except Brad didn't drive toward the chalet or a rental shop. He turned the Liberty onto highway 40.

"What the hell?" exclaimed Lou. "That's the way to Denver."

When Brad got to I-70 and turned east, Lou knew he had been right. Brad was going back to Denver.

"What's he up to?" Sally asked.

"No clue."

"What do we do?"

"We follow, I guess. But I think we're missing something."

"And maybe we've fucked up again."

Sally could not avoid that sense of failure.

"Do you suppose he's decided to skip the part about killing the president?" Sally joked.

"Could have slipped his mind, I suppose," said Lou.

Johnson stopped at a McDonalds in West Vail for a Big Mac and fries, then moseyed on down the pike. It was hard for the red Miata not to stand out. It was the only other car on I-70 traveling 50 miles per hour. When he got to the city Brad drove directly home and went inside. Lou and Sally parked down the block, confused and by now very tired.

Ivanov's men had appeared suddenly out of nowhere and thrown a sheet over Anne the moment Ivanov had toasted her with his glass. They had rushed her struggling down six flights of stairs to the basement where they tied her, still naked, to a chair. Anne was gulping for air. She was dizzy. She knew what was coming.

Alexi, a six-five former Olympic wrestler, had on a black leather jacket and a New York Yankees cap. He was putting on black gloves and a full-length apron.

"Don't want to mess by clothes," he explained, giving his victim a "just you wait" smile.

"I'll tell you everything," Anne said. "Nothing held back."

"That will save us all a lot of time," Alexi said. "Who are these men you brought with you?"

"They're called Team Blue..."

Anne went on from there. Nothing held back. She told them everything she knew.

"Honey, I'm home," Brad yelled, deliberately loudly.

Carla walked down the steps to the family room in a yellow spandex exercise outfit that matched Brad's coat. She had a sheen of perspiration from a workout. She gave Brad a kiss almost as warm as the one she had given Lou Elliott.

"I thought you had to cover the president?" asked Carla.

"You know that stuff bores me. They got someone else."

"But you seemed so excited," Carla said. Brad dismissed that with a wave of his hand.

"Brad, after Lou saw the bug poison, he seemed really concerned. Is there a problem?

"Nothing to worry about," said Brad, "It's safe, honey."

Brad went to his wet bar and made himself a vodka martini, sat down in his lounge chair and tuned his big flat-screen TV to the Discovery Channel. Some girl from India was kissing a cobra.

Moscow police discovered Anne's naked body off the road leading to Sheremetyevo Airport. Because of the condition of her teeth, her fingernail polish and her jewelry, they figured her for a Westerner, maybe even an American. She had not been tortured, an exception Ivanov seldom made. But police found a hypodermic needle piercing her aorta. Her death would have been quick and relatively painless. Whoever had done this was sending a message. What that message was was clearly accented by Anne's corpse still wearing Ivanov's bracelet of cut glass.

When Brad Johnson had not emerged from his home by ten the next morning, Lou and Sally were more than alarmed.

"Something's wrong, Sally."

"If Brad is going to kill the president, he must be planning to do it by telepathy."

What had they missed?

"Sally, maybe he set something up in Steamboat we haven't thought of, maybe can't imagine."

"We followed him, Lou. He set nothing up."

"Maybe he had set it up before."

"Then why drive there at all?"

"We don't know. But this is a man who used wasps to kill Tony Nails. Allegedly. Might he have something similar in mind for the president?"

The word "allegedly" was still echoing in Sally's mind. Was Lou losing faith?

"Lou," she said. "Do you think we're wrong?"

Lou knew a lot rested upon his answer, maybe even Sally's life.

"No, Sal. We're not wrong."

Sally looked into Lou's eyes for some sign of contradiction. Finding none, she turned away.

"I should get back to Steamboat," she said. "Whatever is going to happen will happen there. And I have the credentials."

"What are you looking for?" Lou asked.

"I don't know. But all I can think is he must have lured us back here to keep us away from Steamboat."

Lou danced his fingers on the steering wheel, thinking. It was a reasonable hypothesis.

"OK, Sal. Take the Miata and get there quick. I'll hang with Brad. Maybe he'll tip his hand."

They took a chance and darted over to the condo to retrieve Lou's Landcruiser.

"Sal, be careful," Lou leaned over and kissed her with determination.

Sally pulled away, and put a finger to his lips.

"This is it, Lou. I'll be as careful as needed."

It was not exactly what Lou wanted to hear but it was all he was going to get. Sally took off for Steamboat while Lou went back to Brad and Carla's place. When Lou got there, nothing had changed. The Liberty was exactly where it had been.

Ten minutes later, Brad came out in his pajamas, yawned, put his hands behind his head and stretched. He had had a good night. Carla had been very obliging for a change. He bent down to get the paper and looked up and down the street. There was no red sports car to be seen.

Team Blue had been frantic when they lost contact with Anne. Five minutes later they decided something had gone very wrong and rushed her room. It was empty. When they came out a force of twenty men met them, most armed with AK-47s. Ivanov had decided not to kill them. That could be too much for the FSB to explain away. But killing someone who was trying to kill you is acceptable tradecraft the world over. Besides, he had Anne's confession. He could always use that against the Americans. Now Ivanov knew he had been right to hire Mr. Wood.

A bedraggled Team Blue was packed into a propeller driven plane and flown to Istanbul. Ivanov wished he could see the look in Linda Orvez's eyes when she learned that Anne would not be coming back. He decided to celebrate the victory by returning to his greenhouse. He had some roses to attend to.

Lawrence Naslund was sitting on the ledge of a fountain in the Steamboat chalet when Linda Orvez came to see him. He was in a jogging suit, having worked out in the owner's gym. He was relaxed and alone. The rest of the First Family was in town shopping. It was warm and humid inside. The sweet smell of tropical ferns and plants filled the air. But something was wrong he knew. Orvez was ashen. Her left hand trembled slightly.

The president looked at her with "now what" eyes as she sat next to him.

"Bad news, Larry," she said.

The president raised his eyebrows.

"Team Blue. We lost the leader." Linda explained.

"I am so sorry, Lar," Orvez touched the president's hand. "I have no idea how Ivanov found out. We thought Anne's going with him to her room was safe."

The president leaned back and closed his eyes.

"Now we must assume he knows everything," Orvez said.

"Was she tortured?" the president said with his eyes still closed.

"No. That's how we're sure she told them everything."

The president opened his eyes and looked at Orvez for a moment before he understood.

"Does the press know?" he asked.

"Not yet."

"OK, let's keep it that way," he said.

The president stood. There was a Secret Service man posted just outside the atrium's door. He nodded for him to come in.

"Sir?" the agent asked when he got to the president.

"Time for the pools."

That meant Rendezvous Park, the agent knew.

Rendezvous Park. The mere mention of the place took the president back to a time when he was not president. When he was young and restless and with a woman who was exactly the same. Just the mention brought back memories when he and his girl were broke and happy and feeling that the world could go screw itself. He needed some of that feeling now.

As Lou watched Brad Johnson's home a thought began forming.

He was looking at the chessboard, watching for lines. He was sure Brad had been involved in the killing of Spilotro and Tony Nails. But Lou began wondering if he could he have done it alone. It hardly seemed plausible. He was a reporter, not a law enforcement insider. How could he get locations of protected witnesses?

Another unresolved point surfaced. It had been with him for some time, in the back of his mind. Who was the young woman with black shining hair and a baby-pink complexion who stood beside Steve Brandon at the press conference that buried Sally? He remembered his feeling then that he had seen her before. Where?

Lou scratched his head and closed his eyes. And then something flickered. He had seen her at a restaurant. Maybe a donut shop. Lou wished he could just get out and pace. He was looking at Brad Johnson's house but his mind was elsewhere. More came to him. He thought he had seen the girl in a restaurant near downtown. Some grill. Something. Lou drummed his fingers on the steering wheel. The Mile High Grille. That was it. He and Sally had gone there to listen to some folk music. Neil Young tunes. When was that, Lou thought? August? He had given her a twenty dollar tip. Or was he mistaken? The waitress didn't look pregnant at the time he gave her the tip. How could she be holding her infant in October? But then maybe it wasn't hers. Maybe the whole press conference was a charade meant to cover for Brandon being away at the time of the killings. If he was Brad's partner, he would have wanted to be available. He remembered Brandon was in charge of the Dicerno case so he would have known where Spilotro was, and whether there were any reports that anyone in the Dicerno organization was tipping off police about the murder plan.

The more he thought, the more Lou began to feel he'd been had. When receipts showed Brandon had not been in Savannah or Wisconsin when the killer struck, and when DNA showed he was not the gunman in either the Palermo or Big Bow case, Lou had scratched him off the list. The same with the pack of reporters. They didn't dissect Brandon's story because they had been shamed. What could beat credit card receipts and DNA? The only one who refused to be swayed was Sally.

Lou hit the steering wheel. How could he prove it? Only one way: he had to find the girl. And fast. Lou got on his cellphone and called the Mile High Grille. He told the manager that he was working on a homicide case and that an employee might be a witness. He described the woman.

"There are no black-haired women working here now I would call pretty," said the manager. "But I've only been here two months."

"Think maybe you could look at your records," urged Lou. "Help an old detective out." Lou never claimed to be a "police" detective.

"I'm not supposed to do that, dude."

"I know," said Lou, trying to sound sympathetic. "And I'm not supposed to close down restaurants for health code violations."

The manager gulped. "OK, man. I'll look. You owe me."

"I owe you."

Five minutes later, the manager came up with a name: Lydia Valente.

"She left in November," the manager said.

"You know where she went?"

"We mailed her last check not to her apartment but to some business at 3842 Osage Street. That's all I got, sir."

Lou felt a tingle ripple through his spine. The address was Capricio's.

Ten minutes later, Lou eased his Landcruiser into the lot opposite Capricio's. The club's windows were draped in black, still mourning Danny's death. Inside, it was even darker. Some old-timers long retired from the rackets sat at the bar quietly exchanging some now-unimportant secrets. There were a few families having dinner. Tony Bennett was singing about his lost heart in San Francisco.

Lou recognized her right away, a girl behind the bar, wiping off some beer rings and smiling. Her hair now had purple streaks and she had a stud in her nose. But otherwise she was the same. Lou straddled a stool and ordered a Bud.

When she brought it, Lou smiled and asked in a voice that hint-ed at a Texas drawl: "Hey, didn' I see you on TV one time? Yeah, yeah. It was 'bout some cop?"

"Oh, that. I'm not supposed to talk about it," Lydia said, smiling back at Lou.

"Brandon somebody, warn't that it?" said Lou the Texan.

The girl blushed.

"You guessed it," she whispered conspiratorially. She seemed glad he knew.

"So your name's Lydia, right?

"Right."

"That was a sad story," Lou said in an even lower whisper. "Sorry it got so public. Must-a been tough, fer you I mean."

Lydia continued to wipe the counter although it was now spit polish shiny.

"Yeah," she said. "My folks in San Diego saw the news and wondered what little Lydia was up to."

Lydia held up a finger. "One moment."

She went to serve some of the old men but came back. Lou ordered another Bud.

"Don't mean to be nosey, miss, but that guy, that Brandon whatshisname, he is supposed to be a tough homicide cop as I recall. And you, you are a sweet young thing."

Lou leaned forward, glanced about him as though making sure no one could be listening. "However did you two meet?"

Lydia was game. She gave a "what-the-hell" shrug, rolled her eyes and began talking.

"I used to work at the Mile High Grille on 32nd. Steve came in and had a cup, then got called away on some crazy homicide. A guy named Palermo."

"That's when you met?"

"Yeah, and then he came back later. Anyhow, you know," she said, batting brown eyes under dark eyebrows, "we took it from there."

Lou smiled. "Lydia, you don't mind if I call you Lydia do you? My name is Lou. You are very photogenic. Do you know that?

Have you ever thought about getting back to California? You know, to Hollywood?"

Lydia looked down, almost embarrassed. "I've thought about it. Sure have. I've got to earn some money first though."

"Couldn't you stay with your parents?"

"Naw," Lydia said. "They think I'm a slut for having Brandon's baby. But there's someone who wants to help."

"Oh?"

"Yeah. A guy here who used to work for Mr. Dicerno. Jimmy Fresno. Maybe you know him?"

"Nope, cain't say I do."

Lydia leaned so close to Lou she was just six inches from his ear.

"He's says he's had it with this life. Him, and me we're going to slip away to Oregon. When we got enough money. He says he'll take me to LA. Said things are too dangerous here."

Lou thought maybe he had misjudged Jimmy Fresno.

"Hang in there, Lydia," he said, leaving a five dollar tip.

Back in his car Lou added it up. If Lydia had only met Brandon in June, when Palermo was hit, she didn't have time to have his baby by the time the press conference was held. The story was a lie. And Brandon had found the perfect woman to tell it with. Lydia was desperate, had no local connections, and was hopelessly naïve. Worse, Brandon had steered her to Capricio's, where she could be watched, or killed. And now Jimmy Fresno was going to try to save her.

Lou didn't have great faith in Jimmy's plan. But he had renewed faith in Sally.

79. Burning Rubber

SALLY was dressed Colorado style – jeans and boots and a fur-lined Levi jacket – as she walked up to the Ptarmigan Hotel booth where journalists showed their Secret Service credentials. She was nervous. Were her credentials really still good? If she couldn't get close to the president, what good could she do?

There was a small line. One man from the Atlanta Constitution did a double take when he saw Sally. His eyes asked the question: "What are *you* doing here?" But when Sally winked he turned away. Didn't say anything.

"Next," said a Secret Service man.

Sally had been here before. Just act like you belong, she told herself. She showed him her credentials, and held her breath as the agent typed her name into a computer. He then carefully compared her picture on the credentials against the one in the computer. To get in, they had to match.

"OK," the agent said. "Look straight ahead."

He snapped a photo of Sally, printed it out and laminated it together with a pass. Sally managed to look impatient, not worried out of her wits. The agent said, "Yeah, yeah, I know" and handed Sally her pass. She was in.

Sally wanted to get as close as she could to the chalet where the president was staying. An old man on a street corner, wrinkled, gray and sporting a white cowboy hat, gave her directions. Sally trudged up a hill toward the chalet. There was a check-point to go through before she could get inside the perimeter. A small line of journalists was passing through. Sally got behind it. But as she got to the front of the line a man she knew came out of a booth, talking animatedly with another. It was Steve Brandon. Sally froze. If Brandon saw her, she was history. Sally swung around and bumped into a middle-aged reporter with a huge pot belly.

"Oh, sorry," she said.

The man looked at Sally. He thought of nothing to say and stepped aside. Sally turned and started back down the hill. Her phone rang. She clicked it off immediately.

Lou drove around north Denver, thinking. One thing was bugging him: How would Brad or Brandon have gotten to Tony Nails? That one wasn't Brandon's case. It seemed the puzzle was never ending. He took out his mobile to tell Sally. She didn't pick up. He made another call, but not to Sally this time.

"Ruth Johanson, can I help you?" The voice was gravelly, deep and familiar. Ruth was a middle manager at the local telecommunications company. Pushing sixty, Ruth had soured on the male sex twenty years before when her husband ran off with an exotic dancer to Vegas. But Ruth had made Lou an exception. He had always been correct and courteous when he was with the FBI and he hadn't changed a bit since. He sent her Christmas cards and flowers on her birthday. For Lou's part, he didn't think he was being merely predatory. He liked Ruth and felt sorry for her, and used her rarely. But there weren't many women that age who received flowers from Lou Elliott.

"Ruthie, how are you, you old home wrecker?"

Ruth knew it was Lou right away.

"Me? You're the one who's still breaking hearts all over town."

"Actually, I'm thinking of settling down."

"You must not do that, young Elliott. All husbands turn to shit."

"That's what all women say. Hey Ruthie, I need a favor. Big one. And I need it fast. Can you help?"

Ruth could hear the strain in his voice.

"Sure, shoot," she said.

Lou spelled it out. He needed any calls made from the place where Brandon said he was holed up during the Spilotro and Tony Nails hits.

"Will this get me a new and improved husband?" Ruth asked.

"This could be even better than kissing a frog."

"Oh, my. Promises, promises."

Ruth consulted her computer screen.

"OK, Lou. There were fourteen calls from that first number to Savannah. All were in July."

Lou let that soak in for a minute.

"And in October?" Lou asked.

"Only three. All were to someplace called Bayfield, Wisconsin. OK?"

"OK, Ruthie. Thanks, I owe you."

"You better believe it," said Ruth and hung up.

Lou dug out one of Sally's cigars and lit up, in both senses.

"You prick, Brandon," he almost snarled.

He punched a new number into his phone: the Denver Police Department's Crimes Against Persons Bureau. He asked for Steve Brandon.

"He's not in."

"Can I reach him?"

"What is this about, sir?"

Lou hung up and called Kirkpatrick's direct number.

"Kirkpatrick here."

"Scott, Lou Elliott. I need to know where Steve Brandon is right now."

"What's your number?"

Lou gave it to him. The five minutes it took for Scott to call back seemed like five hours.

Lou's phone rang.

"Yes?"

"He's in Steamboat, guarding our president."

Lou left rubber for thirty yards as he raced down Federal to I-70, all the time struggling with the phone to call Sally. She still didn't pick up. He called O'Dowd. He was out. The computer said that to leave a message, press one. He did, and left a very direct message.

He headed out of Denver and up I-70 at 100 miles per hour, struggling with the phone. He got to the main FBI number in

Denver. After five minutes he was put through to a disinterested-sounding voice. He told the agent that Lt. Steve Brandon of DPD was in Steamboat Springs and was about to try to kill the President of the United States.

"Aren't you the private eye who tried to finger Brandon before and got shot down?" the agent asked.

"This is different."

"I'm sure it is. So let's start from the beginning, shall we?"

Lou was past Idaho Springs before the conversation ended.

He knew it would mean nothing. The agent would pass the tip on to the Secret Service with all the conviction of a Thai hooker.

A state trooper going east on the interstate saw a Landcruiser blasting west. The trooper made a U-turn and gave chase. Lou saw it but couldn't care less. He put the pedal all the way down. He hadn't thought he could handle an SUV doing a hundred and ten miles per hour down the backside of Loveland Pass. Now he knew better.

His phone rang, just as his right tires were lifting slightly off the ground during a left turn. He heard a screech like a thousand nails on a chalkboard. But he landed safely and answered.

"Sally?"

"Yeah."

"It's Brandon."

"What?"

"Brad has a partner. It's Brandon."

There was silence.

"Sally?"

"I'm here."

"So is Brandon."

"I know."

"Think cyanide."

80. Snow Mobiles

SALLY rushed back up the hillside, this time hoping to find Brandon. She had a small derringer beneath an oversized cowboy-style belt. If Brandon moved a little finger she thought she would down him. Sally was out of breath when she got to the check point.

"Where's Steve Brandon?" she asked the agent.

"Where they all are, I suppose," the agent said.

"And where's that?"

"Rendezvous Park."

Sally ran back to town. The old man who had helped her before didn't seemed to have moved an inch.

"How do I drive to Rendezvous Park?" She asked him.

"You don't."

"What do you mean, you don't?"

The old man chuckled: "Cars can't get there this time of year. You ski, or snowmobile."

Sally called Lou. He was nearing the I-70 cutoff for Steamboat, still more than an hour away. Two state patrol cars and one from the Eagle County Sheriff's Department were now trying to close the gap, and other officers were setting up a road-block. Some madman was loose on the highway.

"The president is going to a place called Rendezvous Park up above Steamboat," Sally said. "I've got to rent a snowmobile to get there."

"With luck, I'll see you there," Lou shouted.

He saw the roadblock as he snapped the phone off. The locals had made a mistake. The roadblock was a quarter mile past the turnoff for Steamboat. Lou hit the exit, but still had forty miles to go. It would not be easy. The roads were icy. He was slipping and fishtailing as he rounded corners.

Sally blasted through the door of Rex's Rentals dead on 6 p.m. when rental shops were closed or closing, surprising Rex, who was reading a hotrod magazine. Rex was a hundred pounds overweight, with tattoo-covered arms and a goatee. He could have been any age from thirty to sixty.

"I need a snowmobile," Sally panted.

Rex, who had looked alarmed at first, now smiled at what he thought was a pretty interesting lady. He pulled on his goatee.

"And why would a nice lady like you want a boss mobile?" he asked in what he thought was his best seductive voice.

Sally pulled out her derringer. "Because I need one."

It wasn't exactly pointed at him, but it wasn't exactly pointed away either. The change in him was immediate.

"OK, lady. We've got a big cat out back. I'll fill it up."

She trusted him that he would. The gun ensured he did.

The cops closing in behind Lou were going to be a problem, he knew. He was keeping them at bay but he was not losing them either. They would not buy the story that he was on his way to save the president. They would assume he was out to kill him. Hours later they might know better, but hours later would be too late.

Dusk was fading. Lou gambled. He turned off his lights and drifted left, into the opposite lane. He went all the way over onto the shoulder, but never tapped his brakes. The mountain fell away steeply to his left. The Landcruiser tilted precariously, hit a boulder, then another. Lou was sure he was going to tumble down a mountainside at any minute, maybe way down. Still he didn't tap the brakes. Somehow he managed to level out just as the pursuing officers flew past. They missed him.

Lou swung out and put his foot through the floorboard. He was still fifteen minutes from Steamboat.

The president and his family undressed in a cabin above the hot springs. It was two hundred feet from the cabins down to the pools and the president always wanted to make a run for it. The

Secret Service considered this the weakest point in their security perimeter, and they braced for anything. The first one hundred and fifty feet were the most critical, the service believed. There, the president could be exposed to rifle fire. But after that the all-enveloping fog would ruin an assassin's line-of-sight. The president would simply disappear.

The president and his sixteen-year-old daughter emerged first. She had an overcoat on above her swimsuit but the president only had a tee shirt and trunks on, with a towel draped around his neck. The president liked stepping out nearly naked into the twenty degree Colorado cold and rushing into its wonderful hot springs. President Teddy Roosevelt liked doing the same thing here, and rumor had it that Roosevelt, like the locals, did it naked. Lawrence Naslund remembered doing that too, in a different life.

"Here we gooooooo!" he exclaimed as, holding hands, he and his daughter leapt into the two feet of snow and half stumbled half ran toward the fog below. Agents were everywhere scannnig the trees as the mad dash continued.

The president and his daughter made it to the fog and began to relax. Other members of the first family and the president's top aides were now in pursuit, screaming and hollering at the sting of early January.

As the president entered the fog, Lt. Steve Brandon took out a thermos bottle from his bag, and poured himself some coffee.

"Ready for a cold night, huh?" said George Phillips, standing nearby, nodding appreciatively.

"You bet," said Brandon, recapping the bottle.

He headed out of a cabin and down toward the fog. He was carrying his thermos. No one thought a thing about it.

Sally Will thundered up the road on the snowmobile, snow flying all around her, hair streaming wildly. She looked like a demented jockey on a mechanical horse. Sally had never driven such a contraption before and was certain she would be launched off at any moment. It hadn't taken her long to get the hang of the thing but she was still taking too many risks, dodging trees, boulders and even a startled deer as she careered cross country to reach the park. She went as fast as the machine would go, which to her seemed like the speed of light.

Lou Elliott roared into Steamboat and found a burly man closing up a rental shop with the sign Rex's Rentals over it. "I need a snow-mobile. And I mean now," he demanded.

"Man, we're closed."

Lou took out his .44 and said, "Wrong, you're open."

"Ah, shit, man. Not again."

Lou told the man to move fast. Rex did.

Just as Lou started up the machine and began to move a state patrolman spotted his car. And then spotted him. He got on his bullhorn and demanded that Lou stop or he would shoot. Lou put his head down and accelerated toward the path to Rendezvous Park, barely now visible in the gathering gloom. He heard a series of bangs behind him and the zip of bullets overhead. Lou made-believe he was dodging them by moving his head back and forth. He opened the throttle even wider.

81. Cyanide Death

SALLY prayed to the god of luck that agents would miss the tiny derringer, just as she hoped they would not stumble upon her recent past. She doubted they would warm to her tale. Dismounting from the snowmobile as near as she dared get without being seen she jogged towards the cabins. Agents stopped her at the checkpoint, examined her papers, and ran a metal detector wand over her, discovering pens, breath mint in foil, small change and a big belt buckle. They didn't ask her to take it off. Instead, they waved her in.

Sally asked for Brandon the minute she got to the main cabin. He was gone. She had one chance to figure out where he would release the cyanide. He could release it below, where the presidential party was. She didn't think it likely. He would be seen, be vulnerable to the gas himself, and, only senior Secret Service agents could be that close in. Or so she hoped.

She looked up and saw the column of steam pouring down the mountainside. The answer came to her like a revelation. That's where Brandon would go. He would release the pellets up on the mountainside, out of sight. She didn't know it but she felt it strongly enough. It was a guess but she didn't have any time for doubt. One chance. That's all she would get.

She edged to the perimeter where a Secret Service agent stood guard. She asked him if she could go down a bit. He said no. Then she asked him for a cigarette. As he fumbled for one, Sally took off.

"Stop lady!" he shouted. But Sally kept running.

The agent raised his Uzi, but Sally was already in the cloud. If he shot blindly he could hit anybody. He could hit the president. It was just as well on second thoughts. He really didn't want to hit a journalist either. But she would have plenty to explain when she came out. He barked what had happened into his shoulder mike.

"What do you mean, an unarmed female reporter is crashing the president's party?" the commander thundered.

"Sir, I tried..."

"Shut up, Ralph."

The commander had a decision to make. He could order an evacuation and ruin the president's year-long plan. Or he could order agents into the fog and surround the pool. There was a downside to an evacuation. If there was a plot, moving the president out of the fog could be more dangerous than letting him stay to have his fun. He ordered agents in. It was probably only some recklessly ambitious reporter trying to get some headlines by catching a peek, he reckoned. Crazy woman. She would pay.

Lou arrived at Rendezvous Park fifteen minutes behind Sally and parked his snowmobile out of sight near hers. There was already some commotion. He could only guess what that was. He left his .44 with the snowmobile and walked to the first check-point with no Secret Service credentials.

"Sorry sir, this area is closed," the duty agent said.

"I know," Lou said. "The president's here. I'm a friend of Denver Police Lt. Steve Brandon. I need to speak with him."

He showed the agent his ID and his retired FBI credentials.

"Still, sir, no one can go in," the agent said.

"There's been a terrible accident. Lt. Brandon's wife's been killed. We could have radioed but the family thought I should break the news to him in person."

The agent looked Lou over. He seemed OK. He called to the cabins. Lt. Brandon wasn't there. Agents in the cabin called up Brandon. No response. It seemed his radio was on the blink.

"OK, I'll wait at the cabin until he returns," Lou said.

The agent decided that the retired FBI guy was OK but he wasn't going to take any chances. Every piece of metal on Lou was examined. When his own belt buckle was detected, he, unlike Sally, had to take it off. He checked out. No weapons. The agent radioed ahead. The lie had worked. Lou was in.

The President of the United States floated on his back in one of the steam pools drinking Jack Daniel's from a paper cup. His family frolicked nearby. All around them, hidden in the fog, the Secret Service was positioned. The service thought it was prepared for anything. It was the perfect setup.

Days before, Brad Johnson had relayed the flaw in the Secret Service plan to Brandon. It was the fatal weakness they thought. The hitman would not be outside the fog, as the service thought. He would have to be inside, where night vision equipment would only see an avalanche of infrared. And Brandon would not have a gun. He would have something better.

The idea was to go up the side of the mountain along the path of the descending hot spring water, under the cover of its steam clouds. About halfway up Brandon would pour the specially-coated pellets of potassium cyanide from his thermos into the cascading stream. The thermos was jerry-rigged so that a small amount of coffee was in a sealed compartment at the top, separated from the cyanide pellets beneath. Anyone who saw Brandon drink from the thermos would think it harmless. When he was ready, all Brandon had to do was unscrew and throw away the false top and then simply pour out the cyanide pellets. By the time the pellets dissolved in the super-hot water to release the deadly gas they would be in the pool.

Lou got to the command center chalet and asked about Sally.

"That's the crazy reporter that just headed up the hill," an agent said pointing. "She'll have her tit in the wringer tomorrow."

"Dammit, Sally," Lou said, to himself mainly but out loud, and sprinted into the cloud. Barely had he got there when two shots rang out.

Someway ahead of Lou the sound of the shots stunned Sally. She could barely see three feet ahead. But she knew she must stay inside the cloud because that was where Brandon would be, she hoped. The side of the mountain was steep and rocky. She thought she was in good shape but climbing the rocky slopes at 9,500 feet was a test and she was breathing hard. If Brandon was here she hoped he didn't hear her coming. She took out her derringer.

Not far behind, Lou had made the same deduction as Sally. If Brandon was going to try to gas the president he would start from above. He headed up. The shots that snapped by his head didn't surprise him. That they missed did.

Thirty seconds later, Lou was some several yards behind and many feet below Sally. But he could see no one. He hoped he had guessed right. He knew the shots meant the Secret Service would be coming and wondered if this night would be his last.

Sally climbed ahead, losing faith with every step. Her side cramped, her chest throbbed, but still she pushed on. Still no Brandon. She began telling herself she had guessed wrong, that Brandon wasn't up here after all, that she might as well go down. Brandon had outfoxed her. Maybe the president was dead already. Or maybe that she and Lou had made another terrible mistake. At that moment of indecision she saw a dark blur that didn't appear to be boulders. When the blur moved, she knew it was Brandon. She cocked the derringer.

Steve Brandon had neither seen nor heard Sally. He unscrewed the top of the thermos, removed the false compartment containing the coffee and placed it carefully behind a rock. He, too, had heard the shots and imagined that something might be going wrong. But he didn't think anyone would figure his plan out in time and after that, who cared?

With two unknowns disappearing into the mist, the Secret Service agents way below didn't know what was happening or exactly what to do. None of their training had a scenario anything like this. Assassins didn't usually tap them on the shoulder and ask for permission to go into a secured area to kill the president. Perhaps this was a diversion to smoke the president out into the clear. Maybe not. No one knew. Chaos and panic reigned.

Dozens of agents flooded into the steam, arms drawn. The commander sent a general alert that went all the way to Washington. He waited for some word, anything, about what was happening. An assassination attempt? A lovers quarrel? Some crazed paparazzi scheme? Nothing added up. In D.C. a general ordered a team of commandos from Patterson Air Force Base in Colorado Springs choppered into Steamboat.

Brandon lifted the thermos and inched toward the stream. Any second now. Sally, ten feet behind, got him in her sights. She saw the thermos and knew exactly what it meant.

She leveled the derringer, and shouted: "Stop!"

Brandon froze, not quite believing what he was hearing. Then he slowly turned and saw Sally Will, and the gun. He sneered, the thermos still poised to pour.

"I knew I should have wasted you and your jackass lover," Brandon said.

"Put it down, Brandon," said Sally. "Now. Or I fire."

Brandon knew he couldn't make a move directly toward the stream, now only a few steps away. Sally, ten feet below, would shoot him before he ever got there. Instead, he decided the best course was to launch himself directly at Sally, knock her down, dispense the pellets and run. He slowly and carefully made to place the flask on the ground as she had ordered. But as he moved he suddenly spun round and sprang straight at her. Sally hadn't expected that but reacted just right. She fired and the bullet caught Brandon in the neck. His impetus carried him on top of Sally, knocking her over. They fell together, close to the edge of the hot stream. With supreme effort and a strangled cry of pain, Brandon threw the flask towards the water with one hand and clutching his neck, now streaming blood, with the other.

Barely fifteen feet behind Sally, Lou saw Brandon jump and saw the thermos roll towards the stream after Brandon had been hit. He saw, too, pellets fall out as the flask rolled. Springing forward Lou grabbed the flask inches before it dropped into the stream. Nevertheless several pellets made it into the water. Forgetting their own safety, and leaving Brandon making choking gurgling noises on the ground, Lou and Sally leapt up and scrambled down the mountain shouting, "Get Out! Get Out! Get Out!"

The Secret Service had already taken their own advice on that seconds before when they heard Sally's shot. They had ushered the president and his family out of the pools, but still not quite far enough away from the water. Some members of the party were getting sick. Detectors sniffed the cyanide.

When Sally and Lou got to the pools, the presidential party had gone and men with gas masks and machine-guns had them surrounded. In the background sirens were screaming.

The Secret Service found Brandon's lifeless body and the cyanide flask Lou had intercepted. They gathered up and safely recovered the scattered pellets. The agent named Ralph said he had seen Brandon taking the thermos into the steam just before all hell had broken loose. He also said he had let off a couple of shots up the mountain after Lou when he saw a shadowy unidentified figure appear for a moment out of the fog. Sally explained the derringer and her subterfuge while a call to Washington confirmed that Lou was retired FBI, with a stellar record and a top-secret security clearance.

"I think these two trespassers are righteous heroes," said a man listening to their testimony whom Lou and Sally did not know. "They deserve the Medal of Freedom."

Not only had he said it but George Phillips meant it.

82. Fatal Redemption

FROM the moment he noticed that Sally's Miata had gone, Brad Johnson suspected something was wrong. Lou and Sally were on to something. He had the terrifying thought that they had figured it out. He began to think of the millions slipping through his fingers. It was unacceptable. He hadn't finished with Mr. Wood just yet.

He grabbed his 30.06, jumped into his Liberty and sped away. He passed Idaho Springs then flew through the Eisenhower Tunnel. Cops saw Brad and turned to chase. By then Brad had disappeared on the road to Steamboat. Only a mile from town the radio blared out the emergency warning system. Steamboat Springs was a closed military zone.

Brad slammed his vehicle to a stop at the same rental store visited by Sally and Lou. It was closed, no one was in sight. Brad didn't care. Spotting a suitable-looking snowmobile in the showroom, Brad rammed his Jeep through the front door, shattering glass and setting off alarms. In no time he had fired up the snowmobile and burst through debris as if emerging from hell. Heading towards Rendezvous Park, he hurtled up the mountain on a back way he had learned on previous visits.

Brad got to the park just in time to see paramedics roll Steve Brandon's body into a helicopter. There was no rush, because Steve Brandon was dead while the president had departed very much alive.

Brad Johnson was enraged. The two loathsome creatures who had wrecked his plans were one hundred and fifty feet behind the Secret Service line, his buddy was dead, the president alive, and his career and life ruined. With no further thought than that he wanted Sally Will dead, Brad took out his rifle, and standing, aimed it squarely at Sally's head. He thought he could hit anything at that distance. His blood was flowing hotter than the tumbling mineral spring.

"Goddamn you, Sally Will!" he spat as he tried to keep the sights on her.

Standing beyond the yellow tape where Lou and Sally were being questioned Lou thought he caught sight of something that bothered him, some bright movement. Then he saw a figure standing. And the figure had a rifle. An instant before Brad pulled the trigger, Lou realized what he had seen. It was Brad's yellow jacket. With a yell, Lou tackled Sally to the ground just as a sure-shot bullet whizzed over her head.

Lou scrambled to his feet and pulled Sally up after him, screaming, "That's him, that's the other assassin!"

Without waiting he took off at a sprint towards Brad Johnson and his rifle. The Secret Service agents should have ordered Lou to halt but they were too busy trying to shoot Brad Johnson themselves.

Seeing he had missed and could shortly be cut in two, Brad ran to his snowmobile and cranked the throttle. The only thing on his mind now was survival. He headed down toward Steamboat at full speed.

Lou got to his snowmobile just as Brad passed around the corner and out of sight. Lou set off after him, .44 in hand. Shooting handguns and rifles while flying over mounds and drifts and dips was an art neither Lou nor Brad had mastered. It was even more difficult in the nearly perfect dark of a moonless Colorado night. The men exchanged a few harmless shots well wide of their targets, each nearly losing control as the snowmobiles slipped about like drunken ice-skaters. Above Lou saw choppers, below he saw Johnson pulling away. Lou twisted the throttle to full, expecting to be dead at any moment, either from a crash or Brad's rifle. But Brad didn't fire. Lou thought he must be out of ammunition. That's good, Lou thought, because I'm out too.

As they turned another sharp corner, Lou saw the lights of Steamboat Springs just below. He was gaining on Brad. His mount was faster or maybe he was just more reckless. Whichever it was, before long he had closed the gap until there was almost no distance between them. Brad threw his rifle at Lou and it dinged him. Suddenly Brad turned off the track and headed down a daredevil slope. Only a fool would follow. Lou followed.

It was insane but hormones were now directing matters. Lou drew alongside Brad and thought for a second of jumping over onto the other machine, movie style, but immediately changed his mind. He was not sure he could do it and even if he did what good would it do? Probably only get himself killed. His advantage was not courage or daring but speed. He pushed his machine in front of Brad's and swerved into his path, clipping the front-runners and flipping Brad and his machine high into the air. Brad hit a pine tree at forty miles per hour.

Lou was surprised by the violence of the collision. He had been hoping to catch Brad. He hadn't meant to kill him. Now it looked like he had. He circled his machine back to get near to Brad. He hoped his former friend was not dead. Brad Johnson had killed four men and had tried to kill the President of the United States. But his worst crime, in Lou's eyes, was that he had tried to kill Sally Will.

As Lou got near he saw the machine on its back, still coughing smoke and growling. Nearby was a black and yellow motionless mound on the white snow. He dismounted to see what was left of Brad, steeling himself. He heard a commotion in the distance. The Secret Service was coming. Lou moved to the mound and looked down at Brad's face, deformed from the impact. Blood was everywhere. But just as Lou began to turn away, Brad's eyes opened and he gazed at Lou. Lou was startled. He didn't know what to do at first but then he knelt down by Brad's head, holding his gaze. Brad began to speak, quietly, with a bit of a concussion slur.

"Just one damn lucky shot, that's all you ever had, Elliott," Brad said. It looked like he was smiling. The smile must have hurt but it was genuine. "Just one."

Then Brad Johnson died.

83. America Calling

THE PRESIDENT was whisked from Peterson Air force Base in Colorado Springs to the belly of Cheyenne Mountain that is geared to take a twenty megaton blast. The Secret Service wasn't taking any chances.

Linda Orvez made her way to the president's room inside.

"Linda," the president greeted her, looking happy. For the first time in the past three hours he had a smile on his face. "What a way to end a vacation!"

"Mr. President," Orvez said, looking around at the assembly of military officers in the room. "From what we are getting from Steamboat, the actors were a news reporter and a Denver police lieutenant assigned to your detail. We now know it's the same team that attacked the Witness Protection Program. Apparently the reporter kept a diary. We have it."

"And what stopped them?"

"Remember the Chicago Tribune reporter who did the exposé on the Wasp Man Killer?"

The president drew back his head, raising his eyebrows.

"The one I said had fabricated? What was her name?"

"Sally Will, sir."

"Sally Will," Naslund repeated.

"Yes sir. She and a private investigator figured it out. He's ex-FBI. And, sir, one of the members of the team was the person she originally fingered."

The president let out a whistle.

"I guess I owe Ms. Will an apology."

"We all do," suggested Orvez, displaying uncharacteristic generosity.

"These two didn't plot this on their own, I presume?" the president asked.

"No, sir, it was Ivanov who ordered it. We've intercepted a blizzard of communications inside of Russia. The Russian government is sure it was Ivanov. It was arranged through Vito Borelli in Chicago. Ivanov has been killing off witnesses as soon as he finds them, but we're listening in."

"Linda, do you think Putin knows about Team Blue?"

"No, not for sure – but Ivanov does," Orvez almost whispered. "He has nothing else to lose now. He might go public."

Her hand touched the president's arm.

"Linda," Naslund said. "Could you bring me the phone over there? The red one."

The head of the FSB entered President Vladimir Putin's office.

"There's not a doubt, sir," the FSB man said. "Ivanov ordered the attack on the U.S. president. We've been listening in. This is very bad. I'm sorry sir."

"Why, Sergei?"

"The American president will hold us responsible."

"No Sergei, no," said Putin. "How do the Americans say it? Yes, 'We are in the driver's seat.' "

"How is that, sir?"

The Russian president lifted his feet off the desk and straightened a framed picture of himself and his family. Then he turned to his head of the secret service.

"Because of the fine work you and the FSB have done. You see the American president has played a risky game. We know he sent a team here who killed one of Ivanov's favorites, Slavnik. That illegal act led to Ivanov killing a CIA agent in America itself. To even the score, the American president started killing Russian people on his own soil: Mika Petrovich and Nikolai Boravick. Worse, they then tried to kill Boravick's wife, an American citizen."

President Putin rose slowly from his desk and looked out a window at Moscow covered in snow and ice.

"And as if that's not enough," he continued, "they sent the team – you said it was called Team Blue? – here to kill Ivanov. But instead of killing Ivanov, Ivanov killed the American team's leader, a woman. When all these things went bad, the American president did what they call – I love the term – 'a cover up.'"

"So, sir, what do we do?" the FSB head asked.

"Nothing," said Putin.

"Nothing?"

"Nothing. I will not be surprised if very soon, today even, the American president will be calling me for a favor."

"A favor?"

"I believe President Naslund will want us to kill Ivanov before Ivanov exposes the Americans' incompetence."

"And we will do this?"

"Of course," said Putin. "Ivanov means nothing now. But we will keep our evidence handy for – how do they say it? – a 'rainy day.'

"You see," President Putin continued, "the American leader really set in motion this attempt on his life himself. He started it. And if the American people learn of this they will turn on him. He will never win re-election. He could even be impeached. Right now he's a hero. But tomorrow...?" Putin shrugged.

Just then an aide came in. "Sorry to interrupt, sir, but you have a call on the Red Line."

The Russian president smiled as he walked into another room as the astonished FSB director looked on.

"And how can I help you, Mr. President?" President Putin asked Lawrence Naslund, taking the red phone from the aide.

"You know what happened here?"

"Yes, of course. It's terrible, terrible. Our news says that a police lieutenant and some reporter designed all this. I am shocked, sir. Who can you trust?"

"We know that they were just pawns. The man behind this was someone I believe you know. Dimitri Ivanov."

"No!" The Russian president said.

"Yes," said Lawrence Naslund. "We need justice here, Mr. President. We want Ivanov to pay."

"Mr. President, you take my breath away. Are you sure? Ivanov?"

"One hundred percent sure."

"My God, sir. Say no more. We know what to do. He must pay of course."

"The United States will remember that Russia came to our aid in a time of great trouble," said the American president. "You have my word as an American."

"Sir," said President Putin, suppressing a smile, "we do this for you alone. We expect nothing in return. We will find the criminal and teach him and all of his ilk a lesson they will never forget."

"I will remember this," said Naslund.

"Thank you, sir."

Putin put down the phone and beckoned the FSB man over.

"This could be a very, very good day for Mother Russia," said Putin as he sat back down at his desk. "A very good day."

Lou and Sally got a free trip back to Denver in an army Black Hawk helicopter. They were brought handcuffed into the FBI's headquarters on the 12th floor of the federal building on Stout Street. There they were separated and interrogated by agents from both the Secret Service and the Bureau who learned for the first time about the Italian June Festival and Lydia Valente and how that information pulled it all together.

"Why didn't you tell us this?" An agent asked Sally, leaning across a desk with his hand pressed down in tight fists.

"Would you have believed a fired reporter who your own president said was a liar if I had?".

The agent stood there for a moment, looking into Sally eyes.

"You have a point," he finally conceded.

Lou got the same question, and offered much the same answer. Soon, the cuffs were off, but the interrogation rooms were still guarded by unsmiling armed men.

Both Lou and Sally were questioned for eighteen hours, going over each detail again and again. They each took polygraphs. Finally, a call came to the Special Agent in Charge from the White House. Lou and Sally were released.

84. Vintage Rhythm

IT WAS finally, absolutely over. Back in the apartment Lou and Sally decided it was time to celebrate. Shortly after she had fallen for Lou Elliott, Sally had purchased a good second-growth Château Margaux for $225. OK, it was ridiculously extravagant but she bet that someday it would be appropriate. This day was it.

Lou glanced at the bottle as Sally got out a corkscrew. "You tired?" Sally asked.

"Yes."

"Too tired?"

"Not that tired," said Lou, smiling.

Sally poured. Lou had never tasted a wine so perfect. If wine were wood this one would be antique mahogany. He wondered what she had spent on it.

"Either I'm real thirsty or you picked a pretty good year," Lou said smiling broadly.

He couldn't remember that the classic French red grape was an aphrodisiac but that night it certainly seemed to be, for both of them. A glass later, longing looks were exchanged across the table followed by a stream of discarded clothing leading to the bedroom. There the passion between them was so intense they exploded together within seconds.

"My God," Sally rasped as she gulped down air. "Where did that come from?"

Lou was just as breathless. "We've...been...too...busy with little...things," he managed to gasp.

"Whoa," Sally said, "Let's save a president more often."

While Sally went to take a shower Lou refilled his glass and relaxed. He wondered if he was up for another like that. Silly question, his body replied. Then the phone rang.

"Hello."

"Mr. Elliott?"

The voice sounded refined, possibly British, but more likely someone from some other European country who had learned the English language extremely well.

"Yes?"

"I have information about the Russians who tried to kill the president. Steve Brandon was their agent."

Lou's ardor evaporated instantly.

"Russians? And you want to tell me this because?"

"I want to stop them."

"And you are?"

"Look, Mr. Elliott, I don't trust phones. I am at Tamarack Square, west side. I'm in the only pea green VW Beetle you will see there. Come now, please."

"Can't this wait until tomorrow?"

"No, because they intend to kill others, Mr. Elliott. Maybe even tonight."

"What others?"

"I have a package with information. But you must come immediately. I am in danger. I will only deal with you."

The caller clicked off.

Lou loaded his .44, slipped it into a shoulder holster, put on a jacket and tapped on the bathroom door. He told Sally a client had called and he had to run. It was important. Sally protested but Lou insisted he would not be long. He would be back in an hour or so, no more.

"Keep the wine breathing for me," he said.

Dr. Tsplyev hung up the phone quietly and whistled the "Mary Had a Little Lamb" nursery rhyme. He was whistling it for his pet rat Raspy. He always whistled it when the rat was hungry. He whistled it now.

Tsplyev was sitting in the farmhouse in Last Chance waiting to kill Sally Will. It wasn't his idea. It was Katya's. The whole world was after her father-god Ivanov. And now he could not be reached.

But Katya was in no doubt of what he would want at this moment: Kill the woman who foiled his plan. And make her suffer in doing so.

Lou sped toward Tamarack Square, entering from the east side, examining everything. Nothing seemed out of place. He decided to make his way slowly west, to find the pea green VW.

Katya and Vitali entered Lou's condo shortly after they saw Lou leave. Among Katya's talents was picking locks. The Russians hesitated when they saw the dog but Tika wagged her tail as they entered. This was no guard dog. Katya paused to pat Tika's head and Tika licked the back of her hand in return.

Katya and Vitali crept through the apartment on quiet sneakers. A shower was running. Katya tried the door knob slowly. Locked. It was one of Sally's habits.

"Lou?" Sally had heard something.

Katya held a finger up to her lips. Vitali slowly backed away.

"Lou? Is that you?"

Katya decided to wait her out. They would hide in the bedroom where Katya would hit her with a Taser stun gun while Vitali applied the injection. Downstairs a trunk big enough to carry her to Last Chance awaited.

As Lou got close to the west lot he put his .44 in his lap. He wasn't usually this jumpy but for some reason this time he was. If anything seemed the least bit dangerous, he would engage. But nothing looked dangerous. There was no pea green bug anywhere in sight. Lou decided to park and wait for his informant. He reasoned that he was probably somewhere close by, checking out if Lou had brought reinforcements. Lou turned off the radio and opened his windows. He wanted to listen.

Sally came out of the bathroom wrapped in a towel. She put on one of Lou's flannel shirts he had left over a chair, flipped on

CNN, and flopped down on the couch. She'd decided she'd wait for him here, like this, if he wasn't going to be long. He might just be up for a repeat performance and she couldn't wait.

The news was all about the assassination attempt and a couple of local heroes. She watched for a few minutes until her eyelids grew heavy. She had wanted to stay up but she had a bit of a buzz on and dog-tiredness was getting the better of her. She turned off the set and stretched out on the sofa for a catnap. She heard a noise. A soft "ting" like metal on metal. Maybe nothing but after the earlier sound she thought she'd heard she wasn't so prepared to let this one go. Maybe Tika. Where was Tika? She figured that maybe it was just the dog rummaging around somewhere but she decided to investigate anyway.

Lou was getting antsy. He had been at the west lot for ten minutes and nothing, no pea green Volkswagen had appeared. It was a busted meet. Usually Lou would wait at least an hour to be sure. Sometimes people actually did get stuck in traffic. But something about this meet didn't quite feel right. Lou couldn't quite place it at first but then he remembered the voice with the indiscernible accent. As Lou thought more about it the voice became more menacing in his mind. Then the thought hit him: Suppose the caller's object was not to get him to a meet at all but to get him away from the condo. Suppose he was after Sally.

Slamming the car into drive, Lou peeled out of the lot and dialed Sally. Swerving around slow traffic and passing cars on the shoulder, cutting in, cutting out, spawning pockets of road rage every few yards, Lou prayed he wasn't too late.

Sally's phone rang. It took four rings before she got to it. "Yeah?" she said.

"Sally, get out of there!" a voice yelled at her.

"Lou?"

"Sally, they're..."

The line went dead.

"Lou?"

Nothing.

Sally looked at her phone and realized she hadn't charged it in days. Damn. What did Lou mean, "Get out of there?" Sally got up and listened. Nothing. She began to creep towards the bedroom. She had her snubnosed derringer in the bedroom. Where had that noise come from? Where was Tika? She could not see her or hear her anywhere. Sally could only hear blood pounding in her ears. Her blood pressure must be off the charts. She caught the acrid aroma of fear. Hers. Sally reached the bedroom. Still no one. Lou had yelled for her to get out of there. For a second she thought she must have misunderstood. The two bad guys were dead and she and Lou had been cleared. What could Lou have meant? Still her heart raced. She thought she was seeing ghosts, knowing viscerally that she wasn't. Where was Tika?

By now Sally had her back almost directly in front of the bedroom closet. Silently Katya slowly opened the accordion doors, Taser ready. Something - instinct? the slightest sound? - made Sally turn. She swung around just as Katya pulled the trigger on the stun gun. Katya had meant to hit Sally in the middle of her back where she would be instantly disabled. But her turn meant the Taser hit Sally's right arm instead. Sally's arm immediately went into spasms but she was conscious, and mobile. Sally looked up, unable to get out of the way as Katya came at her. She saw a green-eyed woman and behind the woman a man with a gun.

As Katya swung her right hand like a blade at Sally's neck, something large and silent flew through the air between them. Thank God, thought Sally. Lou has made it home in time. But it wasn't Lou. Tika's powerful jaws came down on Katya's hand before she connected with Sally's neck. Katya cried out in pain as the stun gun went spinning across the floor. Tika then went for the man with the gun. Vitali fired and missed. Before he could get off another shot his hand was nearly severed by the savagery of Tika's bite. That gun, too, went spiraling to the ground where Sally quickly caught it and pointed it at the woman with green eyes.

Katya sprinted for the door. Sally fired but her hand was still shaking from the Taser and she hit nothing but wall. Tika had brought Vitali down and was threatening to do to his neck what she had done to his hand. Defeated, Vitali didn't move, his eyes closed. Tika snarled over him as if she was no longer Tika but a wolf. When the Russian opened his eyes, Tika went for his neck. Vitali closed his eyes.

Sally called 911.

Lou ran into Larimer Place and bounded up the stairs without waiting for the elevator. Midway up, a woman flew by him as if her life depended on it. He got only a glance but he would remember the woman's eyes for the rest of his life. Penetrating, intelligent and emerald green.

85. Russian Steps

DIMITRI Ivanov knew that his failed assassination attempt could cause him big trouble. The American president would try to take revenge. Ivanov thought himself a practical man facing a business problem. Most often his solutions to such problems involved murder, but not always. He had tried and failed with that approach with the president. Now it was time to be creative. Ivanov thought the president also was a practical man. Surely, he would accept a deal that could prevent Ivanov's evidence from being unveiled.

Ivanov retreated to a cabin redoubt in the Urals, surrounded by Russian security guards. The Americans could never strike there with their special gadgets. The place wasn't even on the map. He would write an email to the president and wait for the storm to pass.

"Dear Mr. President," Ivanov wrote.

"I am not sorry for what happened in Colorado. You had attacked me and I was defending myself. But I'm ready to concede victory to you. I will withdraw all operations in America and keep information about your agents and the American woman you killed secret.

"In exchange, you will leave me be. Do we have a deal?

"Dimitri Ivanov."

Ivanov thought it had a chance. A small one, admittedly but it was worth a shot.

And for Ivanov there was another bright spot: The Russian government was leaving him alone. It was bitterly cold in the mountains but he was Russian. He could take it. He could survive anything.

His guards acknowledged him as he made his way out of the cabin. The sun was bright and the mountain air pure. He got the feeling he was on top of the world.

He strode down a path that led to a meadow blanketed in snow. The snow, he thought, was perfect. His long fur-lined boots crunched it as he marched on. Suddenly he had a rush. He had taken on the most powerful man in the world, and he was still standing. He stopped, took in a deep breath, closed his eyes and looked up. When he exhaled he knew he had made his place in history.

But when he opened his eyes a nagging thought flooded into his head with the glare of sun off the snow: Why don't I hear my guards following me as they are supposed to? He turned around to shout reprimands to his sloppy employees. But to his surprise the guards were there. They had formed a crescent thirty yards behind him, where the meadow met the forest. Ivanov squinted. What were they doing?

Then Ivanov noticed something else. They all had rifles raised, and they were raised towards him. Ivanov knew immediately what it meant and fell to his knees in resignation. There was to be no deal after all.

Shots rang out.

86. Diary Dates

THE MYSTERY of why Brad Johnson and Steve Brandon had formed their murderous pact was solved, in part, by Brad's diaries. It all stretched back over the past ten years.

Both men had been drinking buddies at Sparky's, the cop bar where Lou had met Pat O'Dowd while working on the wasp-man case. It was an odd relationship – a cop and a reporter openly fraternizing. Neither cared. Brad was a pro. He never took anything out of Sparky's and put it in the paper unless Brandon gave a green light. The men hit it off, according to Brad's diaries, because they both took a philosophical view of things. Most cops and reporters start out as idealists and end up as cynics. Brad and Steve were different. They had long discussions over topics such as: Was God necessary? Why did time go in a straight line? Did the past exist? According to Brad, they never resolved these questions. Then one day came a crime that changed everything.

A five-year-old named Megan Townsend had been abducted from her southwest Denver home. She seemed a perfect child, with a winning mischievous smile, curly blonde hair, blue eyes that shined with life and dimples that crushed the heart. She was from a middle-class family. Not rich – her father was a junior accountant and her mom a school teacher. But they were handsome parents whose tears seemed to drop right out of the television into family rooms across the metro area.

Brad was on top of the story for the Post while Brandon led the investigation. Volunteers with posters of Megan fanned out all over the metro area. Soon every telephone pole, post box, and bumper seemed to have Megan's picture displayed. Both Steve and Brad held hands with the parents. They began to identify with them. They both openly held out hope while knowing inside there probably wasn't any.

Four days passed with no sign of Megan. Good Morning America interviewed Megan's parents, Jim and Mary Townsend, for fifteen minutes one morning before the sun was even up in Denver. Brad and Steve were behind the cameras. Both quietly shook their heads.

The next day Alajandro Baca, a tourist from Spain, was driving up Turkey Creek Canyon. He needed the bathroom so he stepped over a "closed" sign attached to a chain at the Dakota Campground. His family waited behind in the rental car. The campground had been closed four days before for minor repairs.

Alajandro went to an outhouse and began to unbuckle his belt. He thought he heard something. The stench in the out-house was heavy and the flies were everywhere, but Alajandro decided to investigate the noise instead of just finishing his business. He looked into the dark pit. There was something there. He heard the sound of urine and wet feces sloshing slightly. An animal?

Looking down into the hole, he waited for his eyes to adjust. Finally he saw what looked like a darkened face, but with clear eyes and white lips.

Megan Townsend said weakly: "Daddy?"

Somehow, Megan was alive. Investigators later determined she had stayed resolute for the four days she was in the pit up to her neck, never thinking of death because she had no idea of what that was. She stayed there waiting for her daddy to save her, never wavering in her faith that he would.

She later told Brandon, after she was scrubbed down and in Denver General Hospital, that a "bad man" had taken off her clothes and "put his thing in my pee pee. It hurt me." Then the bad man had dropped Megan headfirst down the outhouse in the just-closed campground.

After the interview, Brandon and Johnson went off to get loaded at a dive in Golden. While the rest of the city rejoiced in Megan's survival, Steve Brandon had a darker take. When he had first started on the police force, Brandon had attended a local Methodist Church. After two years on the homicide squad, he stopped going. The next fifteen years had done nothing to revive his faith. And then Megan Townsend expelled what little remained.

Brandon didn't linger on the strength of the little girl to survive those days in that pit. He concentrated on the evil that put her there. He reasoned that no God would allow such a beast to exist. He was not going to become some silly crusader against evil. Evil, after all, was winning. Steve Brandon became a nihilist, a believer in nothingness. He told Brad Johnson of his beliefs. It became a part of their regular discussions.

The night after the Megan interview, Brad, drunk, pensive and unguarded, shared his own fantasy with Steve. Why not kill for money? If life meant so little, if evil was winning everywhere, why not jump aboard?

"Certainly, we could do a better job than the yo-yos out there," Brad had said.

"Steve, answer this question: Why be good?"

Brandon didn't know that Brad was quoting a German philosopher. At first he was repelled by the idea.

"That would make us just like Megan's 'bad man,' " he argued. But later, Brandon warmed to Brad's fantasy. In a Godless world, why not kill riffraff and make money? Every murder scene he went to convinced him further. Why be good, indeed? Besides, Brad's idea would be interesting.

By the time the day came when Brad told Brandon about the planned hit on Big Bow, he thought it was a fine plan. But Brad did it alone. Bow was just a biker. Cops wouldn't care.

On Palermo, killed outside Maggie's Best, Brad had help. Brandon was head of the investigation. He would keep his boys in check.

Then came the protected witnesses, Spilotro and Tony Nails. For those, the two had to work in concert. Brandon took vacation time around those killings, just as Sally and Lou had discovered. Brad needed Steve to be on hand because Steve, from a PC, could tap into the national crime databases to see if anyone was on Brad's tail.

It was a near-perfect partnership. But their fatal mistake had been in the killings themselves, in the one thing they both over-looked: the filterless Dunhills. They had started smoking Dunhills on that night in the Golden dive. Brad had left his at the murder scenes of Big Bow and Palermo. Brandon had left his at Red Rocks. Brandon had hoped, had intended, to kill Sally that night at Red Rocks, but then goddamned Lou Elliott had showed up.

Then came The Story, Sally's exposé. Brandon had to scramble to explain his absences. He got Lydia.

After Brandon's press conference had put Sally out of the picture, as he thought, Brad and Steve went to work on their biggest, most profitable project – the killing of the president.

By then, Brandon was in it for the rush. Brad, too. He lived only for the adrenaline buzz, the endorphin rush.

They decided that this time, with the president, Brandon should take the lead. He would be the one who could get inside an otherwise impenetrable security blanket. Brad thought of the cyanide.

That was when Lou and Sally had broken further into the team with the discovery of the Bundy mask. Brad was furious that the two had figured it out. Where had that come from? They decided that Brad would act as decoy, luring their main enemies away from Steamboat. That had been a touch of genius, Brad wrote. Lou Elliott and Sally Will had fallen for it.

That was the end of Brad's diary.

The mystery of how Brandon and Johnson cracked the Witness Protection Program was quickly solved. Just as Lou and Sally thought, Brandon had been the lead detective on the Spilotro case. He not only knew where Spilotro was, he had actually visited him.

It was a bit harder to find out how the team knew about Tony Nails. But, in retracing Brandon's steps, investigators had their answer. In the chaos following the Savannah hit on Spilotro, Brandon had rushed to U.S. Marshals' headquarters, which had just sent out a nationwide alert about other witnesses that might be targets. Cables were darting everywhere directing marshals to find witnesses and beef up protection. Secrecy was briefly compromised and at least two cables listed some of the uncoded names and general addresses of key witnesses. Steve Brandon had been in the office when the cables came in. One had some thirty names and addresses. Another was an emergency order to move the most important protected of them all: Tony Nails. His destination was only given as the Apostle Islands.

Epilogue

VITO Borelli was under intense pressure, but federal prosecutors could prove nothing against him and what the president knew from illegal wiretaps was not going to be available, ever.

Borelli told the press he was a simple man who had gotten lucky in the import-export business. To prove it, he said he would move from Chicago and never again consort with those the media unfairly called mobsters.

And that he did, landing in Costa Rica, many millions richer than he had ever been before, owning a mansion on the Pacific Coast near the Playas Manuel Antonio and another on the Caribbean side near Limon. And he discovered a new passion: scuba diving.

Lydia Valente and Jimmy Fresno disappeared quietly to Oregon where they worked in a microbrewery in Portland, saving enough money for Lydia's chance in Hollywood. Acting instructors found her to be a natural, if with rough edges. She won small parts in three movies. One reviewer even predicted a bright future.

Sally Will was again a heroine, a treasure, and the paradigm for truth-seekers everywhere. One columnist in the ordinarily staid Wall Street Journal said that she and her partner, the private eye Lou Elliott, might well be the world's best detective team. There was even talk about Sally's Brandon story, with its "elegant narrative of circumstantial evidence," being nominated for a Pulitzer Prize.

But the most important headline was in the Chicago Tribune. It read simply: "Sally Will finds redemption."

In April, Mel Campbell, the newly-promoted managing editor

of the Chicago Tribune, came to Denver for a vacation. Lou was glad to give him use of his condo while he and Sally took an extended vacation to Costa Rica, courtesy of a greyhound named Rainbow.

Playas Manuel Antonio. No better spot in the world, thought Lou. He and Sally snorkeled, read beach novels and sipped cocktails. In the afternoon, they simply lounged. There was also plenty of sex.

Sally still wondered about the woman who had attacked her, who she was? Lou said he couldn't tell, but with the disappearance of Borelli any threat had probably evaporated.

On their fifth day, an older man emerged from the coral basin, hauling scuba gear and a face mask. A dark-haired woman, striking and tall, followed. They had set up camp not fifteen yards from Lou and Sally. The man and woman stripped off their equipment and settled down on lounge chairs. The old gentleman winked at Sally, as his companion rubbed sun oil over his chest and shoulders. At first sight, Lou and Sally thought this must be his daughter. It wasn't long before the old man's caressing of the girl convinced them otherwise. It didn't matter. Down here, nothing did. The old gentleman finally stretched and came over to talk to Lou and Sally.

"You know," he said, indicating the sea, "you kids should really take advantage of this. It is another world out there."

Lou liked being called a kid. Sally didn't.

"You can rent a boat that will take you out to the reefs," the man said. "And you don't have to swim at all. Just float. There's not a muscle you need to move. The current will take you. You see everything as you drift. It's like a movie. Bright red fish, yellow fish, big fish, schools of fish. I even saw a barracuda. It's like magic. And if you get into it, you can do like me, get a lesson in scuba diving. Then you get to swim with the fishes."

He laughed hard at that.

"I might like that," said Lou. Sally looked skeptical. She also thought she had seen the older man somewhere, but couldn't place it. The older man shot out his hand towards Lou.

"I like your spirit," he said. "What's your line of business?" Lou took the man's hand, and said, "I'm an investigator. Private. And yours?"

"Retired," said the man, not looking in the least fazed. "I had an import-export business in Chicago."

Lou and Sally sat back with the geezer from Chicago, watching sunbeams dancing on the Pacific. All three seemed to think that life could not get any better. Then Sally reached over, took a sip from her Pina Colada, and hauled out a thin black cigar.

"Sally..." Lou started to object.

"Really, hon, this is the last one." Her grin gave away the lie.

~

COMING NEXT...the sequel.

Book 2 in the Sally Will series.

As Katya seeks revenge for the death of Ivanov,
Sally's love for Lou is tested to the limit...

Katya squeezed his inner thigh and rested her head on his shoulder. Tapping the altimeter on her wrist again she turned to look him in the eyes and mouthed:"Ten thousand feet. Three more minutes, you fly with the angels."

Her lips curved in the sensuous way of Angelina Jolie. But her eyes promised so much more. As the earth shrank below them, Argo Anastas, CEO of Newtalagent Inc, a major US defense contractor to the National Security Agency, was already in heaven as he savored the escapism.

At 12,000 feet the woman edged toward the gaping hole in the side of the plane.

"Now come up in front of me."

Anastas' mind raced. He could feel his crotch strain as the beautiful green-eyed woman with the east European accent he couldn't quite place spread her legs around him and snapped on the buckles that would hold them together.

"On three." She shouted a moment later over the roar of the wind and started to rock. "One. Two. Three. Now!"

They fell forward into the abyss, tumbling into the emptiness.

The rush was better than any he had known before. Within seconds the woman had steadied them both as they fell at 120 mph toward the earth, tied together like clams. Anastas' smile stretched full across his face.

The next sixty seconds felt like a surreal eternity. Time stood still. The ground didn't seem to be getting any closer. The panorama was all-consuming. As Anastas sucked in the view he felt the woman fumbling behind his back. The movement jerked his attention away from the scene below.

"Everything all right?" he shouted.

"Sure, I'm about to pull the ripcord. Get ready," she shouted back.

Returning his concentration to the beginning of the ground rush he suddenly felt lighter than before. The ground was coming up fast.

"Come on sexy, pull the fucking cord for chrissakes!" Anastas yelled, a hint of desperation entering his voice.

He turned his head back to see the women. But she was no longer there. As the movement sent him spinning out of control he could see her floating some way above him, her canopy fully open. She was looking down at him and she appeared to be smiling.

Four seconds after the panic gripped him he hit the ground screaming at 120 mph...

The Authors

Fatal Redemption is the product of the unique US-UK writing partnership of Lou Kilzer and Mark Boyden.

Lou Kilzer

Son of a rodeo operator and Wyoming school superintendent, Lou graduated cum laude in philosophy from Yale, has won two Pulitzer Prizes, and has authored two books on World War II history, for one of which he spent some time in Moscow (*see next page*). For a while he was editor-in-chief of the *JoongAng Daily* in Seoul, South Korea, published with the *International New York Times*. Lou spent several years as an investigative reporter at both the *Rocky Mountain News* and the *Denver Post*. He and his wife have recently returned to live in Colorado.

Mark Boyden

Mark is an international business consultant working in Europe, USA, South America, the Middle and Far East. He honed a passion for writing in the hallowed halls of the Denver Press Club in the mid 1990s where he met Lou Kilzer. He moved from writing articles and a regular column for *Marketing Journal* magazine to, with Lou, writing fiction: first a screenplay and then *Fatal Redemption*. Mark now lives back in England, working with Lou on the sequel – and still traveling extensively, including to North America.

BELLA WEST

Non-fiction books by Lou Kilzer:

***Churchill's Deception: The Dark Secret that Destroyed
Nazi Germany*** (Simon & Schuster. 1994)

The never-before-told story of how British Prime Minister Winston
Churchill with the assistance of the British Secret Intelligence
Service successfully deceived Hitler into turning his war machine on
Soviet Russia to save Britain from the Nazi German onslaught.

Reviews
"The gripping story of how Winston Churchill outwitted
Adolf Hitler into invading the Soviet Union – a move that
changed the course of World War II. Pulitzer Prize-winning
journalist Louis C. Kilzer has uncovered documentation
which exposes this great and untold story." – *Goodreads.*

"An audacious rereading of the diplomatic history of WWII... Certain
to be controversial, Kilzer's is an absorbing and cogently-argued original
contribution to WWII literature." – *Kirkus Reviews*

***Hitler's Traitor: Martin Bormann and the Defeat
of the Reich*** (Presidio Press, 2000).

Delving into declassified archives, Kilzer identifies Hitler's
trusted deputy Martin Bormann as the Soviet spy "Werther"
known to, but never named by, Western intelligence agencies
and the man whose betrayal of him Hitler never suspected.

Reviews
"Thumbs up! This non-fiction suspense thriller is recommended for
both history buffs and spy aficionados as a book that merits reading
in the realm of Soviet-Nazi World Way II espionage, for those with
an ear for the deadly symphonies of betrayal." – *Hacienda Publishing*

Both books are available from Amazon.